Two S

Two Steps Away

ACKNOWLEDGMENTS

Acknowledgments and thanks go to my wonderful family: husband Phil, children Lizzy and Beck. Especial thanks to Beck who designed the cover.
Thanks also to my friends and fellow writers who have encouraged, supported and commented on this story: to Sarah, Steve, Izzy, Sheila, and also to all the Rugby Writers.

Two Steps Away

"Most of us are just two steps away from homelessness."

Pete Wayman, Support Worker at The Hope Centre, Rugby.

CHAPTER ONE

Barbara Walters hung up her jacket, pushed her shoes off, and picked up a buff-coloured envelope from the mat. It was the credit card bill demanding the final payment for her living room carpet. She pondered it for a moment. Her local MP had apparently spent nearly two thousand pounds on an ornamental house for his duck pond. I could go to his surgery and demand help to pay for a cheap carpet, she thought, then smiled. She knew she didn't have the nerve to do that, any more than walk down the high street wearing only a yellow polka-dot bikini. She'd just have to economise on duck ponds and other luxuries, like clothes and heating.

Putting the letter aside to deal with later, she went into the kitchen and put the kettle on. As it came to the boil, she rubbed the small of her back and gazed into the garden of her tiny terraced house. A goldfinch, natty in its gold, red and black regimentals, flew onto the feeder near the window and pecked at the niger seeds. Barbara drank her tea and watched it idly, relaxing her shoulders and letting the aches and tiredness from her early start and hours of work fade into the background.

The doorbell rang. Marjorie Fowler, her near neighbour, stood outside, her red lipstick and highlighted auburn hair as immaculate as usual.

"Good. You're in then," she said. "I thought I saw you arrive."

"Oh, hi, Marjorie. Yes, just back from work."

"Having curry tonight?"

"Pardon?"

"Smells like curry."

"Oh, does it?" Barbara exclaimed. "Er, do you want a cup of tea?"

"No, no time. I need to get some spare copies of the CVs printed. I just wanted to remind you about tonight."

"Remind me?"

Marjorie tutted. "The short-listing! Honestly, Barbara, you are coming, aren't you?"

"I hadn't forgotten, you know."

"Jolly good. I just wanted to say... Well, there's someone, called Luke Carmichael, that I definitely prefer."

"Oh?"

"Yes! He's got a very impressive track record. A First in Theology, two years with a New Wine church in Manchester, a year with the YPJT in Derby. Apparently they've been very successful at bringing young people into the church."

"You're going to have to tell me what YPJT stands for, Marjorie."

"Young People for Jesus Trust." She paused. "Anyway, I just want to be sure Luke gets short-listed. All the others seems a bit, well, old. I want someone my boy can relate to."

"Do you?"

Marjorie looked steadily at her, her chin thrust slightly forward. "Barbara, I need you to be there tonight. I need someone on my side. Who thinks as I do. I mean, someone sensible," she added, with a slight laugh.

Barbara raised her eyebrows, then shrugged. "Oh. Right."

Frowning slightly, Marjorie gave Barbara a suspicious glance, then adjusted the terracotta-coloured scarf wrapped around her sturdy shoulders. At the door she turned round.

"And don't forget the PCC meeting to discuss the interviews," she said. "That's just as important."

"I'm not going to forget, Marjorie," Barbara said, smiling.

"You know I've really appreciated you joining the PCC."

"Thanks. I'm glad you asked me."

"You've been very helpful, really. Some of the more - well, flighty - members have some rather impractical ideas, in my opinion. Anyway, I'll let you get on. Enjoy your curry." She strode off, her corduroy skirt swinging and her boot heels clicking briskly on the paving slabs.

Curry? As she returned to the kitchen and put the radio on, Barbara realised the scent of chicken in Balti sauce must be clinging to her skin, shirt and hair. They'd served an Indian-themed lunch in the works canteen so she'd have to shower and change. She really didn't want to go to the meeting wafting an aroma of cumin and stale cooking oil. Especially when Francis Mortimer would be there.

At the thought of Francis, his slightly ugly but intelligent face with his serious grey eyes; at his gentle voice leading the church responses, Barbara paused from rinsing out her mug. Marjorie had, last year, invited her to the celebration meal for an Alpha course. Since Marjorie and her husband George had helped her so much when she'd moved in, Barbara had felt obliged to accept, even though she didn't like the sound of it. After the meal, Francis had stood up to speak. He'd started off by telling a rambling and not hugely funny joke about an atheist and a bear. He hadn't told it well: he'd stumbled over the punchline and then flushed up to the rims of his over-large ears. But as he spoke further, Barbara had listened more and more intently. He'd spoken about faithfulness and love, his voice eager and fluent, with a slight Welsh lilt, his plain face alight with belief and passion. Occasionally he ran his fingers through his ruffled, grey-flecked hair and made it even messier. Now she could barely remember the details of what he'd said, just how she'd felt while listening to him and how much she had wanted to hear him again.

"Here is the six o-clock news," the announcer on the radio said. She jumped and nearly dropped her mug. Day-dreaming about Francis? That wouldn't do. She needed to get ready for the short-listing meeting. At least she didn't have to prepare anything for dinner, just reheat some of the Balti chicken and rice. Despite the spices and fresh coriander, it hadn't proved as popular as they'd hoped, so she'd been able to take some home.

After eating, in the bathroom, Barbara considered then rejected the budget shower gel. It did the job well enough, but smelt like toilet cleaner. Instead, she reached for the bottle of mango-scented gel that had been a Christmas present from Tilly at work. There was only a quarter of it left, but she'd be extravagant, for once. As she let the hot water drench her and clear away the lingering aroma of chopped onions from her skin, she lifted sudsy hands to her face and breathed in the clean, sweet perfume, then washed her hair. Using apple-scented shampoo meant she'd smell like a fruit salad but at least that was better than a late-night take-away.

Once dressed, Barbara dragged a brush through her hair. Her tangle of mousy curls had barely any of the shine and gloss that the expensive argon oil conditioner promised. Could she afford to get it cut and coloured? It would cost forty pounds, if not more. No, she would have to pay the credit card bill first which would leave only three hundred pounds in her account. That didn't seem a lot after seventeen years of working, but buying the house had taken most of her savings. She sighed then applied a streak of brown eye shadow, a bit of highlighter, mascara and lipstick, and stared at herself in the mirror. Her eyes looked brighter, her lips fuller and redder. It didn't bother her that Marjorie would narrow her eyes and frown, but

Francis probably wouldn't even notice. She laughed quietly. What a cliché. How had she become a middle-aged, nondescript spinster with a crush on the vicar?

CHAPTER TWO

Luke Carmichael sat down. Six faces stared at him. It seemed rather a lot. He surreptitiously slid his hands inside his pockets to dry his wet palms before shaking hands with them all. Honestly, he ought to be used to interviews by now. This was his ninth.

One of the interviewers, who wore a dog collar, coughed and shuffled the papers in front of him.

"Well, good morning, er, Luke Carmichael, is that right?" he said. "Er, welcome. Let me introduce ourselves. I'm the vicar, Francis Mortimer, to start with."

Luke lost track of the names and positions half-way through. But the youngest, a woman in her mid-twenties with pinkish-blonde hair, smiled encouragingly at him. He relaxed slightly.

Half-an-hour later he could feel sweat dampening his shirt. The young woman, the vicar, and the oldest man were straightforward, but the other interviewers had fired questions and challenges at him like Tomahawk missiles: "How do you evaluate your work, and why?", "Tell us about a time when you had to deal with a problem with a volunteer", "What risk assessment did you do?" then had scribbled notes and marked crosses in boxes as he had stuttered, hesitated and then corrected himself. Every mistake made him more nervous. He surreptitiously ran a finger round his collar to loosen his tie.

"Can you tell us something about work that you've done with different backgrounds, er, I mean, young people from different backgrounds?" Francis asked, glancing down at the score sheet in front of him.

Luke took a deep breath and considered for a moment. Yeah, he could answer that one, though he knew he'd struggled on the others.

"Oh, um, yeah. Derby, the youth club, there were some kids who were Asian. From Pakistan, India… Some were Christian, but they brought along friends, who were…um, weren't Christian. Hindus, Sikh, Muslim. So we tried to include them, although for some, especially some of the Eastern European children, I don't think they'd been here very long, some of them. So, language was an issue. Anyway, we looked at Diwali, but to be honest, most of them knew more about it than we did. From school, you know." He paused. He couldn't think of what else to say. Francis put something in a box on the score sheet. Luke couldn't see it clearly, but it looked like a zero.

"Um, but, it was really interesting for me," Luke

added hurriedly. "I mean, I didn't know much about it. Or Vaisakhi, or even Ramadan, to be honest. Some of the kids, the Muslim kids, came in Ramadan, and, you know, sunset is late, 8pm, 9pm, in July or August. So some of the older kids hadn't eaten, and if we had food, it was tough for them. So we stopped doing food. But then, some of the other kids, not Muslims, well, there are a lot of really struggling families in Derby, and they were expecting to get fed…"

The youngest woman sighed. "Oh, poor kids," she said. Francis made another scribble on the sheet in front of him. Luke gave up. He couldn't explain it all.

"Right. What skills will you bring to this job?" the square-jawed woman with harsh red lipstick suddenly asked, tapping varnished nails on the desk, and Luke felt as if everything in his memory had deserted him, leaving him gasping for answers like a landed fish thrashing for air.

Yet another failure, he thought afterwards, as he walked down the hill to Merton railway station, his shoulders hunched, his hands thrust deep into his pockets. He got out his phone, thought about messaging one of his friends in Derby or Sheffield, *Car crash interview, mate, no chance,* then changed his mind. The news would get around fast enough. He thought back to the interview and flushed at how he'd stumbled over the basic questions, let alone the killer ones like 'What might be the potential issues of two organisations working together?' He hadn't got a clue with that one.

When the train doors opened at Telford Station

he dodged through the commuters and ran out. He needed to run. He took the steps on the footbridge three at a time, sprinted down the ramp towards the shopping centre and vaulted over the fence at the bottom. The rucksack holding his shoes, jacket and tie bounced on his back, pulling him off-balance. He steadied himself, then took off again, weaving between shoppers and walkers, tight-rope walking along the low rails by the cycle paths. The traffic lights held him up for a moment, but he jogged into the park, jumped up and swung hand-to-hand next to the kids on the high bars in the playground, dropped to the ground, dodged picnicking families and football games, and sprinted onwards.

That had been the worst job interview so far, he thought, as he ran along the suburban pavements. But there weren't many other youth worker jobs around. If he didn't get this one, he'd probably got no chance. He'd have to start searching for bar work, shop work, anything. He jogged faster.

At the cemetery, he leapt onto the top of the wall, five foot above the mown grass and worn gravestones. A cool summer breeze rustled a crisp bag along the gutter. A car went past and the driver hooted at him. The wrought iron gate was open. When he got to the pillar he scrambled up to the top, stood there, breathed in deeply then flung himself across the gap. He grabbed the spikes at the top of the gate as his knees slammed into the wrought iron, and then he pulled himself up, wedging a foot between the spikes so he could reach sideways towards the other pillar. As he scrabbled round it, the cloth of his trousers tore against the rough stones. He balanced on the wall for a moment, breathing in the smells of cut grass, car exhaust, chips and takeaways, then ran on.

At his parents' Edwardian villa, his mother was leaning under the bonnet of their ancient Audi, fiddling with the engine. At the sound of the gate shutting, she straightened up and patted his shoulder with an oil-smeared hand.

"How did it go, darling?" she asked.

"Oh, a bit rubbish, to be honest. Nerves… Where's Dad?"

"Simon's out at the school governors' meeting. Putting the fear of God into the head-mistress, I expect," she said with a laugh.

"Oh. Right," Luke said, feeling relieved. He wouldn't have to endure a post-mortem unravelling of all his interview mistakes just yet. He looked down at the hole in his smart trousers.

"Oh, Luke, you silly boy," his mother clucked. "Ripped on a wall, I suppose? You really should take more care. Well, you'll have to learn to sew, or buy a new pair. But maybe you won't need your interview trousers again. Chin up, darling. You never know."

"Hope so. What are you up to? Need any help?"

"No. I'm just topping up the radiator and checking the oil levels. You pop on in. I expect you need a shower. Dinner will be late."

Luke tossed his rucksack onto the tiled floor, and went into the kitchen for a drink. As the kettle was boiling, he leaned his head against the wall cupboards. *Please, please let me get this job*, he thought. If he got this, at last he would be able to say to his father, "Yeah, they offered it to me. Fairly decent pay, running outreach programmes, youth club and Sunday school, and I get a house to live in as well. Full-time, 40 hours a week. Yeah, it is permanent." And he imagined saying what he knew he'd never say: "Are you impressed yet?"

CHAPTER THREE

When Barbara walked into Holy Trinity church for the PCC meeting after the interviews, Marjorie and her husband George had already arrived and got the tables ready. She said hello, sat down, took her jacket off, shivered and put it back on again.

"Gosh, it's cold in here," she said.

"You wouldn't think it was August, would you?" Marjorie said.

Barbara nodded, noticing that Marjorie was wearing a very un-summery moss-green jumper with a chunky amber pendant. She looked up. The drifting spider's web that she had noticed during the last meeting still clung to the gothic vaulted ceiling and swayed slightly. It seemed longer than before. Barbara imagined the thin legs of a many-eyed spider scuttling down the thread and dropping onto the table in front of her, and she got up and moved to a different chair. The church really needed cleaning, she thought. There were finger-flicked off the tendrils of dust and handed it back to him.

"Thank you, my dear," he said, then looked round at the muddled papers. "Well, we always said we should try 'Messy Church'," he continued, as he gathered up the debris and tried to re-arrange the scattered sheets. "Oh dear. All the CV's are mixed up. I really doubt it's the retired French teacher who lists her hobbies as surfing and Dungeons and Dragons…"

He heaped the papers together, put them on the table and sat next to Barbara.

"Have any of you seen this week's Church Times?" he asked, opening up and smoothing out a newspaper with long, slender fingers. "Essential reading for the upwardly-mobile vicar in a hurry… Anyway, buried in the letters page, between a discussion on the linguistic roots of the word *parousia* and the theological content of John Donne's elegies, there is a fascinating discussion. Look at this question. I am really intrigued by it. 'Why are churches so full of difficult and disagreeable people?'"

"Francis!" exclaimed Marjorie. "For goodness sake, what are you talking about? Are you saying that this church is full of disagreeable people?"

"Oh, Marjorie, no, of course not. The church wardens wouldn't let them through the door, would they? Although I'm sure we would all admit that a few have slipped through. I mean, take Barbara here. We all know how difficult and disagreeable she is," he said, with the ghost of a wink at her.

marks on the glass in the porch, flakes of paint coming off the walls, grit in the corners; the brass was tarnished, the wooden pews dull.

"Anyway, Barbara, I'm glad you're nice and early," Marjorie said, her bangles clunking as she slid a pile of papers across to Barbara. "You need to have a look at these CVs and interview score sheets. Before we decide."

"Yes, of course." Barbara started to read the first one. "Luke Carmichael…"

"Yes, you remember. I told you about him. He's definitely my first choice."

Francis dashed in, his flyaway dark hair blown by the wind and even messier than usual.

"Good evening all," he said.

"You're on time!" Marjorie exclaimed.

"Most unlike me, I know. But I set my alarm to remind me, in case I got distracted. And, oh praise ye the Lord, it worked."

Barbara glanced up at his worn, eager face, with the slight frown lines marking his forehead. He smiled at her.

"How are you, Barbara?" he asked.

"Oh, I'm fine. Fine," she muttered.

Her heart started to beat faster. She bent her head over the pile of CVs to hide the heat in her cheeks. Francis unwound his college scarf then changed his mind. As he wrapped it back around his neck, the pile of papers under his arm fell to the floor. He muttered, "Whoops-a-daisy," knelt down to pick them up, and his briefcase tipped over. An apple, several paperclips, a Bach CD and some pens skittered over the tiles. Barbara ran after one,

"Honestly, Francis," Marjorie said. "Be serious."

"I am always serious, am I not? The point is, that it was an extremely interesting query. With theological implications."

"So? What was the answer?"

"There wasn't one. It provoked a lot of discussion, but no resolution. It was just an open-ended and interesting question."

"Not a very sensible one, in my opinion," Marjorie snapped, and started reading one of the score sheets. "Anyway, we should be looking at these, rather than getting distracted, no matter how interesting the query is."

"Anyone know what *parkour* is?" Barbara said, after a while. "Luke Carmichael's CV - it says his hobby is parkour."

"Parkour?" George said. "Free-running, they call it."

"It's a fascinating hobby," said Francis. "The idea is to move as fast as possible through one's environment, using all the, er, features available. Walls, benches, stairs. Jumping down steps, vaulting walls, things like that, I believe. Completely beyond me, of course, but compelling to watch, I imagine."

The door crashed open as Sophie Tate rushed in, with a flutter of indian-print boho skirts and a faint rattling of her bead earrings. "Oh, I'm really early, aren't I?" she said breathlessly. "Just had my roots done, and there wasn't time to go back home!"

Marjorie stared at Sophie's feathery pink-streaked hair in obvious disapproval as Sophie flopped into a chair.

"Are those the CV's?" she asked, glancing at the pile of papers.

Marjorie nodded. "Yes, Barbara's just reading them."

"Can I have a quick dekko after you, Barbara? Just to remind me? I'm so excited about having a youth worker!" Sophie exclaimed. "Just when two new families have joined us, and they've both got teenagers! God's timing really is perfect, isn't it? It feels as if we've been through a really dark period and now God is going to really bless us."

"Er - I'll get the urn fired up," George said. "Marj, how many?"

"Well, I've only had two apologies. So there should be nine of us."

"Good. Who'd like tea or coffee?"

Barbara remembered the musty smell of mice she'd noticed last time she was in the kitchen. "Not me, thanks," she said.

"Oooh, yes please for me, George! I'm dying for a cuppa," Sophie said. "Just time, before all the heated discussions start!"

"There shouldn't be any heated discussions," said Marjorie. "The choice is obvious."

Marjorie was wrong. The discussions did become heated. Sophie and a couple of others argued vehemently against Luke in favour of another candidate.

"He's older, more experienced," Sophie insisted fiercely. "An ex-teacher, for goodness sake! He'll be able to handle anything. Luke's far too young. I really don't feel like he's the right person!"

Marjorie drummed her fingernails on the table. "Nonsense! It's obvious that Luke is the best man for the job!"

"I know it makes a change for me to agree with Sophie," said Ted Frankland, the church treasurer. "But he is too young, and he didn't come across well in the interview."

"That was simply nerves," Marjorie snapped.

"Terrified by Marjorie, I think," whispered Francis to Barbara. "I know I was…"

"Sorry, Francis? I didn't catch that?" Marjorie said.

"Ah. Well," Francis said, "I was just saying, that, on consideration, I do think that Luke is the wiser choice. I'm sorry to disagree with you, Sophie, but he seems a sensible boy, he's had a good Christian upbringing, he's very likeable. Barbara, what do you think? You've been very quiet."

"Oh, I don't know that I can say," Barbara said. "I've only been on the PCC for a few months."

"You still have a right to an opinion, Barbara."

She glanced briefly at Francis's concerned, gentle expression, and then at Marjorie's frowning face. "Well, I would vote for Luke. I think you are right about him, and he seems nice."

"Thank you. However, it is not an easy choice, is it?" Francis said. "It is very evenly balanced. We could just let God decide."

"You mean pray?" said Marjorie.

"Actually I was thinking more along the lines of tossing a coin. But, yes, we'll pray that God has a preference and will let us know. If not, then we'll fall back on human frailty, as usual. Life would be so much simpler if God directly and unequivocally guided every decision, would it not? Anyway, let us pray."

Barbara dutifully bowed her head, as Francis murmured, "Lord, we come to you, Father of all wisdom, seeking your guidance and, er, wisdom. We ask your help, Lord, to guide our deliberations in this matter."

"Lord, Lord, we ask and pray that we will see your will in this and that your Spirit will lead us to the right decision," Sophie said. "We just ask you for wisdom and for the gift of discernment…"

Her voice tailed off. Barbara was surprised. Usually Sophie would pray out loud for several minutes, barely pausing for breath. In the silence Barbara heard the traffic outside, a passer-by shouting across the street, starlings bickering, the water boiler in the kitchen ticking as it cooled. She knew she ought to be praying but she didn't want to break the quiet and she couldn't think of what to say anyway.

"Can we get on with it?" Ted growled, his moustache bristling so that he looked like an irritable walrus. "Some of us have got jobs to go to tomorrow."

Suddenly Sophie opened her eyes and sat upright, looking amazed. "Oh!" she exclaimed.

"What?" said Marjorie.

"I've just had a vision!"

Ted snorted. "A what? Gordon Bennett, not again!"

"What a loss to the diplomatic service you are, Ted," said Francis.

"Huh?"

"Never mind. Just let Sophie speak."

"A vision of a shattered stone, then Luke's face. Oh, it was really vivid!" Sophie gasped. "Oh, I really really feel this means we're in danger of splitting the church if we choose him."

"Don't be ridiculous!" said Marjorie. "Honestly, Sophie, how can that be possible? We're only appointing a youth worker. You and your over-the-top visions…"

"Now, Marj," said George. "Don't be so harsh. Sophie has a right to say what she thinks."

"Yes, but pretending to have a vision! Honestly!"

"I wasn't pretending, Marjorie. Don't you say things like that! The Holy Spirit really did send me a warning!"

"Marjorie, please," said Francis. "We should take these sort of messages seriously. You cannot limit how God speaks. Sophie, visions can be deceptive, I'm afraid. In the absence of further confirmation against him from anyone else…" He glanced around briefly. "I would suggest Luke. I truly feel he's the best choice; young, energetic, approachable. I'm sure you won't find it hard to work with him. But I think we should wind this discussion up."

"Absolutely," said Marjorie. "It's getting late, and we have got other items on the agenda."

So, can we vote now?" said Ted. "Who wants the greenhorn? I mean to say, Luke?"

Barbara put her hand up along with several others. Marjorie glanced briefly at Sophie's disconsolate face, but nodded. "Good. Six for

Luke. Against?"

Sophie's hand went up, along with that of Ted, Jonathon Roberts, and Ivy Woodings, the oldest member of the PCC.

"I'm not at all sure. I did like the sound of Luke, but I do know Sophie so well," said Ivy, patting Sophie's hand. "I've always found her to be extremely wise. I believe she has a point about his immaturity. And if she's had a vision…"

"Well, vision or not, that's only four against," said Marjorie. "Luke it is."

CHAPTER FOUR

Barbara walked slowly home from work. It wasn't kind, she thought. More than that, it wasn't fair. Three years' work overturned, just like that. As she turned the corner into her street, she saw a group of school children ahead. One of them tossed aside a fast food bag. It landed on the pavement by her lawn and scattered chips and screwed-up napkins over the tarmac. She sighed, went into her house and came back wearing rubber gloves and carrying a plastic bag. Two crows were already strutting cautiously around each other while snatching at the chips. They flew off slowly at her approach and settled nearby, cawing at her. She crouched down and collected up the grease-stained papers and pallid fingers of potatoes. She was foolish to do this, she knew. Don't be such a bloody doormat, her mother would say, let someone else do it. But no one else would. She pushed the bag into the bin. It was only yards away. How could they drop litter rather than walk three yards? They clearly didn't appreciate clean streets. She did.

Barbara had always wanted to live in a well-kept, tidy, quiet neighbourhood, and now at last she did, thanks to a shared ownership scheme run by a local housing association. Her house was at the end of a small terrace in a mixed estate in the north of Merton, with smart four-bedroom houses, a few young trees, black railings in front of three-story blocks of flats and curved roads with block-paving. The estate seemed bare-looking but she appreciated its pristine uncluttered appearance. She liked how the afternoon sunlight shone on the front of her button-neat house, on the glossy painted door, on the clean UPVC window frames.

Marjorie's blue Micra was parked on the block paving outside her and George's detached double-fronted house, with its cream stuccoed walls and columned porch gleaming in the bright sunshine. Barbara paused, looking at the orange-tinged leaves on the specimen acer, the manicured box hedge, the bright arrays of dahlias, red geraniums and asters edging their smooth, green lawn. Her house had a lawn and small border, but somehow her grass was never as green as theirs. But George had lent her his mower and lawn-edger, and in the spring Marjorie had given her a few lobelias and calendulas to brighten her border up. Barbara hesitated, then knocked on their door.

Marjorie opened it. From inside came the sound of 'Fur Elise' being played very slowly on a piano.

"Hello, Mrs Sanderson," Marjorie started to say, then tailed off. "Barbara! I thought you were

Victor's mother, come to pick him up."

"No, oh, I forgot you'd have lessons. I'll go. I won't interrupt."

Marjorie stared at her. "Are you all right?" she said.

"It's nothing. I shouldn't bother you…"

"Don't be silly! Come in. Victor will be done in five minutes. If you don't mind sitting and waiting, then I'll be free."

Barbara sat on the edge of the sofa and listened to Victor's unavailing attempts to master arpeggios and Marjorie's patient explanations and advice. There was a bowl of chrysanthemums on the table and books about playing bridge, growing roses, Hidcote gardens and Handel. Several silver-framed photos of Marjorie and George's only son, Stephen, with his fair hair and hesitant smile, stood on a polished sideboard.

Mrs Sanderson arrived to take away her unmusical son and Marjorie came in with a tray.

"You look like you need a cup of tea," she said. "What's happened?"

"It's work," Barbara said. "They've announced redundancies - thirty percent."

Marjorie gasped.

"And they're closing down the canteen."

"What? Closing it down? Are things that bad?"

"Yes. I'd only been there three years, but they were really nice people, it was such a good job, and it'll all be gone. Gone, in just months!"

Barbara dug her nails into her palms.

"Here, I'll get you a tissue," said Marjorie, going over to the sideboard. "Goodness me, that is a surprise. And a shame. I'm sorry to hear it. But don't get so upset, Barbara! There's plenty of restaurants and pubs around. I'm sure you'll get another job."

"That's the problem," said Barbara, blowing her nose. "I don't want to go back to that sort of work. Long shifts, late nights, not particularly good pay. Bad-tempered, rude customers leaving pennies for tips. At least with this job, I got to know the customers and we got a proper hour off and finished at three-thirty. Even though it was such an early start."

"Hmm," said Marjorie, drumming her nails against the side of her mug. "Will you get any redundancy pay?"

"No, it's sub-contracted out to Elliot's catering. We don't qualify. Elliot's say they've got other work, but it's miles away, in Leicester or Milton Keynes and I don't have a car."

"Oh. George's firm has tea ladies. They might have vacancies. Is that any good?"

"I don't know, it might not be enough hours. Look, don't worry about me. I'll find something. I just needed to tell you. Everyone at work is furious and they're just shouting and angry and it's all horrible."

"I can imagine."

"I wish I hadn't bought the house," Barbara said, rubbing her hand across her forehead. "It feels like I've only just started living in it. I've worked so hard to make it nice, but now I may have to sell and move away. Leave the church…"

"I'm sure it won't come to that. Can you get a

mortgage holiday?"

"I'd already thought about trying that, I might need it. But I've still got to find another job."

Marjorie nodded. "Well, I'll ask around. My friend, Jill, she might know of some jobs in the care homes she manages."

"Thanks," said Barbara, standing up. "I'd better go. I know you're busy. Thanks for the tea. It was kind of you."

"Nonsense! You know I'm glad to help!"

As Barbara opened her front door she saw that there was another buff envelope on the doormat. She opened it and frowned. The electricity bill could be paid, she knew, but then she might not have enough to pay the mortgage if she was going to lose her job soon, not to mention the council rates and the water bill. At least she'd paid for the carpet, and she could look for other work. If she couldn't find another job nearby, something she could get to by walking or by taking local transport, she would have to sell up and move away from Merton; leave the PCC, the church, Francis. At the thought, she went into her tiny sitting room and looked at the pale green walls, the light oak coffee table, the pictures and ornaments she had carefully chosen, the calm oasis she'd created, and she thought how much she'd miss her current job and all the people there. Perhaps she should pray, but she hesitated, wondering if God existed and if he would help her. It was silent outside, not even a car going by. She curled up on the sofa and stayed there, cold and motionless, until hunger roused her and she slowly went into the kitchen to get something to eat.

Next Saturday Marjorie came round, knocking briefly on the door and then walking straight in. Barbara was at the kitchen table, looking through the job adverts.

"Don't get up," Marjorie said, sitting down next to her. "I just popped round to tell you something. Jill, that friend of mine I mentioned, she's a manager for a couple of care homes. One of them, in Willborough, they've got a vacancy for a cook and general assistant. I've got you an application form."

"Really? Oh, gosh, thanks!" Barbara said, leaping up.

"It's nothing! Sit down, don't make a fuss about it. For goodness sake, I'm sure that you'd do the same for me. Anyway, Jill will probably do the interviewing, so I'll put in a good word for you. But it's only thirty hours a week, making lunches and refreshments for two dozen residents and the nurses. The money isn't brilliant, either."

"That doesn't matter, as long as I can live on it. I've not found anything else even worth applying for. I thought there might be something in the schools, but there's nothing."

Marjorie tutted, drumming her nails on the table.

"That's the government for you! Laying off school dinner ladies and putting it all out to private tender, no doubt." She shook her head. "Don't get me started. They're cutting the county music service. Austerity Britain was bad enough, but now it's worse! In my opinion, it's appalling. Anyway, this job. If you get it, it's in Willborough. Do you know where that is?"

"No. I've heard of it."

"It's a tiny village, about six miles south of Merton. The care home is a mile further south. Right in the middle of the countryside. Nice place, actually, one of those places that used to be a big manor house. But, the point is, there's no bus service, not to speak of."

"Oh," Barbara said, shaking her head. "I can't walk that far. I don't think I could even bike it."

"I thought so. I know you don't have a car - can you drive?"

"Yes. Dad taught me, years ago."

"Well, the thing is…" Marjorie twirled a jade bangle around her wrist. "We're going to trade up my car for a slightly bigger one, diesel, better for all those trips to uni we're going to be doing next year, when Stephen goes. So, if you wanted, you could borrow my old one. It's only a Micra, ten years old, but it's in good condition."

"What? Oh - really? Do you mean it? Gosh, thanks. I don't know what to say… That's so good of you!"

"Nonsense! We're glad to help. Don't get up, I'll see myself out. Let me know how the job application goes," and she briskly strode out, leaving Barbara to stare at the door in astonishment.

CHAPTER FIVE

"Off you get, Didymus, make space for Luke," said Sophie, pushing a plump tabby off the faded orange sofa. "Did you know that there are no cats in the bible? You're not allergic, are you?"

"What? No, no worries, I'm fine with cats."

The tabby stretched out its claws on a terracotta and cream dhurrie rug, glared at Luke and slunk under a desk covered with drawing pads, pens and copies of 'Woman Alive'.

"OK, I'll put the kettle on. I can talk to you from the kitchen. One of the blessings of a small house! Tea, coffee?"

"Coffee, please, milk, two sugars," said Luke, looking curiously at a stark abstract painting, in blue and ochre and purple, hanging next to a tie-dyed African banner.

"Right. So, how has your first week been?" called Sophie from the kitchen. "You've had two Sunday services, you've met everyone, you've found your way around?"

"Yeah, sort of," said Luke.

"What do you think of Merton?"

"Merton? It's OK, I suppose. Centre's a bit run down, isn't it? But the people seem friendly enough. Some fun-looking clubs and stuff. Apart from that, it seems just like any other small town."

"I guess it is small compared to Derby. But you'll love it! You'll really love it when you get to know it! It's got some lovely bits. Fantastic flowers, crocuses by the statue in Victoria Park, you should see them! They're just amazing! Lilies of the field, robed in splendour. And the churches are so engaged, really moving out, really working together."

"Um, are they?"

Sophie put a tray of mugs and biscuits by the pile of books on the coffee table. "Oh, yes. Absolutely. Where there's unity, the Lord sends a special blessing and I really believe that for Merton. It's a special place!" she said, sitting on a low wooden stool by the table.

"Oh. OK. Good! I'm looking forward to finding out more about what's going on here."

She leaned forward and cupped her hands under her chin as she looked at him. "Great! You know, I am truly excited about the Spirit blessing us by sending you. I'm sure you'll make a huge difference to our church."

"Well, I'll try."

"Oh, don't worry! Whatever happens, it will work out fine in the end, I know. I mean, you weren't my first choice."

"What?" Luke said, choking on his coffee.

"It's not that I'd got anything against you. It was just that I really felt we should have an older person, someone with a bit more experience. But I was wrong. I think…" She bit her lip and looked thoughtful for a moment. "Yes, I must have been wrong. Anyway, everyone else, well, almost everyone, voted for you."

"Yeah, right. Um, Sophie, well - don't you mind?"

"Mind what?"

"Me being appointed when you wanted someone else."

"Gosh, no. I really believe God sorts everything out, even through our mistakes and confusions. Anyway, have another biscuit. Oh, that was another thing I meant to ask you. Can you drive?"

"No, not yet. I've had a few lessons. That's one of the things I need to do, to sort out a test here."

"Great. Being able to drive will help. Anyway, right, let's talk about the youth club, evening services etc. Hang on, I'll get some paper," she said, leaning over to grab a pen and pad from the desk. "You said that you can play the guitar, didn't you? In your CV. So you can lead worship, which will help."

"Um, yeah, I suppose so. Not brilliantly, but I can manage simple songs. That's all, I'm afraid. I don't like leading the singing, though. I don't think it's obligatory for a youth worker, you know," he said, as she looked disappointed.

"Oh. Never mind, I'm sure that won't be a problem. I can sing, just about. We might need another guitarist. I could ask Gerald."

"Who's Gerald?"

"He's my stalker."

"What?"

"No, not really!" She laughed. "He's a friend, but he's a bit keen on me. Keeps coming to the shop, drinking too much green tea and coffee, hanging around. He's OK, he plays the guitar in a local band, but he's not really a Christian. He's done Alpha, but it didn't seem to stick! Still, he might be prepared to help out on Sundays, if I ask him nicely."

"Great, thanks. Um - what shop? Is that where you work?"

"Yeah. I run a café and crafts shop, called Sea Shells Café, in Pershore Street. You'll have to come and have coffee. You'll love it! It's all seaside-themed, which is ironic when we're about as far from the sea as you can get. Sort of quirky, though."

"OK. I'll do that. Look, Sophie, I know most people think we'll need a worship band to lead the singing in the evening, but I've got some other ideas."

"Fantastic! I knew that was why God sent you! We need new ideas. OK, fire ahead!"

Shouting down the big white phone, that's what Luke's uncle always called it. It sounded funny when he said it, but it wasn't. Luke flushed the toilet again. It was true what they said, sick always did have carrots in it. He hadn't eaten any carrots. Only that donor kebab and a can of lager. At the thought of the greasy meat he retched again. Ugh. He crawled back into bed.

Toast and milk for breakfast seemed to help, but by the evening the toilet had had more use in the past twelve hours than it got in a normal week. He phoned Sophie.

"I can't make it to the youth club. Yeah, I know it's my first session, but I can't help it. Food poisoning. Sophie, I've spent all day on the loo! No, don't laugh! It's not funny! And don't say you'll pray for me! I don't want prayer, I just want this to stop. I feel crap, just crap!"

"OK, Luke, calm down. Just tell me, what have you been eating?"

"A donor kebab yesterday, toast for breakfast but I threw most of that up, a cheese sandwich for lunch… and I haven't been able to face anything since."

"Oh, Luke, you idiot! You haven't stopped eating?"

"Huh? What?"

"Stopped eating! Oh, you poor boy, haven't you ever had food poisoning before? You have to stop eating! Otherwise the bugs just keep multiplying. Didn't anyone ever tell you that?"

"No… What, not eat anything?"

"Clear fluids only, until tomorrow evening. Lemonade, squash, not milk, nothing else. No, don't complain! Trust me, it'll work. And don't worry about the youth club. I'll get Helen to help out and it will be OK."

"Yeah, but missing my first session because of a dodgy kebab! I'm going to look completely stupid, aren't I?"

CHAPTER SIX

As Barbara was sitting at a table in the church hall, arranging paper squares into piles sorted by colour and size, a tall young man with dark hair and pale skin opened the door, peered round uncertainly and then came in. Sophie put down the crate of plastic beakers and bottles of squash.

"Ah, Luke!" she exclaimed.

"Yeah," he said, shrugging. "Sorry, bit late, but here at last. A week late, really, I know, but I finally made it."

"Well, you're here now, that's great. Plenty of time to help set up. Anyway, Luke, this is Barbara Walters. She helps out."

"Um, hi," he said, smiling nervously as he shook her hand. He had a clean, earnest appearance, despite faded jeans and a t-shirt that had seen better days, and his face, with his wide mouth and floppy fringe, had an intelligent, if nervous, expression. He was very thin. Barbara felt he needed to be fed some hearty casseroles before facing some of the kids at the youth club, but she smiled back and said a quiet hello.

"Right, then, well, this is the hall," Sophie said. "I'll give you a quick guided tour."

Barbara finished the paper sheets for the origami, and went into the kitchen to put the kettle on. Luke and Sophie came in. Luke glanced round at the peeling paint and the damp patch on one wall.

"So, what do you think?" Sophie said.

"Um, well, I've seen better to be honest."

"No kidding! It needs new heating, new kitchen, redecorating, everything. It's a nightmare! I keep praying for God to send us some money to sort it out, but nothing so far. Still, we manage."

"How many kids come?"

"Well, it's fallen from eighteen or nineteen to less than a dozen, even fewer some evenings. Me, Daphne, Helen and Barbara lead it." Sophie shook her head. "To be honest, no wonder it doesn't work, with four women, two of them over forty, leading it. Daphne gets extremely irritated when the older kids play up or tease the young ones, Helen tends to favour her two boys – not that I can blame her for that really. Anyway, Helen and Daphne have stepped down, now you're here."

"Helen, Daphne?"

"Helen Stuart. She interviewed you. Along with me, the vicar, Ted Frankland - the treasurer - and George and Marjorie Fowler. Remember?"

"Nope. But I'm getting the hang of who's who. Daphne?"

"Daphne Richards. I don't think you've met her yet. She's on the PCC, been at Holy Trinity for years, one of Marjorie's cronies. Anyway, she and Helen have stepped down."

"Right."

"Oooh, are you making tea?" Sophie said to Barbara.

"Yes, of course. Want some, er, Luke?"

"Nah. Can I have coffee instead?"

"OK," Sophie said. "Er, where was I? Yes, Daphne and Helen have stepped down, but Barbara, thankfully, is staying. She's ever so good with some of the shyer girls."

"No, really…" Barbara said. "I don't think I am. I don't know what to say, to talk to them about, most of the time…"

"Don't be silly," Sophie said, "You do fine." As they went out of the kitchen. Barbara heard her continue. "Anyway, quick tour of the rest, toilets, cupboards and so on. Yes, Barbara is really helpful. Bless her, though, she's so quiet, so unforthcoming that some of the noisier, more riotous kids just ignore her. But she's really kind. She has that 'unfading beauty of a gentle and quiet spirit' that Saint Paul talks about."

Barbara bent her head to hide her reddening cheeks, and stirred the tea noisily. Sophie was right. She did find it hard to talk to the older kids, especially the boys. But now that Luke would be around, hopefully he'd do that and she could stick to doing crafts with the younger, quieter children.

As she went to the cupboards to get out the crate containing the scissors and rulers, Sophie and

Luke came in from the storeroom at the back of the hall.

"Right. OK, that's where the table-football lives," he said. "Crates in those cupboards. Got it, I reckon. Um, do we start at seven?"

"No, half-seven. Can you get the chairs out?"

Sophie started fetching crates out of cupboards and unfolding tables with her usual efficiency. Luke stood in the centre of the hall and looked round uncertainly, then went over to the stack of plastic chairs wedged into one corner. He carried them into the middle and yanked at the top one before Barbara could stop him. They were jammed together. It came free and he fell backwards, crashing into Sophie. She dropped the crate she was carrying.

"Oh, no, sorry!" he said.

"Whoops! OK, it's all right. No harm done, it's only the cashbox and goodies for the tuckshop."

"Tuckshop?" he said, as he and Barbara helped her pick up the sweets and crisps.

"Yes. Oh, Luke, I'm sorry! Those are the wrong chairs! I should have told you. Those are broken - we really should chuck them away. No, the ones we use are in the storeroom behind the stage."

"OK, right," said Luke, stomping off.

"Don't worry, you'll soon get the hang of it all," Sophie called out after him, and gave Barbara a quick, guilty grimace.

Half-an-hour later it was all ready. Barbara and Sophie had done most of it, while Luke had wrestled with a stack of chairs and struggled to unfold and set up a table-football game. Two teenage girls sauntered in. Sophie introduced Luke, they nodded briefly, then sat at a table with Barbara, who started showing them how to make origami boxes for jewellery. They were soon happily folding coloured paper, chattering and giggling, as Luke stood nearby, watching and hovering uncertainly. Some older girls and boys came in. Sophie looked up from the signing-in book.

"Luke, this is Cameron. He wants the Wii set up. Can you do it? Car racing or snowboarding or something. It's all over there, in that corner."

"OK!" said Luke. "Have you got a balance board?"

"Yeah, I think so. No idea how it works though."

"I do. I've used one. Great! We'll do the snowboarding. It's brill. Come on, um, Cameron, give us a hand and we can do the co-op game."

Luke switched the Wii on, loaded the game and got Cameron started on the balance board. As he handed him the remote, a woman swathed in a purple scarf over a green wool coat came in and strode over to him, followed by a slim teenager in a cream hoodie, drainpipe jeans and turquoise high-tops.

"Ah, Luke!" she said. "Glad to see you here at last. It was a pity that you missed your first session. What on earth were you thinking of? Everyone, all the youth, they were expecting you!"

Barbara looked up. It was Marjorie and her son, Stephen. Her strident voice, loud enough to carry over thirty chattering pupils in a school classroom, was unmistakable.

"Yeah, um, sorry about that," he muttered. Barbara could see him flushing.

"Well, I'm glad to see you here tonight, at least. By the way, I'm Mrs Fowler, Marjorie, chair of the PCC. You'll remember; I interviewed you. This is my son, Stephen."

"Hi," said Stephen, nodding laconically to Luke.

"Stephen, I want a quiet word with Luke. Can you go and play table football or something? Right, Luke, come over here for a moment. Now, let me just say I'm still pleased with your appointment. I'm sure missing the first session was just a glitch."

"Um, OK, thanks, Mrs Fowler."

"Anyway, the thing is, it's Stephen," she said, in a quieter voice, but still loud enough for Barbara, and probably Stephen as well, to hear her. "He's very young and easily influenced. I want this youth group and your new evening service to help him stay in the church. He needs mentoring, Luke, by someone near his own age."

"Well, Mrs Fowler, I'll do my best. We're planning…"

"Stephen just needs a bit of guidance. George and I are very pleased that you are taking over the youth club. It's been allowed to drift too much, if you see what I mean."

"Yeah, OK, um, thanks."

"Jolly good! Well, I'm glad you understand me. I've got to go, there's a prayer meeting at eight. I'll just say goodbye to Stephen. I'll be back at half-nine to collect him."

She strode off, nodding briefly to Barbara as she

passed. Luke glanced at Stephen who was lounging on a chair next to a group of girls painting each other's nails, then shrugged. Barbara could tell what he was thinking. Stephen was at least eighteen, and old enough to get to the youth club and back by himself. But then Marjorie was – well, Marjorie was Marjorie, and it was usually easiest just to go along with her. Then a young girl called Shelley asked Barbara, yet again, to show her how to make the jewellery boxes. Barbara folded paper, listened to Shelley's long convoluted stories about quarrels with school friends, helped others thread beads onto wires and glue sequins onto card. Excited comments from the group of boys around the Wii echoed around the hall. Luke seemed to be getting on well with them. The occasional friendly competitive shout of triumph, high-five, cheer and groan, the odd argument about whose turn it was, the laughter as someone toppled off the balance board – the atmosphere seemed much more friendly and encouraging than usual, even if it was louder.

The two hours passed quickly. Barbara was surprised when the kids started putting coats on and leaving, and parents started peering through the doors. Sophie helped Luke get the Wii put away, ignoring the pretend moans as she said that next week they'd put the 'Just Dance' game on and she'd expect boys, as well as girls, to join in.

As the last boy disappeared into the gloomy autumn drizzle, Luke leant theatrically against the closed door.

"First session done, over, finito!" he exclaimed.

"I survived!"

"Yep. Despite Marjorie ticking you off," Sophie said. "Not done yet though. We've got to clear everything away, check toilets, sweep floors, blah blah blah. Don't pull that face. You know it's part of the job."

"Did you enjoy it?" Barbara said to Luke later, as they washed and dried up coffee mugs.

"Yeah, I did, ta. Got to know a few names, improved my Wii skills, talked about school stuff. Interesting bunch of kids."

"Luke, give me a hand with the tables," Sophie said, poking her head through the hatch.

"We're done in here, anyway," Barbara said, folding up the tea-towel. "I'll come and get the floor swept."

In the hall, Luke flipped a table over and tried to fold down the legs.

"There's a catch, you have to pull it," Sophie called as she walked past carrying a pile of chairs.

"OK," he said with irritation. As he tugged, it slipped, the legs swung back and jammed his finger. He swore loudly. Barbara glanced up, mildly shocked.

"Luke!" said Sophie.

He sucked in his breath. "Yeah, sorry, but that … that flipping hurt!" he said, shaking his hand vigorously.

"Oh dear, I bet it did," said Barbara. She looked at his red, squashed finger. "I did that the first time I tried to put those tables away. There's a bit of a knack to them. It's easy once you've got the hang of it. Go and run your finger under cold water.

That will help."

"Poor Luke! I should have showed you how to do them." Sophie laughed. "I thought Christians were born again instinctively knowing how to fold up church tables!"

CHAPTER SEVEN

Rather to her surprise, given how difficult the interview had been, Barbara got the job at the care home. So far she'd spent seven weeks there: running around with trays of drinks, cooking Christmas turkey, mopping up spills, changing beds, chasing lost and muddled residents, dealing with one man's sudden rages and cleaning up the damp patches others left on every seat.

As she dashed into the kitchen one morning, rapidly tying up her work apron, Angela, the supervisor, was scraping margarine thinly onto white bread and piling the slices up on plates.

"Ah, Barbara, there you are! You're a bit late!" she said.

"Yes, I'm really sorry. There was a traffic jam on Commercial Street."

"You should have left earlier, shouldn't you?"

"Yes, sorry."

"Well, never mind for now. Just try a bit harder

tomorrow, won't you?" Angela said, and pointed to several bags of sprouts and potatoes on the counter by the sinks. "Now, get on with peeling those veg."

By the time Barbara had prepped all the vegetables her hands were chapped and dirty. She dashed to the toilet. There was wet paper on the floor and hair in the sink. She picked up the paper, wiped round the sink, washed her hands and tucked the loose strands of her hair back under her cap.

She took the trays of teas and coffees round, going to Jean's room last. She was ninety and she had no memories left, but she always took Barbara's hand, stroking it with her talc-soft fingers, always said, "Are you new here, dearie? You look tired. Have a lie down. I'll get you a cup of tea," then sat down as vacancy blanked her expression. Somehow, though, the fleeting concern in Jean's face, as she peered into Barbara's eyes, helped. Barbara took her time, tidied Jean's bed, put sugar in her tea and gave her a biscuit. Jean was grateful and bewildered, as always. Her daughter had brought her flowers a week earlier and they were wilting, the fragile petals drifting down onto the laminate flooring.

"I'll clear those up," Barbara said, and took the vase to the kitchen. By the time she returned, Jean had drank her tea and was staring out of the window at the grey wind-blown clouds and leafless trees. She stood up, took a few shaky steps forward and gently took Barbara's hand. "Good morning, my dear. Are you new here?" she said.

Barbara's shifts were supposed to be nine to

four, with an hour off for lunch, but most days she was lucky to get a thirty minutes break, and today she didn't leave until after five. As she drove home through darkness and drifting rain, she whispered, "God, if you exist, thank you. Thank you for the job, for Marjorie giving me this car. Sorry I was late. Please help me to keep this job. Please help me to pay all the bills and keep my house." The money was only just more than the living wage. "Please give me a promotion or a pay rise," she added. Prayer felt like talking to nothing, like talking to Jean. It was a waste of time, she thought.

Back home, she had a quick sandwich and went through her bank statement. The three-month mortgage holiday had helped, but now the interest rates had shot up. It was going to be difficult, she knew. Yet again, she looked though the agency sites, LinkedIn, the job adverts but she couldn't find anything. Worries and fears and doubts twirled and scurried through her brain.

Eventually she decided that there wasn't any more she could do tonight, and she had to think about something else, so she went up to the spare bedroom. Rather than a bed, she had furnished it with bookcases and shelves holding several model aircraft and cars. She sat at the desk underneath the window, and adjusted the snake-necked lamp. Her tweezers, fine camel-hair brushes, Stanley knife, paint-pots and plastic sprues loaded with grey moulded shapes were laid out in neat rows. She was half-way through a model of a VW Camper van and she'd wanted to fix the wheels and headlights, and paint the sides.

For a while she was completely absorbed; snicking the flash off the pieces and carefully squeezing trickles of glue onto the surfaces; Classic FM on the radio, her mind quiet. Then, putting the brush down she stretched, opened the curtains and looked outside. The rain had stopped, although scudding clouds still raced behind the wet roofs of the houses opposite. A cat sat on a fence post under a streetlight and stared haughtily at nothing. She hoped the cat wouldn't catch the goldfinches on the feeder. The thought of the birds' cheerful brightness reminded her of when she'd seen the Liverpool 'Razzle Dazzle' Ferry crossing the steel-cold expanse of the Mersey. She still had a postcard of it, so she took it out of the drawer, looked at it, then searched through her pots for red, yellow, black and white paint. Carefully, with her finest brushes, she delicately painted striped, cross-hatched and fragmented camouflage patterns on the van's side. Her brush slipped and a tiny blotch of yellow edged into the red. The little mistake looked huge.

CHAPTER EIGHT

Naomi Robeson came into the narrow hall of their terraced house, dropped her bag on the worn, chipped tiles and wedged her coat in between the others on the rickety hall-stand. Her sister Jessica clattered down the stairs and rushed up to her.

"Nomy! Nomy! I wanna go to this youth club this evening, but Mum won't take me and she won't let me go by myself! She's mean. Mean thing! You'll take me, won't you? Come on, Nomy, Shelley's going and she's, like, it's brilliant!" she said, tugging at Naomi's hands.

"What youth club?"

"In the town centre, at that massive big church. The one by the graveyard place where all the Poles hang out."

"Oh. Really?"

"Yeah, but it's safe, Nomy, it's proper run, they've got proper adults in charge and everything. They do games and pool and have music and stuff.

Shelley says it's real fun. Oh, go on, Nomy, say you'll come with me!"

"What time is it? I'm really tired, Jessie. I need something to eat."

She sat on the bottom step and unknotted the laces of her work shoes, then kicked them under the hall-stand. "I ended up having to do a nine-hour shift today, we were so busy. And short-staffed. Nine hours! And I had to do lifeguard duty for two hours."

"Boring!" Jessica grimaced.

"Yeah. Then I had to clean all the ladies' changing rooms. Someone had cut their toenails in one of the cubicles. Gross."

"Ugh! Poor Nomy! But the clubs not til half-seven, it's ages yet. And it's only two hours long. If you come, I'll make you a coffee and a toastie, I will, I make a brill cheese toastie, don't I?"

Danny Kehinde came out of the back room, leaned against the wall and stared at them, his hands shoved deep into the pockets of his jeans.

"You're nuts," he said. "Go to a church youth club? It'll be full of religious fruit-cakes. I ain't gonna take you."

Naomi glanced into the sitting room. Her mother was lying on the over-large sofa, staring at 'Pointless' on the widescreen TV. There was a glass of beer on the table wedged between the sofa and the wall. Even though it was gloomy outside, the curtains were still wide open.

"You go, girl," said Patience, waving a hand in their direction without looking up. "You both go."

"Where's Walter?" Naomi said.

"Yeah, where's Dad?" Danny asked.

"He done gone to Birmingham with a friend. He said he got some work there for a few days."

Naomi smiled to herself. The less time her mother's boyfriend spent in the house, the better. A pity his son wasn't going to Birmingham too. She went up to her mother and stroked the fresh bruise on her cheek.

"You leave that, child," said Patience. "He swore he didn't mean it. He won't do it again. He a good man, he is."

Naomi shrugged, turned back and looked at Danny as he lounged against the wall. He stared at her with a moody, intense expression, like he always did.

"OK, Mum, I'll go with Jessica," she said. "We'll walk there, and we'll catch the ten o'clock bus back."

"Ace! Thanks, Nomy! I'll go change!" Jessica exclaimed and ran upstairs.

"Fine by me. You go," Danny nodded. "I wanna go into town with Mitch. But I'll meet you both off the bus. I wanna make sure you're safe." He came up to her, wrapped his arms around her, and kissed her neck. She suppressed a shiver. "You take care now," he said.

In their room, Jessica was standing before the mirror and pushing heaps of jumpers and school shirts out of the way with her feet.

"What'd you think?" she demanded, admiring her reflection in a spaghetti-strap top.

"It's OK," Naomi said, taking off her work uniform. "Bit low for you."

"Nomy! I'm eleven. Nearly twelve. Don't be so stupid and boring! I'm gonna wear it anyway!"

"Turn round, then," Naomi said. "Let me have a look."

The green satin was very low. Jessica's thin chest and immature breasts were obvious. Naomi considered her sister, trying to keep her concern out of her face.

"You've got a big spot on your back," she lied.

"No! Have I?" Jessica said, twisting her head round.

"Do you want to borrow my gold shirt? To go over it? Tie it at the waist, like this. Bit warmer too."

"Oh yeah! Brill!"

"And this?" Naomi took a string of topaz beads from the jewellery stand that Danny had given her, a couple of years after he and Walter had moved in.

"Yeah, are you sure? Brill! I'll look ace, won't I?" Jessica pulled at her hair. "Wish I could get it coloured. I hate this bloody frizzy stuff. Shall I get it straightened? I'd look smart with straight hair, wouldn't I? What're you gonna wear, Nomy?"

"Oh, just jeans, I think."

"Nah! Don't be so down! Hey, wear your print dress. This one. You look ace in it."

She pulled a crimson, orange and ivory geometric print dress from an open drawer.

"OK," nodded Naomi. "Why not?" It would be a change to wear something pretty and not jeans or the boring gym uniform. To get away from work, her mother, Danny, the crowded house, for an evening. To give Jessie a chance to go somewhere safe and have a bit of fun with her friends, without worrying about her.

CHAPTER NINE

Red and white striped awnings flapped and clattered against the metal poles of the market stalls. As Luke went by, a burly trader waved a bowl of vegetables at him. "Carrots! Onions!" the trader bellowed loudly, against the background noise of buses, cars and people. Two lads Luke recognised from the youth club were leaning against the window of a burger outlet on the other side of the street. He nodded at them, mouthed, "All right?" and they waved back. As he passed the doughnut stall he hesitated, tempted by the sweet vanilla and sugar scent, but shook his head and walked up the main street, past the charity shops, vape emporiums and drab hopeless-looking clothes shops, with 'Sale' signs shouting from their windows.

He turned a corner and saw a tall, slim girl, with dark curly hair pulled back in a thick ponytail. He thought he recognised her and walked faster towards her. She and her younger sister had come to the youth club a few weeks ago. Her sister had run in excitedly and instantly dashed off to start chatting non-stop to Shelley, but the older girl had walked in gracefully, like a dancer. Luke had gazed at her dark eyes and high cheekbones. She had smooth skin the colour of deep caramel against the ivory and orange of her long dress. Then Jake had dragged Luke off to play a car-racing game on the Wii.

Later, when Luke looked around, she was sitting, quietly drawing abstract swirls on a piece of paper, her calm eyes on her sister, an expression of watchful care on her face.

The girl ahead turned to look in the window of a shoe shop and Luke realised, with slight disappointment, that it wasn't the girl from the youth club. He strode on up the street and into a cul-de-sac and knocked on the vicarage door, for his meeting with Francis to discuss his first few months. Francis led him into the study. Luke was surprised how crowded it was: crammed with bookcases, a massive roll-top desk, and chairs heaped with copies of the Church Times and concordances. A table stood against the wall, its surface barricaded with dog-eared books interspersed with mugs of pens and pencils, and a large tin labelled 'fish food' in black marker.

"Do have a seat, Luke. Oh, let me move that pile. It's the minutes of the 2019 PCC meetings, providing dramatic reading material for several nesting mice, I suspect. Now, tell me," Francis said, sitting opposite him, leaning forward and folding his hands under his chin. "How are you? How are you finding your house?"

"It's OK. It's bigger than my flat was in Derby and it's pretty cool to have it all to myself. There's space for my stuff, my bike and my skateboards anyway. There's a bit of a garden out the back – I ought to try to mow it or something, but I'm not too worried about that. Anyway, it's fine, ta." And it's tidier than yours, he thought, looking at the scarf and gloves on the sofa, the dog-eared novel on the rug, the copy of the Guardian newspaper lying on a chair and folded back to show the part-completed crossword. There was a half-eaten cheese sandwich on the sideboard. Francis noticed him glancing at it.

"Oh, don't mind that," Francis said. "I'm saving it for a practical demonstration for my sermon on the feeding of the five thousand. Anyway, I'm pleased the house is acceptable. Now, how do you think it is going? Now that you've had time to settle in?"

"Oh, um, pretty good. I reckon the new-style evening service will work out, eventually."

"I'm sure it will. There are some in our congregation, of course, who think guitars and drums are the invention of the devil," he chuckled. "And doughnuts instead of biscuits! What are we coming to!"

"Matt Redman and Stuart Townend, I hope. Sophie's friend Gerald is pretty good on the guitar and he helps out. He's not Christian, but he says he really likes some of the songs. Although he will insist on 'Shine, Jesus Shine' again and again."

"Oh… Graham Kendrick? Ah yes, of course, the McDonald's of worship music, as Marjorie calls it. Instantly accessible. Heaven forfend that our songs and hymns should be as easy to pick up as a 'Big Mac'. Anyway, how do you think that the Sunday school is going?"

"Oh, good, I reckon. I enjoy it. There's a couple of the older kids who are really smart. They ask interesting questions."

"And do you think you can handle their questions?"

"Um, I dunno. One of them asked me if I wanted to go to heaven. When I said yes, he said, well, why don't you die then?"

Francis leant back and laughed. "What a fascinating question! I'm not sure I know the answer to that one. What an interesting topic that would be for a sermon. Anyway, back to the evening services. Sophie seems very pleased with them. You've renamed them, haven't you?"

"Yeah, we thought we'd call it something catchy, rather than the 'Church Youth Group Evening Services'. Saves confusion with the youth club as well. Sophie suggested 'Transform', which I thought was OK."

"An inspired name, I must say."

Luke wasn't so sure any more. Most of the teenagers that went had started calling themselves the Transformers and giggling whenever the name was mentioned. But they were stuck with it.

"Um, thanks. Anyway, we've only had five services, but they went OK. About a dozen teens there. More for the last one. We're trying to make it different, friendly, casual, that sort of thing."

"Wonderful. You must keep me informed. I will try to make one. Now, where's my diary?" he muttered, hunting through the piles of books on the coffee table. "I'll be able to come providing I'm not doing the early morning communion, the ten-thirty and the four-thirty service as well… Anyway, that can wait. Tell me about the youth club."

"Going well, I think. There's some new kids coming. Sophie and Barbara are brilliant with the girls, and we've been having some good discussions. In between them messing around, having spats and quarrels, having hissy fits about some crisis or other. Look, Reverend…"

"Please, call me Francis."

"Francis. Look, they are, some of them, really, I dunno, lost, I'd call it. They've got separated parents, there are kids who don't even know who their dad is, girls who think they're pregnant, they go out binge drinking and clubbing until they're completely out of their heads, they try any drugs they can get their hands on. Half of them are going to leave school with practically nothing. Most of them don't believe they'll ever get decent work, let alone a house or home of their own."

Francis sighed, and bowed his head for a moment. "Oh, what a shame. Oh dear. What a struggle they must have ahead of them. I really must come to an evening service and meet some, and hear their stories. But, of course, I do hope - in fact, I'm sure - that you and Sophie can provide them with some of the assistance and support, and role models, that they need."

"I hope so too. We're thinking about starting a Youth Alpha course. Some of them, I reckon, would appreciate it."

"Oh, of course. What a good idea!" Suddenly, Francis stood up. "Tea! I'm so sorry, I forgot to offer you tea. Would you like a cup?"

"Nah – I'm not really a tea drinker."

"Coffee?"

Francis disappeared into the kitchen. Luke stood up and looked out of the window at the shaggy bushes and valiant spring bulbs struggling up through the overlong grass of the garden, then glanced at the yellowing notes, prayer cards, postcards of Lindesfarne and various cathedrals pinned onto a cork-board on one wall. In an alcove on the other side of the fireplace was a large aquarium on a sturdy modern cabinet with brushed-steel handles. It was far more interesting than the watercolour paintings of the Lake District on the walls. Luke watched the bright striped fish darting around, the snail slogging up the glass, and two tiny red shrimps tiptoeing around the rocks and gravel.

Francis came back in, carrying a tray. "Here we are. Milk and sugar and biscuits on the tray, help yourself. I'm afraid the mugs are slightly chipped. I'm still waiting for the PCC to give me a 'world's best vicar' mug for Christmas. Ah, I see you are admiring my fish."

"Yeah," said Luke. "Those shrimps are really cool. And those, they're Tetra, aren't they?"

"Correct. They are very common, but still most attractive, I think."

"What're those called? The ones that you can almost see through?"

"Those? They are Glass Catfish. Amazing, aren't they? How can they possibly live, have blood and guts and muscle like other fish, when they are practically transparent? But my favourite are those male Guppies, with their flamboyant tails. Wonderful!"

"Yeah, I guess so. It's a pretty impressive aquarium."

"Oh, thank you, I must confess that I think so myself. The bishop calls it my second congregation. They are marginally easier to shepherd. More predictable. It is, to be honest, rather an expensive, time-consuming hobby, but they force me to be more organised, more disciplined."

"Do they?" Luke couldn't help glancing at the roll-top desk in the corner. Its numerous pigeon-holes and drawers didn't showcase Francis's organisational skills much: its dark oak surface was littered with stamps, morsels of blu-tack, drawing pins, pens, fragments of paper and a pile of music CDs.

"Oh, absolutely. I have to do daily checks for signs of injury, check the water temperature is right, the lights are working, tidy away dead bits of leaves. Then test the water and change some every week, and clean the whole thing - the moss balls help to keep it all healthy, of course. And every month change all the filters, top up supplies and so on."

"Sounds a lot of work."

"Well, yes, but I often think it's a good model of

one's relationship with God. How one has to put in the discipline of daily prayer and weekly services, and set aside, as my bishop is always reminding me, a good chunk of time every month. But then the framework gives its reward. A continual closeness. Or, in the case of the aquarium, beauty. Look at those pretty little Red Honey Gourami. Careless, happy and calm."

"Yeah, I guess so."

"Of course, the analogy can be stretched too far. But I have learnt a lot from my second flock. One of these days I think I will write a book about it. An 'aquarists guide to spiritual maintenance', perhaps? Anyway, here is your coffee. Er, where were we?

"Um, I dunno…"

"Ah, yes, the youth club! Well, I do hope that your next few months go as well."

"Thanks."

"How are you getting on with Sophie?"

"OK, she's - she's pretty enthusiastic. We get on well."

"Oh, good. I think you will find that she is a very unusual young woman. Despite that rather frivolous pink hair, she has surprising depths to her. And how about the rest of the congregation?"

"Um, OK, I think. The Mitchell's invited me round for a meal, and so did Marjorie and George Fowler."

"Ah, yes. Their son, Stephen, you know him?"

"Yeah."

"He sings in the choir. Beautiful voice. But a confused and anxious boy, I've always suspected, although I'm not fully sure why I think that. Marjorie, she's a pillar of the church, of course. She is a remarkable woman, very capable, very efficient, very loyal. I do not know how we would manage without her sterling input."

Luke nodded.

"Anyway, is there anything that you need help with, Luke? How is your own journey? Your discipleship? How would you say that that is going?"

"Um… well…" Luke thought. What could he say? Sometimes, especially after a trying youth club session, he spent hours on his knees praying for them. Other days he picked up the bible, couldn't decide what to read, put it down again, thinking I'll do it later, and then forgot. Some days he felt God was with him, guiding and sustaining him and that he could do anything in that strength. Other days he was just running on auto-pilot. "Um, sort of OK, I think."

"Well, do come to talk if you need me. God gave me ears as prominent as Prince Charles's, so I'm quite good at listening."

"Um, thanks."

"Although, we really should arrange someone to mentor you. And pray with you, of course. Not me - someone else, so that you have the opportunity to grumble freely about me. I will have a think about that and see if I can find someone suitable. A mature, experienced Christian, I think. I'll try to arrange something after half-term. It's so difficult to get anything done this time of the year. People are either recovering from Christmas or gearing up for Lent. You will be busy too, I expect."

"Yeah. Sophie and I are going to try to organise a party for the youth club, and maybe take them bowling. And a special evening service on the Sunday before Easter."

"Excellent. Well, as I said, I will try to find a mentor for you. Though I must admit I can't think of anyone obvious. But you will need support. After all, you are very young."

CHAPTER TEN

Jessica insisted that she and Naomi went to the youth club every week. Naomi didn't mind. It seemed a friendly, nice-enough place to spend an evening. As they sat down at a table with craft materials, beads, wires and threads laid out, the youth club leader sauntered over. He was a tall young man with dark hair, wearing a navy t-shirt with a faded fish logo.

"Hi. I'm Luke Carmichael," he said, sitting down next to them.

"I know. You've introduced yourself already, ages ago," Naomi said.

"Oh, did I? Stupid!" He laughed uncertainly.

"It's all right." She liked his slight nervousness.

"You're Naomi, aren't you? Naomi Robeson? Your sister, she's Jessica?"

"Yeah."

"Well, anyway, thanks for coming."

He picked up the necklace she'd was making and

started fidgeting with it, pushing the beads up to one end of the wire and back.

"Um, do you like it here?"

"Yeah. It's all right. It's nice. Jessie loves it." She glanced across to where Jessica and Shelley were playing 'digestive biscuit poker' with two boys in the corner, laughing loudly as one of them started to eat, with loud protests and exclamations, a biscuit loaded with jam, cheese, curry paste, mayonnaise and chocolate sprinkles.

A few cyan and turquoise beads slipped off the end of the wire and rolled across the floor. Luke scrabbled after them.

"Here," he said, handing it back to her. "You'd better take it before I wreck it."

"Ta. You a Christian, then?" she asked, threading a pale green bead onto the wire.

"Yeah. Are you?" he said, pushing his fringe back from his eyes.

"No."

"Ever been to church? Got dragged there by your Mum and Dad?"

"Nah."

"Not even at Christmas?"

"Nah, not even Christmas. Mum puts that service on the TV though. On Christmas Eve. The really long one from somewhere in Cambridge. With all those choir-boys in those weird white dresses."

"The Carols from King's?"

"Yeah, that's what it's called. No idea why. Mum always listens to that, but, well, she isn't Christian or anything, really. She believes in fate, karma, horoscopes, that sort of stuff. Our dad, he left when I was ten. Catholic, he was, Mum said."

"He left? Where did he go?"

"Dunno." She shrugged. "Never seen him since. He just walked out, and he's never bothered to get in touch since."

"Sounds a … Not a very good Catholic, I guess. Anyway, what about you? What do you think?"

"Oh, I don't know. I don't think God does a very good job, really. If he exists, well, I reckon he's a bit incompetent."

"Incompetent? I reckon I've never heard anyone say that about God," Luke said, and smiled.

"Don't laugh. I'm serious. Anyway, I liked the Narnia books. I know they're supposed to be about Christianity. But Aslan's a bit more…"

"Competent?"

"Yeah, all right. Competent," Naomi said, shrugging. "He's pretty cool. I loved him when I was kid. My dad read some of the books to me, and then I used to read them to Jessie as well."

"Yeah. They're good. I wanted to be Prince Caspian, when I was ten."

Naomi looked up at his dark fringe, that fell forward and hid his forehead and level eyebrows. He had serious brown eyes and a wide gentle mouth.

"You'd have to get your hair cut first," she said, threading some silver beads onto the necklace. She considered it, then added two deep carmine ones. "But it isn't like that in the real world, is it? It makes it all sound so easy and exciting and perfect. But you don't get talking lions coming to rescue you, do you? Not for real. It's all just make-believe."

"I dunno. Yeah, maybe."

There was a crash from the other end of the hall. Luke glanced around. One of the boys was scooting around on a wheeled computer chair and hurtling into the walls and the table football, while other boys stood round laughing at him and spinning the chair as he shot past them.

"Hey, Jake! That's not a good idea. Come on, guys! Pause it! Honestly, the idiot…" Luke groaned. "Sheesh - it's just one thing after another with him…"

CHAPTER ELEVEN

"It's going well, isn't it?" Barbara said to Luke at the youth club, in mid-March.

"Yeah," he said, looking around. "Everyone seems happy. A success, I reckon."

"Of course it is," she said. There were over a score of teenagers in the hall. Three boys were playing table football, Shelley was making badges and giggling with her friend Jessica, while Jessica's older sister Naomi quietly coloured in some pages from one of the creative art books Sophie had brought. Two boisterous girls were singing loudly and enthusiastically to a karaoke set in one corner. Sophie was talking to a few other girls – probably about God, judging by her earnest expression, but they seemed happy to listen.

"Anyway, I'd better sort out the tuck shop," Barbara said.

"Yeah, ta. Um, I guess I'd be best joining in with the table football."

As he went over to the table, Marjorie Fowler came in with Stephen trailing a few steps behind her. She marched up to Luke.

"I hear you've just failed your driving test? Again!" she said.

"Yeah, um, I have," Luke said defensively, his face flushing.

"Well, that's a shame, but it's also a bit of a problem, in my opinion. How are you going to take the teenagers to the church youth group weekend away next month? I don't think you've got enough time to retake your test and get enough driving experience to be safe!"

"What? Oh, don't worry, Mrs Fowler, we've got it sorted."

"Exactly how have you 'got it sorted'?" she said, her hands on her hips.

"Oh, um, Sophie's taking three, Mr Mitchell another four, and Mr Hazelbury said he'd give lifts to the other three. And I'll catch a train. You see, sorted!"

"I see. Well, on consideration," she said, shaking her head. "I'm afraid that I don't call that fully satisfactory. Three people in Sophie's little Fiat! I don't want Stephen to be crammed in like that. Luke, I'll ask George if he'll help out."

"Well, Mrs Fowler, that would be really kind of you, but…"

"No need to thank me, Luke. I'm sure George will be glad to help. I'll let you know. So, if you don't require me for anything else here, I'll go." She looked around. "You seem to have it all under control, I'm glad to see. I'll say goodbye to Stephen and get back. I've got the flower rota to plan."

"Well, um, OK. Bye. Um, Stephen, do you want to help Barbara with the tuck shop?"

Stephen drifted over to Barbara, sat next to her and listlessly started to arrange the coins from the cash box into piles.

"I don't really need any help," she said. "Why don't you, er, set up the Wii for something? A car game?"

"Yeah, maybe," he said, shrugging, and then mooched over to watch the other boys playing table football.

Luke came over to Barbara and sat down. "Honestly!" he said, running his hands through his fringe. "It was bad enough telling Dad about failing my test again. Sophie wasn't happy either, and then I get it in the neck from Mrs Fowler too! I can't win!"

"Don't worry. I'm sure you'll pass next time. And the youth club is going really well."

"Yeah, there is that. Maybe I'll find Jake and beat him at snooker. That reminds me, where is Jake? I'm sure I saw him come in."

He stood up and looked around. "He's not here… but I can hear someone in the graveyard. No, don't worry, Barbara, I'll go. I'll have a quick dekko."

A few minutes later he came back in with Jake and a couple of other lads, and they started to set out the pool table. Barbara could see that Luke looked very perturbed.

After the session had ended, when the last kids had left, Luke shut the door and turned to Sophie and Barbara.

"When I went into the graveyard, Jake - well, he was smoking something," he said, his face worried. "A spliff, you know, a joint, I'm sure. He looked guilty, he stubbed it out really quickly. The other two were just sitting on the tombstones, hanging around. I reckon they weren't… But Jake… Oh, Christ, drugs…"

"A joint? Oh no!" Barbara exclaimed.

"Jake?" Sophie said. "Oh dear, oh, bless him. I knew there was something wrong!"

"Bless him? But Sophie, it's drugs! How am I supposed to deal with that?"

"You'll just have to talk to him. Tell him it's not a good idea, and not acceptable here. Poor Jake. Such a troubled boy. We should pray for him."

"Troubled boy or not, he's more of a pain than all the others put together. Bloody hell – sorry, Sophie, sorry Barbara, – this is f…flipping hard. It wasn't so bad tonight, but sometimes it's like trying to herd cats on speed."

"I know, but they are good kids, underneath it all, you know that," Barbara said. "And you are helping them."

"I've got an idea. Jake's into board games, isn't he?" Sophie said. "Get him to bring some of those in, get others to play with him. Or teach him some of that free-wheeling parker or whatever it is you do. That'll give him something else to think about."

"Parkour! Are you mad? He's so crazy, he'll break his leg for sure and then I'll be in real trouble!"

"Have a bit more faith, Luke. I'll pray for

protection over him. And you! And you can blame me for suggesting it."

"Yeah, thanks a bunch, Sophie. You nutcase…" he muttered.

"Luke Carmichael, I heard that!" She laughed. "May the Lord have mercy on your soul!"

Barbara meandered around the church, looking appreciatively at the terracotta tiles on the floor, the pale coral and cream sandstone walls, the marble inlay by the altar. As she looked up at the carved corbels, she heard footsteps. She turned and saw Francis coming out of the vestry.

"Ah, good morning, Barbara. Admiring the church?"

"Yes. It's very beautiful."

"Beautiful? Hmm… High Victorian Gothic hubris, to be honest," he said, gesturing at the broad pillars and tall arches. "Built by generous local bigwigs, who wanted everyone to appreciate their donation of a particularly ornamental and glorious building. All that gilt on the mosaic over there and on the altar, all those stained glass windows, and their names on the foundation stone, of course!"

"It's still very impressive," Barbara said, but she noticed that dust lay like talc under the pews, coated the carved wood panels, and blurred the outlines of the stone rosettes. The brass altar rail was dimmed and tarnishing. She itched to polish it.

"Very, yes, one has to admit that. Impressive, massive, and it costs a fortune to heat. But it has its charming corners too. Here, let me show you my favourite."

He led her past an unbalanced pile of chairs leaning against a wall then behind an unwieldy screen that hid a clutter of old hymn books, boxes of candle ends and tarnished candlesticks, and crates labelled 'Sunday School' and 'Mother's Union'. Barbara thought that they could not have been touched for several years, judging by the spiders' webs festooning them.

"Mind the boxes," Francis said, skirting a heap of half-opened cardboard boxes overflowing with scraps of dead ivy, withered ferns and dusty oasis blocks. "I suspect that the flower rota posse are secretly breeding triffids behind that lot. And … ta-da! Here we are."

He paused by a wall memorial with a carved willow drooping despondently over a tombstone, inscribed 'Jeremiah Afhton, died 1792, alfo his dearly beloved wife Louifa, fafe in the arms of God'. He pointed at the window above it, showing Jesus' baptism, with a plump dove drifting over his head, and Saint John standing up to his waist in sapphire and green waters. Odd-looking fish leapt and splashed around them.

"The astonishment on Saint John's face, yet Christ is so unconcerned. And the fish look so cheerful, as if they are delighted to be involved. Do you not think it is extraordinarily charming?"

"Yes. Yes, I do. It's lovely."

"Thank you. I'm glad you like it. The fish are so peculiar, are they not? One day I must show you mine, those in my aquarium, I mean."

An insistent beeping came from Francis's

pocket. He fished around.

"My new phone," he said apologetically. "As you know, I've joined the ranks of the technology slaves. It's … er… it's telling me that I am supposed to be meeting the Area Dean in ten minutes. Ah well. I obey, my master. I'd better go. Are you, er, are you about to go too?"

"No. I'm just waiting to meet Marjorie and George, for the concert."

"Oh, the concert, of course! Well, er, God bless, I'd had better go, I think."

He trotted off. Barbara watched him go, then continued her wandering around the church. It might cost a fortune to heat, it might need tidying and cleaning, she thought, but it was still beautiful.

The pews started to fill up with concert goers. Luke came in carrying two guitars.

"Morning, Luke," Barbara said. "Are you here for the concert?"

"No. What concert?"

"You know, the Saturday lunchtime concert. They're doing two of Mozart's string quartets."

"Oh, yeah, I forgot. I'm just dropping off some stuff for Transform. Helen Stuart's got the car parked outside."

"Do you want some help?"

"Yeah! Ta!"

She helped Luke and Helen ferry music stands, a drum kit, boxes of leads, and a projector screen into the church and put them into a corner pew.

"Luke, this is the data projector," Helen said, carrying in a large black case. "You can borrow it til further notice, but you need to keep it somewhere safe."

"Yeah. Francis says we can leave it on the balcony. No one ever goes up there."

"It must be going well," said Barbara, as Helen left. "All this equipment!"

"Yeah. It's a start."

"Start of what?" said Marjorie, coming up to them and staring at the guitars and drums on the pews. George followed, carrying three takeaway coffees.

"Here," he said, handing one to Barbara. "We thought coffees would be appreciated, and Marj has brought Hobnobs."

"Oh, hiya, Mr Fowler, Mrs Fowler," Luke said. "Um, start of better music for Sunday evenings, modern stuff, songs the teenagers will appreciate, you know."

"Better music?" Marjorie exclaimed, raising her eyebrows.

"Um…"

"Marj, don't harangue the lad," said George. "He means more suited to younger people. Not everyone is a fan of Charles Wesley and eighteenth-century organ music, you know,"

Marjorie laughed briefly. "Right! The younger generation, of course. Even Charles Wesley was once thought too modern! I won't get on my hobby horse. But I must say, I prefer to wait and see if the modern stuff will last. If it's still around in twenty years it's probably worth listening to. Now this quartet… I taught three of them and the violinist in particular is very talented, quite remarkable given his age."

"Anyway, it'll start in ten minutes," George said. "Shall we get seats? You staying, Luke?"

Luke didn't stay. Barbara wasn't surprised – he probably wanted to avoid being browbeaten over music styles by Marjorie. She would have liked him to stay. His enthusiastic face and hopeful energy was a tonic, and she wanted to say something to him about how big a difference he was making to the church and youth club. But he probably wouldn't have appreciated Mozart.

After the concert they lingered while Marjorie congratulated her three protégés. Francis came in hurriedly, looking distracted.

"Where's Luke? Have I missed him? I wanted to show him where to put the equipment for Sunday evenings, but I went and double-booked myself with the Area Dean and forgot," he said breathlessly.

"He's been and gone," said George.

"Oh dear!" Francis exclaimed.

"It's all right, though," Barbara said. "He put the drums and guitars there, and the data projector on the balcony."

"Oh, of course! Thank you, Barbara! That's the best place for it. Of course, I remember now, I'd told him to do that. I needn't have rushed, need I?"

"Yes, he seems a very capable, sensible lad," remarked George.

"Oh, he is. Very. Oh dear, I completely forgot my promise to find him a mentor! Well, that will have to wait until after the Church Youth Group – sorry – the Transform weekend away. Goodness me, there is so much going on. Good stuff, thank

God. I'd best be off. God bless, Barbara, George, good to have seen you!"

George glanced knowingly at Barbara.

"Very distracted, our vicar," he said.

"Yes," she replied, staring after Francis.

"He needs organizing," George commented, adding to Marjorie as she joined them. "Don't you think so? Francis – needs organizing?"

"Oh, yes, definitely. His study!" She tutted. "He told me that the dust gives everything a softer, more lived-in look!"

As they left, Barbara turned to Marjorie.

"Marjorie, can I ask you something, please?"

"Yes, of course."

"Sorry to bother you, but – er – does the church need a cleaner?"

"A cleaner? I should say so! Helen does the loos and the kitchen once a week. But that's all. Daphne and me sometimes have a blitz, but we can't possibly manage it often enough."

"Do you think I could do it? I wouldn't ask very much, only nine pounds or so an hour, for a couple of hours a week."

"Really? Goodness me, Barbara, are you serious?"

Barbara nodded. She didn't like to say that she was struggling to manage on her current salary. Most weeks she only had about forty pounds left after all the bills, rent, rates and mortgage payments had been met. Last month she had been able to pay the mortgage, but, since it was a shared ownership house, she'd had to pay rent as well and it had been a struggle. Even another eighteen pounds a week would make life a little easier. But she didn't want to complain to Marjorie about the poor wages, not when she had taken so much trouble to get her the job in the first place.

"Nine pounds an hour? That's not a living wage," George said.

"Well, it's worth discussion," Marjorie said. "I've said for months that we ought to get a proper cleaner. But you've already got a job, Barbara."

"I know, I was only thinking, I don't know, just Saturday morning, two or three hours. Just to get a bit of extra cash, and I'd like to do it. If it would help, that is."

"Of course it would help. A jolly good idea, in my opinion. What do you think, George?"

"Yes, if you're sure, Barbara. But don't let them exploit you."

"Nonsense! Barbara isn't going to get exploited. I'll see to that. It should be easy to arrange, and get the PCC to agree. Say, three hours, ten pounds per hour, every Saturday morning?"

CHAPTER TWELVE

During a momentary pause in the background sound of conversations, the Wii soundtrack and the click of pool balls, Luke heard thuds and shuffles above him. He looked up at the hall ceiling.

"What's that?" he exclaimed. "There's someone on the roof! On the f…flipping roof! Where's Jake? I bet it's him. The idiot! The priceless idiot!"

Luke ran outside. Jake was balancing on the ridge pole of the church hall, arms stretched out, one foot poised in the air. He saw Luke and waved, wobbling slightly. Sophie came out, looked up and gasped.

"Hi! I'm high! This is brilliant, this parkour stuff!" He laughed. "I'm high! Geddit?"

Luke stared up at Jake. The ridge pole looked precarious, the tiles unreliable. Jake paused, shuffled to the end and then turned round. His foot slipped and he lurched slightly. Luke's heart stopped. His in-depth theology course had never mentioned how to get a loony, reckless teenager off a roof. Jake swayed to and fro, then stood straight and Luke breathed out.

"Jake!" he shouted. "Get down, you moron!"

"What? No way, Jose, I'm high, I tell you! This is bloody brilliant, this is! Ace!"

"I'll have to go up there after him," Luke muttered. "Great, just great. Just hope to God he doesn't fall off."

"Pray, not hope," Sophie said.

"Yeah, right! This was your idea – teaching him parkour – you pray! I'll do something!"

Several screeching girls rushed outside and pointed upwards, with choruses of excited screams, followed by Barbara, Naomi and then the rest of the youth club.

Luke turned to everyone. "Don't even think of joining him. Anyone who does will be…banned! Got it! Stephen, have you got your phone? Get ready to call an ambulance, won't you? OK. Here goes."

As he started to scramble up the drainpipe on the corner, Naomi stepped forward and called up. "Jake! Hi! Hey, Jake, how did you get up there?"

"Easy! From the back!"

"Can you show me? I want to join you!"

Luke groaned. "No, please, no, don't encourage him," he said, but she turned to him with a calm smile.

"I know what I'm doing," she said quietly.

"Hey! Naomi – this way," Jake called, walking along the ridge to the rear. He disappeared over the edge. Luke stared, aghast.

"It's OK, Luke, don't worry!" Sophie said. "It's a flat roof over the extension, he'll be OK!"

Naomi ran to the back of the hall, followed by the everyone else. Luke dropped back to the ground and joined them. Jake stood on the flat roof, looking very pleased with himself.

"See, I got up from that wall over there, then the windowsill and gutter. Easy."

Naomi looked up at him. "Jake, you're brill," she said. "But I don't think I can reach. Come down. Give us a piggy back."

"Yeah, sure!"

Luke thought that he'd lower himself onto the wall. But he didn't. Instead he came to the edge of the roof and stood for a minute.

"Hey, watch me! Everyone get out of the way!" he yelled.

"No! Don't!" Luke shouted. Sophie gasped. Jake jumped, landed on the grass nine feet below, stumbled awkwardly and lay on his back, swearing, then clutched at his ankle, moaning. The other teenagers stood and stared at him. Barbara ran to him.

"Stephen, phone an ambulance!" she said, gently feeling Jake's foot. "I hope it's only a sprain, that's all, but get one anyway. It might be broken."

"Oh, for goodness sake, Ben," said Sophie, turning round to the fascinated onlookers. "Don't take photos of him! And you, Lucy, stop texting or filming or whatever it is you're doing. This isn't entertainment!"

"So, Jake had been taking cannabis?" Marjorie

said, frowning. She'd come round to Luke's house, unasked, the next day. She didn't seem to feel any need to explain why she was there.

"Yeah. But before he came into the youth club! So he said. How was I supposed to have done anything about that?"

"Well, in my opinion you shouldn't have let him in."

"What am I supposed to do? Drug tests on the door? There's no way I could tell. He was being a bit of a pillock, messing around, playing pool with a breadstick, but then half of them are doing stuff like that anyway."

"Nevertheless, you and Sophie are responsible for them. You shouldn't encourage behaviour like that. Nor condone obvious drug use."

Luke ran his hands through his fringe. He wished Sophie was with him, he could do with a bit of muttered praying and moral support.

"Yeah, but we don't," he said. "We do try to talk to the kids about drugs, try to provide alternatives, role models, a drug-free zone, other things to do."

"What, like teaching Jake, what is it, parkour? Hardly a safe alternative," Marjorie snorted. "Now he's broken his ankle, his parents are seriously upset and the youth club is in danger of getting into disrepute. Ted's having kittens worrying that his parents might sue us. But Jake will have to be banned."

"What?"

"Yes. For at least three months, I suggest. Otherwise we might end up having to close the youth club altogether!"

"But, but – that's so unfair!"

"Unfair or not, that's what it's like. It only takes a single accident to wreck everything. Luke, if someone seems to be under the influence of drugs or alcohol, you shouldn't let them in."

"That's going to be difficult."

"I know, but, Luke, you are responsible for the safety and well-being of all the kids that attend. While they are on the premises, at least."

Luke groaned.

"What? All twenty-three of them? Can't I do something easier, like lion-taming or bomb-disposal or something?"

Marjorie smiled and patted his arm.

"I know it's a difficult job, but I'm sure that you'll cope. You and Sophie."

"Ta," muttered Luke.

"However, you have to demonstrate that you take reasonable care to avoid accidents. Which you patently did not, teaching an erratic, impressionable and rash sixteen year-old to jump off buildings." She shook her head. "I had hoped that you'd be a better influence on them. Still, it's early days yet. I'm sure you'll learn from your mistakes."

As Naomi was putting her jacket on at the end of the youth club session, with Jessica theatrically flouncing and pouting about having to leave, Luke came up to them.

"Thanks for your help with Jake," he said to Naomi. "You know. Last week. I thought you were going to encourage him, but, anyway, you helped sort it. Ta."

"That's all right," she said. "Is Jake OK?"

"Broken ankle, not brill but could have been so much worse. Um, I thought you might like this," he said, handing her a book. "It's by C. S. Lewis. You know, the guy who wrote the Narnia books. It's real, though. Not make-believe."

"Oh. Thanks."

She looked at the title: 'Mere Christianity'.

"I dunno. I don't read much these days," she said, not sure that she wanted to read a book like that, although she was pleased that Luke had thought of lending it to her. He seemed to really care for all the kids at the youth group, even those that were absolute pains.

"Neither do I, not much fiction, anyway," he said. "Just the Hunger Games, some of Neil Gaimin's books, Game of Thrones, graphic novels. That sort of stuff. Lightweight. But I used to like that one."

She read the first two chapters the next day. It was pompous and old-fashioned. Then Jessica came in, full of a long tale about some fight between two girls at school, and Naomi put the book aside. She didn't forget it, but picked it up and read a bit more the next day. She had liked the way Luke had given it to her: the slight hesitancy in his voice, the downward glance from under his dark fringe.

At the youth club the next week, when he paused by the craft table, she remembered a bit she'd read.

"Luke, that book, you know. I don't get all that stuff about the natural law, the moral law. What he means about why the moral law isn't just an instinct. Isn't it just something that we've evolved?"

"Oh, yeah. I see what you mean." He sat down by her.

"I don't think it makes sense. Does it?" She explained what she meant, and he listened seriously and intently. As they talked, their eyes met and he paused, stuttered and leaned towards her. Then Jessica reached across the table to grab a box of stickers, and he moved back.

"Um, yeah, you're right. It needs discussion. Can we talk…um…later, about it?"

"Yeah," she said and looked around at the crowded hall. "This isn't the best place."

Having George Fowler's help getting everyone and everything to the 'Transform' weekend away had actually been very useful, Luke admitted, even though his wife had been so bossy about it. There had been more stuff to take than he'd expected: spare bedding, board games, craft boxes, skateboards, flipcharts, pens and notebooks, guitars and music books; the list had gone on and on. Luke would never have got it on the train and in Sophie's Fiat. George had been encouraging, in a quiet way, and hadn't seemed to mind having to drive there and back. At least the venue, a watersports and adventure centre near Northampton, was close to Merton, and the weather had been as good as it could be for late May: sunny and bright, warm enough for t-shirts and shorts on some days. The venue had been a good choice. The kayaking had been popular, and the zip wires and high trapeze had provoked masses of squealing laughter from the girls. Naomi had been noticeably good at balancing on the highest wire. Luke had stared, open-mouthed, as she steadily walked across and back, her head poised, a smile on her face.

He had insisted that they opened up the weekend to the youth club as well, and had been pleased and surprised at how many had come. Mainly, he knew, because their friends had been going.

"Look, it's a Christian camp for the church youth group. There'll be lots of games and sports and fun in the day, and serious discussions about Christianity and religion in the evenings," he'd said, wanting to be totally open, and they'd still come. Of course, the serious discussions had tended to degenerate into loud arguments between the more vociferous kids, but he and Sophie had managed to keep it all reasonably friendly. And they'd finished both evening sessions with hot chocolate, marshmallows and silly games like 'Plum, plum, plum', 'Mafia' and 'Are you there, Moriarty?'

"It's gone well, so far," he said to Sophie, as they collected up the dirty mugs late on Saturday evening. "A real success, don't you reckon?"

"Yes! I told you it would be! Some of the girls have really loved it. I think they've appreciated getting away from their families for a bit. Especially Naomi and Jessica. I truly believe that they needed some Psalm 23. You know, some 'leading beside still waters', that sort of stuff."

"Still waters? Sophie, we took them white water

kayaking!"

She laughed, and picked up the craft box of friendship bracelets.

"That was fantastic, wasn't it? I got soaked! Anyway, home tomorrow afternoon," she said, with a mock grimace. "I'll be really sorry to go, it's been such a blessing! Can I leave you to finish off? We're having a pyjama party in chalet eight."

"Yeah, sure. Have fun."

As Luke put the last few errant pens back into the crates, Stephen stuck a tentative head round the door.

"Can I come in?" he said. "I wanted to talk to you."

"Sure."

Stephen slumped into a chair, with his legs stretched out in front of him and his hands pushed into his pockets. He looked very young. His cheeks were still rounded with puppy fat and he had a slight but definite pout.

"I dunno what to do," he said. "Need to talk to you or someone."

"What is it?"

"Can you be gay and still be a Christian?" he blurted.

Luke wasn't surprised: Sophie had hinted that Stephen was gay. Luke pulled another chair out, swung it around and sat facing Stephen, his arms resting on the back of the chair.

"Well," he said. "Jesus didn't say anything about homosexuality, did he?"

"I dunno. Didn't he?"

"No, not really. There's some bits in the Old

Testament, in Leviticus and so on. But lots of people think they don't apply now. I mean, you know, we don't stone adulterers any more, or execute sons who disobey their parents, or care about eating pork."

"Er, I guess not."

"So, the only bits are those bits in Saint Paul's letters, I reckon. And there's only really three places. Lots of commentators think they can be interpreted differently. Like they think he just means promiscuity or male prostitutes."

"Do they?" Stephen looked up. "Oh. I didn't know that."

"Yeah. Anyway, if you look at the Greek…" Luke started. This is easy, he thought, as he glibly explained what Saint Paul really meant. Stephen looked more and more cheerful as he continued.

"So you reckon it's OK to be a gay Christian, but I mustn't sleep around?"

"Yeah. I mean, I know there's lots of fuss in the church at the moment about gay priests and gay marriage, but I reckon that God doesn't mind homosexual relationships, if they're loving, faithful, all that sort of stuff."

Stephen left, half-an-hour later, looking considerably less sulky. Thanks, God, for that opportunity, Luke muttered to himself, I reckon I've done some good there.

CHAPTER THIRTEEN

Luke opened his door, one evening, to see Naomi standing outside, with fine drops of rain glistening on her coat and in her hair.

"Um, oh, hi, Naomi," he stuttered. "Um, nice to see you. You OK?"

"Hi. Yeah, fine. I just wanted to give you your book back. Sophie told me where you live."

"Oh, thanks. But you needn't have bothered. You could have given it back to me at the youth club."

"Yeah, I know. But I wanted to talk to you about it, and it's just too crowded there, too many kids, you know."

She looked down at her feet. She was wearing thin gold sandals. The skin on her feet was wet, with a sheen like varnished wood, and her nails were painted dark red.

"You look soaked," he said.

"Yeah, I am, a bit."

"Do you wanna come in?"

"Yeah. If it's all right."

Luke wasn't sure if it was or not. All the guidelines were very definite on the subject of youth leaders who played with fire by letting teenagers into their homes. Unaccompanied too. He'd heard dozens of warnings about the slipperiness of the slope. But Naomi was nineteen at least, he thought. It wasn't like she was a vulnerable young girl.

"Sophie told you where I lived?"

"Yeah. I asked her."

That settled it, he thought. If Sophie had given Naomi his address, it probably was fine.

"Well, I guess it is OK. Come in."

In the living room, he moved the skateboard off the sofa, paused the Netflix drama currently playing on his laptop and flipped the lid shut.

"Sorry about the curry smell," he said.

"That's all right. I like curry."

"Do you? Me too. I made lamb jalfrezi last night. Fresh chillis, proper spices, garlic, the works. But it still stinks the place out."

"Smells nice, though," she said, tossing her coat onto a chair, sitting down and pulling 'Mere Christianity' out of her bag. "Here you are. It was interesting, a bit. Old-fashioned. But it doesn't explain lots of stuff."

"What stuff?" he said, sitting next to her.

"Well, like all the unfairness. Gwen, who lived next door to us, she was lovely. Really nice and kind. And she got cancer and died and she was only thirty-seven. But my step-dad, he's a real sod, and he looks like he's gonna live forever. Where's the fairness in that?"

"Um, I dunno. Your step-dad?"

"Well, he isn't, not really. He's me mum's boyfriend. He lives with us, but they're not married or anything like that."

"And he's a real sod?"

Naomi looked at him steadily.

"Yeah. He hits me mum, takes her money, that sort of stuff."

Luke flinched. "Does he hit you?" he asked.

"Nah. Not after the first time, anyway. Not now. Nor Jessica either. I told him, if he touches her, I'd call the police. Anyway, why doesn't God give him cancer and leave people like Gwen alone? It isn't fair."

Luke thought of all the pat answers he'd learnt at church, college, youth groups and Christian courses. None of them seemed capable of satisfying Naomi's earnest gaze.

"Well, I reckon it's because of free will," he stuttered.

Naomi laughed.

"I knew you'd say that! That's what Mr Greggs, the R.E. teacher says. It's crap, and you know it. C'mon, Luke, this book doesn't say anything, and I wanna know. Why is it all so unfair? C'mon, what do you really, really think?"

She leaned towards him.

"I really want to know," she said.

Luke was bewildered. There were so many arguments and counter-arguments in his head, but which one did he really believe?

"Um, blimey, Naomi, I don't know. But, well, this sounds a bit wacky, but sometimes I think – what's God supposed to do? Kill off all the sods, like your step-dad? Like Hitler, Jimmy Saville, that guy in North Korea, the Syrian president, Isis bombers and terrorists, all those greedy bankers?"

"Well, yes, he should."

"Yeah, but then where does he stop? All, I dunno, all the murderers? All the thieves?"

Naomi kicked her sandals off, curled her legs up, and gazed at him.

"I dunno," she said, slowly. "I never really thought about it like that." She looked as if she was really interested in the issue.

"Well, what do you think?" he said, twisting to face her, and trying not to stare at her mouth, her legs, her eyes. "Tell me what you think about it all."

Luke's phone chimed, startling him. He stopped kissing Naomi. They were half-lying, half-sitting on the sofa. Naomi's bra was undone and her skirt askew. One of his hands was on her back and the other enthusiastically exploring inside her shirt. His phone said quarter past ten. They'd been talking for ages and they'd shared a couple of cans of lager. Then - he wasn't sure how it had happened - they'd moved closer together and she'd kissed him, or he'd kissed her.

Naomi adjusted her skirt. She stood up.

"I need to use the bathroom," she said. "Where is it?"

"Upstairs, door at the top," he said, as he checked his phone. It was only a message from Ben about meeting up tomorrow at the parkour spot on Whitefield Road. He switched his phone off and stood up. His heart was beating fast and he couldn't get the feel of her skin and lips out of his head.

He heard the toilet flush and glanced upstairs. Before they'd got … distracted they'd been talking about 'Game of Thrones'. She hadn't seen Season Five and he'd promised to lend it to her. It was on the bookshelves above his bed so he went to get it. Naomi was on the landing, looking into his room.

"Oh my God, Luke, are you for real?" she said. "Your room's so tidy!"

"Um, well, my Dad used to be in the army," he said. "He sort of got me into the habit…"

"Wish I could get Jessie into the habit. We share a bedroom and she's real messy. Oh wow, you've got all the Jason Bourne films, Lord of the Rings, and Harry Potter? I thought Christians weren't supposed to like Harry Potter?"

"Yeah, some don't, but I reckon it's OK. Good versus evil, and Dumbledore's a bit like God, isn't he?"

"But gay."

Luke laughed.

"I really like that poster," she said, stroking Sean Bean's face as he sat disconsolate on the iron throne. "Poor guy! He gets his head cut off, doesn't he?"

"Yeah." Luke went to the shelf and got the DVD and a book. "Here you are. Do you want the book too? The first one?"

"Yeah, ta."

She sat on the bed and started flicking through the book.

"Hey, Luke, which Game of Thrones character are you?"

"I dunno. Never really thought about it."

"Haven't you done that online quiz?"

"Nah. There's so many of those sort of things that I couldn't be bothered."

"I'm Arya Stark, I reckon. Well, I'd like to be like her."

"Why?" said Luke, sitting next to her.

"Cos I like the way she fights."

Bright daylight, glowing through the curtains, and the sound of cars and buses, woke Luke up. He squinted at the clock. Nine am. Bloody hell. He looked at Naomi, curled up on her side, with her arm flung over him. Her breasts were bare, her skin deep brown and smooth. The quilt was tangled around them. The pillow lay on the floor next to scattered clothes and underwear. His father would be appalled that he hadn't folded up his jeans and t-shirt. His father would be appalled, full stop, he realised. He supposed he ought to get up and tidy his clothes, but images, textures, astounding memories from last night slipped into his mind as easily as he and Naomi had slipped into bed together. He remembered how he had woken in the pre-dawn light, reached for Naomi in dazed and urgent need and whispered, "Can we do it again?" She'd rolled into his arms. He remembered smooth skin, soft lips, sleepy but determined hands caressing his back and down to his thighs and pulling him into her. Why had he never done this before? Why had God created such a drowning, overwhelming experience for Luke to reject and postpone it?

Naomi stirred and snuggled nearer to him. She was beautiful, he thought, running his fingers over her face and shoulders. Her closeness warmed him. "Luke," she murmured, "Luke," and gazed at him. Her dark eyes were wondering and happy, her soft mouth reached to kiss him. He couldn't help himself. He wanted to taste the miracle again, to submerge himself in her, even if he broke every guideline and rule he'd set himself. He pulled her closer.

An hour later Luke stumbled to the fridge, pulled out the orange juice and drank straight from the carton, cold sharp gulps. His hands were shaking. Naomi was upstairs, getting dressed after having a shower. She was so calm, yet he was still trembling with the realisation. He sank to his knees.

"Oh God, oh God, oh God," he said. Why had he done that? What had been the point of all his puritanical, high-minded resolutions when he'd tumbled so easily? All the teaching he'd had about sex had been so straightforwardly simplistic. Wait, wait until marriage. That had been the message and his intention. He'd known it would be difficult, and there had been times when, holding a keen and attractive girlfriend in his arms, it had been very difficult indeed, but he'd been determined. He was going to wait, to prove himself strong, restrained and faithful. Like Toby, the leader at Luke's Sunday school. He'd taught again and again about waiting and had waited himself. When Toby had married Lynn, it had been obvious, from their excited eyes and Lynn's blushing face, how much they were looking forward to their first night. Even Luke's mum had remarked on how keen they were to leave the reception and drive off to the hotel. Luke had wanted to be like Toby. To be persistent and obedient and wait, knowing it would be worth it. Oh, what a fool he'd been! It would have been worth it! He stood up and leant against the worktop, his fists clenched, his head bowed. It should have been his wedding night and now he had wasted it.

Naomi came into the kitchen, smiled quietly, and slid her arms round his waist, kissing him silently and rubbing her cheek into his chest. They stood, arms around each other for a few minutes. Luke knew he ought to say something, but he couldn't think what. 'That was fantastic', 'thanks', 'I love you'? Nothing seemed right. 'Have you done this before?' he wanted to ask, but he knew she had. She had been so sure, so deft, so confident. It had seemed familiar territory to her. She was nineteen; a normal, attractive nineteen-year old woman; she'd been with several boyfriends, no doubt. What an idiot he was! This would be routine for her. Normal. Not a discovery. Nothing special.

A snatch of Shakira tinkled from Naomi's pocket. Luke let her go and stepped back. She pulled out her phone.

"Um, Naomi, won't your mum be worried?" he said.

"Nah. Mum won't even have noticed," Naomi

said, her eyes on her phone. "This is Jessica. Hang on, I'll just text her."

"Don't…" Luke started to say.

She looked up.

"I won't tell her. I'm not stupid. I'll say I was at Hannah's. It'll be all right."

Her fingers darted over the screen.

"Luke, have you got anything to eat? Any toast or summat? I'm starving."

"Yeah. Sure."

"Thanks," she murmured, as she carried on tapping at her phone.

As he buttered some toast, she put the phone back in her pocket.

"There. Sorted," she said. "I've got to get back home, get my uniform. I've got to be at work at eleven."

Luke poured himself some rice crispies, sloshed milk on and took a spoonful as he stood by the sink. Naomi perched on a stool by the worktop, eating the toast and watching him.

"Hey, Luke, relax," she said. "It's all right."

"No! It's not!" he burst out. "I shouldn't have done that! For crying out loud, Naomi, I'm a youth club leader, a Christian youth worker. I'm not supposed to sleep with…"

"With what?"

"With girls! With anyone! Let alone someone from the youth club!"

Naomi bit her lip.

"Oh. I see," she said.

"Oh, bloody hell, what a mess. We shouldn't have done it."

Naomi turned her head away and stared out of the window at the overgrown garden and drenched grass.

"Don't tell anyone, please!"

She turned back. Her head was held high and her face stony.

"I wouldn't anyway."

"And, oh no…" He hesitated, then blurted out, "What if you get pregnant?"

"I'm on the pill."

"What? Oh yeah, of course you are! I'm an idiot, aren't I?"

He pulled the fridge door open, shoved the milk inside, and slammed it shut. Naomi reached out her hand to him. He ignored it.

"Luke, I…" she said.

"You what? You're sorry?"

"No… Nothing. It doesn't matter. Yeah, like you said, of course I'm on the pill."

"Good for you. So we can just pretend this never happened."

"Never happened?"

"No! We'll just forget it. For Christ's sake, I know I was stupid! I'll get your coat and bag. I just hope no one sees you leaving. That'd be all I need."

He watched her walk quickly down the rain-drenched street, her hood pulled up over her head. She didn't look back. Then he went upstairs, stripped the creased, stained sheets from the bed, put them in the washing machine, knelt on the tiled floor of the kitchen and tried unsuccessfully to pray.

Phone calls to his mother were always an encouragement. Luke rang her the next evening. He needed some unquestioning support.

"Five families at Messy Church! How wonderful, darling! You must be delighted," she said. "Wait, here's your father, you can tell him yourself."

"Um, OK," Luke said, reluctantly.

His father came on the phone.

"Luke, my boy! Tell me, how's my young apprentice doing?"

"Fine, um, fine. It's going well. I was just telling Mum."

"I'll get the news from her then. Did you get the Alpha course started at the youth group?"

"Yeah, just a couple of sessions."

"Great! How many of the youth are coming?"

"Um, only three, actually. But we've only just started."

"Only three? Ah, well, that's a shame. Any of them going to church? Any signs of any of them coming to Christ?"

"No, sorry, not really."

"Don't worry, my boy, it's early days yet. I'm praying hard, so I'm sure you'll see a harvest. James – did your mother tell you? – James is running a Pilgrim course at St. Bartolph's and they've had a dozen new converts from it."

Great, thought Luke. Just what I wanted to hear. Big brother the vicar is scoring points again.

"That's good," he said, through gritted teeth. "Well done him."

"Maybe you should do that. Oh, by the way,

you'll be pleased to hear Iain's job with Shell is working out fine. And Charlotte's been offered a job as a chief fund-raiser for the Meriba Fresh Water Trust in Chester."

Bully for her, Luke thought, but "Has she?" was all he said.

"Yes, we're very pleased for her. She's glad to be moving out of Stevenage and, of course, Chester is a beautiful town. Tell me, any more news your end?"

"Nah, not really, just jogging along. Doing the stuff, you know."

"Keep up the good work, then. I have got to go, I've got an allotment holders meeting. I'll say cheerio and God bless, my young apprentice!"

Luke said goodbye, then slammed the phone down. He hated that joke. When he was younger, his father would introduce his family to guests, always starting with his two older brothers James and Iain, then his sister Charlotte, and finally, "this is Luke, the youngest." His sister, five years his elder, would usually add, "the baby of the family!" and everyone would laugh and nod, smiling down at him.

CHAPTER FOURTEEN

He might be the baby of the family, but the dreams and fantasies he was having about Naomi were very adult indeed. Maybe he should try to find a girlfriend? A safe, not-too-challenging Christian girlfriend, to keep him on the straight and narrow. What was it Saint Paul had said about the best remedy for lust? To marry? The idea startled him. None of his siblings, none of his school or uni friends were married. They all seemed a bit young. But why not? He was twenty-three. His parents had married before they were twenty-two. No, he shook his head. It was a stupid idea. Stupid.

But it wouldn't go away. Perhaps it would be a smart idea to be the first one to get hitched. It'd be one up on James, Charlotte and Iain anyway. Luke considered the members of the church congregations that he knew. Where were all the young unattached Christian women? There weren't many of them around, and a surprising number were already single mothers. Of course, there was always Sophie. She was fairly pretty and they did get on all right.

He texted Sophie. "Fancy going to the cinema next week?"

An hour later she replied.

"Yes, love to, rom com, Fri half-seven?"

Rom com – well, OK, he could deal with that. He should have known Sophie wouldn't go for the latest slick Matt Damon thriller or superhero movie.

As it turned out, the film wasn't as soppy as he expected, and, predictably, Sophie loved it.

"Wasn't Tom Hiddleston brilliant?" she exclaimed, as they came out from the cinema into the August night.

"Yeah, um, which one was he?"

"Honestly, Luke, you're terrible!" She said, giving him a friendly shove.

When they reached the junction, Sophie said, "My car's parked down there. Shall I give you a lift home?"

"Nah," Luke said. It was bad enough that she wouldn't let him pay for her: a lift home would be too patronizing. "I wish I'd passed my test and got a car – I ought to be giving you a lift."

"Luke, don't be so silly. That doesn't matter. And I'm sure you'll pass your test next time. I am praying for you!"

"Yeah, maybe. Tell you what, it's only half-nine. Come on, I'll buy you a drink." He gestured to a nearby bar.

"OK! But it'll have to be non-alcoholic."

"Fine. Coffee? How about hot chocolate?"

"Fantastic! Do they do hot chocolate in there?"

They found a sofa, pushed back into a dark corner, to sit on. Luke got Sophie hot chocolate and had orange juice with vodka. He had a feeling he was going to need it. Although she had clearly dressed up a bit, in strappy sandals and a flower-sprinkled floaty dress, and silver earrings with a matching necklace instead of her usual blue glass cross, she wasn't making it easy. She laughed, chatted and teased him. She relaxed back on the sofa next to him, with her shoulder touching his, but there was never a moment when he could put his arm around her or lean in close. This is hopeless, he thought. Maybe later.

Sophie drank the last of her chocolate.

"Yum!" she said. "Thanks! Come on, I'll give you that lift anyway. No arguments! It's late."

At the car, she turned to him.

"Thanks ever so, Luke. That was lovely. Lovely to go out, do something non-churchy."

She stepped closer and suddenly it was easy to put his arms around her and pull her close into his chest. And it was fine. She had some sort of perfume on, he didn't know what, but the scent was subtle and pleasant. She stayed in his arms for a second, then moved back slightly. He loosened his hold and she said, "Gosh, Luke, I didn't think you were the hugging type."

Now or not at all, he felt. To his surprise, it was natural to kiss her cheek then go the extra step then kiss her mouth. Briefly, but definitely.

"Hey, steady on, Luke," she laughed. "I'm glad

you're Anglican, at least. No tongues!"

"Don't laugh. I'm serious," he said.

"What? Oh, Luke, you sweet boy! What do you mean?"

"I'm serious. You and me. Really. You know…"

"Oh, be merciful to me, Lord, for men hotly pursue me! Psalm fifty-six!" she exclaimed. "First Gerald, and now you!"

"Sophie!"

"Are you really serious?"

"Yes!" he said loudly, almost shouting.

"Gosh, Luke, oh my goodness. I never thought. Really? Like … like going out together?"

"Why not?"

"I dunno, Luke. Look, seriously, I like you, but that's all. And I've always felt, very strongly, that it's wrong to just go out with someone unless there was something, I don't know, a potential, a possibility of a commitment."

"You mean – like marriage?"

"Yes! I'm not going to get together with anyone for, you know, a casual going-out relationship unless I truly felt it was possible that we'd marry. It's a Christian thing, I guess."

"Yeah, sure, well – I suppose you're right. Um, I'm not, I mean, I reckon I don't see why not. Why it's not possible."

"Oh Luke, bless you! You really are so sweet! But, honestly, Luke, that's not going to happen, is it? You find me irritating sometimes, don't you?"

Luke hesitated a fraction too long.

"Um," he said. "No, not really."

"Oh come on! Quoting bible verses, having

visions, that sort of stuff? It's not quite your thing, is it?"

"Um…"

"It's fine, Luke! But it is my thing and I'm not going to change. No, it's not going to happen, Luke. I'm sorry if you're disappointed."

"OK," he said, looking at the pavement, putting his hands in his pockets and shrugging.

"I can see the relief on your face, Luke Carmichael!" she said. "Come on: friends, fellow-workers, but that's all. OK? Shake?"

He pushed his fringe back and smiled ruefully.

"I guess so."

She shook his hand.

"I suggest you look elsewhere," she added. "Naomi Robeson, for instance."

He stared at her. But her expression was one of simple friendliness.

"Naomi?" he exclaimed.

"Yes. But I'm not saying any more! We'd better go. Hop in!"

Outside his house, she stopped the car and turned to him.

"Luke, there is something I've been meaning to tell you. Something about Stephen. Just a hunch, a warning from God, for both of us. Be careful with him."

"What? Be careful? Do you mean he's, like, dangerous?"

"No! Just be careful, be wise in your dealings with him, in what you say to him. I had a vision – but I'm not going to share it – but it's a warning for us, for me, and for you. Just be wise, OK, Luke?"

"OK. Sure, I'll be sensible. I'll be careful," he said, as he got out.

"Good. So, I'll be seeing you. Goodnight and God bless. Thanks!"

As he let himself into his house, he tried to remember what he had said to Stephen at the weekend away. He'd been wise, hadn't he? Anyway, it was too late now. Stephen would be going to York University soon. It would be fine, he was sure. And Sophie always was a bit over-dramatic with her dreams from God and wacky visions.

CHAPTER FIFTEEN

Naomi had liked Danny initially, but his father had frightened her from the first moment she'd met him. She'd been twelve, Jessica only five. Patience had stumbled through the door late one afternoon, while Naomi was heating tinned chicken soup for dinner for her and Jessica.

"Girls! Hey, girls, come and meet me new fella! This is Walter," she'd said and stepped aside to reveal a tall black man with arrogant eyes. He had a slight paunch and a scar cutting a paler line across one arm.

"Them your kids? They're real pretty, they are. Like their mother."

"Girls, now then, say hello. I done brought him home to meet you."

Naomi and Jessica dutifully chorused, "Hello." Jessica hid behind Naomi's skirt as she peered up at the big man with his overpowering voice.

"Come on then, Patience. I wanna get to the

club before six, I'm meeting Jacob there."

"Now, Naomi, you look after you sister, won't you? Be a good girl. I'll be back by ten."

But it was nearer twelve when Naomi was woken by Patience coming in, giggling and staggering up the stairs. Thankfully, she couldn't hear the big man as well. But the next week he came in with Patience and was there at breakfast, sitting with his elbows in the crumbs on the table and filling the cramped kitchen with his shoulders, his body and his voice.

"Tea, then, woman. I'll have tea."

Patience was wearing a heavy gold necklace. She noticed Jessica staring at it.

"Does you like it, child? Walter bought it for me. Tis real gold, it is. Real gold," and she patted it and smiled as she tipped two fried eggs onto Walter's plate.

His visits became more frequent, the jewellery he gave Patience more ostentatious and gaudy, the breakfasts she cooked for him more substantial. A year later, Patience came into Naomi's bedroom and flopped heavily down onto the bed. She sighed. "You room is so tidy, child. You a good girl. Naomi, honey, Walter's going to be moving in tomorrow, he is. So Jessica will have to go in with you here. We can put her bed there, in the corner."

"No!" Naomi exclaimed. "I don't want him here!"

"Shut you mouth, child! He's losing his flat, he is. So he's coming here. Him and his child, his boy, Danny."

"Danny?"

"Yes, Danny. His son. Nice boy, he is. He's coming too, and he needing his own room, cos he's twelve. Twould not be fitting for him to go with you or Jessica."

Naomi protested, but Walter and his son moved in anyway. Danny was a slight, big-eyed lad, barely an inch taller than her. He smiled at her, a careful, wary smile, then sat on the edge of the sofa, watching her and Jessica. The telly was on. Bob the Builder was fixing yet another trivial problem: building a summerhouse for some old lady. Jessica was at school, but she still wanted to watch Roley, Spud and Bird create chaos with diggers and dungarees.

Danny leaned forward.

"Why're you watching this? It's baby stuff," he said.

"I like it!" Jessica said, twisting round to stare at him. "Go 'way! It's my house and my telly!"

"All right then! I only asked," he said, leant back and glanced cautiously at Naomi. He spent the next few months being so polite, diffident and shy that Naomi unbent. Then he bought Jessica a stuffed Bob the Builder toy and became her favouritest boy in all the world. A year later, as he sat between them on the sofa watching 'Frozen', it felt like he'd always been there. Walter was more impermanent: staying for a few months, vanishing to do some 'work for a mate in Lunnon' for a few weeks, reappearing with a wad of cash and a dozen bottles of beer.

That Christmas Eve Danny and Naomi made a den by covering the dining table with an old sheet and hid together under it. Patience was sprawled on the sofa cushions half-awake, Walter had gone out to the pub, Jessica was in bed watching hopefully for Father Christmas, and James Bond was raising one eyebrow at a villain on the telly.

"Give me a kiss?" Danny whispered in the dim light. Naomi looked at him and considered. He'd got thinner. His cheekbones were sharper, his eyes large and nervous. "All right," she said. His mouth tasted of peanut butter sandwiches and his nose bumped hers. She pulled back and looked at him.

"Was that right?" she said.

He nodded.

"Do it again," he said. "If you want to."

"OK," she said.

That was her first proper kiss. Then there was another first time, two years later. Naomi had heard shouting in the kitchen and the crash of crockery. She rushed in. Walter was shaking Patience. Her purse lay wrenched open on the table and shards of a broken plate were scattered over the floor.

"Where's the money, woman? Where's it all gone? You told me you had twenty quid! There's nothin' in here, nothin'!"

"Walter," slurred Patience. "I'm sorry, Walter. Don't, don't'..."

"You fat slag. You spent it on booze, you cowin' slag."

He smacked the side of her head and she slipped down onto the floor, crouched down and hugged her sides, rocking to and fro. Naomi ran to her.

"Don't!" she shouted at Walter.

"You keep out of it, you little bint," Walter said.

He moved towards her, his hand raised. Danny came in, ran forwards and grabbed his arm.

"Leave her, Dad!" he shouted. "I've told you - you leave her alone. Don't you touch her!"

"OK, son," Walter said, stepping back. "OK, take it easy."

"Walter, I got some money. I done put some in the tea caddy. There's a tenner in there. You can have that. I'm sorry, I'm…" Patience started sobbing. Her tears ran down her face and trickled over the stains on her jumper.

Walter pulled the note out of the caddy.

"See, honey, I didn't…" she moaned, holding her head.

Walter tucked the note into his pocket then turned on Danny and Naomi.

"Get out of here!" he growled.

As Naomi scuttled out, she looked back. Walter was kneeling on the floor, stroking Patience's hair and muttering, "Honey, honey, there, don't cry. You shouldn't have pushed me to it, you shouldn't have…"

In the hall, Danny pulled Naomi closer to him. She was shaking. He put his arms around her.

"I won't let him hurt you," he said. "I'll look after you. Hey, come up here. Leave them to it."

Naomi could hear her mother's incoherent murmurs, and Walter grumbling and muttering. Danny's large eyes were nervously watching her.

"Yeah, OK," she said, as he took her hand and pulled her upstairs into his room.

"I made summat for you," he said.

"What?"

"Here. I made it in D & T."

He picked up a badly-painted red and green wooden board and pushed it towards her. It had brass hooks screwed into it at uneven intervals.

"See. It stands up and you can hang your stuff on it. Necklaces, rings, stuff."

"Oh. Thanks. That's nice of you."

She put her arms round him and kissed him.

"Thanks too, for – for, you know," she said.

"I won't ever let him hurt you, you know," he said. "Naomi, please, come here. Sit down."

He sat on the bed and pulled her hand to make her sit down next to him.

"Naomi, you're so pretty," he said, running his finger along her cheek. "Will you, you know, be my girl?"

"What do you mean?"

"Well, you know. Have you ever, actually, ever done it?"

"No. Have you?"

"No. But, look, Nomy, shall we?"

"What – do it? Like, sex, you mean?"

"Yeah. Do it together, first time."

"But it'd be weird! You're like my step-brother!"

"No, I ain't! They ain't even married. You kissed me, didn't you? You like me, don't you?"

She nodded.

"I like you. Come on, Nomy, come on. Let's see what it's like. Don't you want to?"

"I dunno…"

"Come on. I'll look after you. You'll be my girl, my girlfriend. We'll keep it secret, like, so they don't know. Come on, it'll be fun."

He leaned in close and looked at her. Naomi looked at him, and then stared at the dust bunnies on the floor. He had put aftershave or something on. It was piney, woody; like fresh soap. She did like him. He'd been a nervy, gentle, big-eyed boy at thirteen. Like Bambi. Now he was taller, surer, confident. He'd grown up fast in secondary school. As he pushed her back onto the bed and ran his hand inside her t-shirt, feeling for her bra strap, she wriggled down and started to undo his shirt buttons. Better with him, here, in his bedroom, she decided, than against a rough wall in an alley with a drunken sixth-former like her friend Hannah. Better to do it now, safely, and see what it was like.

"Yeah, all right," she said. And it was all right. He was nice to her. At first, anyway.

CHAPTER SIXTEEN

One by one Barbara took down, from the shelves beside the desk, her collection of completed models: Minis, the Razzle Dazzle Camper van with the corrected mistake, Cadillacs, Spitfires, Hurricanes, a square-rigged tea-clipper that had taken her weeks and, at the back, her very first model. A Dakota, painted rather clumsily, with crooked decals and blobs of glue adhering to the wheel struts. She had been twelve when her father, Liam, had given the kit to her. He'd burst into the house; all deep voice, corduroy coat, leather driving gloves, whiskey smell and bear-hug arms.

"How's my little girl?" he'd roared, swept her up into his arms and pressed the stubble on his chin into her cheek. "Mother of God, I've missed you, me darlin'. Three bloody months on the road!"

"We was expecting you yesterday," said her mother Janice.

"Got delayed, didn't I? Any road, I'm here now.

Babs, me darlin', look what I've got fer you."

Like a magician pulling rabbits from a hat, he revealed present after present. A teddy bear, a Lego set, doll's house furniture made of real wood, and lastly the Dakota kit.

"Got it from a shop in Liverpool," he said. "No idea why. But I always liked them Dakotas. Big noisy brutes of a plane. Saw them flying over Crawley to Normandy. Never forgot it."

Janice tutted. "Don't talk rubbish. You were a kid of four, living in some god-forsaken Irish farm. Bloody liar, that's what you are."

"Ignore her, Babs. Course I saw them. Come on, honeypots, let's make it together."

Barbara picked up the Dakota as she remembered. He'd helped her cut out the first pieces and put the wheel frame together. Then he'd got up, patted her on her head, told her she was his darlin', and went off to the pub; reappearing two hours after her bedtime, staggering and beer-filled, to kiss her goodnight.

That was the pattern of her childhood, swinging between the slovenly carelessness of her discontented mother, and the brief eruptions of her huge, indulgent father; home for a week or so and then back on the road, buying and dealing in Irish and Scotch whiskey, ferrying van-loads from County Louth or Dalwhinnie to Manchester, Birmingham or Coventry. God knows what he'd seen in her mother, or vice versa. It was no surprise when he had an affair and moved out.

Barbara had moved up to Aberdeen with her mother, but as soon as she was independent, she'd returned to the Midlands to be nearer her father. Janice had snorted, "You're joking? Moving to be near him? Well, I always thought you were a Daddy's girl with no sense, but that takes the biscuit. I warn you, Babs, you'll regret it." Liam was living with his mistress in a rented terrace house in Stafford. When she eventually and inevitably left him, he moved in with another woman in Liverpool, a tedious three or four hour journey up the M6. Most of the times that Barbara visited him he was drunk, even at eleven in the morning. He always exclaimed with delight at seeing her, but now she was beginning to notice that he never made any effort to phone her or drive down south to see her. She realised that he probably cared very little for her. Even so, she folded the Dakota carefully in foam and bubble-wrap before putting it on top of the others in the cardboard box.

There was a knock on the door. It was George, with Stephen.

"Come to help you load up the rest of the stuff," he said.

As he and Stephen came in, he added, "By the way, Barbara, I'm sorry to hear the Micra failed its MOT. Hope it wasn't too expensive."

"No, it wasn't too bad. Thanks for asking." Barbara said. She felt compelled to lie. It had been bad. Four hundred and seventy-five pounds for the brakes, lights, and a new clutch cable, but she couldn't tell George and Marjorie that, not when they'd been so generous to someone like her. When she'd moved in, Marjorie had lent Barbara milk, teabags, sugar and biscuits, and carried suitcases and boxes upstairs. George had helped unpack and fit together her new flat-pack furniture, telling her about how he played the organ in the church and how proud they were of their son's singing in the choir, as he slotted in the shelves with long, careful fingers. And now he was helping her again.

"Shame to be moving out," he said, as he twirled the allen key in the bolt on the bookcases. "I remember helping you put these together."

Barbara nodded, surreptitiously wiped a drop of moisture from her eye, then started to pull her shirts and trousers from the wardrobe and shove them into a cardboard box.

George and Stephen started carting boxes out to the van. Most of her furniture had gone to the flat already or been given to charity shops or sold. The flat she was moving to was smaller, but she ought to be able to afford it, as far as she could work out. But she still owed the building society over six thousand, as well as several hundred to the housing association. The debts had started in January with a defaulted payment and subsequent bank charges, and the same thing had happened again in March. After paying for the car MOT, it was clear she could not afford the rent and mortgage, not with the little that she was earning. Then the house had sold for three thousand less than she had paid for it. When she'd explained about it being a shared ownership house, the estate agent had shook his head and said that, in that case, if she needed a quick sale, she'd have to drop the price by ten thousand. Her original deposit, all her savings, everything, it seemed, had disappeared into the black gap between income and outgoings that she'd found herself in after nine months work at the care home.

She should look for better paid work, but Angela was relying on her and always grumbling about how difficult it was to get good staff. And the thought of another interview, after the one at the care home, made her squirm. She had been embarrassingly aware that she didn't seem to have any strengths or achievements, and she couldn't answer questions like 'What are four positive things your boss would say about you?' It was clear she'd only got the job because Marjorie had put in a good word for her. And where would she get a decent salary anyway? Who else would employ her – with just a Level 1 Diploma in Hospitality and Catering, seven years kitchen work, and eight years at Thomson's, and nothing else worthwhile to show at all?

George interrupted her thoughts. "Barbara? All the boxes, is that right? What about the pictures on the walls?"

"Oh, sorry, I'm such an idiot – I completely forgot to pack them!"

"I'll do it," said Stephen. "No problemo…"

"Thanks! It's so good of you. I know I'm being such a bother."

"Don't be silly, Barbara," George said. "You know we're glad to help."

Half an hour later they took out the last few boxes and bags.

"That's it, done and dusted, van's packed," said George. "Stephen, are you OK to walk? There's only two front seats."

"No, it's fine, I'll walk," said Barbara. "It may seem silly, but I just want to, you know, say goodbye to my house."

"Right. We'll drive over and meet you there, then. Pass us your flat keys, and we can start unloading. Oh, and this is for you, from Marjorie."

He handed her an envelope. As the van drove off, Barbara went upstairs, walked slowly around the vacant bedroom, the cleaned and emptied bathroom, the cleared-out study. She looked out of the window at the tidy complacent houses, the smart street, the specimen trees on the front lawns. As she leant against the glass a great weariness settled on her. Probably she would never look out at that cultured, quiet, suburban view again. Someone else would move in. She rubbed her forehead, sighed and walked slowly downstairs. Mechanically, she checked all the kitchen cupboards, fished a last spoon from the back of a drawer, glanced at the unmown lawn, empty bird-feeder, straggly asters and starved hydrangea, then turned away and went into the living room.

She realised Marjorie's letter was still in her hand. She opened it. Inside was a 'Welcome to your new house' card, with a black and white photo of a old Volkswagen Beetle, the roof piled high with suitcases, chairs, rugs and boxes. Marjorie had written 'We hope your move goes well and you are happy in your flat. God bless' and included a cheque. Barbara unfolded it, her hands trembling. A hundred pounds! She collapsed to her knees and stared at the amount and at the scrawled 'M.

Fowler' signature. It was real. Marjorie was so kind to her! She curled up on the floor, hugged her knees and allowed herself to cry a little. Then she sat up and shook her head. After all, it was her own fault she'd got into such a financial hole. At least she had the chance of a fresh start and this gift would help. Barbara looked round at her cream carpet and green walls. The flat, in a square block on Bristol Street, had a blotchy greyish carpet, which was heavily stained, and dull magnolia walls, pock-marked with holes from drawing pins and picture hooks. There was no garden, but it did have a parking space. It was up two flights of stairs, but Barbara didn't mind that. It was just that it was small, grubby and rented. She squared her shoulders, wiped her eyes with a tissue and went out, locking the door behind her.

The rent was two-thirds of her previous rent and mortgage payments, and seemed high for such a small, tatty flat in a depressing, neglected suburb. But paint, at least, was cheap. Barbara spent several days cleaning, with the windows wide open to clear out the stale cigarette smell. She filled nine bin bags with rubbish left by the previous owners: scraps of packing paper, dirty socks, used tissues, broken mugs, newspapers, discarded underwear and worse; she washed and scrubbed and scoured, then headed to the nearest DIY store. Two tins of pale sea green brightened the walls considerably. As Barbara hung the curtains back up, she noticed something wedged behind the storage heater under the window. She fished it out. It was a ten-pound note.

A good omen, perhaps? She sat on a chair, stared at the ominous stains on the carpet, and decided she couldn't face the grubby gloom any more. She needed some encouragement. Ten pounds was enough for a tiny treat and seeing Sophie would be a blessing. She put it into her pocket, put her coat on, and walked into town.

The Sea Shells Café was empty, and Sophie was sitting at a table, biting her nails and staring out of the window, with a folded newspaper next to her. She looked unusually morose, Barbara thought, as she came in. Sophie looked up, her face brightening slightly, and pushed the newspaper aside.

"Hi Sophie," Barbara said. "I was passing, I thought I'd pop in. Are you all right? Where is everyone?"

"I'm fine, Barbara, fine, just a bit – never mind, I'm fine. I have to keep telling myself, 'weeping may endure for a night, but joy cometh in the morning'. Psalm thirty. Jenny, she helps out, she's done her shift and gone home. It's always really quiet after half-four on Saturdays, especially during the school holidays. Everyone's finished their shopping and left. Even Gerald hasn't come in for his green tea and toasted tea-cake."

"Would you like him to come in? I thought he was your stalker?"

"He's all right. I only call him that as a silly joke. Anyway, can I get you anything?"

"Two teas – one for me and one for you, please. And shall we have two slices of that coffee and walnut cake? You seem a bit low, if you don't mind me saying so."

"Thanks. I have to admit it, yes, I am. I'm not usually like this, am I? I'll tell you in a bit."

Sophie went behind the counter and got cups and teapots out. While she was busy, Barbara looked at the paintings for sale on the walls. There were three seascapes in pale turquoise and lavender shades, pretty if rather amateurish.

"Did you do these, Sophie?"

"No. I can't do watercolours at all, and I hate them anyway. They're so insipid! No, that's mine, on the far wall. It's been there two years – not even Gerald will buy it. I probably ought to take it down."

Barbara went over and studied the large oil painting. Dozens of deep green, blue, brown and purple crosses were arranged in a grid, each one on a dark-coloured rectangle. Some had ornate Celtic knots, complex mehendi-like patterns, or spirals and whorls decorating them; others had fine silver or gold outlines. Near the bottom left was a single rose-coloured cross on a pale pink background. The label underneath said '63+1'.

"Sixty-three plus one? I don't understand. What's that mean?" Barbara said.

"Did you know that sixty-three Ethiopian immigrants died trying to escape Libya to get to Italy? Their boat ran out of fuel and a uncaring b… no, I won't say it, an uncaring rat of a captain on a French ship saw them and did nothing. Nothing! Sixty-three desperate people dying of thirst! And yet all the front pages were just about a missing blonde-haired toddler. You remember? I felt so cross about it. I thought that the deaths of all those people, women, children too, were just as important. Just because they were African… It took me ages to paint it. Anyway, tea and cake's ready."

Sophie stirred sugar into her tea.

"Well, er, what is it, Sophie? What's wrong?" Barbara asked.

"Everything! Well, lots of things. It's such a battle sometimes, and it really seems like Revelation twelve - 'the devil has come in great anger, knowing that he has little time.' Look at this in the local news!"

She pointed at a police photo of a young teenager, under the headline 'Yob convicted of brutal attack'.

"I knew him. He used to come to the youth club. And now he's in prison for beating up an East European! I tried to save him, I tried to tell him about Jesus, but he didn't listen. I prayed for him so much! And now look at him!"

He did look particularly vicious, but then police photos weren't flattering.

"I'm sorry, Sophie. It's not your fault though," Barbara said.

"I know. Maybe prison is what he needs. It's just that I didn't save him. I've never managed to save anyone! Not really. I pray and do all the stuff, you know, say stuff, but it seems to just slide off them. Even Gerald. I thought, when he went on Alpha, that it would work, but he's still as completely uninterested as ever. I try to bring people to Jesus, but they just don't seem to want to know!"

"Oh, Sophie… I don't know, I thought you were

all right. I don't know what to say…"

"There's so much need! It's just overwhelming! Pregnancy and drug counselling, support for single parents and divorced fathers, alcohol-free clubs, anger management classes, all that sort of stuff. The list goes on and on of what we'd like to do. Oh, Babs, those youth club kids are so lost and need God so much and we just can't do it … we can't help them, we can't save them…"

And to Barbara's astonishment, Sophie, the ever-optimistic, ever-visionary Sophie, burst into tears.

Barbara hunted through the built-in closet for her dark jacket and black skirt, put them on, combed her hair and checked her appearance in the tiny mirror, moving to and fro so she could see herself despite the flecks and corroded silvering. She'd not been to many funerals, and wasn't sure whether her pale blue shirt was sombre enough, but it would have to do.

At Holy Trinity she looked around and was relieved to see that she fitted in. Others were wearing purple, dark navy or grey as well as black. George started playing the organ: a mournful and slow piece in a minor key. Francis stood at the altar, facing the congregation, and shifting from foot to foot. He looked nervous. Barbara wondered if he hated doing funerals. He fidgeted with his collar, and his hair on one side stuck up. She itched to go and smooth it for him, and to take his hand, to calm him down. But she stayed in her pew as the coffin was brought up. Such a humble pine box to hold all that was left of Mrs Woodings.

Two Steps Away

She'd only had three months in her retirement village; with its library, conservatory, restaurant, croquet lawn; and she'd so been looking forward to it. But to die quietly in your sleep aged seventy-nine was probably the best end one could hope for.

Francis stuttered throughout most of the eulogy. "Of course, I didn't know Ivy very well, only for the last five years. But I always found her to be encouraging and cheerful. She had been a Christian, of course, for over sixty-two years. An impressive record. Not many of us can claim that. And she had read her Bible, prayed, served God and worked hard. She was a founder member of the local Mother's Union, and after she lost her husband, in her fifties, she went to South America for six years to help with the Tearfund mission work there. She was a wonderful, faith-filled example to us all. Now, can we all join in with the final hymn, which she chose herself, 'Abide With Me'."

At the end of the service, only a few family members followed the coffin. Just a god-daughter, some nieces and nephews, and a couple of their children, according to Marjorie. But there were over thirty other people in the pews, some of whom were weeping into black-edged handkerchiefs. Mrs Woodings would obviously be much missed. Barbara wondered if Francis would miss her, if she were to die in her sleep next week. Probably not.

CHAPTER SEVENTEEN

At the PCC meeting, after everyone had got their coffees and teas, grabbed biscuits, found their agendas and notebooks, and Helen had said an overlong opening prayer, they read the apologies and then Francis announced, "Firstly, I'd just like to say a quick congratulations to Luke for passing his driving test."

Marjorie started to drum her fingernails on the table, but stopped herself. Patience, she said to herself, looking around. She wouldn't be the only one waiting for Francis to get to the point, and fill in all the details after his unusually terse and elliptical email. Of course, Luke's fan club were more interested in him finally managing to get his license. As if it was something out of the ordinary! she thought, as Sophie exclaimed, "Oh, yes, that's brilliant, Luke! I was praying for you all the time. I knew you'd manage it! It's going to be so useful, you being able to drive!"

"Yeah, um, thanks," Luke said. "Third time lucky, I guess."

"Anyway, yes, well done, Luke," Francis said. "You'll be trading up the skateboard for a Skoda, no doubt. And also I must say a thank-you to Michael Stuart, Helen's husband, who you all know anyway, of course you do, for joining the PCC to replace Ivy."

Everyone nodded and murmured thanks to Michael, who dutifully nodded back. Marjorie nodded very briefly. Despite the fact that, after two elderly PCC members left, they had had to co-opt someone, she wasn't sure she was happy with him coming on board. He had very modern evangelical ideas, and had even been heard to say that Stuart Townend was a bit old hat and his songs rather dated. But Francis had suggested him and no one else objected. Marjorie had learnt the wisdom of picking her battles, so she had shrugged and accepted him.

"Also, Barbara, bless her little cotton socks, is going to do the minutes," Francis continued. "Thank you, my dear."

Marjorie noticed Barbara's cheeks reddening as she looked down and scribbled 'thanks were expressed to MS and BW' on her notepad.

"Firstly, I've received apologies from Jonathon Roberts – yet again, I'm afraid. Now, I believe you all received my email about Ivy's legacy," Francis said, with a smile on his face. "It is, indeed, wonderful and very unexpected news. Such a change to have a happy treasurer, isn't it, Ted? So encouraging!"

"It certainly is," said Helen. "But the question is, what do we do with it?"

"Definitely," said Marjorie, unscrewing the top of her fountain pen. "In my opinion we should – no, I'll wait. Francis, first, please, go through the details. And tell us the amount, for heaven's sake!"

"Ah, yes, of course. Ivy, as you may well have heard on the church grapevine; before my email even reached you, no doubt, given the efficiency of our local gossip machine: anyway, she left us almost all of her estate. There were some small bequests to other charities and to her nieces, nephews and god-children, but she had no direct descendants. It was all very sad, I believe. She and her husband would have loved children of their own. Of course, I never met him, but I've been told he was an extremely godly man."

"Get on with it, Francis!" groaned Ted. "You don't half waffle sometimes!"

"Do I really waffle, Ted? Oh, I'm so sorry, you should have said earlier. Anyway, back to the sainted Ivy. She wasn't exactly impecunious and, as you know, she sold her house and moved into the Beeches retirement village three months ago. We are extremely fortunate that she did so. No one has to deal with all the complications of selling her house. The money is in the bank, as it were. The solicitor contacted me last week, and gave me the exact amount, after our blessed government have taken their cut in inheritance tax. Er, I have it somewhere…" he said, shuffling through a large notebook crammed with papers and newspaper cuttings.

"How much?" exclaimed Helen. "Don't keep us all in suspense!"

"Hmm…tempting… No, I'll put you all out of your misery. Drum roll, please. Two hundred and fifty-one thousand, three hundred and seventy-eight pounds. Approximately. Ta-da!" Francis looked round in satisfaction, and tossed a letter onto the table.

Marjorie stopped writing and dropped her pen on the table, as Barbara gasped and Helen stared at Francis with her mouth open.

"Goodness me!" said Daphne, picking up the letter and glancing at it. "Really?"

"Yes, really."

"Praise God!" said Michael.

"Wow!" said Luke. "Quarter of a million! Bloody hell!"

"Blimey O'Reilly!" said Ted, leaning back and folding his arms. "Good old Ivy!"

"And what are we allowed to do with it?" asked Marjorie. "Will it have to go to the diocese?"

"Our dearly beloved bishop can't touch it. Ivy stated, in her will, that the money is to go to Holy Trinity Church, Merton, for the advancement of God's kingdom, in any way that the vicar and the PCC see fit."

"Excellent," said George. "Means we can do more-or-less what we like."

"Fantastic!" exclaimed Sophie, grinning at Luke. "Isn't God good! So amazing! Over quarter of a million… Poor Ivy, but she will be so pleased. Luke, think what we could do!"

"Yeah, I am," said Luke. "Yeah!"

"Hold your horses," said Ted. "It's not yours, you know!"

"Quite right, Ted," said Marjorie. "Luke, it's the PCC's decision."

"Oh, yes, Marjorie," said Francis. "Coming back down to earth, it needs thought. That's why I asked for this meeting. And also because I wanted to see the expression on your faces. Gob-smacked…such a delightful word. So, it needs careful prayer, thought and discussion. After all, it is a theological question. What is the kingdom of God, and how do we advance it?"

By ten o'clock Marjorie was starting to feel more and more angry. The discussion had gone on for far too long. Everyone had their own ideas and pet projects. Luke and Sophie wanted drug counselling, youth work, better music facilities and a sound desk; Daphne said some new toys for the toddlers, 'proper good quality wooden ones', and then went on to talk about how a revamped kitchen with a café would be nice; Ted wanted the office computers and the hall heating improved; Helen and Michael wanted youth work and improved toilets.

George was quieter than usual, his face tense. All he had said was, "The organ is starting to deteriorate. It needs some money spent on refurbishment," but no one had listened. Marjorie knew how important it was to him, but he wouldn't fight for it. Very well, she would. She wouldn't let Luke and Sophie waste money on ungrateful teenagers and faddish worship services.

"We've been discussing this for," she glanced at

her watch, "two hours, fifteen minutes. It's about time we made a decision. Can I remind everyone of the plans that we had drawn up, several years ago, for church re-ordering? If you remember, we had an architect make some proposals that would give us a kitchen, a cafe, new toilets, a better church office, with money left over for the organ restoration. We didn't have the money then, but we have now. I think it's about time we realised those plans."

"Ah, yes, of course," said Francis. "I wasn't here, then, but I have seen those plans."

"They were exciting," said Daphne. "Inspiring. I'd forgotten them! Thanks for the reminder, Marjorie. Of course, they are just what we need."

"Very opportune," said Ted.

"But not necessarily what Ivy meant by advancing the kingdom of God," said Francis.

Marjorie tutted. "The church is the kingdom! We've had enough discussion about that. Everyone's had their say. The way I see it, it's between those who want to use this legacy on young people; drug counselling, pregnancy advice, modern-style evening services with sound desks and what not; and those who want to improve and preserve the facilities, the organ, the buildings of Holy Trinity for the public and future generations. A simple choice. So, I suggest we vote."

"Yes, perhaps you are right, Marjorie," Francis said. "It is getting late. A moment of quiet prayer, of reflection, then, as Marjorie says, we will vote."

"And no visions!" said Daphne. "I don't want anyone manipulating others by claiming 'God said to me'!"

"I don't manipulate others!" Sophie retorted.

"Did I say you did?"

"Please…" said Francis. "Guns away, please! Perhaps if one of us has a vision or a word from God, they should ask God if they are meant to share it. And I know, we all know, that Sophie is not that sort of person."

"Course she's not!" said George. "Honestly, Daphne, that was way out of line!"

Francis turned to Sophie and quietly said, "A little Matthew seven, I think? Don't cast your pearls before swine?"

Sophie bit her lip and nodded.

"Right!" Marjorie said. "As Francis said, a moment's reflection. Then I'll ask everyone to say what they truly feel this money should be best spent on."

She watched the second hand go around twice as everyone sat with their eyes closed. The church filled with silence. As she waited, she sent a quick prayer heavenward, then deliberately picked up her pen, pulled her notebook towards herself and cleared her throat.

"Barbara, I know you're taking the minutes, but this decision is so important that I will make some notes too and share them with you afterwards. Just to ensure we've got it all correct. Now, it is a simple vote: youth work or church facilities. We can argue over details another evening. It's nearly ten, we'll just all quickly say what we think. Sophie?"

"Youth work."

"Yeah, youth worth too," said Luke.

"Luke, you don't have a vote," snapped Marjorie. "You can listen, advise and suggest, but you don't have a vote."

"OK, sure. I forgot."

"Barbara?"

"Oh, Marjorie, I'm sorry. I did like the sound of having a café but I feel that the work Luke and Sophie does is so good, I'm, well, I guess I'm voting for them."

Marjorie raised her eyebrows at this, but said nothing.

"Michael? Helen?"

"Youth work, absolutely," Michael said and Helen nodded. "Yes, same here. What Luke's doing is very impressive and we must support it,"

"Ta!" said Luke.

"Right. Daphne?"

"Playgroup and church facilities, without a doubt. Especially better storage, toys, toilets and an improved kitchen. It would make such a difference to the toddler and Sunday school groups, it would bless local parents, and be a good outreach."

"Ted?"

"Church re-ordering, of course! We'd be idiots to neglect this chance to fix it!"

"George?"

George hesitated, looking at Luke and Sophie, then shook his head. "Has to be the church facilities."

"Me too," Marjorie said. "Francis?"

"Er, well, I do think that what Luke and Sophie are doing is truly advancing God's kingdom.

Reaching a lost generation. It is vital, in my view. So I will opt for the youth work."

Marjorie snapped her notebook shut.

"Right! So that's five to four. Youth work it is," she said, and glared at Luke, Sophie and Barbara.

Holy Trinity's pews were hard, made of oak darkened by age and with no concessions to comfort in the form of padding or cushions. The wood felt cold and waxy beneath Marjorie's hands as she placed them on the back of the pew in front, feeling the grain, worn smooth by decades of polishing. A scent of lilies drifted from two dramatic arrangements of white and cream flowers, foliage and trails of variegated ivy that stood on high iron stands on either side of the steps to the altar. Wherever Marjorie looked, light glinted on the polished brass of candlesticks, rails, gilding on paintings and icons, and on the giant eagle forming the lectern. The church definitely seemed a bit brighter, the brass shinier, the floor tiles glossier, now that Barbara was cleaning for three hours every Saturday.

The choir entered, shuffling and self-conscious in white surplices over red robes. The organ poured out reverberating chords and their voices rose; clear tenor and high alto, the resonances of song and music combining with the perfume and gold and glory. Tears pricked Marjorie's eyes. She hadn't heard this introit for over thirty years. Her grandmother had loved it. Marjorie bowed her head and listened. This was what it was all for. This was what she would do anything to keep.

Two Steps Away

At the end of the service, George played his favourite Magnificat Fugue by Pachelbel. The lower D sounded slightly off-key, and a faint breathy wheeze came from one of the pipes, as if it was packed with cotton wool. George was right: the organ was disintegrating. Suddenly she was aware of every tiny flaw in its sound. She winced as discords crept into the harmonies, as jarring and insistent as a magpie's cawing. She looked around. No one else seemed to have noticed. George would have done though. She could see a frown on his reflection in the slanted mirror over the keyboard. She saw Luke and Sophie, laughing at something. They weren't even listening. And the music would get worse and worse, now that Luke had persuaded the PCC to spend that money on youth work instead! Youth work – wasting it on feckless teenagers, when the organ, the finest musical instrument in Merton, was falling apart!

CHAPTER EIGHTEEN

"No. I can't any more, Danny," Naomi said. Her knees felt like they were about to give way. She fought to keep her voice firm.

"What? Why not?" he shouted, trying to pull her into his bedroom.

"I don't like it. I don't like what you wanna do."

"How'd ya mean, you don't like it?"

Naomi just shook her head. She couldn't tell him about Luke. About what an oasis that night with him had been. About the sweetness of his uncomplicated, naïve lusts. About how enthralled and easily delighted he'd been, compared to Danny's increasingly complex and twisted desires.

"It's just ... Nah, I can't explain it!"

"There's someone else, ain't there?"

"No! But ... Christ, Danny, it was fine at first, but..."

"But what?"

"I don't like that sort of weird stuff. It's just – I

don't wanna do it anymore!"

"What weird stuff?"

"That you get off those sites – those porno sites."

Danny let go of her arm.

"Oh, is that it? You just want straight stuff? Just a simple, normal, boring time in bed, like we did when we were kids? I can still do that. I can well do that…"

"No! no, no – not any more, Danny. Please … just not today."

"I dunno what the hell's up with you. Haven't I bin good to you? Don't I look after you? I stop Dad hitting you and Jessie, don't I?"

"Yeah, I know, Danny, but…"

"Ain't I good to you? I dunno what's up with you these days, Nomy. Come on, come on…"

He leaned forward, stroked her cheek and nuzzled her neck.

"Nomy, Nomy, come on… I want you. I'll be, I'll do what you want. Honey, come on…"

"No!" she said, pulling away.

She could smell the weed on his breath and clothes. Ever since he'd started smoking joints, five years ago, he'd got more and more unpredictable: suddenly erupting into rage, swearing and smashing his fist into the table and storming out into the dark. Now his face changed. Primal terror snapped into her blood at his expression.

"There's someone else, I bet. You've been two-timing me, haven't you, you cowing slut! Come on, Nomy, tell me who it was!" he said. He lashed out and hit her. Her head cracked sideways and slammed into the edge of the door. Sharp pain stabbed her temple. She cried out.

"You screwing-around little tart! I'll kill you…" he snarled in her face. He seized her arms. His eyes were burning into her. "Tell me who it is!"

He grabbed her hair and yanked it.

"No one! No one!!" she screamed.

"If there is, I'll find out," he hissed, his hand lashing out at her again and again. She tried to get away, but it wasn't any use. In the films women fought back, like Arya in Game of Thrones. She tried to kick him, to thump him, to trip him up and to run out of his way. But the films lied. It didn't work. She couldn't do anything to protect herself.

The beating went on until she felt blood trickling down her neck and bruises rising. She could feel her eye swelling up and her side throbbed with pain. Then he stopped and stared at her as she crouched on the floor. He knelt down.

"Oh God, Nomy, oh God. I didn't mean to."

"Go away," she sobbed. "Just go away."

"Lemme help you. Oh, God, Nomy, I'm sorry. I didn't mean to hit you, but you pushed me to it." He swore, again and again, his head bowed, then looked at her and stroked her cheek. There were tears in his eyes. "Nomy, I'm sorry, I really am. Don't tell anyone, will you? It was a mistake. I didn't mean it."

Naomi was silent. She rubbed her face where it ached from his fist.

"You – you know I didn't mean it. Come on, Nomy, I've said I'm sorry, haven't I? I'll get you fixed up. Lemme get you a plaster or summat."

She shook her head.

"Christ, Naomi, what the hell do you want me to do?"

"Just leave me alone. Don't you touch me again."

"OK, right! If that's what you want! But, you remember, you're still mine. My girlfriend. You don't touch, you don't even look at any other guy, or I'll do worse. You remember what I've done for you and your sister! I keep Dad off your backs, don't I? I protect you. And Jessie. Don't you forget it!"

With an effort, Naomi, pushed herself upright and stared defiantly at him.

"You keep Jessie out of this," she said. "You leave her alone."

"Right! I will, but don't you tell anyone about this. I'm going out, but when I come back, you get yourself fixed up and you remember - I'm your boyfriend, I'll be good to you, I'll look after you, but you – you sleep with me. No one else! And I won't screw around with anyone else. You remember that, you're with me, no one else, or else. You think about it. Jessie's here too, ain't she? Don't you want me to look after her too? My kid sister?"

"Jessie doesn't need your sort of looking after, you - you - I hate you! Don't you even think about touching her!" she hissed, and sat up. He tried to help her stand up, but she pushed his arm away. "You leave her alone! I mean it. I do. You touch her – you hurt her, you even touch her and I'll kill you. I will. I'll tell the police. She's only fourteen and I'll tell the police and I'll hurt you back so much you'll never be able to move again. You leave her and me alone! Leave us alone!"

"Fine! If that's it – fine! Have it your own way, you and your precious little sister!"

He slammed his fist into her face again. She collapsed. Her cheekbone sliced against the edge of the door latch as she fell. He pushed her aside and ran downstairs. The front door slammed.

She lay on the floor, dizziness numbing her. When it passed, she crept to the bathroom and tried to clean up the worst of the blood. At least he'd gone, but what was she going to do? Call the police? They wouldn't help. Boyfriends beating up girlfriends? Not interested. He'd have to break her arm or half-kill her before they'd do anything.

Oh, God, she looked terrible. She had bruises on her face, a purple blotch on her cheek and a cut lip. Blood trickled from her cheekbone and from another cut over her swollen, reddened eye. She scrabbled in the bathroom cupboard to find antiseptic, cotton wool, plasters. The antiseptic stung and she gasped. The cut on her cheekbone looked deep. It might need stitches, she thought, sticking a large plaster over it.

If only Luke... Luke had what? Not thrown her out? Not avoided her every Youth Club evening since then? He didn't care two hoots for her, that was obvious. He wouldn't help. Nor would her Mum. Still besotted with Walter, accepting the words and harsh blows as normal, even as proof that he cared. At least Walter left her and Jessie alone. And Danny was, usually, pretty kind to

Jessie. Please, God, please don't let him touch her! But she couldn't stay here, not even to protect Jessie. She wouldn't stay to face Danny's violence again. If he ever found out that she really had slept with someone else, he'd murder her.

Despite the trembling in her arms and hands, she packed a bag with some clothes and toiletries, and a few of her most treasured items: a friendship bracelet Jessie had made for her, the soft velvet panda her Dad had given her before he'd run off, her diary, and the posh laptop Danny had got her for Christmas. God knew where he'd got the money for it – drug-dealing? Shoplifting? She hadn't asked, she'd been so pleased to get a decent computer at last. She shoved in her phone and purse. There was only a few pounds in her purse, and about sixty-five in her savings account left after helping Mum pay the bills. Not enough. But she knew she had to get away. Somewhere Danny wouldn't find her. He knew all her friends, where she worked, the youth club, everything. And what he didn't know, he'd find out from Jessie or Mum. She'd have to leave work, but she wouldn't stay here. She wouldn't stay a moment longer in the same house as him. She'd find somewhere, a hiding place, somewhere. As she pulled her coat on, she realised who would help: Sophie. She'd know about stuff like this.

Naomi sat on the bed and waited until four o'clock, reckoning that by that time the coffee shop would be quiet and Sophie about to close up. But Jessie came through the front door, calling, "Nomy, I'm back! Shelley's Mum gave me a lift!"

Naomi sighed. She had hoped to be gone before her sister got back. She thought about hiding - she didn't want to have to explain it all. Maybe she should warn Jessie? She shook her head. If Jessie started avoiding Danny he'd just get more enraged. She'd just have to hope that he was so obsessed with her that he wouldn't bother with her sister.

When Jessie walked into the bedroom and saw Naomi she screamed.

"Nomy! What happened to you?"

"It's OK, Jessie, it's nothing, I just fell over," Naomi said. "I've got to go out. I'll be all right. Don't worry, OK? I'll be back soon, I think. Look, get yourself dinner, OK? Do yourself a cheese toastie or something. And don't tell Danny that I've gone, right?"

She grabbed her coat and the bag and ran out. It was drizzling. She pulled her coat on and ran, ignoring the pain in her side and face, until she got to the Sea Shells Cafe. It was still open with light pouring from the windows. Sophie was wiping tables. No one else was there.

"Oh, great God in heaven, Naomi! Oh, my goodness! Oh, you poor, poor girl, what happened? Did you get mugged?" Sophie exclaimed as Naomi came in. "Come in, sit down. Oh, Lord help you, should I call the police or take you to hospital?"

"No, no, Sophie. It's not as bad as it looks. Don't call the police, there's no point. It's not like that. Look, I need some help. You've got to help me. I figured you'd know what to do. And you'd know where I could go. You'll know this sort of stuff. You did a sponsored run, didn't you? Last year, for that women's refuge place in Leamington?"

CHAPTER NINETEEN

"Bread of heaven, bread of heaven," Marjorie sang defiantly, dashing along in the sparse mid-week traffic on the A1, with the windows wide open and 'Keswick Praise' playing on the CD. Her fingernails tapped the steering wheel in time to the music as she overtook a sluggish lorry. Stephen had texted to say he'd left his swim kit behind, as well as his winter coats and shoes, and he needed an alarm clock. So she'd decided to nip up to York to see him, and take him a few extras too: a hot water bottle, a fleece blanket, a decent pillow, a mattress topper. She'd been horrified by the thinness of the mattress the halls of residence had provided. George was working overtime since he had an imminent deadline for a wind turbine installation, so she went on her own, taking advantage of a half-term Wednesday with no piano lessons. She'd missed Stephen far more than she expected. She'd even missed washing his socks and underwear.

Weekly phone calls were insufficient. He'd been gone three weeks now. She and George were 'empty-nesters' and she hated it. Hated Helen saying "I expect you're really enjoying your freedom now", hated the vacant chair at dinner, hated not being able to put a pile of cleaned ironed shirts and jeans on his bed and have him smile "Ta, Mum" and, most of all, hated not hearing him sing in the choir. At least Stephen had told her that he'd found a friendly Anglican church to go to, one popular with the uni students. He'd sworn that he was going to go regularly.

"Don't worry, Mum," he'd said. "I'm not going to go all pagan on you."

"Yes, but do they have a choir? What about your singing?"

"It's not that sort of church, Mum, but it's OK. It's cool. Luke would like it. He knows the worship leader. I went last Sunday. It was pretty good," he'd said, and relief filled her.

She ran up the stairs of the residence block, two at a time, and knocked on his room. No answer. It was still only eleven, he might be at a lecture. She'd said she'd arrive at twelve, but the traffic had blessed her. A cup of tea would be welcome, and she could use the kettle in the shared kitchen just down the corridor.

Through the narrow glass strip in the kitchen door she saw Stephen. He was sitting with his back to her. He'd had his hair cut and cropped stubble softened the nape of his neck. She paused to look at him for a moment. When he'd been four he'd had blonde curls that tickled her cheek when she hugged him, and he'd cried and cried when they'd decided to cut his hair the week before he started school. She'd even kept one of the curved strands, tucked up in tissue paper in her jewellery box.

Another lad was in the kitchen. He wore nothing apart from a loose pair of grey jogging trousers that were sliding down his narrow torso to his hip bones. Marjorie hesitated before going in. The boy sauntered over to Stephen and flung an arm around his shoulders. Stephen said something and put his hand on the boy's naked spine, ran his fingers down the boy's side and slipped his hand inside his trousers. Marjorie could see her son squeezing the smooth globe of the other boy's buttock. Then the boy bent over and they kissed.

Marjorie dropped her handbag and stepped back. Her heart thudded against her chest like an animal crashing into a cage. She stared into the room with her hand to her agonized throat. She tried to breathe, fighting not to shout, or swear, or collapse.

Stephen opened the door and came into the corridor.

"Mum?" he exclaimed. "Mum! Are you all right?"

"No! Of course I'm not all right!" she spluttered. "Stephen, what the hell were you doing with that boy?"

"What boy?"

"Him! Him – in there! In the kitchen!"

"Oh, you mean Dave?"

"Is that his name? Dave? Yes, him!"

She stepped away from him with her hand still

on her throat, until she was leaning against the wall.

"Stephen, you were – you were kissing him! You and him – it's disgusting - fondling his – oh God, Stephen…"

She gulped. Stephen stood with his hands rammed into his pockets and his shoulders hunched. His face flushed as he stared at the carpet.

The kitchen door opened. The boy came out and glanced at them both.

"Er, Steve, what's going on? Should I stay …" he said.

"I dunno!" Stephen said. "I dunno… Look, Dave, er, this is my Mum. No, Dave, maybe you'd better go."

"Fine," Dave said, looking at Marjorie with hostile curiosity. "Steve, I'll come round later, or call you or summat."

He walked down the corridor. Marjorie shrank back against the wall as he passed.

"Mum," Stephen said. "Mum, please…"

"Stephen, just tell me – tell me it wasn't what I thought it was!"

"Mum, I thought you knew. I thought you'd figure it out that I was gay," he said. "I didn't try to hide it, I didn't! You knew I didn't like girls – not like that, anyway. I thought you'd realise. I thought you must know."

"You're gay? Knew you were gay! How the hell was I supposed to know? You never said! You never did anything like that at home – how was I supposed to know?"

"I dunno…"

"You didn't dare tell me, that's it, isn't it? That's why you never said anything. I didn't even think for one moment that you were gay. You know that! And now you've let me find out like this! Finding you with some boy!"

"Oh Christ, Mum, sorry, I mean… Oh no, no, Christ, no…"

He sank to the floor, hands still stuffed into his pockets as he sat, his back against the door.

"Don't blaspheme! Don't say Christ like that!"

"Mum, what does it matter? I'm gay! Dave is my boyfriend! I mean it - I'm gay. Mum, I'm sorry, but I can't help it!"

He stared up at her. There were tears in his eyes but his expression hardened into a defiant scowl.

"No, you're not! You can't be. You've just – chosen it! A bloody life-style choice. God would never have given me a - *homosexual* - for a son." She spat the word out.

Stephen covered his face with his hands.

"Right! Stephen, you'd better come home. We'll get you treated. We'll sort this out together. Come on, Stephen." She held out her hand to him. He ignored it and shook his head.

"No, I'm not going to get fixed. I'm not broken. No, I'm staying here. God made me like this, Luke said."

"What! Luke – Luke Carmichael?"

"Yeah…"

Marjorie drew in a deep breath. She could barely believe it.

"Luke?" she exclaimed "He knows! And he didn't do anything about it? Nothing? He should have! He should have, at the very least, told me or George! The - the devious, lying... I can't believe it. He knew? Did he encourage you?"

"Yeah! He did! He said it was all right to be gay. And to be a gay Christian. He said I should join the G.L.C.O"

"The what?"

"G.L.C.O. The Gay and Lesbian Christians' Organisation."

"Oh God, is there such a thing? And you're in it – Luke told you to join? I suppose he's in it too!"

"I dunno, Mum. Look, Mum, I can't help it. Luke says God just makes some people that way and as long as I love God first it doesn't matter who else I love and how..."

He petered out. Marjorie stared at him coldly, as he looked down at the laminate flooring of the corridor. She picked up her handbag and stood up straight.

"Are you going to come home with me?" she said.

"Come home? No. I'm not leaving. I want to stay here – at uni."

"With Dave – and all your depraved gay friends, no doubt!"

"They're not depraved!"

"They are. And so are you. Right! If that's what you want! Don't bother coming home, Stephen, until you've stopped this – this disgusting, horrible..."

"What! No, Mum, you don't understand! I can't! I can't help it! You're not listening to me!"

She turned and walked away.

Once in the car, she sat and stared through the windscreen. Students were going to and fro, laughing, running to lectures, bicycling to the town centre. One, a tall brunette in a green coat with a bright rainbow scarf, pushed a baby in a modern pushchair, all black tubes and clever knobs and levers. The baby slept while a mobile of yellow plastic fish and shells dangled above him from the pushchair canopy. Marjorie had daydreamed of Stephen at a church wedding with a sensible, pretty bride, of becoming a grandmother, of holding a tiny baby again, of George becoming a grandfather. He'd have been a wonderful granddad!

And now this.

Luke had told her son it was fine to be gay. He had encouraged him. *Seduced* him. He was probably gay too. The image of Stephen's fingers caressing the other boy's bare flesh scorched her mind's eye, burning into her memories. Oh God, sodomy, sodomy, she thought. Foul, foul. How could Luke and Stephen have done it, have even thought about it?

Marjorie saw Stephen coming towards the car park, his face pale but determined. She got out of the car.

"Have you changed your mind?" she shouted.

He shook his head.

"No, Mum. Mum, you've got to listen to me…"

"Right!"

She threw open the car boot and started heaving out the things she'd brought him; the kettle, his swimming kit, his coats, the blanket, the fleece;

piling them onto the tarmac. She threw the pillow on top.

"There's your stuff. Don't come home until you can tell me that you've stopped this – this depravity," she snapped.

She got in the car and drove off, leaving him standing alone next to the heap of boxes and bags.

Marjorie didn't tell George. She couldn't bear to. So she just nodded and said 'OK' when he asked about Stephen. As she brooded on it all, she remembered something she'd heard one of her pupil's parents say about the park on Whitefield Road. Luke went there, didn't he?

A few days later, she phoned Daphne.

"Daphne, tell me," she said smoothly. "Have you ever noticed anything odd, suspicious, not quite right about Luke's behaviour at the Youth Club?"

"No. What do you mean, not quite right?"

"Oh, I don't know exactly. It's just a sort of hunch I've got that's been bothering me. By odd, I mean, not appropriate, you know the sort of thing. Have you noticed anything?"

"Should I have done? What's going on, Marj?"

"It's probably nothing. But you know he's always going to Whitefield Road. Meeting boys from the Youth Club there."

"What of it? It's where they do that parkour stuff, isn't it? The free-running place?"

"Yes. Well, apparently it's well known, so I've been told, as a pick-up spot for local … local homosexuals," she said, twirling her bangle around her wrist. "Queers. A – what do they call it – a cruising spot."

"No! Really? Is it? Well, I never! And Luke always seemed such a nice, clean boy. Well, you never can tell, can you? Although I've always thought he might be gay. It is odd that he's not got a girlfriend. You'd have thought he and Sophie – anyway, well, Luke! Who'd have thought it?"

"I don't know, Daphne. I might be wrong."

"He *has* been spending a lot of time with Jake. In fact, I heard Jake agreeing to go to Luke's house. Luke's got all the phone numbers of the boys at the club, now I come to think of it…"

"I'm sure there's nothing to it. And don't say anything to anyone about me telling you this, will you?"

"No, of course not."

"Anyway, Daphne, just keep an eye open, would you? My main concern, of course, is that the kids at the Youth Club are properly protected."

"Oh, I know, Marj. I quite agree. Yes, the children. We do have to be careful. Yes, of course I'll keep an eye open."

Marjorie put the phone down. It was so easy. It was frightening how easy it was. That was all she needed to do.

CHAPTER TWENTY

Barbara rubbed 'Brasso' into the altar rail, lost in her thoughts, when Luke came up to her.

"Mind if I squeeze past, Barbara?" he said. "I want to put these two loudspeakers up there."

"Sure," she said, standing up. "Are they for the evening service?"

"Yeah. We've got a new sound desk coming tomorrow. And another data projector!"

He sounded as excited as a little kid at Christmas.

"Is it going well, then?"

"Brill! We've got all this new kit for Transform, and Sophie's looking at finding a place to set up a pregnancy advice centre. And we're linking up with the Rebekah's Well Counselling Centre in Kenilworth to set up something similar here, for teens. Specially to help drug users."

"That's wonderful."

"Yeah! Plus we are thinking of starting an

alcohol-free night club in that empty café next to the Post Office. Sophie's just buzzing with ideas and plans."

"Good, oh, good, bless her."

"Exciting times!"

"And the youth club?"

"Still good. It's been a bit quieter than usual in the last two or three weeks, but that's probably because of the darker nights, I think. Anyway, see you, Barbara, I've got to drop the songs for tomorrow night round to Sophie's."

He put the speakers down and dashed off.

Barbara finished the rail and looked with pleasure at its clean, gleaming surface. Next would be the lectern. A substantial and arrogant-looking eagle, it was going to take a lot of 'Brasso'.

"You've done a good job there, lass," said Henry Somers, one of the bell-ringers. He came up close to her, standing so near that she could smell beer and cigarettes.

"Thanks."

"You can come and polish my brass anytime, love," he smirked.

"What?"

"That was just a joke! Don't look so prissy. Eh, that was Luke Carmichael, wasn't it? From the Youth Club?" He gestured back to the porch with his thumb.

"Yes."

"Humph. I'm surprised he's still around. That they're still letting him run the Youth Club. Not with the way he's been going on."

"What do you mean?"

"Oh, come on, girl, you must have heard." He winked at her. "Daphne Richards told me. He's been interfering with the kids at the club, ain't he? Getting their phone numbers, having them come to his house, meeting them at that Parkour place on Whitefield Road. Bloody disgusting, it is, how they're letting him get away with it."

Barbara stared at him. "No! No, I don't believe it!" she exclaimed.

"Oh, it's true, all right. Daphne told me. She's seen him, she has. Touching up the young girls, looking down their tops. Disgusting, it is. Disgusting!" he repeated with relish as he walked off.

Barbara couldn't, wouldn't believe it. She'd been with Luke at the Youth Club for dozens of evenings. He was always friendly, cheerful, but she'd never once seen him even touch a girl on the shoulder or give a boy a friendly pat on the back. He'd seemed to have set himself a rule not to be even the tiniest bit physical with them. No, it couldn't be true, she thought, shaking her head. Sophie trusted him totally, and she'd know instantly if there was anything wrong. It was just a horrible rumour spread by nasty-minded people and hopefully it would die down soon.

It had been four weeks since Naomi had come to the youth club. Yet again, Jessica had come with her friend Shelley. Yet again, as she walked in without her sister, Luke felt the heavy thud of disappointment in his stomach. He could no longer pretend that it didn't matter. He went over to her.

"Hiya, Jessica," he said, trying to make his voice sound relaxed. She looked up at him suspiciously. "Um, how are you? You've missed a couple of sessions, you been OK? And your sister, Naomi, not seen her for a while. I guess she's stopped coming?"

"Yeah," she said. "You mean you don't know?"

"Know what?"

"That she's run away?" she said, her voice breaking. "Me... me and Mum, we're ever so worried. Danny is, like, frantic. He's like, out of his head about her."

Luke felt his knees give way. He had to sit down next to her.

"Run away!" he exclaimed.

"Yeah, we dunno where she is."

"When?"

"Five weeks ago. She went out when I came back from school and she never came back."

"Yeah," said Shelley. "She's just vanished! It's dead mysterious!"

"Have you told the police?"

"Course we have! They ain't any help," said Jessica. "They said she's told them not to tell us where she is. But we've had some texts from her, well, I did. They said she was OK, not to worry, she was safe."

"Police won't do anything cos she's, like, she's adult and she's been in touch," added Shelley.

"But it's awful," Jessica exclaimed. "Why would she leave like that?"

"Oh God," said Luke. "Oh God..."

"I really miss her. I'm dead worried about her!

We dunno where she is. And the last time I saw her, she looked like she'd been beaten up. She had these bruises, a cut on her face, blood…" Tears formed in Jessica's eyes. Luke gasped. He couldn't help it, he leaned forward and put his arms around her as she sobbed into his T-shirt.

"Let me know if you hear anything," he said. "Please."

Over her head he caught sight of Daphne Richards. She was staring at them both. He wondered why she was looking so suspicious.

"Oi! What you doing? You leave her alone!" someone yelled.

Luke released Jessica and looked up. A young man, who he didn't recognise, had come in with Jake and was striding towards him. He looked furious. Luke stepped back.

"Hey, it's OK, it's cool," he said. "She was upset about her sister."

"Yeah, well, we all are. You keep out of it."

"Sure, steady on. Cool it," Luke moved further back. He lifted his hands in a placating gesture and the young man relaxed slightly.

"Yeah. Right," he grunted.

"I'm Luke. Don't think I've met you before?"

"Nope."

"Danny, don't be such an arse," Jessica said. "Luke, this is my sort of brother, step-brother anyway. Danny."

"Well, Danny, good to see you."

"I ain't staying. I just came to bring Jessie."

"Fine."

Danny glared round at the kids playing board

games, at the PS3 consoles, at the tuck-shop table covered with sweets and fizzy drinks.

"I ain't gonna stay here, Jess, not with all this kid's stuff. I'm going into town, but I'll be back later to bring you home."

"OK," Jessica said. "Please yourself."

"Don't you go back on your own without me!" Danny said. He turned to go. Luke hesitated then put his hand out to stop him.

"What?"

"If you hear anything, anything about Naomi, can you let us know?" he said. "We're worried about her."

"Like hell I will. What's it to you? Ain't none of your business, you and all the other weirdo religious nutcases," Danny growled, and walked out.

Marjorie did not want to lead the delegation to the vicarage, but she need not have worried. Daphne strode through the door ahead of her and Ted, obviously eager to be the spokeswoman. She flicked a church newsletter off a cushion and flounced down on the sofa in the living room.

"Well, Francis," she said. "Like I said on the phone. As church wardens, we've got to do something."

"Before things go seriously wrong," said Ted.

"What things?" asked Francis.

"Luke!" said Daphne, folding her arms. "I told you that was what we needed to see you about!"

"I said from the start he was too young," Ted growled. "Should have put experience first, not appointed a baby-faced greenhorn who takes risks. We're getting into choppy waters."

"You had better explain," sighed Francis, leaning back and steepling his fingers together.

"First of all, you have to understand, Francis," Marjorie said "That our main concern is for the welfare of those kids at the Youth Club and the Sunday School."

"Yes, yes, of course it is, yes," said Francis. "So what is the issue?"

"Cannabis!" said Ted. "That's the issue."

"What? You don't sugar-coat bad news, do you?"

"Yes, drugs, cannabis, which is a gateway drug, let me remind you!" Daphne said. "And there are impressionable kids, barely ten, at the youth club!"

"Not Luke?" said Francis, horror on his face.

"Well, actually, no, it was the lad - you know, the one who broke his ankle falling off the roof."

"That was a lawsuit waiting to happen," muttered Ted. "We got away with it, thank God."

"He was on cannabis, you know! Cannabis! And apparently he's not the only one. Dozens of them, in the churchyard. Cannabis, and worse."

"Yes, but I heard it was only Jake," bleated Francis. "Luke spoke to him, warned him, and he's been much more sensible since then. And there was no question of him actually using drugs at the youth club itself."

"Did Luke tell you that?"

"Yes…"

"And you believed him?" said Daphne, jabbing her finger at him. "Well, Francis, you really should have checked your facts on that!"

"It doesn't make much odds if it was at the youth club or the church yard," said Ted. "We only need a couple of drug-dealers turning up and we're in serious trouble. And that's not all."

Daphne shuddered theatrically. "It's creepy. He's definitely over-friendly with the the kids, you know what I mean? Especially to the boys. Pretending to pray with them, inviting them to go round to his house, stuff like that."

"Not very professional, in my opinion," said Marjorie.

"And I've heard that someone saw a girl, at least they think it was a girl, leave his house one morning."

"Heard from who?" asked Francis.

"A neighbour. They told someone else who told Mrs Cartwright, and she thought she ought to let me know. And that was at the church house, may I remind you, Francis! It's clear he's making arrangements to meet them at all hours, corrupting them!"

"What, Luke? No, I don't believe it!"

"Believe it or not, the whole thing could be a legal minefield," said Ted gloomily. "If he's had minors there, alone; drugs, booze; it doesn't bear thinking about. That lad's got no self-control, as far as I can see."

"Steady on, Ted," said Francis. "I understand your concerns, but there's no real evidence."

"Don't be more naive than usual, Francis! And that parkour of his – it's just an excuse to meet them alone, unsupervised; to get close to them."

"Henry, he's seen them at the parkour place," said Daphne. "Stripped to the waist, hugging each other, cans of beer, hanging around til after eleven, doing God knows what."

"Henry? What on earth was Henry doing there that late?" interrupted Francis, but Daphne steamrollered on with obvious relish.

"Oh, I don't know, probably walking his dog, but that doesn't matter. I'd go on Henry's word, rather than Luke's any day. You're far too biased about that lad. I've seen him at the Youth Club – he's always hanging around the younger girls, and the minute any new boy arrives - Luke's in there, gets his phone number. According to Amy, Christine told Alison that Luke tried to get her to go to his house, alone, and that he was chatting her up, fondling her… Completely inappropriate behaviour!"

Despite a faint qualm, Marjorie was impressed, and satisfied, at how the lies about Luke had sprung up like weeds. She had heard the original remark at the Youth Club last month. From a single comment by Christine, along the lines of 'I reckon Luke fancies me', Daphne and Amy had constructed a beautifully damning hearsay accusation. It wouldn't stand up in a court of justice for a second, but it worked in the vicar's study.

"Luke… Such an open, friendly boy," sighed Francis. "I don't believe it."

Ted grabbed a Church Times off the coffee table and waved it at Francis.

"That's irrelevant! You don't want to see it on

front page headlines, do you? 'Drugs and sex orgy at church worker's house'?"

"No, I suppose not," Francis said.

"You should have kept a closer eye on him. What happened to that mentor scheme you were always on about?"

"Procrastination, pure and simple, I'm afraid. There were always more urgent tasks."

"Procrastination! Well, that's typical of you, Francis! That takes the biscuit!"

"It might not have made much difference," said Marjorie. "The point is, it's got to be investigated. The rumours, the hints… We need to know what's been going on."

"It's a bit dodgy, to say the least," said Daphne, nodding.

"Oh dear, oh dear," said Francis, his shoulders slumped. "I do find it hard to believe. Luke, of all people!"

To give Francis credit, Marjorie thought, he did take some persuading. But Daphne and Ted's mendacious concerns were effective. After another twenty minutes Francis was looking beleaguered and convicted.

"You'll have to call a PCC meeting on this, Francis," Ted said. "At the least, talk to Luke."

"Yes! Sort it out! I really think he'll have to go!" added Daphne, standing up.

After Daphne and Ted had left, Marjorie lingered.

"A private word, please, Francis," she said. Francis nodded.

"It's not your fault, Francis," she said. "It was a

PCC decision."

"Yes, yes, you're right, I know. But still … I can hardly believe it."

"In my opinion, Francis, much of it is gossip. But there is no smoke without fire. I am sure there is something in those stories about someone at his house. Call it a hunch, if you will."

Francis slumped down onto the sofa, his head bowed. He sighed.

"Francis, as the safeguarding officer, can I give you some advice?"

"Yes, of course, please do, Marjorie."

"Well, there is a serious allegation in the midst of it all. That Luke seduced … spent the night with one of the youth club members."

"I suppose there is," Francis nodded sadly. "I suppose there is."

"Francis, you have to do something. Go and ask him. If he admits it, if it's no one underage, and I would be very surprised if it was, then ask him to leave quietly. There hasn't been any official complaints, so it can be - well, hushed up. Just do it quietly. Otherwise, it will have to be a matter for safeguarding, for the church wardens and the PCC. Possibly even the police. And we - the church - can't risk that."

CHAPTER TWENTY-ONE

Luke thought that Francis wanted to see him about the long-promised mentoring proposal. But Francis looked particularly grave and unsure as he gestured towards a chair.

"I'll go straight to the point," he said, sitting down on the other side of the desk from Luke. "It has reached my ears, well, that is to say, I've been told of some serious – er, very serious allegations. About the youth."

"Allegations? If it's about Joshua, Helen's son, and Lucy saying she's seen him drug-dealing, it wasn't anything. It turned out that all she'd seen was him giving his younger brother his hay fever tablets."

"Hay fever tablets? Goodness – anyway, no, it's not about that. No, Luke, I am very sorry, but it's about you, and the teenagers at the youth club."

"Me?"

Francis ran his finger around his dog-collar.

"Oh dear, this is very difficult. I do wish I didn't have to do this, but, Luke, I'm very much afraid that I have to ask you. There are allegations of inappropriate behaviour against you. Very inappropriate. Apparently you have abused your position and slept with some of the youth."

"What? No! Never! I'd never do that. Never!" Luke said, standing up as rage poured through him. But he remembered Naomi. Oh, Christ help him, he had, hadn't he? He sat down, his head in his hands.

Francis regarded him steadily, his elbows on his desk and his fingers steepled together.

"Luke..." he said gently. "Is that true? Is there something? Have you slept with any of them?"

Luke nodded.

"Oh God, I'm such a fool, such an idiot... It's so complicated... I'm sorry," he groaned.

"Oh dear. God and all his angels help us! I am so sorry to hear that," sighed Francis.

There was a long pause. The clock on the mantelpiece ticked on and on. Francis bowed his head, and his lips moved silently. Then he stood up, came round the desk and sat on the chair near to Luke. He gently patted Luke's shoulder a couple of times. "Oh dear. Oh dear," he said, shaking his head sadly.

"It was just once. It wasn't anyone under-age, or forced, or anything like that," Luke blurted out.

"I sincerely hope not. I could not believe such a thing of you, Luke, anyway. But who was it?"

"No, no – I can't say."

"Well, I don't want to force your confidence, but

I do need to know something about, er, the circumstances."

"I suppose so. I suppose you do. That you've got a right to know." Luke ran his hands through his hair "Um … it was a girl from the youth club."

"A girl?"

"Well, young woman, she's at least eighteen. Nineteen, I think. She brings - used to bring her sister. We got talking, and we met. At my house. Um, you know…it, um, just happened."

"Over eighteen. Hmm… If she was bringing her sister…Was she in loco parentis, Luke?"

"I dunno, what does that mean?"

"I mean, was she looking after her sister, and being the, er, responsible adult?"

"I guess so. She is. Well, she was."

"Who is she?"

"Naomi Robeson."

"I don't know her, I'm afraid. Are you still - are you still involved with her?"

Luke sat for a moment, his head in his hands. Then he looked up. Francis was leaning forward, gazing at him, with concern but also with a faint frown on his face. He wondered whether to tell Francis about Naomi being missing, but what good would that do?

"No. No, I'm not." Luke shook his head. "It's over anyway, I think. Even so, I know. I should never have done it!"

"No. You shouldn't. Frankly, consensual, over-age, finished or not, I am still really disappointed in you, Luke. You may have kept within the letter of the law – gracious, I can imagine the headlines if you hadn't! Child abuse inquiry into church youth worker?"

"Child abuse!" Luke leapt up.

"That's what the newspapers would say. Sit down, please, Luke. It's not what I would say. But the headlines… It doesn't bear thinking about. Oh dear, oh dear, what a tangled web! However, er, where was I?" Francis paused for a moment, then continued. "Er, anyway, the fact remains that you have committed - er -fornication. You must be aware of how you, we, should strive to set an example. Chastity, abstinence prior to marriage, complete faithfulness within marriage."

"I know." Luke hung his head.

"I'm aware how hard this teaching is. I can honestly say, I understand. Why, I myself … No, no, that is not to the point, but Luke, you know also that forgiveness and a fresh start is possible. If we confess our sins, He is faithful and just and will forgive our sins and purify us from all unrighteousness. You must know that verse."

"Yeah, I'll know. I'll try. Start again, I guess," Luke said.

"A second chance is always given. Read Psalm fifty-one. It may help."

"OK, yeah. I reckon I need some help. It's bloody, I mean, flipping hard. So hard."

"Yes, I know. I'll help, if I can, of course, but, goodness me, Luke, I don't want to lecture you. Not on sex, marriage, relationships – such a complex, controversial subject. Er, anyway, Luke, to return to this. It's not clear what will have to happen next. Because you have admitted it, I do not have much choice. And the circumstances are a little unclear, a little too close to the youth club, I think. There will have to be a PCC meeting about this, an investigation, and we will have to consider your position."

Luke clenched his fists tightly and closed his eyes for a moment. He thought of the consequences. If he got sacked like he deserved… Guilt pressed like a dead weight on his throat. He tried to pray, but what could he say? There wasn't really any choice for him now.

"No. You don't need to do all that," he said eventually, looking back up at Francis. "There's no need for that. I'll resign."

"What? Fall on your sword? Oh, Luke…" The sorrow on Francis's face echoed the anguish Luke felt.

"Yeah. I guess I've got to. I've wrecked it all, haven't I?"

"No, of course not. Well, somewhat, perhaps. But if you resign, it does make things a little easier. Thank you. We can avoid a formal disciplinary procedure and any publicity. I can't risk the local papers getting hold of this. Oh dear. What a shame. What a disaster. We had such hopes of you."

Luke shook his head. He knew that. He'd had such hopes himself. He thought of what his father would think. He thought of leaving Merton; of abandoning their plans for the evening services and the Youth Club; of saying goodbye to Sophie and all the teenagers he'd met; of returning in disgrace to Telford. He thought of Naomi. He couldn't leave.

"Can I have a few months' grace to get another job before I leave?"

"You can't carry on working for us, not for Holy Trinity. Not for any church, I think."

"No, I didn't mean that. I meant staying in Merton for a bit, looking for work."

"I can't give you a reference for youth work, not now."

"I can see that. I'll have to look for other sort of work, not church work – Christian work, anyway. Something, anything, shop work, bar work, anything. But I don't want to leave Merton, not straight away."

"Well, since you are resigning immediately, with no palaver, I can give you a reference. Then we can put this all behind us. Thank God, it was no one under age! I have your word on that? That the young lady is, er, adult?"

"Yeah, I mean, yes. Adult, consensual – that's what it was, you know. Um, Francis, please don't tell anyone about her, about who it was, about it being Naomi. I, um, I don't want gossip about her."

"Of course. There is no need for me to go into details with the PCC or anyone. There hasn't been any formal or official complaint, so we don't have to go into all the safeguarding issues, so what more can be done? Given what you have said, I will accept your assurance. Anyway, er, where was I?"

"References?"

"Oh, yes, of course! I would be more than happy to give you a reference for suitable work. We can simply say that you found the youth work uncongenial."

"Um, OK, thanks."

"And, on consideration, if you need to, there is no need for you to move out. At least, not for the time being. No one else is likely to want to move into the church house." He leaned back, looked out of the window and sighed. "In fact, given the strangely hostile attitude in the PCC, at the moment, towards the youth work generally, I think it is unlikely that we'll appoint a replacement for you. A shame, a real shame…"

CHAPTER TWENTY-TWO

Barbara sat in the church office and tried to ignore the cluttered shelves, untidy heaps of files and half-empty coffee mugs. She'd cleaned the office a week ago, but Francis had left his sermon notes, a cup of cold coffee, his phone and his favourite Parker pen on the desk again. Heather Robinson, the parish administrator, only did three mornings a week and was far too busy with rotas, newsletters, diaries, answering emails and queries to do any sorting out herself. Much as Barbara would like to tidy up after Francis, she had to get the PCC minutes from last night typed up, and then the toilets had to be done. Someone, probably a kid, had missed their aim in the man's cubicle.

It had been an interesting PCC, to say the least. Luke wasn't there, for a start; but Daphne and Ted were, airing all the unbelievable and slanderous rumours going around about him. Sophie had been doing her best to defend him while Marjorie had been noticeably silent, a strangely satisfied look on her face. Then Francis had dropped a bombshell with Luke's resignation.

"Oh… Oh, my God, no!" exclaimed Sophie, her hand over her mouth.

When Francis told the PCC that Luke had admitted sleeping with one of the youth club members there was a chorus of shocked gasps. Sophie bit her lip and turned her face away.

"I told you so!" exclaimed Daphne.

"Apparently the other – er – partner, was not underage, and it was, as he put it, consensual, so there is no question of an illegal act, thanks be to God," Francis said.

"Just as well!" said Ted. "I can imagine what would have happened if Luke had been found to have abused or had sex with a minor. We'd have heard sirens dashing up James' Street."

"Yes, or worse. Not to mention my personal disappointment at discovering Luke to be so, er, such a sinner."

Marjorie had gasped at the revelation, and her face had blanched. She dropped her pen, and as she bent to pick it up, Barbara had heard her mutter, "The sod! The absolute, bloody sod! How could he?" Barbara really couldn't put that in the minutes. Instead, she had written a terse paragraph about Luke's resignation, and added, 'There was some discussion about this, and the chair proposed that the Youth Club be temporarily closed.'

Barbara consulted her notes. She, Sophie, Helen and Michael had voted against this, but they'd been outvoted. Similarly with Marjorie's next proposal:

that money saved by Luke's resignation and the youth club closure be spent on restoring the organ. Of course, George had voted for that, as had Daphne, Ted and Jonathon Roberts, who had said nothing, as usual, but had simply raised his hand. Francis had listlessly given Marjorie his vote, as if he had lost all heart for it. Barbara wondered how much the unholy trio of Daphne, Ted and Marjorie had bullied him. She had longed to say some word of encouragement to him, or to be allowed to put her arms around him and comfort him. She finished the minutes and, while they were printing, allowed herself a few moments of daydreaming.

The door opened, startling her. She looked up, half-hoping it might be Francis, but it was Marjorie.

"Ah, Barbara. Done the minutes?" she asked.

"Yes, I'm just printing them out. I was going to put them in the pigeonholes."

"I'll take mine now," Marjorie said, peeling the top sheets off the pile on the printer tray.

"I'm so sorry about Luke," Barbara said. "It's hard to believe that some of those rumours were true. I'm sure the worse ones weren't. I can't believe he's that sort of person."

Marjorie grunted, her eyes on the sheets.

"You've mis-spelt 'admitted'", she said. "It has two t's."

"Oh, blow! Sorry!"

"Don't bother correcting it. It'll do."

"OK, thanks. You must be very disappointed about Luke. I am. I really liked him. He was doing such wonderful work at the youth club and that sort of stuff, and he was so popular…"

"Disappointed!" snorted Marjorie. "Of course I am! And that you voted against me, as well!"

"Oh, yes, Marjorie, I'm sorry, but I really felt that the youth work should carry on."

"Who with? Sophie and you? I don't think so! No, I think we've learnt our lesson. To discover that such a trusted person had been … well, been deceiving us all like that!"

"Oh, no, I'm sure he didn't mean to deceive everyone. I mean, er, he made a mistake, but…"

"Don't you start defending him too, Barbara. It was bad enough Sophie singing his praises and insisting he be given a second chance! Don't either of you realise just how serious all this is? For heaven's sake, just cos he's good-looking doesn't mean he's all right! Don't you get seduced too!"

She walked out, slamming the door behind her.

"Francis said it was a pity," Luke said, as he sat in Sophie's living room a few days later.

"A pity? It's a bloody, bloody shame! It's wicked, that's what it is!" exclaimed Sophie.

"Steady on, Sophie," said Luke, "I deserve it. I've got to man up, haven't I?"

"Oh, Luke!"

"I mean, I did break the cardinal rule of youth work, didn't I? I did sleep with one of them."

"It was Naomi, wasn't it?"

"What? Blimey, Sophie, how did you know?"

She merely raised her eyebrows at him.

"The usual way," she said.

"You mean…"

"Yes. God told me."

"Oh. That way. Sophie, does God tell you everything that I do?"

"Don't be silly, Luke! Of course not!"

"Huh. Anyway, Sophie – about Naomi. Do you know where she is? Don't suppose God has told you that, has he?"

Sophie looked at him for a long time. Then she leaned back in her chair. Didymus jumped up onto her lap and started kneading and purring as she stroked him.

"God hasn't told me that," she said, eventually. "What are you going to do, Luke?"

"Stay in Merton, for a bit, anyway. I've got an interview for a supermarket night-shift, shelf-stacking, and a couple of others. Bar staff, waiting, that sort of thing."

"Good."

"I need to find Naomi, Sophie! I can't just walk away, not knowing what's happened to her, not knowing if she's OK."

"I know. Luke, I know. But you shouldn't have had to leave. You shouldn't have been treated like that by the PCC."

"But – well, they're justified, aren't they? I've got to go, haven't I?"

"For one mistake? It isn't right how much some of them are gloating! Judging you. You'd have thought they'd never read the Sermon on the Mount."

"Oh. Sophie, it's tough."

"You bet. Some of them…" She shook her head. "Well, it's almost as if they're delighted you've made a mistake like that. Gloating, rubbing their hands together with glee.

"I know I was wrong, but that's a bit too much to take! I reckon that they're sods, real sods, to be like that!" Luke said loudly, slamming his hand on the sofa arm.

"Well, I wouldn't go as far as that. Forgiveness, you know! Not that it's easy. Anyway, you know that they've co-opted that slime-ball Henry Somers and voted to stop all the good stuff we started. All of it, Luke! All the counselling, my pregnancy crisis centre, the evening service, youth Alpha, even Messy Church – the Youth Club... It's all stopping, Luke!"

"What? Oh, that's utter - Sophie, I'm sorry. It's all my fault!"

"No, it's not. It's Daphne and Ted – the – no, I have to say it!" She drew in a deep breath. "Petty gutter-minded power-hungry overbearing nasty gossiping, narrow-minded bigots! Sods!!"

"Sophie!"

"Yes! And worse! Hypocrites! Saying 'oh, we must pray for Luke' with great smiles on their faces. The gossip and back-biting is bad enough, but they enjoy it so much! Francis tries to stop them, to get them to cool it, to be charitable, but he may as well try to stop an avalanche."

"Yeah, well, I guess I'm better off out of it then."

"Helen and Michael have told me that they are seriously considering leaving Holy Trinity and going to the Westland's Evangelical Fellowship. There'll be others too, who decide to leave. Especially with the evening service reverting back to boring, ancient Book of Common Prayer. Such a – a disaster!"

Suddenly, she pushed the sleeping Didymus off her lap and stood up. The cat stalked over to Luke, after a brief irritated meow at Sophie, and leapt onto his knees. Sophie went to the window and stared out.

"What is it?"

"I've just remembered! God told me this would happen. That the church would split. But I thought God was with us and nothing could be against us. But now look! Oh, don't worry, Luke," she said, turning round. "It's not your fault. The cracks were always there, under the surface. But why did He warn me?"

She sat down and put her hand to her mouth. When she took her hand away Luke saw bite marks on it.

"Why? And what am I supposed to do?" she whispered. "I can't stop it. I can't do anything – there was nothing I could have done to have stopped this happening."

She shook her head.

"Nothing …nothing. Luke, I'm sorry. You'd better go. I'm glad you're staying in Merton. I'll come round to see you next week. And I'll pray for all your job applications. But, do you mind? I feel … feel, really, that I just have to get alone with God. I can't even pray with you. Sorry... sorry..."

It was only a few days after the 5th of November. A stray firework flew into the sky, bursting into bright chrysanthemums against the sunset-lit clouds, as Luke walked slowly up Deeping Street, past the blocks of flats, the school playground, the takeaways, the 1950's semis. How had Francis found out? Maybe someone saw Naomi leave, maybe Naomi had told her sister. And where was Naomi? Every time he remembered she was missing, it knocked him again with as much force as it had the first time he'd heard. The only trace of hope he had was her text to her sister.

He leaned against the fence by the bowls club, bent his head and prayed for her safety and that he'd see her again. But he had no right to see her. He'd practically thrown her out. Young idiot, as his father would say. If only he'd – he'd what? Slept with her every night for a month or more, started going out with her openly, been honest, told her how he felt? Suppose she had run away because of him? He couldn't bear the thought. And now that the work he and Sophie had been doing was destroyed, Jake and all those other damaged, needy kids were back on the streets with no help or hope or advice. The evening service had collapsed, the church was in crisis, even Sophie was dispirited and despondent. It was all hopeless, he thought, kicking the fence post as hard as he could.

A wind was growing, sending scraps of litter racing over the grass verges and shaking the trees.

"Jesus, I've failed, haven't I?" Luke said out loud. "What an absolute almighty mess. I know, I've just screwed it all up, haven't I? And I don't know what to do now. It's just a wreck, isn't it? And it's all my fault! Too cocky, too proud..." He swore violently and punched the top of the fence again and again, until pain raced up his hand and arm.

He needed to run. He didn't know what else to do anyway. No work, no purpose, nothing to do except wait to see if he'd get one of the jobs he'd applied for. No point in going back to his house. He'd only slump on the sofa, watch repeats of The Big Bang Theory, drink lager, and vegetate. He turned round and started jogging back down the road, across the traffic crossing, going faster up the hill to the suburbs. He headed out to the bypass, sped up, and ran and ran and ran.

Dripping with sweat, his legs trembling, he got back home two hours later, having run until he could barely put one foot in front of the other. Exhaustion helped. To drink glassfuls of cold water, to stand in the shower, feeling only the aches in his legs, the stitch in his side, the numb tiredness spreading through him, and then to collapse onto his bed and sleep; that was all that he could cope with.

Luke woke at four in the morning, after dreams of crashing towers and bricks falling on him as he tried to run away; his legs struggling to push through air suddenly thick as treacle, his heart pounding with strain. He'd left the curtains open and the room was bright with moonlight. Luke had the strangest sensation that just before he'd woken, he'd heard someone speak. He lay still, listening, expectant. But it was silent. There was not even any traffic noise. As he stared at the pale strips of cold light on the walls and ceiling, Luke whispered, "I don't know what to do, Jesus. I wanted to serve you, you know, to do something great. But I've failed."

Success is over-rated.

Luke's eye's widened. Had he really heard that? Or was it in his head?

"What? What?" he said out loud, and the reply came: Some of those I love grow through failure.

Luke didn't know if those were his own words and thoughts, or if they'd come from outside him. From God?

My grace is sufficient for you, for my power is made perfect in weakness. He heard that, as clearly as if someone was in the room with him.

Oh, no. He was turning into Sophie.

CHAPTER TWENTY-THREE

Her head down, Barbara scuttled past the group of smokers clustered on at the top of the stairs by the entrance to the block of flats. Once inside, she put the kettle on, filled three saucepans with water and put them onto boil as well. Despite asking several times, the landlord still hadn't fixed the immersion heater, and she needed a wash. Yet again, she'd have to do the best she could in a bathtub with a few inches of lukewarm water. While the saucepans warmed up, she flopped onto the sofa to gaze absently at the landscape poster she'd put up to cover some of the worst cracks on the walls. Several unpacked boxes were stacked under the poster, left unopened until she could afford some shelves or cupboards or some sort of better storage.

Barbara glanced at them for a moment. The one on the top was labelled 'model cars'. She knelt by it, ripped off the tape, and lifted the lid. The Dakota was on still on top. She carefully removed the bubble wrap from around it. Despite the packing, it had been damaged in the move. One of the wheels had broken off and the wing was crooked. She held it gently, turning it over and over as tears prickled her eyes.

Suddenly her mobile rang.

"Barbara?" Sophie said. "I thought I'd call you. Are you OK?"

Barbara wasn't sure she could trust her voice. "Er, Sophie?" she said, eventually. "You want to know if I'm OK?"

"Yes, I just thought - it's like I had a hunch something was wrong. Like God told me to phone you. So, are you all right?"

"Gosh, oh I don't know, Sophie." Barbara looked over at the broken Dakota. "Thanks for calling. Er - I'm not sure. It's OK, I don't want to bother you."

"Don't be silly! What is it? You can tell me, if it would help. Remember, if two lie down together, they will keep warm, but how can one keep warm alone? Proverbs…Or is it Ecclesiastes? Anyway, you know what I mean."

"Well – it's just that Dad died last week. You knew, didn't you? The cremation's next week, in Liverpool. I phoned Mum to tell her and she…"

"She?" Sophie prompted, after a long pause.

"She laughed. She just laughed." Barbara drew in a breath. She didn't want to burst into tears over the phone. "Sorry, Sophie…Honestly, it's fine. Fine. Really."

"Oh Babs, poor Babs. It's not fine, is it? Look,

I'll close up the shop in half an hour and come over. Put the kettle on. We'll have a cup of tea and talk about it, and pray together. Cast all your cares on God, you know! See you in a bit."

Sophie had been a comfort and a strength, Barbara thought, as she drove back from Liverpool, three weeks later. Still, it had been difficult. She added up the cost of the cremation in her head. It was £1,863, or was it £1,873? £1,873 and she had been almost the only mourner. The only one under fifty, anyway. A few old men from the pub, someone from the betting shop, a couple of neighbours, that was all.

Eighteen hundred pounds! And she knew, with fatalistic pessimism, that Liam would have left nothing but unpaid debts, worthless furniture and empty whiskey bottles. He certainly hadn't bothered with life insurance or savings accounts. The woman he'd gone to Liverpool with had long since gone; having left him after three years for the dentist who veneered her front teeth. His third mistress didn't turn up. She had been a blowsy, over-made-up woman with false eyelashes and a desperate cleavage. She'd cleaned him out with her demands for holidays and meals out and theatre trips, and credit card bills for jewellery, facials, gym membership and sun-bed treatments that he hadn't even known she'd bought. Barbara went to console him, the day after she'd walked out, but he'd only muttered, "No fool like an old fool", as he tore up the credit card statements, then hugged Barbara, adding, "Come on, honeypots, let's get to the pub.

At least I can get completely bladdered tonight, now I haven't got that snarky cow complaining at me." She'd had an orange juice, then after an hour, she'd given up and left him there, downing his eighth pint, and he'd barely noticed her leaving.

Concentrate on driving, Barbara told herself, not on fruitless regrets and speculations. A fine drizzle fell. She'd got caught in jams in Liverpool, but at least the traffic wasn't too bad on the M6. But, just past Birmingham, the cars ahead slowed down and bunched up. There was a police car on the ramp, with a speed camera, Barbara assumed. She thought nothing of it - the Micra struggled to get over seventy even going downhill. But as she passed, the police car switched on its siren and moved into the lane behind her. They can't mean me, she thought, I'm only doing sixty-eight. But they tailed her, flashing their headlights at her, their siren wailing loudly. She pulled onto the hard shoulder and stopped. Her heart pounded. As two officers slowly got out and came up to her she gripped the steering wheel tightly, telling herself to calm down. It's OK, it must be a mistake, that's all. Stay calm. Say calm, oh God, keep calm!

The first one, an efficient-looking woman, tapped on the passenger-side window. Breathing deeply, with her hands trembling, Barbara lent over and wound down the glass.

"Yes, officer," she said. Her voice shook. "Er, I wasn't speeding, was I?"

"No, ma'am. But can you confirm your registration number?"

"Er, of course. T 516 JKL, no, JLK. Sorry, I

always get them the wrong way round."

"Right. Do you have your driving license with you?"

"Yes, hold on, it's in my purse. Yes, er, here it is."

She glanced at it and passed it back.

"What's wrong, please, officer?" Barbara asked.

"Is this your car?"

"Yes."

The second officer, a tall severe-faced man, came up and stood behind the first, staring intimidatingly down at her.

"Are you aware, ma'am, that your car isn't insured?" the first officer asked.

"Insured? But it is. I'm sure it is. I'm sure…"

"Well, according to our records your car is not insured."

"That's a serious transgression," added the tall officer. "We're cracking down on uninsured drivers in this area."

"But … but it's supposed to be renewed automatically. I'm with Star First Insurance, and they are supposed to renew it and tell me. I insured it last year, I know. And they will have renewed it, I'm sure!"

"Do you have their renewal letter?"

"Oh God, no. Oh no! I've just realised. I forgot to tell them I moved house!"

"They should have sent you a reminder or a renewal confirmation."

"I moved house - I haven't had any letters from them! Oh no. Oh, no! What an idiot I was!"

She bit her lip hard, and screwed up her eyes.

She wasn't going to start crying, begging for sympathy. The first officer looked taken aback, but the other one was unimpressed.

"Nevertheless, driving without insurance is a serious offence," he said. "Now, ma'am, if you will get out of the car and give the keys to my colleague here, we will escort you to the nearest service station."

Barbara couldn't believe this was happening. It seemed like a nightmare: being driven in the back of a police car then marched into the service station café, one officer either side of her, as if she was a criminal. She supposed she *was* a sort of criminal. As they took her name, address, and license number, as they explained her situation to her, as they gave her a leaflet and charge sheet, she could barely understand them or answer them. Finally, they stood up.

"What happens now?" she whispered. "Where's my car? How do I get back home?"

The first officer turned to the tall one.

"We can't just leave her here, Gerry," she said. "I reckon she needs a bit of help. Bit more explanation. Cup of tea, perhaps."

"Tea and sympathy? What a waste of time. You're a soft touch, Liz, you are. Come on! We've got to get back on the beat."

"Five minutes won't hurt."

"Suit yourself, then." He shrugged. "I'm going to have a pee and get a coffee."

He strode off. Liz sat down next to Barbara.

"Have you got any money on you?" she said.

"You need to get a friend to pick you up, or get a taxi."

Barbara stared in a daze at her.

"Taxi? Oh, I suppose so… I don't know. I've got some cash, a bit, I think."

"Good. There's a payphone over there. What you need to do is get yourself home, phone the insurance company, get that car insured properly. OK?"

"Yes, I think so. I'm sorry to be such a bother. I can't think how I came to be so stupid."

"Well, we all make mistakes. Not to worry. You get yourself home, get the insurance sorted, phone up the number on that leaflet and get your car back. Once you've done that, it'll be fine. There won't be any charges. Not if you get it sorted straight away. You just made a simple mistake. Like lots of people."

"Thank you. I moved house… I just forgot about the insurance."

"At least you remembered to tax it. Right. I need to be off, before Gerry starts playing the gambling machines. Now, you sure you'll be OK?"

Barbara dabbed a tissue to her eyes, and breathed in.

"Yes, officer, I'll be fine. Thank you for your trouble."

Barbara sat at the table and stared round at the bored teenagers, weary adults, slumbering babies, and efficient businessmen with open laptops. She bit her lip. She mustn't cry, not here. But the tears came, nevertheless, and she fled to hide in the toilets.

When she had calmed down, she drew a deep breath, washed her face, emerged into the bright emptiness of the service station, and bought a cup of tea, wincing a little at the price.

She tried to think who to call. It was strange how few friends she seemed to have. She'd got on well with some of the neighbours round her old house, but not so much that she could phone them at eight in the evening from a motorway service station and ask to be rescued. She didn't know her work colleagues at the care home enough to ask any of them. From Thomson's? She'd only seen Tilly and Pavithra a few times since they'd closed down the canteen. And now she lived in that tiny, gloomy flat, she didn't feel she could ask them round. Pavithra was into nightclubs and bars anyway, which were not really Barbara's thing. She phoned Tilly, but there was no answer. Perhaps she'd better wait. By ten she'd tried Tilly nine times. She must be away, visiting her son or on holiday.

The thought of Marjorie and George crossed her mind, but she couldn't let Marjorie know what an idiot she'd been about the insurance. They'd help, doubtless, but Marjorie would be patronisingly kind, and probably a bit irritated too.

Francis? Oh, if only he'd appear, like a miracle, strolling through the automatic doors, his dog-collar clean and white, his hair slightly messy, his gentle face smiling at her predicament!

Barbara was starting to feel light-headed. It was no use, she'd have to eat. She bought the cheapest meal she could: soup, a roll, a small coffee with plenty of sugar. The tinned mushroom soup was lukewarm, the roll was dry, the coffee weak, but it still cost over seven pounds. She pulled her coat around herself, tucked her handbag into her lap, and laid her head on her arms.

Someone, a cleaner, poked her. "Hey, lady, you can't sleep here!" he said. It was one in the morning - too late to risk a taxi and she shuddered at the thought of what they'd charge. The service station was a half-empty mausoleum of exhausted drivers and wandering lost souls like herself. Somehow, she got through the night: sitting at a table until a waiter started to wipe those next to her, hiding in a toilet cubicle then loitering around the car park in the three o'clock cold; orange streetlights glaring down at her, empty paper cups skittering past her over rain-drenched tarmac, car headlights spotlighting her, idle truck drivers gawking at her.

By morning she knew there was only one person left who could help her. Firstly she called the care home and, stuttering as she lied, told them her car had broken down and she was stranded in Liverpool. Then, reluctantly, she dialled Sophie's number.

Back home, after Sophie had rescued her, Barbara read and re-read the leaflet the police officer had given her. It seemed straightforward, but she'd have to pay to get her impounded car released. At least she'd got the insurance sorted, although it had taken hours. If only she'd forked out the money to have her mail forwarded! It was only late afternoon but her eyes itched from lack of sleep and she felt so weary she could sleep for hours. She decided to tackle getting her car back the next day, even though it would mean another specious excuse to the care home.

"OK. Have you got your incident number?" the efficient voice on the other end of the line rapped out, next morning.

"Er, yes… it's on my charge sheet, hang on…" Barbara read it out.

"Great. I'll just key it in … Right, that's correct. Now, your car is being held in the privately-run Coventry pound. I'll give you the address and opening times later. Your car will be released on full payment of the impounding charges. That's a hundred and five pounds for the impound fee plus another hundred and thirty-five pounds per day and part day thereof. Will you be paying by debit or credit card?"

"Oh, so, that's, er, two hundred and forty. Two hundred and forty pounds? How am I going to manage that? Oh, Christ help me! Oh, God! Sorry… er, I'll have to pay by credit card. Er, let me fetch it out. It's Visa…"

"Right. The full total is five hundred and ten, plus five pounds credit card handling fee. So that's five hundred and fifteen pounds in total. Can you let me have the number on your card and its expiry date? Hello? Hello?"

Barbara stared at the phone. Over five hundred pounds? Had she heard correctly?

"What? Sorry, I don't understand. Five hundred

and fifteen? But that's more than the car is worth!"

"The fee is one hundred and five pounds, plus a hundred and thirty-five pounds per day or part day. It's a fixed fee. We've had the car for Tuesday, Wednesday and today: three days; five hundred and fifteen pounds including card-handling fee."

"But I can't afford that!" Barbara exclaimed.

"Well, you don't have to redeem the car today, but the charges will continue to accrue for every day that it is impounded," the brisk, pitiless voice continued.

"What happens if I don't pay?"

"Right. The car is held for one month and then sold at public auction to defray impounding costs."

"What? But that's - that's so unfair!" Barbara clenched her fists. "That's just not fair! You can't do that! It's my car! How can that be legal?"

"Well, it is, I'm afraid."

"Legal? How can I possibly afford five hundred pounds? You can't do this to me! What am I supposed to do?"

There was a pause, and then the implacable voice continued. "I'm afraid, madam, I cannot advise you. Do you wish to continue?"

Barbara hung-up. It's not fair, she thought angrily. How could that be right? To lose her car like that? What was she supposed to do now? And how could a loving and just God do something like this to her, for a single, tiny mistake?

As she sat in the living room, mindlessly watching the news on the TV, the phone rang again. It was probably the care home. Barbara knew she'd have to answer it eventually. Wearily she switched off the TV.

"Yes?" she said, picking the phone up.

"Barbara? Barbara! Where the hell have you been? I've been trying to get hold of you for days. What the hell's up with you?" demanded her supervisor, Angela.

Barbara stared around at the smudged walls and out through the window at the grey sky laden with heavy clouds. She hadn't been out for six days. She'd barely eaten and barely slept. There wasn't any point in trying to pretend everything was fine.

"Sorry," she whispered. "I, er, I lost my car. I couldn't get in."

"Lost your car? How can you lose a car? Do you mean it was stolen?"

"No, er … no, not stolen. I've just, er…" Barbara's voice tailed off.

"Well, have you lost your car or what?"

"Er, yes. Sorry, Angela. It's gone. I don't have a car. I'm sorry, I couldn't get to work."

"Blimey, Barbara, you might have let us know! It's been a real pain trying to find cover for you, not knowing if you're coming in or not, not being able to get hold of you! So what are you going to do about it?"

"Sorry. I don't know. I don't know what to do."

"Well, it isn't good enough, Barbara. You've been a good worker, you really have, but we can't have this sort of unreliability and lack of communication. I'm afraid, I'm really afraid, that we're going to have to let you go."

CHAPTER TWENTY-FOUR

It was likely to be a very satisfactory PCC meeting, Marjorie thought, even though she was irritated that Barbara had turned up late and Jonathon Barton had sent apologies again. He wasn't much loss, she thought, he never said anything and always voted with the vicar. If Barbara didn't turn up soon, Marjorie decided that she would take the notes. She didn't trust Francis to do them. But Barbara had arrived, with unkempt hair and a grubby cardigan and only a minute to spare, and was sitting scribbling frantically as Ted summed up his proposals. Both he and Daphne looked complacent. Only Sophie seemed discontented. She had a large plaster on her hand and kept rubbing it.

"At least we don't need to go through all that faff about applying for a faculty," Ted said.

"Remind me, what's a faculty?" asked Sophie.

"It's one of those fiendish jurisdictions that make the Church of England so charming," said

Francis. "An arcane and complex procedure to make it as difficult as possible to make repairs and alterations to church buildings."

"Well, no one should be able to change things willy-nilly!" said Marjorie. "Sophie, because these plans require significant re-ordering of the church and the church hall, we need permission from the diocese before we can do them. It's sensible."

"Sensible! It was ridiculously complicated! Dozens of forms!" exclaimed Daphne. "In my opinion, we should be able to do what we want with our church, without having to jump though hoops like that."

"You're telling me!" said Ted. "It was a bloody nightmare getting it. It was almost five years ago, before your time, Francis. We had the plans, we got planning permission, which I kept renewed, thank God, we had big fund-raising ideas and we reckoned we'd get the cash. But the money never exactly poured in, and then we had a change of vicar and it all got put on ice. But we've still got the faculty."

"And now we have the funds," said Marjorie. "All we need to do is vote - again! - on whether to spend Ivy's legacy on the church re-ordering or on youth work. It is important, very important, in my opinion, that we reconsider where this church is going, in view of the disastrous recent events with Luke! So, let's discuss it!"

After half-an-hour of discussion, she decided that it was time to force the issue. She glanced ostentatiously at her watch.

"Right. We've had long enough. Everyone's had

a chance to say something. It's about time that we had the vote."

Marjorie was not surprised to see Francis voting against the building work, along with Sophie and Barbara. But it didn't matter, now that Helen and Michael had left. Marjorie knew that she could count on Daphne, Ted and the others to support her.

"Carried," she said. "Five votes to three. Good."

Sophie sighed. Francis shook his head.

"I really do feel that we shouldn't be making a decision of this importance with only eight people," he said.

"It's quorate, Francis," said Ted. "Perfectly legal. Stop fussing."

"We've had enough discussion," Marjorie said. "What else can we do? I know we've lost people, but we've still got to carry on with the church business until we can get some more people co-opted. We're fortunate that Henry has agreed to come on board. Now, we've all had a chance to have our say, we've voted according to procedure, so can we move on, please? Ted, perhaps you can take us briefly through your proposed timetable?"

"Sure. I'll start by seeing some local builders, get some quotes. Now I'm retired, thank God, escaped the rat race at last, I'm happy to project manage it."

"Thank you, Ted. That's very good of you. It's a big thing to do, I know,"

"No problem. I'll draw up a full timetable." He leaned forward and tapped on his tablet, nodding with satisfaction. "Be glad to get started on it, now that I've got time on my hands. More fun than endless gardening and home improvement projects for the wife, at least. I expect that we can start on the new kitchen, toilets and under-floor heating in the church hall within a month, no problem. That cafe, what with the roof and stuff, will take a bit longer and it'll need a bit more planning. Pretty bloody ambitious, I reckon."

"But worth it!" said Marjorie.

"Absolutely! And that under-floor heating's going to make a big difference," said Daphne. "We should find it much easier to rent the hall out, once we have it. Especially with a new kitchen, decent warm toilets, and those lovely huge storage cupboards for the toddler groups and uniform groups."

"Jolly good," said Marjorie. "When do we think it will all be done?"

"Three to four months. Say March, April, I reckon," said Ted. "I'd estimate early April for the church hall. There's bound to be some snags along the way, job like this."

"Fine. And the new kids' area and re-done church office?" asked Daphne. "We need those as well!"

"Start them just after Christmas. Probably finish late April as well."

"And not a moment too soon, I reckon!"

Francis sighed, leaned forward, his hands steepled together. "Oh dear. It's going to be so much upheaval. I'm really not sure about this."

Marjorie noticed Ted rolling his eyes towards the ceiling.

"Well, we're committed now," she said.

"George, what's the situation with the organ restoration?"

"I've got some quotes," George said. "The firm we usually use to tune the organ also do restoration work. They seem very helpful and efficient. They say allow about a month overall, and they can start some work now, but seeing as we're planning serious building work, we should delay the last bit. Don't want to get dust in the pipes. I imagine they won't be able to put it back together until May. So that will probably be June or July."

"Oh, that's a shame that it will take so long," Barbara said. "I expect you were really looking forward to it being restored."

"Yes. Good thing I'm a patient man - I'd hoped to play it for the Christmas carol service. Worth waiting for, though."

"Well, when it's done, perhaps we should have some sort of announcement in the local press, or maybe even a special concert, to mark the occasion," Marjorie said. "I'll have a think about that."

"I can't wait!" Daphne exclaimed. "I'll be so glad to have organ music again, especially in the evening, instead of guitars and drum machines! Incidentally, did you hear about Luke?"

"Nope. What about him?" said Ted.

"He tried to join the youth groups at St. Bart's but Pete Williamson had to ask him to leave."

Francis leaned forward. "Daphne," he said, warningly. "That sounds suspiciously like gossip to me. I really must protest at this continual harping on about the boy. He's resigned, it's done. Leave it."

Daphne shrugged. "It's not gossip, it's just information. I'm just letting people know. For prayer," she said. "And the churches need to share information, don't they? Especially with this situation. To ensure their kids are protected! That is important, isn't it? Right?"

"Which reminds me, Francis, we shouldn't let Luke stay in the church house," said Ted. "Is it appropriate, given the circumstances?"

"There is no harm in him staying there for a few months, until he is sorted with his own house. No one else wants to live there."

"Humph," said Ted. "I still don't like the thought of him still hanging around. We don't want him coming into contact with young kids, do we?"

"He's working - hard to believe, I know! - as a shelf-stacker!" Daphne whispered to Marjorie.

"Really?" said Marjorie. A twinge jabbed her conscience, but she ignored it. She might have started this snowball of malicious gossip, now rolling and gathering rumours of its own volition, but she didn't care. Luke deserved it. As Henry and Ted added their own snide remarks, and Francis fruitlessly tried to intercede, she thought of her lost son. They could blacken Luke's name as much as they like, it wouldn't restore Stephen.

"Poor Luke," murmured Francis.

Sophie drew in a deep breath.

"Poor Luke! Yes - it's just not fair!" she exclaimed. "All this … It's just gossip! Nasty, unfounded gossip, and you know it. For heaven's sake, the poor guy makes one mistake, that's all, and he resigned over it anyway, and now everyone's treating him like he's the worst sinner out. What happened to 'judge not'? and forgiving others? It's horrible, the way you all enjoy it, horrible!"

"Well, it's clear whose side you're on!" said Daphne. "He's got you wound around his little finger, hasn't he? One of his fan club, are you?"

"Daphne!" said Francis. "Daphne, that was far too harsh. Sophie has a point. There is far too much unfounded talk - gossip! - going around about Luke. We should be charitable. Marjorie, perhaps you would care to move on to the next item on the agenda? The new bell ropes?"

"Yes, of course," Marjorie said. She paused, and shuffled through her notes. "I'll just let Barbara catch up with the minutes, while I find the letter. Ah, yes. This is a request from the bell-ringing group for funds for new ropes. Also they have asked for the bearings to be renovated, a wall heater, improved lighting for the ringing chamber, and some money for publicity - advertising for new members and so on. Estimated cost about three and a half thousand. And well worth it, in my opinion."

Beside her, Henry nodded with complacency.

"We are fortunate to have such an experienced, committed group of ringers," Marjorie continued. "Any objections?"

"Over three thousand pounds? Yes, I have!" said Sophie. "Two objections!"

"Oh, Gordon Bennett, here we go again," said Ted. "Not another over-the-top prophecy. What is it this time? The steeple falling down and the bells crushing the altar?"

"Ted!" said Francis. "Please! Your ministry of discouragement really needs to be reined in. Sophie, carry on. We are listening. All of us!"

"Thanks! Firstly, I'm a bit - well - surprised, to say the least, about this! It looks to me as if this is a bribe. We all know who wanted Henry co-opted onto the PCC, and now look! He and his group suddenly get a nice fat grant! It's simony, that's what it is!"

"A bribe? How dare you!" exclaimed Marjorie. "This request was made months before Henry joined us!"

"Well, it's the first I've heard about it. And I don't like it! I don't like Henry's group suddenly getting over three thousand pounds barely a month after he joined the PCC. We all know he'll vote through whatever you want!"

"Sophie, don't you even suggest things like that! Henry will be impartial, and he's been a member of this church for years before you came along! I'm not even going to listen to an accusation like that. And I don't think you even know what simony is!"

"That's way out of order, Sophie, and you know it!" said Daphne.

"I don't care! It has to be said. And even so, I definitely don't think we should be giving money away like that!"

"And what's your other objection?" said Marjorie.

"Oh, yes! It's just that, well, I really want to say that I don't feel this is the right thing to do - to spend so much on the bells, when we've cancelled all the youth work, closed the youth club, changed the evening service. I mean, what sort of message are we giving? I really, really feel it shows, not just that we don't care, but we're losing our vision of God's kingdom. We're becoming - well, exclusive. Inward-looking. And it's wrong!"

"What, no visions?" said Henry. "Well, I'm disappointed in you. I'd expected something a bit more juicy."

"What?" exclaimed Sophie.

"I heard you produced a good one about young Luke. Although it didn't come true, did it? Lost your touch, have you?"

Marjorie heard Sophie wince and suck in her breath, as if physically punched.

"That's … that's just not true! It did! It did! Oh, heavens above, don't you all see it? God was right!"

"What do you mean, Sophie?" asked Francis.

"The church did split!"

"Don't be ridiculous!" said Daphne. "Honestly!"

"But it did!"

"You'd better explain, Sophie," said Marjorie. "We don't know what you're talking about."

"For heaven's sake! God warned us. And now - the Mitchell's have gone, Paula College and her kids, Helen and Michael, Dave Packham, Patel Mistry, Haiyan Zhang, they've all left. Go on, tell us. You're the treasurer, Ted. Money talks, doesn't it! So how much less are we getting?"

"The collection is down," admitted Marjorie. "Ted, you have to admit that you did tell us that we'd lost several significant regular donations."

He nodded.

"So what if we have? We can manage," Daphne said. "Money isn't everything. I'm sure Sophie would be the first to say that!"

"Yes, I would! But the point is, the church is divided. Damaged. Really damaged. And not a single one of the kids who used to come to the Transform services has stayed!"

"No great loss," muttered Henry.

"Henry! You can't say that! I can't believe you said that!"

"Well, bloody disrespectful lot; lounging about, swearing in church, never giving owt to the collection, talking and whispering and nose-studs and tattoos. Coming in stoned out of their minds. Girls with thongs like strippers. Load of idle hoodies and wasters."

Sophie shook her head. She looked as if she was about to cry. Barbara reached over and patted her hand.

"I'm sorry, Sophie," she said. "It's a shame, I agree. You and Luke, what you were doing - it was good, I think."

"Henry, we should not judge them," Francis said. "Not by what they wear, how they talk. Those teenagers - God loves them just as much as you. Sophie has a point. We have lost some key people recently, and some very damaged vulnerable youth who we should have helped."

"Vulnerable? I don't think so!" said Ted.

"This is not the time or place for this discussion, in my opinion," said Marjorie, snapping her notebook shut and tapping her pen on the table.

"What's done is done, and there's no help for it now. We should move on. Any other business?"

"No! We shouldn't just move on!" Sophie exclaimed. "We should try to fix it! We've messed it all up, but it's not too late. We should repent and pray and change what we've done!"

"Sophie, your comments have been noted! Now, can we carry on?"

"Steady on a moment, Marj," said George. "We should listen to Sophie."

"Er, yes, Marjorie, perhaps Sophie has a point," said Francis.

"What? Might I remind you, Francis, that we have just decided properly, in the PCC, by voting, on the course that this church would take. We are committed. We can't just shilly-shally around because of one over-wrought would-be prophetess and her imaginary visions."

Sophie leapt up, biting her lip.

"What! Would-be prophetess? That really hurts, Marjorie! I don't know how you can say such things. Listen, I told you that God warned us!" She hesitated. "Oh, I know that I've got to - to be faithful, to stick it through, whatever names you call me. Francis, I just really think it's all going - not wrong, but we're drifting away from God's purposes. Oh, I can't - I can't, just can't, do this! I just can't! I've prayed and struggled but it's all so wrong!"

"Sophie, I think I understand," said Francis. "Maybe you can come and discuss this with me, at some point."

"Thanks. Maybe, but even so, I'm just going to

have to resign. Yes. Resign. From the PCC."

"Sophie! Resign?" said Francis.

"Yes, but I won't leave the church. I can't! I really don't feel I can be on the PCC though, but I'm sure, just positive, God doesn't want me to give up meeting altogether. I'm not a church-hopper, I won't quit, but I just can't help on this any more! It's all so wrong!"

She shook her head, gathered her diary and pens, coat and bag, and walked out. Barbara stared after her, then stood up, saying, "Oh, poor Sophie. Oh, I'm really sorry!" and went after her, putting an arm around her shoulders as they stood in the porch. Sophie leant into Barbara's embrace, her face hidden from them. Marjorie watched them, then turned back to the others. Ted and Daphne looked pleased but they were, to give them credit, trying to hide it. Henry smirked, Francis looked grief-stricken.

Marjorie put her pen down emphatically. George glanced at her and shook his head, but she avoided his eyes.

"Well, that is a pity, but perhaps it is for the best. Rather an emotionally-unstable woman, I think," she commented. "Did you see the bandage on her hand? And the marks on her arms? Self-harming, I'm sure. I've seen the signs before, on a girl in Stephen's class."

"Oh dear. We must pray for her," said Francis.

"Yes, of course. Now, any other business?"

CHAPTER TWENTY-FIVE

George came through his front door, took off his coat and shook the raindrops from it.

"It's not still raining, is it? My geraniums are getting drenched. Anyway, how was work?" Marjorie called from the kitchen.

"Yep, still raining. Been a long day," George said, shrugging. "Bloody IT – you know this new graduate we've had for three weeks now? They still haven't got him a PC. They promised it would come today. Poor lad's getting bored stiff reading manuals and there's nothing else I can give him to do. Talk about frustrating. We need him to get started on the efficiency calcs for the LV510 turbines."

"Your IT department is a disgrace, that's what it is," Marjorie said, coming into the hall.

"Tell me about it. At least we've got a graduate. Brexit isn't doing us any favours, business wise. Orders down - the usual story. And you? Good day?"

"Fairish. Mrs Sanderson has finally accepted that Victor is never going to master arpeggios or scales, or get beyond grade five, and so she has cancelled his lessons. So now I've got space for Helen's boy."

"Right. Good. How long's dinner?"

"Bout thirty minutes."

"OK. I need a bit of Chopin," George said, going into the front room. He put aside the Rachmaninov concerto that he'd been practising, and started hunting through the music books. It had been one of those days: when the meetings, the deadlines, the frustrations all mounted up and pulled tension into his head. He could feel an incipient headache threatening his temples. Sometimes only Chopin would do. The steady beat of the 'raindrop' prelude, the perfect melancholy of the C minor prelude, the dreamy melodies of the nocturnes.

As he came to the end of his favourite nocturne, he heard Marjorie quietly come in. She stood behind him, her hands resting gently on his shoulders.

"Better?" she asked.

"Yes."

"It was good," she nodded. "Very good. Like you always are. Wish I was that good."

"Hmm," George said. "Maybe. Not perfect, some of the appoggiaturas weren't quite right. I need to practice them."

"Well, the C Minor prelude was beautiful. George?"

"Yes?"

"About the organ?" she asked earnestly. "You are pleased, aren't you, that it's going to be renovated? It is worth it… It does matter, doesn't it? And the new building work. The heating, the toilets, the kitchen."

"What? Of course it matters," he said, turning to look at her concerned and questioning face. "What are you asking for?"

"Oh, nothing. I just … Nothing. Just wanted to know."

"Pity about the youth work. But to lose the organ… Well, I'm glad the PCC voted as they did."

"Me too. Anyway, can you help me lay the table?"

George took the napkins out of the drawer and put them by the knives and forks neatly laid out on the dining table. White damask napkins and personalised napkin rings! He'd always thought them a bit pretentious but Marjorie had insisted. Her grandmother, who'd bought her up since she was thirteen, had always used them.

He'd got out all three, without thinking. As he put Stephen's back he wondered, yet again, how the boy was really doing. Apart from a couple of terse phone messages and a short email a month ago, saying, "I'm doing all right. Lectures are fine. Tell Mum I'm eating properly and going to church, like she said," they'd not had any communication from their son for weeks.

"Heard anything from Stephen?" he asked.

"No," Marjorie said, getting the glasses out.

"You haven't phoned him like usual, have you?"

"No! George, the boy's left home. He's too busy

with uni friends, I'm sure. He's got to have his independence. I'm not going to keep him tied to my apron strings!" she snapped and stalked back into the kitchen.

"Hmm," George said. There was something wrong, he was sure. Marjorie was crashing saucepan lids and chopping parsley with unusual vigour.

After they'd eaten, and George had loaded the dishwasher while Marjorie had cleared the table, he put the kettle on.

"I'll make coffee. Decaff?" he said.

As Marjorie sat in the living room, George put the coffee on the table, and then picked up one of the silver-framed photos of Stephen. He looked at it, then put it carefully back. Marjorie pointed the remote at the TV but George took it from her.

"Later, Marj. Now, what's up? You haven't phoned Stephen for weeks, not since you came back from seeing him. You've barely said anything about him since then. What's up? Is he all right?"

She wrapped her hands around her coffee mug and stared into it.

"I'm not stupid. I know there's something wrong. I just want you to tell me what it is, before I phone him."

Sharp raindrops flurried against the windows and streamed down the glass. Marjorie put the mug down and sat hunched up on the edge of the sofa. She twisted her bangle around her wrist so that it wrenched and pulled her skin into concertina folds.

"Stop that," George said, sitting next to her and

seizing her hands. "Tell me what's up! It's Stephen, isn't it? What's wrong with him?"

"I can't see him. I can't see him any more. He's not my boy any more. I won't see him! I won't accept what he's done!" she said, her voice steady, her face hard.

I bet he's got a tattoo, George thought. "What's he done?"

Marjorie shook her head. "It's too – too awful."

"For crying out loud, woman, tell me! I've got a right to know. He's my son too!"

"I know! But… You're right. I suppose you'll find out anyway. I'm not trying to protect him, George. I just can't bear it. I can't bear to think of him doing that…"

"What? Doing what? Tell me!" George said, standing up.

"He's homosexual, George. He has a boyfriend. He has…sex…with other boys. It's horrible, horrible!" Her mouth twisted, and she turned away to stare at the streaks of rain striating the window panes.

"Oh. Oh, so that's it. He's gay, is he? Oh. That makes sense." George sat down. Now he understood it. Now he realised why Stephen had never had a girlfriend, liked Mika and Tchaikovsky, and spent so long gelling his hair and ironing his jeans. Not that gelled hair was any indication, he knew. George supposed he ought to feel surprise, shock, even repulsion, but instead he felt as if the last missing piece of a jigsaw puzzle had been found and slotted into place. Or as if a piece of music that he was trying to play had been mistakenly printed as G major and now he'd discovered that it was actually F minor.

"Right. I understand now," he murmured. "Poor Stephen…"

"Poor Stephen?" Marjorie exclaimed. "He's chosen it – don't you waste your pity on him!"

"I don't think it's a choice, Marj. I think some people are just made that way."

"I don't believe it! It's a – a bloody lifestyle choice. A depraved, corrupted, evil choice! I don't believe that God makes people gay. Look at the bible! Look what He says about queers. What the punishment is. Look at Sodom and Gomorrah! Oh, Stephen! Not Stephen! Not my boy!"

She started to cry. George put his arms around her.

"Steady on, old girl, steady on. Stephen's still our son. And I'm sure he hasn't chosen it, that he can't help it. I read somewhere that it's mostly genetics. Or the way someone has been brought up…"

"Are you saying it's my fault?" She wrenched herself out of his arms and stood up. "No! Never! Never! I was - we were good parents to him. It's not our fault!"

"No, of course not!"

"No, if it's anyone's fault, it's Luke's. Bloody Luke Carmichael. Sod him!"

"What, Luke, the youth worker? What's Luke got to do with our son?"

"He seduced him, George! Told him it was fine to be gay. I bet Luke slept with him… Luke, seducing our boy! Having sex with our son! Our only son! I'll never forgive him! Never!"

George stared in astonishment at her. He found it hard to believe. From what he'd seen of Luke, he would have thought he was straight. And Sophie trusted him, and that counted for a lot. But he had voluntarily resigned from the youth work and there had been some nasty gossip circulating recently about him.

Marjorie strode over to the sideboard. She grabbed all the photographs of Stephen and threw them into the bin.

"I asked Stephen to stop – to stop seeing his boyfriend. But he refused. He'd rather sleep with depraved perverts than listen to me. He's not coming home, George. He's not our son any more, George. He's not our son: our lovely, pure, only son!"

CHAPTER TWENTY-SIX

School day, work day, church day, gardening day; the routine rolled over Marjorie, despite the empty bedroom and silent phone. George said very little. She knew he'd phoned Stephen, but she wasn't going to ask him about it. What could be said about him anyway? There was a void now instead of a son. She would live with it. She taught Mozart and Handel to the same unappreciative teenagers and enthusiastic six-year-olds, nodded hypocritically as hopeful parents said, 'of course she'll practice, fifteen minutes a day, of course,' groaned quietly as yet another mother asked, 'well, he'd really like to learn something modern' or 'can you teach him that song from Lord of the Rings?' She went into the schools to take A-level music classes as usual, she cooked dinners and swept up leaves, she dug up the dahlias and packed them in compost to overwinter in the shed, she signed the PCC minutes and tidied the church office, she invented work to swamp the time with busy-ness, anything to keep her mind from brooding.

Christmas loomed up, a cold scarlet and green iceberg in the sea four weeks ahead, but she did not know how they'd deal with it. She pushed the thought of it under water and carried on. At least there was plenty of work. The specialist renovation firm had taken the organ completely apart and she could talk to them about its restoration. Or she could spend as many hours as she wished going through the church hall and kitchen plans with Daphne and Ted, helping to arrange builders, checking estimates and bills, and inspecting the work.

If anyone asked about Stephen, Marjorie put on a hard, fake smile. "Oh, he's doing fine, doing really well," she'd say, adding another layer to the brittle shell around the canker of confusion, fury and aching inside. She'd lost Stephen. What if she lost George too? Or God?

She lay awake for hours, unable to stop the thoughts, regrets and anger circling round her brain. Either God had made Stephen homosexual or Stephen had chosen it voluntarily and was in rebellion against God. Either option was a terror, to be suppressed and fought against. Prayer became a battleground. She could only say, with mechanical stubbornness, "Our Father in heaven, thy will be done." When she came to the line "as we forgive others" she thought of Luke. No, forgiving him was not feasible. Apparently he was still around, doing some menial shelf-stacking job at one of those cheap German supermarkets. Francis had said that Luke could stay in the youth worker's house for another six months. Francis might be weak and conciliatory, but she wouldn't be. She was glad that Luke had been sacked. He'd lost his job, his purpose, his visions – but what was that compared to her loss of her only son?

George snored peacefully beside her. She wished she could have his straightforward view of it all, but for her it wasn't that simple. She opened her eyes and glanced at the clock by the bed. The alarm would go off in an hour. There was no point in trying to go back to sleep. She got up, went to the dark, silent kitchen, drearily made a cup of chamomile tea, pushed it aside, sank to her knees on the cold tiled floor and curled up in sorrow and regret.

"I've been to see Stephen," George said, coming through the door and hanging up his coat.

"What?" Marjorie exclaimed. "You've been to see Stephen? But I thought you were working!"

"No. I took the day off and went to see him. I assumed you wouldn't go, and I wasn't going to have the hassle of telling you beforehand."

Marjorie said nothing, just folded her arms defiantly. She wasn't going to ask how Stephen was, if he was eating properly, if he was studying, if he'd done what she wanted and decided to try to be normal.

George looked at her with his eyebrows raised, put his keys and wallet on the side table, and took her shoulders.

"He's coming home for Christmas," he said.

"No. No, no, he's not."

"He is." George shook her slightly. "He is. There's no two ways about it. He's coming home and you're just going to have to accept it."

Marjorie shook her head. "I can't, George. I can't!"

"You'll have to. He's coming back on the 23rd, for a week, and that's final."

"But I can't, George! I can't bear to think of him like that! And he won't change, will he? Suppose he brings his boyfriend here? No! I won't!"

"You'll have to, Marj. I'm not having our son turned out of his own home. Not at Christmas too. I mean it. We'll make up his bed, have dinner, presents, Midnight Mass, turkey, the usual. What we normally do."

"Don't be so stupid!" She slammed her fist on the side-table. "How can we possibly carry on as if there's nothing the matter? I can't do it, George! I can't!"

"I expect you'll manage."

"I won't forgive him, George. Never."

"I'm not bloody asking you to forgive him! Just give him a bed, a room, meals, that's all! I don't expect he thinks it's going to be easy either. In fact, I had a job persuading him to come home at all. Even for just a week. I'm not sure he can forgive you either."

Marjorie stared at him. Stephen talking about not forgiving her? It didn't make sense.

"Not sure I can forgive you myself, come to that."

"What? Forgive me? What for? George, you

don't understand. You didn't see him with that boy. It was sickening – sickening! And it's all bloody Luke's fault. Encouraging him, seducing him. Leaving me to find out like that! I'll never forgive him, either!"

"I think you're right. Luke should have told Stephen to tell us. But you'd have still done the same, wouldn't you? I don't know why you're so hard on the boy! It's not as if he was a drug addict or skipping school to go shop-lifting or car-jacking, or stunts like that."

The phone rang. Marjorie was glad of the interruption. She couldn't bear the intensity of his voice, and how was she supposed to deal with an unrepentant Stephen at home over Christmas? Was she supposed to buy him - and his boyfriend! - presents?

"I'd better answer that. It might be important," she said.

"Fine. I've said my piece. I'll go and make a coffee," George said, stomping into the kitchen.

Marjorie picked the phone up.

"Yes? Who is it?"

"Barbara. Er, hi, Marjorie. It's Barbara."

"Oh. Hi. OK, well, Barbara, what can I do for you?"

"Marjorie, I'm really sorry to bother you, but I need some help, and I don't know who else to go to."

"Help? What sort of help? I don't think I can persuade Jill to let you have the care home work back. Not after you let them down like that."

"No, I know, I'm sorry. But I couldn't anyway,

you know I lost the car…"

"Yes, I heard about that!" You were a careless, ungrateful fool, losing the car I gave you, Marjorie wanted to say, but she held her tongue. There wasn't any point unleashing any anger on someone as weak and pathetic as Barbara. She took the phone into the front room and shut the door so George couldn't hear.

"Oh, Marjorie, I'm so sorry, and it was so stupid of me. But, the thing is, I'm really struggling now to pay the rent. I'm trying to find work, but it's really difficult."

"Yes, I can imagine. Bankrupt Britain…" Marjorie said. "Of course it is!"

"Most of the shop work and waitressing – well, they're giving it to school leavers and people under twenty-one so they can pay them the lower minimum wage. Or it's part time and it just won't pay enough. I don't know what to do!"

"Well, I don't know what you suppose I can do. I can't get you a job."

"No, I suppose not."

There was a long silence, then Barbara blurted out, "Marjorie, I hate having to ask, but I'm desperate. The landlord's put the rent up. Can you lend me some money? Six hundred pounds for this month's rent, until I can find work?"

"What? You're joking. Six hundred pounds! We've already given you a car and a house-moving present. Wasn't that enough?

"Yes, and I really appreciated it, I'm not ungrateful, but I really need help. Just to borrow something, to tide me over. I'll pay it back, I'm sure."

Marjorie drummed her nails on the sideboard as she listened. She'd helped Barbara enough, surely? She'd found her a job, helped her move house - even given her a car! Which she'd gone and lost! No, dependency, that was what it was called. Help someone out too much and they start to assume you'll always help. They'll stop trying to sort the problems out themselves.

"No, I won't lend you anything," she said. "How do I know you'll be able to pay me back and that you won't be in a worse situation next month? I'm sorry, but not this time. It's your problem, not mine."

"Oh, yes, I know, but…"

"You'll just have to cope. I mean, if we give you six hundred pounds, then that's six hundred less we can give to charities - don't you realise that? There are other people who need help and they won't get it if we help you. Honestly, Barbara, you got yourself into this mess, and I'm not sure I should help you anymore."

"Oh, Marjorie, I'm really grateful for what you've done, but, please…"

"Why don't you try Sophie? Or your precious Luke, since you're so fond of him? See if he'll help, the filthy bloody shirt-lifter!"

"What? I'm sorry?"

"You heard me. He's a homosexual, he seduced and slept with boys from the youth club. You know very well that he's admitted it. I'm sorry to disillusion you, Barbara, but it's true. He's gay. A bloody depraved homo. It's true, damn him!" and she slammed the phone down.

An hour later, she phoned Barbara back. "I've changed my mind," she said curtly. "Give me your bank details and I'll transfer the money. You'll have to wait a few days, though, until after George's salary comes in."

CHAPTER TWENTY-SEVEN

"I'm given you a few extra hours. You were supposed to be out by noon, missie," the bailiff said, as he stood on the doorstep. "Come on, I've got stuff to do here…"

"Just ten minutes! Please! I'm almost there, I just want to finish this one box," Barbara said, but the man shook his head. She dashed back to the bedroom, grabbed as many things as possible and shoved them into a rucksack. Then she jumped like a startled rabbit as the bailiff strode in and stared around, followed by a subdued younger man who glanced apologetically at Barbara, then stared down at the floor, his cheeks flushed.

"Right. Glad to see you've left the furniture, the TV, the white goods, electrical goods, microwave, kettle, everything else. They're distrained, so you can't take them. Come on, hurry up!"

"Give her a break," muttered the other man.

"We can't, sorry, mate. That's just how it is.

We've got to clear the flat, and we've gotta have time to get that lot sorted. Right, lady. Got yer stuff? Good. Gimme the keys."

Barbara heaved the rucksack onto her back, grabbed her coat and handbag from the hall, lifted the box, walked between the two men with her head down, and out of the flat.

The box was heavy, even though it was only two-thirds full. She'd filled it with DVDs, her radio, CDs, books, a bible, her diaries, paint tins for her models, mugs and plates, saucepans, cutlery, scarves and hats and gloves and anything else she could grab. She'd been stupid. Why take the DVDs when she couldn't take the TV or DVD player?

In the street twilight was falling. It was getting cooler. As the street lights flickered on, Barbara sat on a bench by the market place. She rummaged through the stuff in the box, found her diaries, the bible, and the warmest jumpers, scarves, socks and so on, and then shoved them into the rucksack and a couple of carrier bags. Then, with a twinge of guilt, she left the box outside the door of a charity shop, and walked to the church.

As she cautiously unlocked the door and peered in, she gasped and tears filled her eyes. She'd forgotten that the flower rota posse had planned to decorate the church for Christmas that morning. The building was empty, but glowing with warm, flickering lights, and the scent of pine needles, oranges and snuffed-out candles filled the air. Many-coloured fairy lights on a huge tree glittered and reflected off the baubles and tinsel, off the stained glass of the windows and the brass of the lectern, memorial plates and candlesticks. Christingle oranges from the children's advent service decorated the window ledges and glowed warmly from within wreaths of ivy and foliage on the side of the pews.

Barbara dropped her rucksack and bags on a pew and stood for a while. Then she went to the Christmas tree, gently touched the branches and gazed at her distorted tear-stained face mirrored on one of the baubles. She felt strangely calm now. It was almost a relief that the worst had happened. She had been in constant dread awareness of impending eviction, like a child trying to sleep despite its terror of the monster lurking in the dust and shadows under the bed. And now the monster had surfaced, grabbed her, snarled with vicious teeth, tore her flimsy home into fragments, and gone.

The church clock struck five, startlingly loud in the silence. Barbara realised she needed to hurry, before someone came in to get the church ready for the evening service. She grabbed her bags and ran up the stairs to the balcony. That morning she had got up at four and spent hours trudging with aching legs and arms carrying laden boxes and suitcases from her flat to the church, until nine when she realised she had to stop before Heather came in to open up the church office and saw her. Now her cardboard boxes of clutter, suitcases full of clothes, carrier bags and bundles of bedding were all secreted in obscure seclusion upstairs, behind two screens and the high back of a dark oak pew. The balcony was gloomy, but she didn't dare put a light on. She put the rucksack down, and dropped the bags onto one of the boxes behind the screens. It collapsed slightly and she heard something break. She opened the box, took out the newspaper-wrapped object on top and unwrapped it. It was the Dakota. The crooked wing had snapped. She wasn't sure why she kept it anyway. Sighing, she slowly re-wrapped it in the newspaper, put it back into the box and closed it up.

Kneeling on the dusty floor, she took out a couple of blankets from the boxes, her duvet and a pillow, and arranged them on the narrow strip of worn floorboards between two pews. She stood up, went back to the top of the stairs and surveyed the balcony. Her makeshift bed and her boxes were hard to see, and she could move them so that they'd be even more hidden behind the pew and the screens. If she was discreet, she could keep her illegal nest secret and sleep here. It would be a hard mattress, but she'd manage for the first night. Tomorrow she'd get a mat and sleeping bag; she still had twenty-seven pounds left in her purse. During the day she could cover the makeshift bed with the cardboard boxes and it would probably be safe enough. No one ever came up here. Not since Luke left. His data projector, sound desk and drums were still in an untidy pile near the staircase, but no one had touched or moved them. She had the church keys, she was still doing the cleaning work; she could carry on with that, wash in the toilets, get her clothes cleaned in a launderette, shower in the local sports centre if she bought a swimming ticket. She would have to cope somehow. What choice did she have? The social security worker at the local benefits office had made it clear that she was not entitled to any help.

"Let me make this clear. You had a job, but you were asked to leave because you didn't turn up for several sessions?" the cold-featured woman had insisted.

"Yes, but I couldn't get there, I'd lost my car," Barbara said, but it was wasted.

"That doesn't make any difference. You walked out of an existing job, so you are not entitled to housing or unemployment benefit because of the circumstances of you leaving your work."

"So what am I supposed to do?"

"Get another job? Not my problem," she'd said, looked past Barbara at the queue behind her and barked, "Next please!"

Barbara's account was now so overdrawn that she had thrown away all her bank cards. At least Marjorie had arranged for Heather in the office to pay her cash for her three hours cleaning a week. Food would be a problem but she would live on cold baked beans and unbuttered cheap bread if she had to, rather than admit to Francis, Marjorie or anyone else how low she'd been pushed. And she'd get another job, she'd even look for work in Coventry or Nuneaton, then save a deposit for another flat and escape this trap. It would only be temporary. It had to only be temporary.

CHAPTER TWENTY-EIGHT

At least it was all over, George thought. Christmas and New Year were over, and Stephen had demanded to be driven back to York on the first day possible, at eight o'clock in the morning. He'd thrown his stuff into the boot, ignored Marjorie standing motionless and silent on the doorstep, slammed the car door and hadn't said anything except, "Let's go! Can we go?"

Now, after thirty minutes on the M1, George decided it was time to break the silence.

"Quite an interesting Christmas, all things considered," he said, as they passed Leicester.

Stephen only grunted.

"Glad you came to the Midnight Mass?"

"Yeah, sure."

"And carol singing?"

"Suppose so."

"Good."

George overtook a dawdling Renault.

"Your mother will come round, you know."

"You're joking! I don't think so."

"We'll see. Anyway, I'm glad you came back. Aren't you?"

"No," Stephen muttered and turned his head away to stare obstinately at the queue of toiling lorries in the inside lane.

"Don't be so sulky. You survived, didn't you?"

"Yeah, whatever. Sure I did. It was wonderful. Best Christmas ever."

George had to smile at the sarcasm in his son's voice. It had been the worst. Marj had amazed him with the venom she'd been able to put into the simple question 'would you like some sprouts?' Her saucepan-clashing skills had reached impressive heights. In the middle of the uneasy truce and the noticeable absence of mutual presents, cards, hugs and good wishes, he had gritted his teeth, uttered soothing platitudes and escaped to peel potatoes or wash up as often as he could, while Stephen hid in his room.

"She won't come round. She hates me!" Stephen burst out. "She's thrown out all those photographs of me, hasn't she? All the ones on the sideboard?"

"They're not thrown out. I've put them in the drawer. Mark my words, she'll want them back some day, and there'll be more, no doubt. When you graduate."

"Huh. I'll believe that when it happens."

"Give her time."

George could only hope that time would do something to change her attitude. Arguments probably wouldn't work. He had to admit to himself that he couldn't understand her. It wasn't as if she was the sort of motherly baby-mad woman who was always planning for their son's marriage, sizing up potential daughters-in-law and talking about grandchildren. And the way she blamed Luke for it all? It seemed odd.

Another ten miles passed. They crossed the river Trent, flooded with late December rains. Stephen reached forward and fiddled with the radio.

"Anything rather than bloody Classic FM," he said.

"Fine," said George, wincing as Radio One enthusiastically filled the car. "Just turn it down a tad, will you? I want to ask you something."

"What?"

"You know Luke's left, don't you?"

"Yeah, I heard. I didn't hear why though. Why? I thought he was doing a brill job. Pretty ace guy, I thought."

"Francis said – and this is in confidence, Stephen, don't you talk about this with anyone. Seems to me there's been enough gossip going round. Anyway, Luke had sex with someone – or several, I don't know – several of the youth club. The kids, that's what the rumours are saying. You know."

"Sh…eeet! Not Luke! No way! That's – that's gross!"

"No way? Stephen, Luke admitted it. Look, turn the radio off a min. I hate having to do this, but I have to ask you." George tightened his hands on the steering wheel. "Marj said you and Luke were, er, well, was there anything between you and Luke?

Your mother, she thought that there might be, that, er…"

"What? That we - what?"

"Oh, blimey, Stephen, you know what I'm getting at. I need to know. You can tell me it's none of my business if you want, but I'd like to know if there was anything behind Marj's hints."

"Mum's hints?"

"Er, well, she said that you and Luke had slept together."

"What? I never - Luke never touched me. He's straight! He's not gay. He fancied Naomi Robeson anyway."

"He's not gay? How do you know?"

"I just do. Come off it, Dad, even you must have heard of gaydar."

"What? Gaydar?"

"You just get to know. If you're gay – it's like, hints, things people say. I'm not gonna explain it. But trust me, Luke's straight."

"Oh. Right. That's strange. I don't understand where Marj got that idea from. She said, well, her exact words were, that Luke seduced you. Odd way to put it, now I think about it. She said he told you it was fine to be gay and he seduced you."

"I dunno what she means by seduced. He did talk to me. I asked him about… He said he thought it was fine. That God made some people gay and still loved them. He told me about the G.L.C.O."

"Sorry?"

"The Gay and Lesbian Christian Organisation, dur! He told me about it. That's all. That's probably what she meant."

"Right. I think I'm beginning to get it."

"OK. Are we done? Can I have Radio One on now?"

"If you must."

On the way back, listening with relief to a long Beethoven symphony on Radio Three, George pondered it all. He didn't understand all the reasons behind Marjorie's hostility, but she'd have to accept Stephen as he was. What a huge drama - tragedy - she'd made of it all. It sounded as if Luke was a not-completely innocent casualty in a tangled, hopeless muddle. He probably hadn't deserved to lose his job. But there wasn't much George could do about that. There would be enough of a challenge ahead to reconcile his son and his wife. He frowned. There wasn't any obvious way. To be honest, he thought, after a Christmas like that, it was definitely going to be a relief to go back to work on the Tuesday and immerse himself in something simple, like finite element analysis of wind turbine blades.

CHAPTER TWENTY-NINE

"Brrr... Freezing, isn't it?" Sophie said, as she came in to Luke's house. "Why haven't you got any heating on? It's almost as cold in here as it is outside!"

"You'd better keep your coat on. Stacking shelves only pays peanuts and I haven't got any more work yet. I can't afford to heat the house all the time."

"Oh! Luke, oh, I'm so sorry! How are you managing?"

"Oh, just about. Don't worry. I'm hoping that they'll give me some more hours or some overtime next month."

"Right. I'll pray that you get some!" Sophie said, as she pushed aside a pile of used plates and mugs to perch on the edge of the sofa. "You can't live like this. Anyway, Luke, I came round, to see you and how you were, but also - also because I think I should tell you something about Naomi, but I'm not sure..."

"Naomi? What?"

"I know where she is."

"You know! You know where she is! For Christ's sake, Sophie, you … You told me you didn't know. You lied to me!"

"I didn't lie! I speak the truth, Luke Carmichael, I always do. Well, as much as I can, generally… I try, anyway. You asked me if God had told me where she was. And I said no, because he hadn't! I just knew through ordinary, not heavenly, knowledge."

"That's just nitpicking, Sophie! Honestly, I can't believe you did that!"

"I didn't do anything wrong. At least I don't think I did. And I'm glad I …" She paused, holding the blue glass cross on her necklace and gazing thoughtfully out of the window.

"You did what? You lied?"

"Misled, prevaricated, whatever. It doesn't matter, though, because I can't tell you anyway."

"I don't believe this!" he said, and thumped the sofa arm. "Why ever not?"

"I'm not going to say why not either."

"Oh, come off it, Sophie. If you're not going to tell me where she is or anything, what's the point in you telling me in the first place?"

"Because I don't know what to do!" she said earnestly, leaning forward. "I think, I feel, I believe God wants me to tell you – I have this sort of feeling, like a nudge… Do you know what I did this morning?"

"No, of course not!"

"I've always thought it was silly, doing it, using the Bible like a magic eight ball. But I did the random verse thingy, you know, opening the bible at a random page and stabbing a verse with a pencil. I prayed first, really prayed, just prayed like mad but I wasn't getting anything other than this sort of nudge. But then I got this really weird verse, and it just felt like a confirmation."

"What was it then?"

"I'm not going to say, not yet, anyway."

"Sophie, stop being such a…"

"Such a pain in the arse? Oh, I know I am, Luke Carmichael, but honestly, I'm trying to do the best I can! It's really really difficult! And I don't know what to do! Oh, I just don't know! I don't know!"

"I do. Sophie, please, just tell me where Naomi is! Forget the blasted bible verse and tell me, for crying out loud!"

"Why do you want to know?"

Luke stood up and walked round the room, running his fingers through his hair.

"I just do, I really do. It's driving me nuts, not knowing where she is or if she's OK. I'd give anything to see her. Look, can't you at least tell me she's all right? Not, I dunno, in prison or emigrated or hospital or, I dunno, worse…"

"Worse?"

"You don't know what I've been imagining. That's she's dead, or kidnapped, or sold into the sex trade or drugged up in some seedy brothel. Just tell me, Sophie, put me out of my misery! Is she OK?"

"Yes, she's OK. She is, honestly. It's nothing like

that. Anyway, you know that she's texted her sister. Several times."

"Yeah, well, that could be faked, her phone stolen. I know you probably think I'm daft, but that wasn't enough." Luke sat on the chair opposite Sophie. "Come on, Sophie. Please?"

She looked down. "I'm trying to decide," she muttered. "It's hard to know what to do. I've been praying…"

"Me too. For Naomi. I've prayed and prayed…I've prayed for her, for her safety, that she'll find God. Or at least, I've tried to, but I just end up praying that I'll find her. That I'll see her again… Oh, it's hopeless. Please, Sophie?"

Sophie stared out of the window, twisting a lock of her hair between her fingers for a moment, then turned back to Luke.

"OK. Well, she is OK. She's not kidnapped or anything like that."

"She's OK? Really?"

"Yes, she's safe. But it's complicated. I can't explain. Not yet anyway."

"But she's all right?"

"Yes. Luke, just keep praying for her."

"I do!"

"Well, really, really pray for her. I'll see. Anyway, I think I see what to do. I'd better go. I'll try to call her and I'll let you know what I can. I promise. But, Luke, you really should clean up this place," she said, gesturing at the half-empty glasses, used socks, trainers, t-shirts and cornflake bowls on the floor. "It's turning into a dump. It's not like you!"

After she'd gone, Luke looked around. Maybe

she had a point, he thought, picking up a smeared plate and curry-encrusted fork. If Sophie really did know that Naomi was safe, and knew where she was, and would tell him, better still, let him get in touch with her, it would be worth tidying up.

Three days later, Luke got a text from Sophie. All it said was, "Meet me at Martha's Café, Leamington Spa, 3pm Tuesday." He might have passed his test, but he couldn't afford to run and insure a car, so he had to take a day's holiday and catch two separate buses to get there. Even allowing an hour for the trip, he arrived ten minutes late. He couldn't help wondering why Leamington, and why didn't Sophie just give him a lift?

Martha's Café was a little, Christian-run café in a side-road, with several jolly, curly-haired ladies in their fifties at the counter. Church volunteers, Luke assumed. The menu announced healthy flapjacks and vegetarian soups, the counter displayed cakes and scones on mismatched crockery. Invites for local Alpha courses, old copies of 'Woman Alive' and 'Spring Harvest News' were wedged into magazine racks on the walls.

And, sitting alone at a table at the side; below a pinboard tiled with adverts about a mission to send Christmas presents to Romanian orphans, a talk on 'Do Science and Faith Mix?' and a prayer group knitting for pre-term babies, was Naomi.

Luke stopped in the doorway. She had a mug of tea and a book open in front of her. As he waited, she looked up and saw him. He couldn't move. She was there, her dark eyes steady on his face, her mouth gentle, her skin as smooth as caramel. Except for a scar running over her cheekbone. Seeing that broke the paralysis. He went to run to her, to take her hands, to pull her to her feet and hold her. But a cheerful woman at the counter intercepted him, saying, as he went past, "Hello! Can I help you, dearie? Tea, coffee, juice?"

"Um, what? Yeah, in a mo," Luke said, and he paused. He didn't have the right to kiss Naomi, or do any of the things he wanted to do. He remembered what Francis had said. Self-control, boy, he told himself. Grow up!

But he couldn't stop himself gazing at her, drinking in her extra-ordinary luminance, reaching up to briefly touch the pale scar as he sat in front of her.

"Naomi! Are you all right? I wasn't expecting you, I thought Sophie would be here. Naomi, for God's sake, I mean – what happened to you? That scar? Where did you go? Did someone hurt you? Why did you run away?"

Naomi only sat, looking down at the book in front of her. As he fell silent, she closed the book and looked up.

"Game of Thrones," she said. "I'm on volume four. You got me reading them. Er, anyway, hi. Hi, Luke. D'you wanna get a drink, a coffee?"

Luke turned. The cheerful volunteer was looking pointedly at him.

"Um, spose so." He went to the counter and ordered a coffee.

"You OK, then?" Naomi asked, as he sat down.

"Me? No, not really. No, it's all gone a bit crap recently. But at least you're OK. I was really worried about you, when you vanished. You are all right, aren't you?"

"Yeah. Just about."

"What're you doing here?"

"In this café?"

"Um, yeah. Were you waiting for Sophie?"

"No. For you. Sophie said you'd be coming here."

"Oh! Did she? She didn't tell me you'd be here or anything. She's being really cagey these days. She wouldn't just tell me where you were or anything. Bit weird, weirder than usual for her, anyway."

"Don't dis her! She's a good person, she is. She helped me get here."

"Huh? What, to Leamington?"

"Yeah."

"Why? Naomi, what's going on? Why did you run away? What're you doing here?"

"It's a long story," she said, slowly stirring her tea.

"OK. Well, please, tell me. Go on," he said.

"Right. Look, Luke, it's not easy for me to say. I'm in a refuge."

"A refuge?"

"You know, a women's refuge. You mustn't tell anyone about it. That's one of the rules."

"A refuge? But - I don't understand. Why?"

"Oh, come off it, Luke. Why do you think?"

Naomi paused as the volunteer brought over a coffee to Luke and he stirred sugar into it.

"Refuges, Luke, women's refuges!" she said.

"Use your brain. You know what they are for."

"Oh… Oh, no. Not - your dad? Your step-dad?"

"Nah. My step-brother. Danny. He beat me up."

"Christ! Oh, no, no! Danny? It was Danny! Naomi, are you OK? How badly did he hurt you? Aren't you going to tell the police?"

"No point, is there? It wasn't like he broke my arm or anything. But I couldn't stay in the house, I thought he'll really hurt me, really seriously, if I stay. He's, like, it's like he's half-crazy, sometimes. He loses his temper, and it's really scary. I was terrified. Blood everywhere, my side hurt, bruises all over me." She touched the scar. Her voice trembled slightly. "I had to have stitches where I hit the door. Sophie helped me, took me to A & E, got me into this refuge place."

Luke took a deep breath as his hands tightened into claws. He clenched his jaw. He couldn't trust his voice and he didn't know what to say anyway. All he could think of was what he would do if he found Danny… He wanted to hold Naomi, to help her, but she looked down at her mug, avoiding his eyes.

"Is it all right? The refuge place?" he asked, eventually.

"Yeah. Sort of. They're kind. It's safe. But it's a bit boring."

She looked up at him. "Luke, you said everything had gone crap. What did you mean, crap? You not OK, then?"

"Nah, not really. It went all pear-shaped. I lost my job."

"What? The youth worker job?"

"Yeah. They sacked me – well, I resigned first, before they did."

"What?" Naomi stared at him. She reached across to take his hand, but drew back. "Luke, why? Why would they sack you? Jessie thought the youth club was brilliant."

Luke hesitated. But he may as well be honest. He couldn't lie to her. Not to her earnest, examining gaze.

"It's really hard to explain, Naomi."

"Go on, tell me. I'm sure you didn't do anything terrible. Not you."

"Um, they think I did. They, I mean Francis, the vicar, and the PCC, they found out about us. You know, that night. I dunno how they found out. But that's why I got sacked. Well, resigned."

"What! They sacked you 'cos of that? But that's so unfair! Luke, that's not fair! We didn't do anything wrong! Did we? Did we?" Her voice rose and she grabbed his arm. The woman at the counter turned to stare at them.

"We did! Well, I did! I told you, remember. Youth leaders aren't supposed to do that! It's just – just the one thing you can't do. The real big deal, big sin, mistake, whatever you want to call it."

"I don't call it a mistake. Are you saying it was - that it was sinful? A big sin?"

"It was! I wish we'd never done it!"

Naomi bit her lip, stood up and shoved her book into her bag.

"I wanted to see you," she said. "To, I dunno, get something sorted. Not to hear you going on and on, again and again, blah blah blah, about how you're sorry about sleeping with me. How you wish you'd never done it." She took a deep breath, then slung her bag over her shoulder and grabbed her coat. "Well you can just get lost, Luke Carmichael," she said, her voice loud. "I wish we'd never done it too. I really wish I'd never even seen you!"

She strode out. Luke stared at the swinging door. He stood up to run after her, but the woman at the counter frowned at him, and he paused. What could he say anyway? He'd spoken the truth. Part of the truth, at least. Suddenly he realised how it had sounded to Naomi. A big sin? How could he have been so crass as to say that? Stupid, stupid mistake! What an idiot he was! To do that, not once, but twice. And what was he hoping to get by seeing Naomi anyway? Reassurance that she was still alive? Oh, a double, treble idiot, he thought, as he realised why he'd really wanted to see her. And now he'd blown it again. Francis had talked about having a second chance. He'd blown it, hadn't he? There would be no way he'd get a third chance.

On the bus back to Merton he leant his forehead against the cold window and watched the bare trees and empty fields pass. He'd thought he ought to be honest. Telling the truth was a Christian virtue, wasn't it? So he should have been honest about his regret for that night. But he hadn't been honest, he realised. The truth was that he didn't regret that night. He regretted losing his job, that was all. But not that night. No, the memory of that stirring warmth-filled darkness and the hope that there would be other nights of such depth and desire – he didn't regret that. He should have told Naomi that. He should have told her, took her hand, asked her out, stroked the scar on her cheek and told her how he really felt.

Danny had given her that scar? It looked vicious. He must have punched her really hard. At the thought, his stomach tightened. He ought to have done something to help her. But what could he do? If he wasn't a jobless, hopeless mess; a failure, an arrogant and over-cocky idiot, he'd have asked her to go out with him properly, straight off, instead of going on and on about his regrets. Now it was too late, he desperately wished he had asked her, and even more that she'd said yes. That would have been brilliant. Absolutely brilliant! But it might have been a struggle staying chaste…

CHAPTER THIRTY

Barbara walked back from the Jobcentre to the side entrance of the church. Behind the barriers a crane still blocked most of the path between the church and the hall as it dangled huge sheets of glass over the new roof. Builders and surveyors were constantly in and out of the church, yet her concealed nest of sleeping bag, duvet, boxes and pillows remained undiscovered. It probably wouldn't be for much longer, she knew, but she never would have believed that she'd get away with it for so long. Or that not having an address would make it so hard to find work, or that it would take the social services so long to even consider helping her find somewhere to live.

The hall doors were open so she glanced in. Two carpenters in blue overalls and belts weighed down with spanners and screwdrivers hammered wooden cupboard frames onto the walls. Another spread plaster on the walls of the new toilets. Noise, dust, saws, toolboxes, work benches and stacks of timber surrounded them. Barbara nodded to them, then went into the church and into the office to collect her pay.

At the door she paused. Marjorie and Ted were there, gazing like tornado survivors at a chaos of strewn paper, pulled-out drawers and files, and overturned chairs. Pens and pencils were scattered on the carpet like shards from a wrecked building.

"Oh, my goodness! What on earth has happened?" Barbara exclaimed.

"Burglary, that's what," said Marjorie, standing four-square in the middle of the debris with her hands on her hips. "The church's been burgled. Last night, as far as we can tell. They took the laptop, the petty cash, Francis's mobile – I keep telling him not to leave it in the office! At least that's pin-protected, and the laptop will be password locked. Most of the data is safe. At least we archive daily, don't we, Ted?"

"Yep, Heather sorts that out," Ted said, nodding. "And she's pretty good at it."

"Archived to the desktop and they didn't take that, thank God."

"Too old, not portable or saleable, I expect," added Ted. "They nicked the candlesticks though. Those two big silver ones on the altar. But we might be able to trace those if they try to sell them. They're antiques. And they're insured."

"Everything is insured, Ted. I saw to that years ago," Marjorie said.

Barbara looked round at the turmoil. Last night? They must have been in the church while she was asleep, but she hadn't heard anything. They could have come upstairs and found her. She shook at the thought.

"Oh no," was all she could say.

"Oh no indeed! It could have been worse though," replied Marjorie.

"Worse? What do you mean?"

"They didn't find the safe. It's behind all the robes in the vestry. They took the collection box though. I find that pretty disgusting, to be honest. To take the collection box! The laugh's on them, though, it never has anything more than a few coins in it."

"Oh. Well, that's a mercy, I guess," said Barbara.

"Yep," said Ted. "Since we've lost half the congregation to Westland's Evangelical Fellowship and St. Bart's up the road, the collection is noticeably smaller."

"Well? What of it? We're better off without them, I reckon!"

"Do you want any help clearing up?" asked Barbara.

"What? No, of course not. We'll manage. Are you here for your pay?"

"Er, yes, if it's not too much of a bother. I can see you're going to be busy."

"Well, Heather's gone down to the police station to sort out the incident report and paperwork, but Ted can give it you. I'd better phone the insurance company. I'll have to go outside, I'll get a better signal on my phone than in here."

Ted handed an envelope to Barbara. "Here you are. Heather had put it in the safe. Lucky for you they didn't get it, eh? See the mess they've made of the office door? Jemmied the lock, they did, thieving sods. That's going to be a pain to fix. But we can't figure out how they got into the church itself, which is odd."

Barbara opened the envelope on her way out. Thirty pounds in precious notes and coins. Her stomach had given up rumbling by now. She hadn't eaten properly for a couple of days. Only an overripe banana, some squishy tomatoes, a pint of milk and small pack of ham on its 'best before' date from the reduced shelves at the supermarket on Wednesday. They had been cheap enough, but even so they had only left her a few pennies. Now she had a fat purse. And she knew which café did the biggest breakfast, with unlimited coffee and toast; almost enough food to last for an entire day. It was worth £3.79, even if it took four pound coins and only left twenty six pounds and twenty-one pence. Or was it thirty-one? No, her maths was better than that. Twenty-one pence!

Two hours later she came back to the church, feeling the simple comfort of a full stomach. Hopefully it would be quiet. She'd creep upstairs, grab her bag of soiled clothes and head for the launderette. It would waste another three pounds but she couldn't bear wearing her stale blouse for one more day.

She unlocked the vestry door as quietly as she could and slipped inside, holding her breath. Mercifully, the church was empty, the office vacant and tidied, Marjorie and Ted both gone. Barbara breathed out and went upstairs to the balcony. She paused on the last step.

The church wasn't empty. Someone was there. It was Francis. A tingling rush of fear and shame swept through her and seemed to stop her heart. She couldn't breathe. She reached out to hold the newel post to keep herself from falling.

He was crouched by her nest of bedding, his head bowed, sorrowfully turning over her pillow, her duvet and her pyjamas. The suitcase and cardboard boxes that held the remnants of her home were opened and the contents exposed. Her rucksack was gaping. Her jumpers and blouses had been pulled out into a careless pile. Someone had emptied out her hairbrush, toothbrush and flannel from her toiletries bag. Even her neat cotton bag of sanitary towels and liners was lying unzipped and examined. Two tampons had tumbled from it and rolled into the grey dust on the dirty floor.

Barbara put her hand to her mouth. She gasped. Her heart started up, fast and loud. She had to run, to get away. But Francis had heard her. He turned, saw her and stood up.

"Barbara! What are you doing up here? Is all this yours?" he exclaimed.

She couldn't say anything. Her mouth was dry, her heart hammering against her ribs.

"I thought I recognized this cardigan," Francis said. He gestured towards her pale green cardigan where it lay, folded up by the pillow. "But I couldn't believe that it was you that had left these things here. Barbara, my dear, are they yours?"

"Yes," she stuttered.

"Oh. Oh dear. Don't worry. I haven't told the police whose they are."

"The police! Oh, God help me," Barbara whispered. Tears came and she couldn't stop them.

"What is this, Barbara?" He reached a hand out towards her. "What is all this doing here? Are you in trouble?"

"No, no, it's nothing," she whispered, stepping back. "I'm sorry. It's all my fault. It's nothing. I'll clear it up."

"It is all right, Barbara, my dear. Don't worry so much."

"How did you find it, how did you know…"

"The police were here, because of a theft last night. Someone left the church open, they think, and someone, thieves, got in and forced the office door."

"Oh, I see, I mean, I know about the burglary…"

"Do you? Anyway, the police were here, and they said we needed to check everywhere for missing items. I remembered poor Luke's data projector and drums on the balcony. They were fairly expensive, as I recall. So we came up here and found – well, I'm so sorry, Barbara," he said, looking sadly around at the ransacked boxes. "They insisted that they searched through everything, to see if they could find out, well, whose it all was, and whether there was anything - er, anything suspicious. Any drugs, stolen goods, I think that they meant."

Barbara staggered sideways and sat down on a pew. She wrapped her arms around herself to try to stop herself trembling from the cold horror of it all.

"You and the police? The police… Oh, God, did you tell them it was me?"

"No, as I said, of course not. I didn't realise it was you at first, and even when I thought it was you, I didn't say anything. But they were very suspicious, I must say. Suspicious and rather astonished that we should apparently have a tramp sleeping up here and not know it. Especially a, er, a female tramp."

"A tramp!"

"I don't mean that you are a tramp, of course not! That was their term, not mine. But they think the thieves must have been let into the church by an accomplice. By someone inside the building. They said if we had a tramp sleeping inside the building, then that was probably who it was. Since not all the locks are deadlocks, it would be easy enough to let thieves in."

"And you think it was me?"

He hesitated for a moment. "You? No, of course not. But I didn't know what to think. I found it hard to believe that it was you. No … I'm sure it wasn't you…"

He sounded too unsure. She realised that he had thought it was her. He had, even if for a short while, thought that she was a thief. She lurched forward and grabbed her rucksack. Frantically she rammed her toiletries and hairbrush to the bottom then started shoving her clothes on top. Her hands were shaking. Humiliation burned in her cheeks. She pulled out the two carrier bags holding her used and grubby clothes and underwear from behind the boxes. Thank God, at least, Francis hadn't emptied those out and looked through their contents as well.

"Honestly, it wasn't me, but I shouldn't have slept here, should I?" she blurted. "I'm sorry, I'm so sorry. It was all a mistake. It was just supposed to be for a few days. Just a few days!"

"Barbara, my dear, what was supposed to be for a few days? What is the matter?"

"Nothing, nothing! It's all my own fault anyway. I'm sorry, I'm so sorry," she gabbled as she scooped more of her possessions into the rucksack.

"Barbara, slow down. Please, please, stop. The police don't suspect you."

"But you do. I know you do." She clutched her bags to her chest and stood up. Tears stung and trickled coldly down her cheeks. She could barely make out the unsympathetic pity on Francis's face, but it was there, apparent even through the salt water blurring her eyes. "It wasn't me, but I shouldn't be here anyway, should I?" she whispered and stumbled down the stairs. Francis called something, but she ran through the empty church, flung her keys down onto the vestry floor, dashed through the door and sped out into the bitter winter air.

A cold wind blew the acrid scent of a bonfire over the frosted lawns, as Barbara sat in the Marriot Gardens, gazing blindly at the empty flower beds and the lone council worker sweeping up rime-edged leaves. She clutched her handbag, rucksack and bags closer to herself. Now what, she thought? Go to her mother in Aberdeen and ask for help? Goosebumps rose on her arms in the chilly breeze. She had sat, silent and unmoving, for an hour, getting colder and colder. Suddenly, she remembered shivering with bare feet on pine boards, the sharp smell of iodine, the icy sting of gentian violet on her blisters. She must have been about five, and had been standing, in her knickers, on the kitchen table.

"Keep still, can't you?" her mother had said, slapping her leg. "And don't pick them! It makes them spread!"

"But it hurts!"

"I can't help that. Bloody school, bloody teachers. It's only impetigo, for crying out loud. Why the hell are they making such a fuss?"

"Where's Daddy?" Barbara had said. She looked down at her tummy. It was blotched with scabs and dabs of purple.

"Swanned off to Ireland again. Business, he said. Bloody doubt it though."

"I want Daddy!"

"Christ, you're such a daddy's girl! Well, he'll be back next week. And if you believe that you'll believe anything. Keep still, and let me finish. You don't want him to come back and see you all covered in spots, do you? Stand still and let me put this stuff on it, or it'll get worse and worse until you look horrible. Like a monster. Daddy won't like that, will he? His little girl all covered in spots and scabs."

There would be no comfort if she ran back to

Aberdeen, to her unsympathetic, irritable mother and her partner, the well-paid financial planner who clearly thought Barbara was a waste of space . Anyway, Barbara wasn't sure she could even afford to travel that distance. It would be seventy, eighty pounds or more by train. She would have to look somewhere closer to Merton for help. But where? She couldn't afford even one night's bed and breakfast. Marjorie said she'd help but hadn't. Sophie might but she'd already rescued Barbara once and she knew Sophie wasn't well off. She couldn't ask her again. And there was no one else. How could she have ended up like this, being thought a thief, with nothing left except a rucksack and two bags of clothes? Where did she go wrong? She sat, shivered, and thought and thought until darkness fell.

CHAPTER THIRTY-ONE

"Right, Francis," Marjorie said. "Yes, I see, all right! Calm down, stop going on about her. There's bound to be some perfectly normal explanation. OK, I'll tell him. Right. Goodbye!"

Marjorie put the phone back carefully. She sat on the chair in the hall and thought for a while about what he'd said. Perhaps Barbara had got into real money troubles again? She suddenly remembered that she had been intending to lend Barbara that money when she'd asked last year, but that she'd forgotten. All that fear and sorrow over Stephen, all that miserable, stress-filled Christmas had driven it from her mind. Maybe she should have tried harder to remember Barbara's request. But six hundred pounds was such a lot, and Barbara hadn't reminded her or asked again. And she was in cahoots with that vile, corrupting Luke anyway. Getting up, Marjorie went into the sitting room.

"That was Francis," she said. "He's got a real

bee in his bonnet. Apparently, Barbara's gone missing."

"Barbara missing?" George said, looking up from the crossword.

"Yes, so he says. She didn't turn up to clean the church nor to collect her pay. She hasn't been seen for days. He's making a bit of a fuss - typical Francis! I said I expect she's ill, got flu or something, that's all, but he's been round to her flat, and apparently she's moved out."

"Moved out?"

"Yes, and without leaving any forwarding address, and she hasn't told the office, or me, or anyone where she's gone."

George folded up the paper and put it aside.

"That's odd," he said. "Not like her to be so thoughtless. Sure she hasn't gone on holiday, or - isn't her mother up north somewhere? Perhaps she's had to go and see her. Illness, something like that."

"That's what I told Francis. But she ought to have said. Even just a phone call or something, not just gone off! She'd have told Sophie, anyway. Francis tried Sophie, but she doesn't know. Apparently Barbara goes pretty regularly to her cafe, but she hasn't see her either, not for days."

"Hmm. We should do something. Hope she's all right."

"Of course she's all right!" Marjorie said, sitting on the sofa, reaching for the newspaper, then tossing it aside. "For goodness sake, she's a grown-up. She can look after herself. There'll be some perfectly normal explanation and she'll turn up. I expect she's probably just given up here and gone back to her mother in Cumbria or Scotland or wherever it was. He was talking about phoning round all the local hospitals. Silly old woman!"

"Phoning hospitals?"

"Yes! In case she's ill! Fussing and clucking like an old hen. Honestly, I've got no patience with the man. I can't see why he's making such a commotion about it. When that other girl ran off, you know, the one from the youth club, he barely noticed."

"Well, Barbara is part of the church, isn't she? He has to notice. It's his job."

"Humph. He should concentrate on being a vicar instead of fussing about absconding parishioners. His job is to lead the church!" She jabbed a finger into the air. "Not run around after attention-seeking missing women or allow disgraced youth workers to carry on living rent-free in church properties. You know, George, I'm really going to have to raise that issue at the next PCC. It isn't right that Luke Carmichael is still there - in that house - six months after he's been sacked!"

"You've really got it in for that lad, Marj, and I've never quite understood why," replied George leaning back, crossing his arms and looking at her quizzically. "Leave it. You should just leave it."

"What? I haven't got it in for him!"

George said nothing, just carried on looking steadily at her. She hated it when he did that. The man rarely argued, just looked.

"You know I haven't!" she snapped. "You know what he did."

"Well, that's just it. I don't. You said something about him and Stephen, but Stephen says not." He shook his head. "Says that's not true."

"Huh! He's just protecting him! Luke admitted it. He admitted it!" She stood up, went to the window and adjusted the position of one of her deep red amaryllises, turning it towards the light.

"Just what did he admit?" George said.

"That he'd - he'd slept with someone in the youth club."

"And you assumed it was Stephen."

"No! Yes! Stephen was so - I don't know, George, I just assumed it was!" she exclaimed, turning back. "I can't remember why! Anyway, that's not the point. Luke admitted sleeping with the youth, which, - may I remind you, George - is a huge thing anyway! It's an utter, complete betrayal! It's appalling! Whether it was Stephen or not! Child abuse!"

"That's too strong, Marj. I don't believe it was child abuse. There's no suggestion, apart from all the gossip, that it was. Francis isn't daft, he'd have got you, as safeguarding officer, involved like a shot if it had been anyone under-age."

"I don't care! It could have been … We don't know what was going on. He can't be allowed to get away with it. Give them an inch… And he still corrupted Stephen. He should have told me, not encouraged the boy; corrupting him, lying, telling him it was fine, that God didn't mind!"

"I wish you'd drop it, Marj."

"Drop it?"

"Oh, leave off. Stop going on and on about

Luke and trying to blame it all on him. It isn't his fault."

"It is!"

"Leave off, woman! Leave the poor guy alone!"

"Leave him alone? No! He's…" she clenched her fists.

"You're getting hard, Marj," George said, standing up to face her.

"I'm not!"

"You are, you know. Barbara's missing - your friend - and you don't seem to care. You've really got it in for Luke. And your own son. You can't be like that, Marj. You're just going to have to accept Stephen as he is."

"I can't! I can't, George. I can't and I won't!"

"You'll have to. He's not going to change."

"Oh, he is going to have to. He is," she said, folding her arms defiantly. "It's his choice, George. I'll make him. He'll have to."

"How? Don't be so stupid, Marj, it's not like getting a different hair cut! Have a bit of understanding, for God's sake!" he said, shaking her shoulders.

"I don't want to understand him. No! Not - not something as horrible, evil, as what he does!"

"Bloody hell, woman, you're treating him as if he's a mass murderer! For God's sake, all he's done is get a boyfriend - a partner. Why the hell is that such a crime?"

"It is! I don't know! I just can't bear it, George!" She couldn't help it, now the tears would come. Not just at the thought of losing Stephen, but now George too. She pushed him aside, grabbed a tissue, wiped her eyes and strode out, slamming the door behind her.

The church was empty. Marjorie sat in the pews and stared at the windows, the organ, the gilding and brasswork, the ornate tapestry on the altar. It had been there since she had starting coming with her grandmother, thirty-six years ago. A place of clean holiness. A refuge for an unhappy child of a discordant and destructive marriage, taken, after a vicious divorce, to the welcome peace of her grandmother's 1950's semi in Merton. She had started going to the local grammar school and her grandmother took her to church twice every Sunday. The ritual, the music and the quiet had soothed her. Pure, serene voices; high-pitched and soaring over the deep organ notes; the measured tones of the vicar; the repeated liturgy; the formal responsive psalms; the incense and the flowers: looking back, Marjorie realised how healing it had all been. How peaceful, slow and gentle her life became. In the church, under the echoing vaulted ceiling, listening to the familiar words, Marjorie had come to believe in God. In the God of music, calmness and subtle ritual; the God of the lifted silver chalice, the fragile broken wafer, the sprinkled water from the stone font.

Now she was alone in the church and needing another refuge from the discordance within her. She dropped her head down, hiding her face in her hands. "George. Stephen," she whispered. "Stephen, Stephen…" It was no use, she couldn't pray about him. It was too murky, too disturbing.

Two Steps Away

At church with Grandmother, when she was older, she had learnt about how the homosexuals of Sodom tried to break into Lot's house in order to rape his visitors, and the fire and brimstone that God had poured out onto them. Grandmother was always sure that God would punish all homosexuals. And now the thought of Stephen had the same poisonous stain, the same cold and dreadful fear.

CHAPTER THIRTY-TWO

Luke free-ran from the station to Coventry Cathedral. Despite his hampering rucksack, he hadn't been able to resist the lure of the 1950's shopping centre. The underpass, the low walls, the railings, the steps, the covered litter bins, the concrete tubs holding frost-withered bedding plants: it could have been designed with parkour in mind. His breath smoked in the cold February air as he ran from the precinct into Broadgate, glanced up at Lady Godiva's statue and wished he dared leap up onto her horse's back.

In the gloomy ruins of the old cathedral he paused and checked his watch. Nine-thirty pm, perfect. He hoped this would work out all right. It was another one of Sophie's daft ideas. But then she had told him where Naomi was, so he reckoned he ought to follow her advice. At the thought of Naomi, his stomach tightened. He'd heard nothing from her since that day in

Leamington Spa, and he hadn't dared tell Sophie how he'd blown it. Although she probably knew. God had probably told her that too.

On Mondays the Coventry Winter Shelter was in the cathedral undercroft, so he ran down the steps, glanced curiously into the cafe area where a dozen men were sitting around tables; talking, drinking coffee and playing cards; and poked his head into the kitchen

"Hiya," he said, to a man washing-up a pile of crockery. "I'm Luke, Luke Carmichael, here to help the night shift. First time here. What do I do?"

"Oh, hi, great, I'm Gregg," he said, putting out a sudsy hand for Luke to shake. "I'm just finishing off. I'll find the night team leader, Mark, he's around somewhere. Just let me get these plates done."

"OK, where do I put this?" Luke said, swinging down the rucksack that held his sleeping bag, underwear and toothbrush.

"Dump it there."

"Fine. Um, I haven't done this before. How's it work?"

"What, a Winter Shelter? It's pretty simple, really, you know. Fifteen folding camp beds, different church hall every night, each church sorts out its own team and catering and laundry, we cart all the beds and bedding between each one so each guy gets their own bedding. It's all piled up in the corner, we need to start making up the beds soon."

"Different halls?"

"Yeah, last night they were at the Salvation Army, tomorrow it'll be the Methodist Church centre. We've given them a supper, and there'll be a team in to do the breakfast, around 7am. You just need to make sure it's all OK overnight."

"Will I get any sleep?"

"Oh, I expect so. A bit, unless you're unlucky and we have a bad night. You never know what it's going to be like. Anyway, I'm done, we'll find Mark and he can show you around, talk you through it all and so on."

Ten minutes later, Luke helped Mark set up camp beds and put pillows, sleeping bags and towels on each one.

"We've got seventeen booked in tonight," he said. "A bit too many, should only take fifteen really, but we couldn't turn them away. Not when it's this cold. There's a couple, though, that haven't turned up. One of the guests thinks they've managed to fix it to stay with a friend."

"OK," said Luke,

"You sleep there," Mark continued. "We've got two women who were sleeping rough, they'll be in the other room, through that door at the back, with Sue. Sure you'll be fine? You might not get much sleep. Terry's a bit hyper, more than usual, anyway. But he'll calm down, eventually."

"OK, ta."

"Right, let me introduce you to the guests."

Mark took Luke around the tables, saying names too fast for him to follow as he shook hands with the men. A mixture, a real mixture. A scrawny young man who asked him if he was a Christian and then, without waiting for Luke to answer, launched into a rapid, continuous tirade about a sect in the United States, the cyclones, the Yemen, and what was God going to do about them until Mark said, "Just pause a mo, Terry, let me carrying on introducing Luke to the others." Two lads, barely eighteen, they could've come straight from his old youth club. A grumbling scarred man with an almost unintelligible Somerset accent, a lanky Polish man with a bird tattooed on his temple, two Romanians, a tidy man called James with a wheeled suitcase and a dark coat who looked like a manager or teacher. Luke wondered what on earth had happened to him, that he was sleeping with homeless guys in a Winter Shelter.

The door to the back room opened. Luke turned. Coming out, wearing a faded dressing gown, her hair messy and uncombed, her feet in crumpled grey socks, was Barbara.

"Luke!" she gasped, dropping a towel and sponge bag onto the parquet.

"Barbara! What on earth are you doing here?" Luke exclaimed.

"Oh, do you two know each other?" Mark said. Luke nodded.

"Barbara, are you OK? Is that right? You know Luke?"

"Yes, I do. I know Luke, I know him from Merton." She looked at him then, clutching her dressing gown, glanced at the doors behind him. "Luke? Why are you here?"

"Um, I'm volunteering."

"Are you? It's just you…there's no one else from Merton, is there? Francis…er, or Sophie?"

Luke shook his head. She looked relieved.

"Sorry, but I need to check," Mark said. "Is there any problem with Luke being here?"

She bit her lip, looked down, picked up her towel and bag, then eventually she looked up and shook her head.

"No, it's all right, really, Mark. Er, Luke, hi, nice to see you again. How are you? I was really sorry about you losing your job. Are you still in Merton?"

"Yeah, but, Barbara, what are you doing here? I heard from Sophie that you'd gone and no one knew where you were. That was weeks ago! Why are you here? What on earth happened?"

"Mark, can I talk to Luke for a bit, please?"

Mark nodded. "Yes, of course. He's here all night, so as long as you're both bedded down and quiet by eleven, there's no problem. I'll leave you to it. Luke, it's fine, I don't need much help for this stage of the night, so take your time."

Barbara sat down at an empty table on one side of the cafe, and Luke sat opposite her. He could see that worry lines had deepened around her eyes and forehead, and that her face was paler and thinner.

"Don't tell them! Please, Luke, you mustn't tell them!" she said urgently, as Mark walked away.

"Tell who?"

"Francis, Marjorie, the church. Don't tell Francis, or anyone, that you found me here!"

"Why not?"

"Why do you think? Do you think I really want them to know that I'm…" she hesitated, and glanced around at the other guests, "that I've ended up in a place like this? That I look like this?"

"Um, OK. If you don't want me to."

"Thanks. Is Francis OK?"

"Yeah. He was really upset when you vanished, so Sophie said. Barbara, what happened? Why are you here, of all places?"

"It's all my fault. It's a long story." She paused and shook her head.

"Are you all right?" he said. It was a stupid question. Of course she wasn't. "Francis, George, they've all been going on and on about you disappearing like that. They were really worried about you, according to Sophie."

"Were they?" Barbara's face lightened.

"Yeah. They've even stopped talking about me, 'cos of you. So, thanks there."

"Luke, I know," Barbara said, reached out and patted his hand briefly. "I know. I'm sorry about what happened. There were all sorts of rumours about you."

"Do you think I don't know!" Luke exclaimed, running his hands through his hair.

"I overheard Daphne and Ted talking about you in church once. When I was dusting the bookshelves. Daphne said that she was going to ask her small group to pray for you. And she told Henry, the bell-ringing guy and he told me. He said awful things about you. They said you were a… Oh, Luke, I hate saying it."

"Saying what, for God's sake?"

"A … a paedophile. That you were grooming the under-age boys at the youth club."

"What! What the ….!" Luke stood up and swore loudly. "They said that! Bloody, bloody hell! No wonder!" He kicked at a chair, knocking it over. The other guests turned around at the noise and clatter, and Mark looked up from the pillow he was shaking into a case and frowned. Luke muttered "sorry", picked up the chair and sat down, staring at Barbara.

"Is that really what they said? Who said it? It's not true, you know that, don't you!"

"Of course I do. But at the time, all everyone knew was that you'd left the church, been asked to stop doing youth work, so they all thought – well, you know."

"That explains it! I went to St. Bart's for a couple of Sundays. No one spoke to me, they all seemed to be avoiding me, and then the vicar asked me, very politely of course, to find somewhere else. Said he didn't think I'd find his church very – very fitting for me. Sod!"

"Did he? Oh Luke, I'm really sorry. What did you do?"

"Left! Wasn't going back there. It was like, really, like God had thrown me out. Like he had thrown me to the wolves and walked away. So I didn't go back. Not to anywhere. Gave up on the whole bloody lot of them. Churches, Christians, religious hypocrites, the whole damn lot of them."

"I don't blame you," Barbara sighed.

"Cept Sophie, though. She's all right. She stuck by me, even though everyone else seemed to think I was – what's it called – persona non grata."

"Oh, Sophie - that's just like her! She is such a nice person. So kind!"

"Yeah, nutty as a fruitcake, but, yeah, a nice

person. She's the reason I'm here, you know."

"Sophie?"

"Yeah, I was just about ready to give up on the whole God thing. I mean, I'd tried. Really tried. And it was all just a hopeless mess."

"Like me. We're both in a state, aren't we?" Barbara plucked at her faded green dressing gown and stared sadly down at her sagging socks.

"Yeah, guess we are. Maybe the only way is up now. I did think about going back to Telford, but Dad… Anyway, I couldn't. Francis said I could stay in the house for a few more months, until they'd found someone else, then I heard they had stopped all the youth work anyway. I'd still got my supermarket job and so even though it was all such crap, and I never wanted to see the inside of a church again, I thought I'd stick it out at Merton for a few more months. In case – well, I dunno. Just in case, I guess."

"Oh. In case what?"

"Oh, I dunno. Just in case. I just wanted to stick it out for a bit longer." He put his head in his hands, and stared at the cracked Formica table for a few moments. He didn't want to talk about Naomi, about yet another failure he'd notched up.

"Anyway," he continued, lifting up his face. "Sophie said something to me – you know, this is going to sound really weird. She said she'd seen a vision of me on my knees in the chapel here in the cathedral – the Gethsemane one. You know? With the crown of thorns and the angel holding the cup?"

"Yes, I know it."

"It seemed to click. Like God had abandoned me but he hadn't really, you know?"

"No, sorry, I wish I did."

"Oh, I dunno, Barbara, I know this isn't making sense. Sophie said that the angel turned into me with a mug of soup. So I should volunteer in a soup kitchen for the homeless. I said she was loopy. But she insisted that if I did, the soup would become a river of healing. Daft, like I said."

"But you learn to listen to her, even if it does sound daft, don't you?"

"Yeah, so I asked around. The Merton Winter Shelters wouldn't touch me, but Sophie and Francis gave me a reference for the Coventry one. So here I am."

"Serving soup – well, supper – to the homeless. Like me." Barbara smiled wryly.

"Yeah. Barbara, you're the last person I would have thought would be here. How did you end up in Coventry? Just checking - you're not volunteering, are you?"

"No, Luke. I'm sleeping here. I really am homeless, I'm sorry. But I didn't want anyone in Merton, anyone who knew me, to know, so I came here."

"Why not?"

"I couldn't bear it! I mean, look at me, Luke!" She held out her hands. Her nails were dirty and bitten short, the cuffs of her dressing gown stained and frayed. "I'm a mess! Practically destitute! All I've got in the world is in a rucksack and two bags in that room over there."

"What happened?"

"I couldn't pay the rent. Simple as that. I had no savings – almost everything I'd got had gone on buying and furnishing my house, four years ago, and I lost all that when I lost my job and had to sell it. The council said it was my fault, that I was intentionally homeless." She shivered. "And they classed me low-risk, because I'm not an addict or a prostitute or alcoholic or pregnant."

"What! That's so wrong! That's just completely wrong and unfair!"

"Yes, but that's what it's like. I didn't know what to do, and I didn't want anyone in Merton to know. I couldn't bear…" She paused, wiped her hand over her eyes, then took a deep breath. "Anyway, so I ran away, and went to Coventry. The Winter Shelter leaders and Salvation Army are going to try to find me a flat. I'm not sure they can – I've got no money for a deposit, and having been evicted once…"

"Didn't anyone in Merton help you?"

"No – I couldn't ask them! I can't go back. I'm sorry, I know it seems stupid, Luke, but I just can't! I can't bear them knowing!" She twisted her hands together as she shook her head.

Across the room, Mark, who'd been chatting to the men around the table, stood up.

"It's getting late, everyone," he said. "Can you start bedding down, please? Lights out and quiet at eleven, remember."

Barbara grimaced. "It's like being in a boarding school, but without the camaraderie and midnight feasts," she said. "I'd better get myself and my bed sorted out."

"Me too. Look, Barbara, please, I'll talk to you in the morning. Sophie said something about you, when you vanished, which, I dunno, I think I should tell you."

"Did she? What?"

"That you were a pearl of great price. It's something Jesus said. One of the parables. Do you know it? About a merchant looking for and finding a pearl and selling everything to get it?"

Barbara stared at him, and blinked hard.

"Oh. Yes, I know the one you mean. A pearl of great price? Gosh, I don't think so. Me? No, not me, no, not really. I don't know why Sophie would think that. But, thanks anyway, Luke. Er, goodnight, hope you sleep well," she murmured, then picked up her bag and towel and headed towards the bathroom.

CHAPTER THIRTY-THREE

As Barbara cleaned her teeth and tried to scrub her nails in the cold and inadequate toilets the tears stung. A sudden image of her father; running into the house, calling out for his precious colleen, his angel Babs, his pretty little daughter; had come into her mind. She thought of the merchant seeking the beautiful pearl, and shook her head. Her father wouldn't have gone out of his way to find her, she knew, despite his words. She tried to imagine what it would be like to have a father who really did think that of her. Who would search for her if she was lost. Who would sell all he had to save her from this homelessness. She wasn't worth it, she knew. But even so, the words 'a pearl of great price' kept echoing in her head as she spread out her sleeping bag on the rickety canvas bed. She fell asleep almost immediately, despite the restless tossing about of the other homeless woman and the faint hiss of music coming from the ear-buds from the volunteer's phone, and slept long and deeply, with no dreams, for the first time since she'd run from Holy Trinity.

By the time she woke up, the other woman had packed up and gone. She got dressed quickly and went into the cafe. Only two men and Luke were there, eating breakfast as the morning team cleared plates from around them.

"Morning! We didn't want to wake you," said one, a rotund older woman. "You looked so peaceful. I don't need to leave too early, so we've got a bit of leeway. There's still plenty of coffee and tea over there. I can do you some porridge, if you want."

"Yes, please, thanks."

As Barbara sat down and added milk to her tea, Luke came over to her table with plate of toast and a mug.

"Hiya," he said. "You OK?"

"Yes. I slept well. How about you?"

"Just about, but I only got a couple of hours sleep, I reckon," he said, adding two spoonfuls of sugar to his mug and stirring it. "It was a bit of a disturbed night. Some of the guys didn't settle down until late. There was an argument between two guests about a toothbrush, of all things, but Mark quietened them down. And one guy snored. Still, it was OK. I reckon I can do another night, next week. At least I get breakfast. Can you pass us the jam?"

"I'm glad you're still here. I wanted to say something to you. Something else about all those rumours, something I've realised."

"Oh, yeah. Those. What?"

"I didn't believe them, you know that," Barbara said, as another friendly volunteer brought some toast over to her and trotted back to the kitchen. She paused, spread butter and marmalade on the toast, then glanced around. The volunteers were all busy and the two other guests were packing their bags away. No one was likely to hear them talking. "It just didn't seem possible, not you, not knowing you like I did. But I think you did need to know just what was being said."

"Yeah, thanks," he said indistinctly through a mouthful of toast and jam. "But I dunno what to do about it."

"But, Luke, I'm sorry to ask, but why did they sack you?" she said in a whisper. "You're not homosexual, are you? I mean, you didn't sleep with the boys in the youth club, did you? I'm sure you didn't."

"No! I didn't!" he said, gulping down his mouthful of toast. "And I'm not gay. That wasn't why I left. I wasn't sacked, I left. So that was just a blatant lie! Why do they think that?"

"I don't know either. I just know that Marjorie was really angry with you. Furious."

"Marjorie Fowler? Really?"

"Yes. She, er, I phoned her once, and she said something awful about you. Said you were a homosexual and that you'd slept with boys from the youth club. And that you'd admitted it."

"But - but I didn't!" Luke said loudly and thumped the table. Coffee spilt from his mug. The two men in the corner turned at the sound. "Why?"

he continued, in a quieter voice, running his fingers through his fringe. "Why do you reckon she'd say that?"

"I don't know. She sounded like she really hated you. Oh, she was pleased enough about you; at first, anyway. But when the PCC voted to spend that money on the youth work, she was pretty cross with you. And Sophie. For a while, that is."

"Oh yeah, she was always a bit off-hand with me after that. But why did she pick on me? Why say things like that? She must have known they weren't true."

"I don't know. Anyway, that's when the rumours started, a few weeks after that. I've realised that she must have started them. Or her friend Daphne. I think you should know. They came from her, I'm sure, the rumours that you'd been - well, been involved with boys in the youth club."

"Oh - so that's why Francis asked me! That's what it was all about!" Luke exclaimed.

"What – what did he say?"

"He asked me about my relationships with the youth, and said there were accusations that I'd slept with some of them. And I couldn't say no, because I had. Only once, but I had."

"I know. That's what Francis said that you'd said."

"Yeah, but it's not what you think, it wasn't a boy. Don't tell anyone. And it wasn't anyone underage. It was a mistake, sort of. Oh, Barbara, it's such a muddle! It's so complicated!" His shoulders slumped as he thrust his hands into his pockets and stared at the spilt coffee in front of him.

"Is it?" Barbara reached out a hand and briefly stroked his arm. He looked so young and so worried. "It's OK, you don't need to tell me. But, Luke, tell Francis! Tell him the truth, whatever it is, ask him to scotch the gossip, give you your job back!"

"Yeah, maybe," he said, looking up. "Fat chance, I reckon. But why do you care, Barbara?"

"Cos you're too nice a lad to be treated like that, Luke. You and Sophie were doing a good job with all those kids and it's all gone to pieces."

"Oh. OK, reckon I'll – well, maybe. I'll think about it. Maybe you're right."

He stood up.

"I'd better go, my train goes at nine. But, Barbara, what about you? What are you going to do?"

"Oh, I'll be all right," she said, taking a gulp of her tea. "I'm getting fed. I've slept. I've got porridge on order, which will be nice. I think I'll be able to sort myself out. It's just temporary. Don't worry about me. And, please, please, don't tell Francis or anyone!"

"Can I tell Sophie? She was really worried about you."

Barbara nodded. "But, please, tell her to keep it secret."

"Why? It's nothing to be ashamed of."

"Oh, it is. It's my own fault. I'm sorry but I can't bear people knowing. Except Sophie. I know she can be trusted. She doesn't gossip."

"Yeah, she's good. Will you be here tomorrow? I

mean, at the Winter Shelter?"

"Probably. I can't see why not, barring a miracle. It's at the Methodist Church, isn't it, tomorrow?"

"Yeah, I forgot how it works. Look, I'll tell Sophie, and come back tomorrow - no, flip, I can't, I've got a night-shift. I've got to do it, I've been asking for some extra hours, and I need the money. Tell you what, I'll come the day after. Wednesday night. I know it's another day, but is that OK?"

"Yes, of course."

"Where is it on Wednesday?"

"I think it's at St. Edward's church."

"Right. I'll come and I expect Sophie will come too. We'll help, we'll do something, I promise. Just hang on, OK?"

"Er, OK. What else can I do anyway?" she said, with a rueful smile.

"Can I get you anything?"

"A French manicure, maybe?" She looked at her nails with a grimace. "No, don't worry. I bet you don't even know what that is. I'll be OK."

"Yeah, well, even so," Luke dug into his pocket and pulled out some notes and coins. He shoved them across the table to her, and put on his coat. "I reckon you'll need those. Don't know if it's enough for a French manicure though. And I've got an older sister, so I do know what that is. See you Wednesday. Take care."

"OK. Thanks. Er, God bless?"

"Yeah. God bless."

Barbara watched him walk out. He was a good guy, she thought. The rotund grey-haired volunteer brought a bowl of porridge over to her.

"There you are, Pearl, bless you, you get some sugar on that and get that inside you. It'll do you good."

Barbara stared at her kind, concerned face.

"Sorry? What? Er, I think you've got my name wrong. I'm Barbara," she stammered.

"Are you? Oh, gosh, of course, so sorry. I'm sure I don't know why I thought you was called Pearl. I do get muddled with all the names, getting old, you know! Getting forgetful! Pearl - what was I thinking? Now where did that come from?" she said, shaking her head. "Anyway, you're Barbara - I'll try to remember. Here's the milk, sugar's there, you've got a spoon, haven't you? Anything else you need?"

Barbara shook her head. The volunteer bustled back to the kitchen as Barbara sat, amazed and speechless, thinking, why did she call me Pearl? Pearl! How did she know? Did Luke say something to her? No, he wouldn't have done that. She couldn't have overheard either, she wasn't there last night. No, it must just be a coincidence. But how could it be? That name! Awe tingled down her spine and she put her hand to her chest. Her heart beat fast. It was almost frightening. She could almost imagine that an angel had touched her. It felt ominous, as if a heavy veil had been torn between the material world and something strong, unpredictable, and immense.

CHAPTER THIRTY-FOUR

Wednesday's Winter Shelter was at St. Edward's, a 1940's red brick Methodist church, with a bleak, unheated hall attached. The volunteers were apologetic.

"I know it's a bit chilly, dear," one said. "And it needs a lick of paint. But we've put you and the other women in the prayer room at the back and you should be a bit warmer there."

Barbara nodded.

"Honestly, it's fine," she said. "It's warmer than outside, anyway."

"Oh, yes. Brr - it's freezing! Been like this for days! Terrible weather… I don't know how you survive. How do you keep warm?"

"It's difficult," admitted Barbara. It was an understatement. Barbara had spent the bitterly cold day queueing fruitlessly at the Jobcentre yet again, hanging around the library, wandering around the shopping centre and sitting in a Day Centre called

Matthew's Place, with other homeless people, drinking cups of sugary tea and hoping for a chance to use the washing machine. She felt sick of the endless futility and boredom and fear, but she said nothing, just nodded to the volunteer. And Luke had promised that he would come. Maybe Sophie too. Maybe they'd be able to help her.

As she ate the jacket potatoes and baked beans that seemed to be standard fare at the Winter Shelters, she listened for the door. Every time it swung open she looked up then back down at her plate, disappointed again. The tidy man in his dark coat, James, chatted to her about the weather, the news, the latest faux-pas by a Westminster MP, but she answered mechanically, her eyes watching all the time for Luke.

The volunteers cleared supper and folded the tables and chairs away, Barbara helped make up the beds, then she cleaned her teeth and washed her face, and went to spread out her sleeping bag. Still no Luke, no Sophie, no Francis, no rescue, nothing. The night shift took over, closing the doors and switching off the lights. She lay wide awake for hours, nails dug into her palms to stop herself sobbing so she wouldn't disturb the other women sleeping beside her.

Thursday was drearily identical, apart from an overnight fall of heavy snow that made her feet damp as she trudged into the city centre to meet a different person and hear a different excuse at the Jobcentre. The winter shelter was a different church hall: a modern Baptist Church in Earlsdon.

At least it was warm inside, away from the frost that glazed the snow with a thin film of crackling ice and made her shiver despite her coat. But there was still no Luke and no word. At breakfast, she lethargically poured milk on a bowl of cornflakes. Terry, the scrawny and long-faced young man, came and sat next to her.

"You don't like cornflakes, do you? How can you? They's disgustin'. Like little bits of cardboard. I like bacon, I do, but they don't do it here, do they?" he said, in a rapid staccato, giving her no time to respond. "And you gotta keep the pigs right, they should be in woods, now, shouldn't they? With oak trees, yeah. Like nature, y'know. Huntin' for truffles or acorns or whats-its, or rabbits, now, rabbits, they're OK, but you have to tame them, you know. D'you like rabbits? Or guinea pigs? D'you have pets? I had gerbils, in Bradford, in a flat, big old cotton mill, did you know it? Full of them machines, it was, once. I hates machinery. Do you?"

James came and sat opposite.

"No, Terry, oh no. Not like that," he said. "Grilling poor Barbara like that! That is not the best way to start the day. What you should say is 'Good morning, Barbara, I hope you slept well?' and give her a chance to answer you."

Terry stared at him. James deliberately put sugar in his tea and nodded at him. "So, Terry, let me demonstrate. Good morning, Terence, did you sleep well?"

"Yeah, er, yeah, I did. But I woke at five, I were dreamin' of watermelons and motorbikes and

Tommy Cooper and me ears were freezin'. I thought they'd dropped off."

As Terry burbled on, Barbara shot a grateful glance at James. She was glad he'd deflected Terry. She didn't feel she could cope with his weird volubility so early in the morning, not with everything else and the prospect of another dull, cold, pointless day once they left the shelter.

After a long walk along snow-covered pavements that afternoon, Barbara found Friday's Winter Shelter: a draughty Victorian hall hidden away in the suburbs of Foleshill. By ten Barbara had given up on Luke and his promises. James, at least, was friendly. When he went outside 'for a fag' she put her coat on and stood by him, staring up at the sharp white stars against the dark orange city sky.

"Freezing again," James said, holding out the cigarette packet. "Real brass monkey weather, as they say in Yorkshire. At least it's not snowing. Would you like one?"

"No thanks," she said.

"Good for you. It's a terrible habit, I know, but, Jesus Christ, at least it makes you feel warm," he said, taking a long drag on his cigarette.

Terry came out and stood with them.

"Fookin' hell, it's bloody icicles, icicles, ain't it? Fookin' freezin'. Like Titanic, d'you see that film?" he said, pulling a bottle out of his pocket and taking a long swig.

"Yes, I did," said Barbara. "I thought it was wonderful."

"Yeah, the bit where it cracks and sinks, but Kate Winslet, what a drip - hey, get it? What a drip! Hey, Babs, want a bit? Warms you up good and proper."

Barbara looked at the bottle.

"What is it?"

"Brandy, that's what, but don't tell anyone, I nicked it from Sainsbury's. Sainsbury's fookin' basics brandy, ain't that a laugh? Bloody stupid, ain't it? They do basic smoked salmon, too, bloody ridiculous, fookin' basics cheapo smoked salmon. Hey, I went to Ireland once, salmon ladders they were, but I never saw no salmon, but the river, lots of fish, in the dam, loads of fish. Loads. I hate fish. Too bony. Hate the scales too. Did you ever go to Ireland? The Titanic, launched from Belfast, it were."

"You're almost making sense this evening, Terry," James said and flicked his cigarette end into the bin. "Anyhow, I'm going in."

"Too cold, ain't it, mate? Too bloody cold. Me nadgers are gonna freeze off if I stay out here much longer," Terry said, flapping his arms around and hopping from foot to foot.

Barbara went to follow James, but Terry grabbed her arm.

"Hey, Babs, look at the stars," he said. "Like that bit where Rose is singin', ain't it? Here, go on, have a bit."

Barbara looked up. The moon, a thin slice of silver, was rising above the roofs of the houses and shone, even against the flat sodium glow of the street lights. Her breath smoked in the cold air. It was beautiful, the moon and stars, but what good did it do her? Tomorrow she would be trudging the streets again, being humiliated and chilled and pushed aside. Luke, Sophie, they obviously weren't going to help, and she didn't deserve it anyway. Mechanically, she took the brandy bottle that Terry was holding out to her and swallowed. She coughed, but the burning warmth in her throat and stomach felt like the best thing that had happened to her for days. She took another gulp.

"Hey, steady on, darlin'," said Terry. "Bloody good stuff, though, ain't it? Basic's brandy! Yer gotta laugh. Good, though, ain't it?"

"Yes. Thanks."

"Here, look at the label, it's French brandy, though, not English, not Scotch. They do whiskey. Whiskey, brandy, saké. Hey, they don't do brandy in Japan, do they, only saké, noodles, raw fish, that and kimonos, big cushions on their arses, eat with chopsticks, not forks, weird, ain't they? Here, have some more, darlin'."

Oh, it was good, Barbara thought, taking a long pull at the bottle. It was like glowing fire, like heat, like strength. Maybe she should get bladdered, just once. The rising haze of alcohol warmed her and blurred the bitterness inside. Suddenly, she felt light-headed and dizzy. Terry put his arm around her shoulders.

"Go on, have a bit more. You look like you need it. Bloody good, go on, that's right, drink up. Hey, you're pretty, ain't you? Like Kate Winslet, a bit, not like that other woman, the old one with the necklace, the blue one, in the water, and I'm

Leonardo DiCaprio, ain't I?"

"Yes, sure." Barbara couldn't help laughing at the thought. "You're Leonardo and I'm Kate."

"On the Titanic, looking at the stars. You and me, darlin'."

He pulled her close. Suddenly he was too close. He smelt of sweat and brandy. His arm was tight around her. She squirmed and tried to break free, but he twisted her round and clamped his mouth on hers. One of his hands scrabbled at her coat and pulled it open. His unshaven face scraped her skin, his breath reeked, his hand clawed at her breast. She retched as she struggled to push him away.

"Don't. Don't!" she gasped. "Get off! Get off me!"

"Yeah, sure, sure, you bloody cow. Come on, Babs, darlin'," Terry mumbled into her neck. He staggered back, taking another gulp of brandy. "Come on, you had me brandy, I want a kiss, I do, a kiss for more brandy, French, like Paris, like those postcards, I've got some, they've got the Eiffel tower on and girls on bicycles, come on, darlin', give us a kiss, a bit of some, yer know!"

"No! Leave me alone!"

He reeled in front, between her and the door, but she dodged past him. He grabbed her arm. For a frightening moment he wrenched her back and wrapped both arms around her. She couldn't move. He rammed one hand over her mouth. She twisted fruitlessly then, frantic with fear, she lunged forward and bit his fingers as hard as she could. He yelped and dropped his hand. She wriggled free and ran inside, dashed to the toilets, locked the door and hid, breathing fast, shaking, until one of the volunteers called, "Lights out in fifteen minutes." She crept out, told the volunteers she was inside, and crawled into her bed. Her whole body trembled. The exhaustion and the terror and the brandy flooded her. She closed her eyes and drifted into swirling fears and nightmares and, finally, the relief of unconsciousness.

By morning, she had slept well enough to feel a little braver, despite a pounding headache. Brave enough to face another day's pointless meandering, but not brave enough to face Terry at breakfast. She stayed in the women's room, sitting on her bed and staring at the grimy linoleum. One of the volunteers came in followed by Emma Carrington, the support worker at Matthew's Place Day Centre.

"Ah, Barbara," Emma said. "Now, I don't like doing this, but Terry said you were drunk and you had a bottle of brandy with you, last night. You know the rules and you signed the consent form, so I'm very much afraid that Julia here and I have to search your bags."

Barbara looked up. "Brandy? Oh, but it was his … Oh, I'm sorry, I shouldn't have…"

Her head throbbing, feeling sick, she watched silently, as they efficiently but pitilessly went through her things. In her coat pocket was the almost-empty bottle.

"Oh no!" Barbara said. "No! I don't know how it got there. It's not mine. Terry - he must have put it there!"

"Hmm," said Emma. "Well, it's your word

against his. He's gone, now, so I can't ask him. But Julia says you looked, and smelt, like you'd been drinking last night, She didn't like to say anything then, but you had been drinking, hadn't you?"

"I had, yes, I'm sorry, but it was Terry's, honestly, it was!"

"Have you had breakfast?"

"No."

"Go and have breakfast. Then I'll talk to you. Explain the procedure and your options."

"Are you going to arrest me?"

"What? Of course not! Don't be daft! Now you go and have something to eat, for goodness sake!"

It was nearly nine and all the other guests had left. Barbara managed to force down some lukewarm lumpy porridge and a cup of coffee, before Emma came and took her aside into an empty room at the back.

"Now, you know the rules about no alcohol, no drugs, no drinking, don't you?" she said.

Barbara nodded.

"We have to enforce them. We're over-subscribed as it is, and we can't make exceptions. We've got seven on the waiting list who need beds. I hope you understand?"

"Yes, I see."

"I know there seems to be some doubt, and I know Terry isn't exactly whiter-than-white himself, but we can't show favouritism. Much as I'd like to. The standard procedure is a seven-night ban from the Winter Shelter. Sorry, but that's what it is. I don't have any leeway."

"Seven nights? A seven-night ban?"

"Yes. Until next Saturday night."

I can't survive, thought Barbara. I can't do it. I might as well be dead.

"Are you OK, Barbara?"

"No, not really. What am I going to do?"

"You're from Merton, aren't you?"

"Yes."

"Any friends, any family there?"

"No, no family. Er, friends, I'm not sure."

"They've got a Winter Shelter scheme. You might be better off there."

"Yes, maybe," thought Barbara, but she knew she couldn't. Someone on it would recognise her and it would be bound to get back to Holy Trinity. She shivered at the thought of going to back to the people she knew in Merton, asking them for help and facing their visible sympathy and invisible criticism.

"Hmm," said Emma. "Well, get your things together. Come and see me at Matthew's Place, about 2pm, and I'll see what I can sort out for you."

Seven nights on the streets of Coventry! Barbara knew she wouldn't cope. Anything, prison even, would be better than that. But what were her options? Drugs, prostitution, prison? Maybe prison would be a good idea. One of the homeless guys at the shelter had just come out of prison and told her that he wanted to go back. "It's the routine, init?" he'd said. "Yer get yer meals, yer can do vocational trainin' and stuff, it's safe, see?"

The streets were crowded. Barbara wished she

could find somewhere to hide her rucksack and two carrier bags, so she was less obviously homeless. James had the right idea; with his dark buttoned-up coat and wheeled suitcase, he looked like a business man returning from a conference. Barbara put on another jumper and a scarf from one bag, shoved a hat and gloves from the other into her pockets, and was able to push her bags into the rucksack and hoist it on to her back. She felt hot and looked overweight, but at least it meant she was less noticeable.

Trying to look confident and normal, she walked into the camping shop in the precinct. If she was going to try to get arrested it might as well be for something she needed. And there it was: a single 'all you need to start camping' kit. Tent, mat, sleeping bag and pillow, all in one convenient bag. Barbara glanced around surreptitiously. She didn't want to make what she was doing too apparent. And now it came to it, she wasn't sure being arrested for shoplifting was a good idea. She'd probably just get a suspended sentence. To guarantee a warm night in a prison cell she'd probably have to attack a policeman or hold up a bank with a gun. She looked at the camping kit, at the unlikely cheerfulness of the man crouching in front of the tent on the cover picture, then she grabbed the handles, picked it up, and walked rapidly out.

Nothing happened. No one stopped her, no one shouted, no security guard ran towards her. Her heart beating furiously, feeling sick and dizzy, she kept on walking. Outside the precinct she took a gulp of the freezing air. Grey clouds had moved over the sky, threatening snow later on. Barbara threaded through the shoppers, past the statue of Lady Godiva, along Trinity Street, through the streets and car parks and back alleys and under the ring road until she got to Matthew's Place.

"I don't want to stay in Coventry. I think I'll have to go back to Merton," she told Emma, that afternoon. "I've got a tent and I can camp in the woods. They're fairly close to the centre. It's a smaller town. I know it better than Coventry. I'll be fine, I think." She thought of the canal near the woods, of its dark calm waters.

"Are you sure?" Emma said. "Camping in this weather?"

"Yes. It will be just as cold being here. And better than the streets, isn't it? Also I think the Jobcentre there will help me, more than here, because I come from Merton."

"Well, there is that. And they might have got a couple of spaces in the Winter Shelter there, you know. If you need it. I'll phone them up, and let them know that you are going to be around and might need their help."

She shut down her computer, stood up and pulled her coat on.

"Have you got enough money for a train ticket to Merton?" she said.

"Er, I think so. I've got, er, a few pounds left."

"Just a few pounds? Right. Well, this time I'm going to break one of the rules. I'll give you a lift to the station and buy your ticket. OK? Wait for me in the lounge, while I just phone up the Merton guys."

At the station she insisted on buying Barbara a sandwich and a hot chocolate, as well as her ticket.

"You look like you need it. Oh, and I nearly forgot. This is a grant from the emergency fund," she added, handing Barbara a white envelope. "Right. I'm off. Stay safe, won't you? Keep off the brandy?"

"Yes, thanks, thank you. I'm so sorry to have done that…"

"Don't be daft. There but for the grace of God, you know."

"What? No, I don't know."

"Oh, you know. There but for the grace of God go I. We're all really only two steps away from homelessness. Well, all of the 'just about managing' folks, which is most of the country. It doesn't take much! Redundancy, divorce, greedy landlords, illness, addiction, and then the odds are stacked against you. The benefits system, the universal bloody credit system, everything," Emma shuddered theatrically. "Come the revolution… Anyway, forgive the rant. I'd best be off. Hope it all works out for you."

Once on the train, Barbara opened the envelope. She gasped and put her hand to her mouth. It contained five ten-pound notes.

CHAPTER THIRTY-FIVE

It was after midnight by the time Luke had finished unloading fresh vegetables onto the shelves and tidying the packing area. It had been a long shift. He'd got back to Merton Tuesday morning, had an hour's sleep, then had to get to work. Now he just wanted to get home and crash out. Tomorrow he'd call Sophie and talk about how to help Barbara. Maybe she could move in to his house. It was daft that he was living alone in a house with two bedrooms and a box room, when she was on the streets. But he'd have to ask Francis as well. It shouldn't be a problem. The PCC shouldn't complain - though they probably would, just 'cos it was him suggesting it.

As he stepped outside, thinking about what he could do to help Barbara, he shivered and zipped his jacket up. Dark clouds of mist and fog drifted through the car park and streets, muffling sounds and glazing every surface with frozen droplets of ice. Luke walked down East Lane and past the Salvation Army church, towards Old Hilton. The freezing air stung his skin and he wrapped his scarf around his neck and walked faster down the alley and through the back streets. He came round the corner to Lime Street, just as three young men, two white and one black, came out of the old Railway Club and walked towards him. One, the black man, hesitated and stared at him. His full lips, dark eyes and close-cropped hair looked familiar.

"Um, hi," Luke said. "I know you, don't I?"
"What? What did you say?"
The young man stopped still, his hands thrust deep into his pockets. He glared at Luke, his eyes wide and menacing. He looked wired and edgy, Luke thought. On drugs, or something. He stepped back. The other two lounged against the wall, watching. One was tall with a leather jacket, cropped blonde hair and a steel ring threaded through his eyebrow. The other was sturdy and shorter, with a shaven head, pale blue eyes and straining muscles visible through a tight-sleeved t-shirt.

"Hurry up, Danny," he said. "Leave it, we gotta get to town."
"Yeah, I know, but hold on a mo!" Danny growled. "I reckon I know this guy."
"Danny?" exclaimed Luke. "You're Danny! You - " He remembered the cut on Naomi's face and the trembling distress in her voice, and he clenched his hands and moved towards Danny. The other two stood up and came closer. Their faces were fierce and their fingers curled into ominous fists.

Luke hesitated.

"Yeah, I know who you are now!" Danny said. "You're that smart-arsed youth worker. Luke somebody. Yeah - you're Luke. Where is she? Where've you got her, you scumbag?"

"I haven't got her! She ran away of her own accord! From you, you - you beat her up! You hit her!"

"So what if I did?" Danny sneered. "She ain't nothing to do with you! Tell me where she is!"

"What, so you can beat her up again? You sod!" Luke shouted, trying to throw a punch at Danny's face. Danny caught his arm, pulled him off balance and kicked his side. The other two leapt forward. Luke wrenched himself away.

"Sod, am I?" Danny shouted. "Yeah, maybe I am, but I'm gonna teach you to touch her. I'll kill you! Get him! Come on, get the son of a bitch!"

Luke looked at the murderous expression on his face, turned and ran. He skidded on frost-covered ice on the corner, fell, righted himself and wheeled into Lowman Street. It was more public, he thought. He'd have more chance there than getting himself cornered in an empty alleyway. All three were chasing him. He had a sudden idea and dodged left into Little Fenn Street. As he remembered, it was a dead-end with a locked gate between it and a petrol station forecourt. Luke vaulted the gate rapidly and easily. The petrol station was closed, so there was no help there, but at least his hunters were slower than him getting over the gate.

Luke sped towards the main road. Two taxis and

a lorry passed, holding him up. Danny ran close behind him, shouting incoherently. He was too close. They were nearly on him.

Luke dashed over the road, hurled himself over the barrier in the middle, and sprinted towards the town centre. He needed to find crowds, the taxi rank, a policeman, some help, before they caught him. He glanced back, and saw, through the haze of the orange-lit night, that the three were still chasing him. Danny was in the lead. His face was contorted, his eyes raging, his voice loud and furious. Even in the heart-pounding fear that flooded through him, Luke could not understand how Danny knew about him and Naomi.

But, now, he had to run.

He scrambled over a fence into the library car park and dashed along the front of the building. They were close behind him, but he knew a few parkour tricks. He jumped up onto the brick wall by the steps and ran along it. There was a six-foot drop at the end. He launched himself forward, landed, rolled quickly into a somersault, leapt up and sprinted onwards. Snowflakes were starting to fall around him.

Danny and the other two paused at the drop.

"Stairs! Get him!" Danny roared, turning back.

Luke had gained seconds on them now. He was faster and he could fool them. He sped across the car park, over a hedge and a brick wall, and past the backs of the shops. More snow was starting to fall, a steady swirl of larger and larger flakes. He slipped on a sheet of snow-sprinkled ice, crashing down onto his shoulder and elbow. Bruising pain tingled along his arm. By the time he'd got up, they were so near he could see Danny's breath steaming in the cold and his teeth showing in a grimace of rage. His fists were clenched, his face manic.

Luke turned and fled. But in his panic he forgot. It was the middle of the night. The shopping centre was closed and its glass doors locked against him. It was a dead-end. They were on him. There were steps at the side up to a door. Luke scrambled up them. The door was locked too.

"Gotcha!" the blonde-haired man said, and laughed. "Right. Let's have some fun!"

"Gonna teach you a lesson," Danny snarled. "Teach a religious nutter like you to keep your filthy hands off my girl…"

They advanced. As Danny came up the stairs, Luke saw a chance. He grabbed the stair rail, pushed up, flung his legs round and kicked. His foot slammed into Danny's chest, knocking him back against the other two. Luke swung over the rail, landed and sprinted on, as they stumbled and fell.

He heard their curses and shouts fading behind him. He kept going, towards the market square, where the taxi rank was. His heart felt overloaded, his breath panting and gasping, a stitch was jabbing into his side. He should have done more training recently.

In the square taxi drivers skulked in their cars, away from the thickening snowfall. A couple leant against a shop door with their hands wrapped around cigarettes. A few late-night clubbers staggered along, clutching each other. One peeled off to throw up in a litter bin.

As Luke paused and tried to pull in enough air to shout for help, he heard Danny yelling, "Stop him! Thieving bastard! Get him!"

The two taxi drivers ran forward. The clubbers laughed and lurched around. They spread their arms wide to catch him. Luke could see they weren't going to help. One lanky youth made a grab for him. Luke ducked and swerved, dodged past Danny, and ran back up the High Street. He jumped from bench to bench, flying across the gaps, but they relentlessly came on, hunting him.

Luke turned left and sprinted through the alley to the Masonic Hall and through its car park. At last, he thought, a stroke of luck! The far entrance, with its high wrought-iron gate, was locked. It would be easy for him. He dashed at it, launched himself upwards, reached up for the top rail one-handed, swung up, grabbed with the other hand and pulled upwards. The blonde one tried to reach his shoe. Luke kicked out and hit his ear, then yanked himself up, scrambled over and dropped.

His ankle twisted as he landed. As the jarring pain shot up his leg, he fell sideways and cried out.

Danny and the others struggled to get over the gate. They're not tall enough, thank God, Luke thought, twisting round to look through the falling snowflakes to see where they were. He heaved himself up onto his knees. Abrasive tarmac rasped his hands as he tried to stand, staggering as his ankle gave way. He crawled forward.

"Go round," shouted Danny.

Ignoring the shards of pain in his ankle, Luke

forced himself up and limped on. He stumbled down the path to the cemetery and hauled himself over the wall. Danny and the others shot out from the alley towards him. Their shouts and curses rang in his ears. They were getting closer. A homeless man, lying under snow-sprinkled cardboard on a bench, sat up and stared at Luke as he half-ran, half-limped through the tombstones and yew-trees. He knew he couldn't go much further, not with a wrenched ankle. There was a toilet block between the cemetery and Chapel Street. He climbed onto the cemetery wall, leapt forwards, caught the parapet of the toilet block and clambered up onto its flat roof. He didn't think Danny or his friends would be able to easily climb up. He knelt down, gasped and rubbed his ankle. At least he might get a breathing space to call for help.

The three of them circled the toilet block, looking up at him.

"Cornered, ain't'cha?" the burly man said. "A little rat in a trap."

Luke crawled to the parapet. In the cemetery he could see the homeless man standing up and watching. A police car drove past, blue lights flashing cold on the swirling snow around them. It didn't stop. Luke stared down at Danny.

"What the hell's this about, Danny?" he yelled. "What've I done?"

"Don't you know?" Danny shouted back. "I'll know about you two! I'll teach you, you and that bitch, when I find her!"

That bitch? Luke remembered the scar on Naomi's face, how she'd told him with a trembling and scared voice, what Danny had done to her. Rage filled him. His heart raced faster, his face flushed. He clenched his hands, hobbled back a couple of paces, took a deep breath and threw himself off the parapet down onto Danny. He tried to hit him, to hurt him, to punish him for what he'd done to Naomi, but Danny fought back, his vicious fists and feet thudding into Luke's side and stomach. Suddenly Luke saw the cold glint of sharp metal in the other's hand. He twisted out of reach. They both tumbled sideways, rolling in the ice and grit and frozen puddles on the pavement. Luke flailed at Danny, trying to push him away, trying to avoid the knife in his hand. Voices; yelling, cursing; surrounded them. He realised that the homeless man was there, holding back the blonde man and shouting incoherently.

Danny smashed a fist into Luke's shoulder and then the burly man was there, kicking at Luke's chest and leg and head, kicking again and again. He stamped on Luke's ankle and Luke screamed as the agony speared up his calf. He tried to roll into a ball, but Danny knelt on his chest, pinioning him. His hand slid out, the steel tip of the blade reflecting in the street lights. He cut sideways, down; the blade stabbing through Luke's jacket and into his side. Then the other man's boot smashed into the back of his head and the pains and noises faded into dark confusion.

CHAPTER THIRTY-SIX

It was twilight and Barbara's breath already formed clouds of mist in the cold air. She sat down on the sleeping bag and wrapped her coat around herself. The tent couldn't be said to be cosy, despite how small it was. She'd found a clearing in the wooded areas near the canal. There were no paths to it, so she thought she'd be safe despite the council estate less than a mile away. Shivering in the faint twilight, barely able to read the time on her watch, she realised she had no choice but to stay in the tent. Without a torch, she'd never find her way back through the trees and frost-rimed shrubs. It was after five, the sun was setting, it would be dark for fourteen hours. She wriggled into the sleeping bag and lay down, waiting for the time to pass and the next day to start. Hunger pains pulled at her. Her feet ached from the cold. Sleep was impossible as heat leached away.

Animals made rustling noises through the

shrivelled leaves and dead twigs on the ground outside. An owl flew past, its low hooting echoing through the tree trunks, then a dog barked roughly. It sounded so close that she sat up, her heart racing in sudden fear. There were voices nearby: laughter, sounds of conversation, shouts, swearing. She huddled, clutching her trembling knees, as she held her breath and listened. She didn't know what she would do if they found her tent. At last the voices faded into the distance. Barbara waited as long as she could, but she needed to go to the toilet. It was silent outside, apart from the whispering noises of the undergrowth.

She shoved her feet into her shoes, went outside and crouched in the bushes, came back and put on another jumper under her coat, pulled some gloves over her numb fingers, dragged on an anomalously cheerful red knitted hat, and another pair of socks. Crawling back into the sleeping bag, she curled up and tried to ignore the sounds and the cold. She shivered uncontrollably. The chill rose from the ground, through the thin mat and sleeping bag, and seeped into her blood and into her bones until they felt like freezing water turning into icicles inside her. She dipped in and out of sleep, aware even as she dreamt of the icy touch of frost on her face and cheeks.

Eventually grey early light filtered in and she gave up trying to get back to sleep. Outside, she heard a chattering blackbird fly past the tent. Her hat, the sleeping bag and walls of the tent were damp from condensation and dribbles of water slid down the canvas. Pallid goosebumps spotted her arms.

She peered out of the tent. The sky was starting to fade from indigo to turquoise and the stars were faint dots of light, disappearing as the light grew in the east. Pale frost lay on the grass and dead leaves, amidst the remaining patches of frozen snow, and every branch of every tree had a filigree of rime edging it. She dressed, got her bag, and zipped the tent closed with hands that shook with cold. At least she could leave her belongings in it, and she could buy a torch, so the next night might be easier.

As she shivered and stumbled along the road into the town centre, her hands trembled and hunger pains grabbed at her stomach. A sudden black dizziness flooded her vision. She stopped and leaned against a wall until the faintness passed. A corner shop was open at the next street and she bought a pasty, coffee, a chocolate bar. She sat on a bench in a small park nearby and devoured the sweet chocolate, then the waxy pastry, chunks of potatoes and greyish meat, washing them down with gulps of hot, bitter coffee.

In the town centre she rested on a bench by the market square, until the clock in Holy Trinity chimed eight times, then she crept into the back of the church. It was Sunday. There would be an early morning communion service. She could hear Francis one last time. She hid behind a pillar and listened as if his words held the secret. He was discussing Jesus's saying, 'Ask and it will be given to you'. Barbara snorted in quiet derision. Hadn't she asked and asked and asked again? For something as basic as shelter, a job, food? God had clearly given up on her, despite telling her she was a pearl of great price. If you don't do something, soon, God, she said, I'm going to give up. I can't live like this.

She didn't go up to the altar rail for the bread and the wine, and the temptation to linger past the end of the service and speak to Francis was easily resisted. The closing blessing came. She waited for the words, 'The Lord bless you and keep you, the Lord make his face shine on you', then she tried to slip out unnoticed, but Francis saw her as she stood up.

"Barbara! Oh, thank goodness, Barbara!" he called, and started forward, ignoring the astonished congregation. "Barbara, wait…please, wait!"

She couldn't help it. She ran. How could she face him? She knew she was filthy, her breath would be rank, she must stink of sweat and slept-in clothes, she hadn't brushed her hair, let alone washed it, for days. He would be pitying but he would be revolted, she knew, though he would hide his revulsion well. The thought was unbearable. As she scuttled out and ran down the street, she could hear him frantically calling to her, but she ran and ran and didn't look back.

Alternatively drinking coffee and dozing, Barbara spent most of the day in the library and in supermarket cafes; with a carrier bag containing a torch, a fleece blanket, batteries and fruit. She put another bag with milk and cereal bars on to the table beside her to show she was a bona fide shopper and not a tramp. She shouldn't waste money on coffee, but where else could she go that would be warm? And buying a drink, discussing decaeff or skimmed milk, and exchanging a few words with the assistant about the weather; it was a bit of human contact and some relief from the enervating boredom and powerlessness of it all.

As night fell, she trudged the two miles back to the tent and crawled inside. Her belongings were all there, strewn damply around as she had left them. She hunted through her rucksack, fished out her bible, wrapped the fleece around her shoulders, munched on a chilly and tasteless apple, and tried to read the bible using the pale light of the torch. But there was no comfort there. How could there be? Francis was so sure God existed. He said the evidence was almost incontrovertible, and spoke with passionate belief of history, the gospels, the moral law, the origin of life and his own experience. But Barbara had no such faith. God, if he existed, had dropped her into the mire and sent no help. She could no longer go on in this isolation and cold pointlessness. She shivered. Tomorrow, barring some miracle, she would end it. The canal was nearby. She would let its frigid waters take her. She thought of how the cold would bite and seize her, of the brief agony and the chilling shock, and how they would slowly fade. How she would float, carried by the icy water. How the numbness as her sluggish blood congealed would lull her to sleep and her eyes would close and darkness relieve her.

"God, I'll do it!" she muttered fiercely. "I don't care any more. I don't care if it's giving up! You've shown you either don't exist or don't care about me after all. That thing about being a pearl was - it was a lie! If you don't give me any help, any sign that you care, anything to stop me, anything, I'll do it. Tomorrow morning."

CHAPTER THIRTY-SEVEN

When Luke opened his eyes, he saw pock-marked polystyrene ceiling tiles and a fluorescent light above him, and heard shoes pattering on hard floors, faint beeps and whispered conversations. He lay on his back surrounded by faded grey and blue curtains. His ankle stung, his head pounded as if he had a hangover from a dozen beers and his side throbbed with pain. Even his toes were aching, and his body felt hollow with exhaustion. Warm fingers clutched his hand. He tried to lift his head and look round. Someone gasped beside him.

"Luke? Luke, oh, Luke, you're awake! Oh, thank God, thank God!"

"Mum?" he murmured. "Mum, what happened? Where am I?"

"You're in hospital. You were attacked, and they had to give you…"

Her face shrank and her voice faded as if she was receding into a tunnel. Luke tried to stay awake and to hear her, but the overhead light darkened and the dimness muffled him in heavy silence. He slept, a strange sleep full of odd dreams. He was going on a pub crawl round Merton wearing a purple wetsuit and a dog collar, then being chased by hairy yetis in bobble hats, yelling 'Don't you touch Naomi ever again!'

"Naomi," he tried to say, but his throat was dry. Someone leaned over and put a straw into his mouth.

"Water," they said, as he drank. The lukewarm water tasted of stale plastic.

"Thanks. Thirsty…"

"That's a good sign. I think you're getting back to us, aren't you?" someone said. He opened his eyes. A woman wearing a blue nurse's uniform with an upside-down fob watch, and a concerned look on her face, bent over him.

"Hospital. How long?" he whispered.

"A few days. You were pretty badly hurt. Surgery to cauterise your liver, six units of blood, broken ankle, CAT scan for brain damage, the lot. You had a fairly serious extradural bleed, from a blow to the back of your head, so we had to put you into a coma to allow it to clear. But you've recovered well. Anyway, I'll go and get your meds. You've got a visitor."

"Luke!" Sophie screeched. "Oh, praise the Lord, I've been praying and praying and praying for days for you! Oh, Luke, bless you, I'm so thrilled to know you're going to be all right! At last!"

"Sophie? Steady on. Days? What happened?"

"Well, you've were really hurt. They really did

beat you up, you're blessed to be alive, you know. You lost masses of blood."

"Blessed? Don't feel blessed…" Luke tried to sit up but a jabbing pain in his side made him wince, and he collapsed back onto the bed.

"Oh, you are, you know! It's all a bit of a mystery, a real mystery. Anyway, you're better! Your parent's have been here all the time, they're staying in the Travelodge. Your Dad's gone back to Telford, but he's coming back tomorrow, and your Mum is here, she's gone back for a rest, but she's coming to see you this evening. They've been so worried, but we knew you were going to be all right last night, your eyelids flickered. I never thought I'd be so glad to see that!"

"Why?"

"Apparently it meant you didn't have brain damage. And then you started breathing on your own."

"Huh?"

"You were on a ventilator. Oh, Luke, you were in ICU, tubes and things and drips everywhere, down your nose and mouth, in your hands, it was horrible. Really scary! I don't think I've ever prayed so much, I was so worried for you. I can't believe how badly you were hurt!"

Luke shut his eyes. He could only remember snapshots of that evening. The glint of light on the blade, the foot crashing down on his ankle. The desperate running through the snow. The tiredness, the effort of breathing.

"Sorry, Sophie, feel whacked. Got to sleep…"

Luke snapped his eyes open. He remembered everything about that night and the day before: Danny and his thugs chasing him, before that, catching the train back from Coventry and, before that, the Winter Shelter.

"Sophie! Barbara!" He struggled to get up. "I have to tell you about Barbara! Sophie, she's…"

"Sophie's not here, darling." It was his mother's voice. "She came yesterday, and said that she was speaking to you and then you fell asleep."

"Mum? Oh, Mum, get her! I've got to tell her something!" He threw the covers off frantically.

"OK, darling! Don't worry! She'll be here soon, she's gone to park the car and walk round. The car park is miles away, so she drops me off and then has to find a space. Luke, come here, please, let me hug you! We've been so worried, so frightened!"

Luke let himself be held. Being in his mother's warm, unquestioning embrace helped. He felt stronger.

"I'm OK, Mum. I feel better. I've got to do something about Barbara…"

"Yes, I know, but it can wait a few minutes, can't it? You're in no state to get up."

He pushed himself into a sitting position, then collapsed back onto the pillow. His ankle felt oddly heavy. He reached down and felt the rough texture of plaster around it.

"I broke my ankle, didn't I?" he said. "Falling off that gate."

"Yes, but it could have been so much worse. Oh, I'm so pleased you feel better. So relieved! They say it will be a week or so before you're fully recovered, apart from your broken ankle. They'll get you some crutches soon, because you'll have a cast on that, and a limp for a while. Oh, look, here's Sophie! Sophie, Luke's awake! He's sitting up!"

"Hey, that's great! You're sitting up! Oh, Luke!" Sophie leaned across and hugged him, and kissed his cheek. "Welcome back. You look so much better. It's hard to believe that you could have been in a coma, and on a ventilator, and lost masses of blood and been knocked unconscious and stabbed and now look at you! It's like a miracle!"

"In a coma? You make it sound like an episode of Casualty. It doesn't feel like that. Apart from my ankle and my side."

"The nurse says that you're young, fit, you've had so much blood pumped into you, they expect you to recover really quickly. But it's still wonderful! Right, I've got grapes, chocolates, bottles of water and juice and, Petra, I called in at the cafe and got us some coffee. Right, let's have a picnic!"

"Sophie, look, I've got to talk to you. It's urgent. It's about Barbara."

"Barbara!" Sophie leapt up, spilling grapes over the bed. "Luke, what is it? Do you know anything? We're so worried about her, we don't know what to do, or where she's gone. It's been so long! Francis is - well, Luke, I've never seen him so upset. He's practically frantic. He thought he'd seen her, but if it was her, then she ran off. Oh, it's been like we've been attacked! First Naomi, then all the gossip and the church splitting, then Barbara disappearing, and you being so seriously hurt. I really feel that we have to pray God's protection over us."

"Yes, yes, Sophie, pray all you like but for God's sake, listen first! I know where she is!"

"Calm down, Luke. You need to rest!" said his mother. "Please, don't worry. I'm sure she'll be OK and it will wait."

"It won't wait. I promised her. I promised her I'd help her! She must think I'm a real sod, to have promised and then just walked away."

"Luke, tell me!" Sophie exclaimed. "What is it? Look, Petra, he won't be able to rest, will he, until he's told me?"

"I met her! In Coventry. In the Winter Shelter."

"No! You're kidding! In the Winter Shelter? Really?" She sat down and grabbed his hand.

"I'm not. Look, let me tell you."

As Luke finished. Sophie stood up, wiping her eyes with a tissue.

"Poor, poor Barbara," she said. "I'll go. I'll tell Francis. We can go to Coventry together, this evening. We'll find her, Luke, don't worry."

His mother left later on, having sat with him for an hour, holding his hand, saying very little at first, except about how worried she and his father had been.

"And furious, too. If he'd caught those young men - thugs, I should say! I've never seen him in such a rage."

"What happened to them?"

"Well, the police turned up, and an ambulance. There was some man there, he'd been sleeping on a bench in the cemetery, and he'd shouted for help. They think he'd actually phoned for help, but there's some mystery about that, according to Sophie. No one knows who phoned the police."

"Yeah, I remember him. A homeless guy, on the bench. He tried to get them off me."

"Did he? Anyway, he shouted so loud these men from the pub came over to help and they caught hold of those brutes, while he tried to stop you bleeding to death. He must have known some first aid, thank God. If he hadn't…" She paused, squeezed his hand, and took a deep breath. "Anyway, as soon as the police arrived and arrested them, and you'd gone off in the ambulance, he seems to have vanished. We wanted to find him, to thank him, but there was no sign of him. Not even anything left on the bench. It was as if he'd never been there. It's all a bit odd. Sophie says he was an angel. But she - well, bless her, but she is a bit melodramatic, isn't she?"

"Yeah, that's her. Angels and miracles everywhere. So Danny's been arrested?"

"Yes. You know his name? You know who he was?"

"Yeah, but I don't know why he went for me - least, I don't think I do. No - I can't tell. I suppose there'll be a court case, or something."

"Oh, no. The police have been to see us, though they'll want to interview you at some point. Anyway, the point is, they say, is that he was carrying a knife and class-A drugs, and there are plenty of witnesses to the attack, even some CCTV. And it's not his first offence. He's pretty well known to the police, they said, shoplifting, car theft, stuff like that. They said that he's pleaded guilty. He'll go to the Crown Court and then straight to prison, almost certainly. And probably both his accomplices. So that's a relief, at least."

That evening his sister Charlotte phoned him.
"You all right?" she said.
"Yeah. Getting there."
"Good. How's your ankle?"
"In plaster. But it will be OK, they say. After a few weeks."
"OK, good. Honestly, trust you to get beaten up."
"Yeah. Trust me."
"I told you church youth work could be dodgy, didn't I? You should have listened to your big sister."
"Well, yeah, but I still would have gone for the job."
"Really? Getting chased through the streets by knife-wielding maniacs was on your list of 'what I want out of my job'?"
"Um, maybe not. How about yours?"
"A bit less exciting than yours. Going all right, I suppose. I've got masses on my plate getting ready for the end of year accounts. Might be only a few weeks away but it's panic stations here. I'm not supposed to get involved, but it seems like I'm the only person in the office who can work a spreadsheet."

She rattled on for a few minutes about the idiosyncrasies of company tax returns and the successes she'd had applying for trust fund grants. "Landed a big one, 50K, last week. Made up for missing out on two others the month before. Of course, the disadvantage is having to buy cakes for everyone. Go me, though."

"Go you. So it's going well?" Luke said.

"Yes. Well enough. Wish Dad thought that. He's talked about nothing but you, you know, recently. I got so fed up with him going on and on about how well you were doing last year," she said, her voice bitter. "You and James, it was like you were the bloody golden boys. He never says anything about what me or Iain are doing. It doesn't seem to count, with him, cos it's not church work. And now you get yourself mugged, and it's like you're all he cares about. He was on the phone for hours yesterday telling me about you."

"What?"

"Oh, yes, don't you just know it! I'm glad you're getting better, really, though. Sorry to sound off like that about Dad. It bought it all up, somehow. Anyway, I've got to go, work tomorrow. See you. I'll try to get to Merton next weekend, come and see you. Get well soon, God bless and all that, you know."

He found what she'd said hard to believe. His Dad boasting about him to Charlotte? It didn't sound likely at all. And he'd failed anyway, hadn't he? Failed completely. A fallen church youth worker, reduced to stacking shelves, getting beaten up in revenge for sleeping with a girl from the youth club. A useless, complete and utter failure.

CHAPTER THIRTY-EIGHT

When the sun rose, the world glittered. Thick frost decorated the edges of the grass and dead leaves in frills of pale lace, and sparkled upon the dark lines of the branches and twigs. Barbara hadn't expected to sleep, but she had, despite the frigid air and the twitching, rustling noises of the woodland. She had woken early, pulled on a woolly hat, shoes and gloves, wrapped a scarf around her face, crawled out of the tent and stood shivering in the bitter cold, staring at the clearness of the sharp blue sky and the brightness of the snow and frost. Despite the glacial chilliness enveloping her, despite her numb feet, and fingers that ached with cold, she felt strangely peaceful and almost happy. This morning would end it. God had proved as unreliable and distant as her own father.

As she threaded her way through the wood, knocking the filigree of icy crystals from twigs and branches, she heard birdsong. Cheerful, twittering sparrows flitted above her, looking for and finding the last few berries of the winter. A grey squirrel scolded her from high above before lolloping away along a slender branch, its tail flicking behind it. She unwound the scarf and pushed her hat and gloves into her pockets. The morning sun was glowing low on the horizon. Its light blinded her and its faint but persistent warmth seeped into her skin and thawed her face. The blood came tingling back into her fingers. She came to the footpath that led to the canal, crossed a field with two stamping horses blowing clouds of mist into the cold air, then climbed the stile to reach the towpath.

And paused, dazzled.

Bright sunlight reflected from frozen water and flooded the open reach between the snow-covered ridged fields and leafless hedges. It was quiet and still. There were no noises from cars or trains or people. Even the horses and birds had fallen silent. The sky and the polished water shone with glaring light, except where the bare trees encircled the canal with drooping branches. Reeds and grasses by the path incised dark blades against the whiteness of the frosted surface. Barbara went to the edge where the water was clear of frost, making a deep brown border to the pale expanse. She knelt down and touched the water. It was solid, cold, transparent ice. Pale green stems of bullrushes and reeds stood rigid in it. She could see silvery bubbles spread through the glassiness, and below them mud-coated pebbles and leaves on the bottom.

Carefully, she stepped onto the ice. It didn't move. She tiptoed further out and still the ice held.

She walked slowly into the centre and stood motionless, hardly daring to breathe. The canal felt like a great sheet of mile-thick Antarctic ice bearing her weight as if she were as light as a snowflake. She stamped her feet and still the ice remained as unmoving as a glacier. A dust of snow crystals skittered across the surface and around her feet in a faint breeze.

"I'm walking on water," she whispered into the chilling silence.

It seemed God did want her after all. That he would freeze the whole world to keep her alive. She lifted her head and gazed upwards. A strange optimism filled her. It stayed with her as she walked down the centre of the canal. The sun shone on her back and warmed her. The sky blazed pale blue above her and the path ahead was strewn with frost crystals over the frozen waters. It was a clear path. It was obvious. She had to change her mind, admit what a predicament she'd got into and let people know what she needed. She had to find Sophie and ask her for help. Even if Sophie hadn't come to Coventry, so probably didn't care that much about her, she should still try her. And Francis too, she thought. It would mean owning her shame and failure, and giving up that embarrassed stubbornness that didn't want people to know her mistakes and problems. It was a sort of proud self-reliance, she supposed. A sin. What had she really got to be proud about anyway? Just that one phrase, and one frozen canal. If God saw her as a pearl of great price, then she supposed she'd manage to ask for help. She'd manage to survive, even if Sophie, Luke, Francis and Marjorie didn't want to help. Even if she had to go to the Merton Winter Shelter, it would be a step on a way back to a normal life.

She walked back to the edge of the canal, back to her tent, packed some stuff into a bag and zipped up the tent. Then she stood up, breathed in deeply, straightened her shoulders and headed through the wood, up the steps by the bridge and along the road into town.

At the cafe Sophie was just opening up. When she saw Barbara she ran to her, hugged her and exclaimed, "Barbara? Barbara! Oh, praise the Lord, hallelujah! We've been desperately worried about you! Where were you? Luke said you were in Coventry - did you know he was in hospital? Francis and I went to the shelters in Coventry, yesterday evening and they said you'd gone back to Merton. Emma Carrington told us that you might be camping. In this weather! She said she thought you'd probably end up going to the Winter Shelter, but we couldn't find you there or anywhere! We've been frantic! Where were you?"

"Luke was in hospital?"

"Yes, he got mugged, he said he'd seen you, but he was unconscious for days, then he told us. Oh, Barbara, we spent all last night looking for you. We were going to search all the woods, this afternoon, to see if we could find any trace of you. What happened?"

"You looked for me? Did you? Really? Oh, Sophie, oh, thank you! Oh, gosh, Sophie, it's such a long story! I shouldn't have run off, not without telling you. I've been such an idiot."

"Never mind that, at least you're back. I'm going to have to tell Francis! Just let me phone him, OK?"

Barbara hesitated. "Yes, OK, but..." She gestured at her clothes. "Oh, Sophie, I need a wash! I'm filthy! I've been sleeping in a tent, I haven't even cleaned my teeth for three days…"

It was inevitable, irresistible and a relief beyond bounds. She dropped her bag, sat down at one of the cafe tables, sunk her head into her hands, and released all the pent-up tears of the past hurts, sorrows, and struggles of her life.

Much later, she sat curled up on a chair at Sophie's house, with Didymus on her lap and strong sweet tea in a mug on the table in front of her. Just to be clean again was a delight.

"Right! I've got the spare room set up. You can stay there, until we can sort out a flat for you," Sophie said, coming into the room and collapsing onto the sofa.

"Thanks. You are so good, Sophie."

"Don't be silly. Not really. Anyway, it's not me. It's…you know, Christ in me."

"Thanks anyway. I'd like to see Luke. Poor Luke! Fancy him being beaten up like that! Knifed, you said? Oh, gosh, poor boy. It isn't fair, is it, Sophie?"

"I don't know. I don't know what fair is. I think God moves in mysterious ways. There will be some reason for it. Anyway, shall we go to see him tomorrow evening? It's a bit late tonight. And I think you're exhausted, aren't you?"

"Yes, I have to admit it, I am. I haven't been sleeping that well." She shivered again, at the memory of the freezing air in the clammy tent and how it had seeped into her bones until she felt she'd never be warm again. She sipped gratefully at the steaming mug of tea.

"Right. Early night for you! And tomorrow, or maybe the weekend, we'll get the rest of your stuff. Rescue your tent, you know. We can't leave it all there."

"Thanks. Oh - Sophie, I stole that tent!"

"What?" Sophie sat up and leant forward. "Really? Babs, are you serious?"

"Stupid, but I thought it was worth the risk. Honestly, by that time going to prison seemed like a safer option. So I shoplifted it. I'll have to own up, pay for it, shouldn't I?"

Sophie laughed. "Sorry, but I just can't see you as a shoplifter! Don't worry, I'll keep your guilty secret. Tell you what, we'll find some way to give the money to the shop. And we can give the tent to someone."

"Someone homeless. Like me." Barbara wrapped her hands around the mug and sighed.

"Chin up, Babs," Sophie said. "You won't stay homeless. Which reminds me. We need to talk to Francis, and decide what to do. We really really need you back at the church! It's filthy, you wouldn't believe it!"

"What? I've only been away, what, three weeks?"

"OK, well, maybe that's a slight exaggeration. But we'll get that cleaning job back for you. And

Francis wants to see you. He says he owes you an apology."

"Oh, no, he doesn't…no. There's no need for that. I think I need to apologise to everyone for all the trouble I've been. And thanks. Oh, and thank you for what you told Luke. About me. About being a pearl. It, well, I think it means something."

"Gosh! I'd almost forgotten that! I'm so glad Luke told you. Did it help? Did it make sense?"

"Yes. Really. I can't explain it all, but it did. It's strange, but it did."

"Oh. You know, that is such a relief. That it wasn't just random, that it helped." She stared out of the window for a while. "I was beginning to think that God - well, it's just as if it's been a desert time. As if God has walked away from me. It was so hard! Oh, it's silly, but I always thought of myself as a prophet. Not an appreciated one, it's true. And then everything seemed to go wrong, and all the words I got from God were wrong. That about a pearl - I was sure it was God speaking, and I mentioned it to Luke, I don't know why, I meant to tell you anyway, and then you vanished! So I was so, like, just confused. Really confused. It was awful."

She clutched at the glass cross on its cord around her neck.

"I had that word about Luke splitting the church, but what was the point of that? There wasn't anything I could do to prevent it. It was like a train wreck! All I could do was stay faithful. It was awful! Worst part of my life. A really dark time."

"Like a dark night of the soul?"

"Yes, I guess so. Look."

She sat forward, and pushed her sleeves up, showing her forearm to Barbara.

"Barbara, you're not the only one who gets into a mess. See that?"

Barbara leant forward. All along Sophie's arm were faded irregular-shaped bruises. One, near her wrist, was a circle of dark marks. It looked like a bite.

"Sophie, what on earth are they? What happened to you?"

"Don't tell anyone. It's stupid, I know. Christians aren't supposed to do this, are they? But I get so low, like really depressed, and I think that God isn't there, or isn't speaking to me, or doesn't care, and I do that to myself. Then I have to hide it! So stupid! Why don't I trust him a bit more?"

"Oh, Sophie! You poor thing!" Barbara exclaimed. She'd always thought Sophie was the most confident, positive person in Merton. So sure of God, of the bible, of everything. "How can you get depressed? You?"

"I know. I hide it well, don't I? But some days it's just such hard work, just keeping going. Keeping praying, talking to people, smiling. I manage, I keep working while the day lasts, then the night comes. Then I come back here and it all goes to pieces. I just curl up in the corner, with the lights off, I can't even pray, and…"

She shook her head. "No, it's too bad. I won't go on and on about it. But I thought you ought to know. We're all in the same boat, all of us in a mess. Me too. Anyway, sufficient for the day is the evil thereof. Maybe you can pray for me. And I'll pray for you."

"Bear one another's burdens…" Barbara said. "Yes. All right."

CHAPTER THIRTY-NINE

It was quiet in the hospital. Luke's mother had decided to return to Telford for a couple of days and come back mid-week. The nurses changed Luke's dressings and took out his stitches, the doctors cut down on his painkillers, and the occupational therapist made him get up and practise walking with crutches. The consultant had promised him that he'd be out within a few days. But between the hospital routines, stuck in a side ward next to a somnolent man recovering from a broken hip, all he could do was lie there, listening to music on his phone, posting photographs of his cast onto the internet, or just stare at the ceiling tiles, thinking, longing for something, anything. Some purpose, some point to it all.

The next afternoon, he started walking up and down the ward with a single crutch. The therapist had told him not to put any weight on the broken ankle for a minimum of four weeks, but at least he was allowed out of bed and could move about. He reached the window, stared out at the frost-sprinkled roofs and the grey clouds covering the early morning blue, wedged the crutch more firmly under his arm, swung round his foot, feeling the heavy weight of the cast, and set off again. It was getting easier.

Suddenly Luke stopped. Naomi stood in the doorway, watching him with serious eyes. She'd put her hair into a thick ponytail. Her fingers twisted the hem of her jumper.

"Er, hi Luke," she said.

He stood, balanced on one leg and his crutch, looking at her. With her hair pulled back her slanting cheekbones were clearly marked, throwing shadows on her cheeks. She looked older and thinner but as beautiful as ever. His heart beat insistently on the wall of his chest.

"Naomi! You're back," he said, but he couldn't think of anything else to say. All he wanted to do was lurch forward and hold her. She took a step towards him.

"I just wanted to see if you were all right," she said.

"Um, yeah, fine," he replied.

"Can I, I don't know, can I stop a bit? Talk to you?"

"Yeah, sure, of course. Um, there's a couple of chairs next to my bed."

He turned round and hobbled back to his bed in the corner of the ward. Naomi took off her coat and sat on the edge of one of the chairs. Luke slowly lowered himself onto the other chair, leaning the crutch against the bed, and watched her, remembering how she'd shouted at him and stormed off the last time they'd met.

"I shouldn't have said that," he started to say, but Naomi spoke at the same time. "I heard about you being attacked. Danny really hurt you, didn't he?" she said.

"It's all right."

"I heard you'd broken your ankle and got stabbed and knocked out. That's not what I'd call alright."

"Oh. Suppose not."

"No, it's not alright. Not really, is it? I'm sorry. It was 'cos of me, wasn't it?"

"Well, I dunno - I suppose so, in a way, yeah. But it's not your fault."

"No, maybe not. But I still didn't want something like that to happen to you. And it wouldn't have done, he wouldn't have done that if I'd…"

She stared down at her feet.

"Whatever, I wish he hadn't gone for you like that. He's got so vicious, these days. He used to be all right, you know. He could be really sweet and gentle, when he was younger."

Luke thought of the twisted, hate-filled expression on Danny's face when he was stabbing the knife in.

"Why's he changed?" he said.

"Drugs, I think. Anyway, he's in prison now. That's why I came back."

"Came back? You mean you've come back to Merton?" Luke sat up and leaned closer to her. She smiled slightly.

"Like my mum always says - it's an ill wind. Yeah, it's safe now. I'm back at home. With Jessie."

"Bet she was glad."

"Yeah. She made me a 'welcome home' card. As big as this." She held her hands a couple of feet apart. Luke laughed.

"That's great. Literally," he said. "At least something's come out of it."

"Luke, but he knifed you, him and his mates. They pretty nearly killed you."

"Nearly did, yeah," Luke said. "I was sh… I was really scared, honestly, Naomi. I don't think I've ever run so fast in all my life."

"You must have been terrified."

"Yeah! I just walked around the corner, and there he was. And as soon as he recognised me, he just flipped. He wanted to know where you were and then he went for me. He said he was going to kill me."

Naomi shuddered. "I hate him. I really do," she exclaimed.

"I don't really understand why. I mean, why'd he go for me like that? He said he'd teach me to touch his - his bitch. Sorry, but that's what he said. He meant you… But he's your brother!"

"Step-brother, sort of, but not really. His dad never married my Mum, so I'm not sure what you'd call him. But he's not my brother! It's not like that. And I'm not his. But he thinks I am. Er, Luke, don't hate me for this. But we used to sleep together."

"What?" Luke gripped hard on the arms of his

chair. "You - and him?"

"Fraid so. Last year. Then I wanted to stop, and that's when he beat me up."

"Naomi… Oh, what a mess. God help us, Naomi. What a mess!"

"Yeah. I'm sorry - really sorry, Luke. Suppose I should have told you about him. But I never told him about you, honest! He got hold of Jessie's phone, made her give it him, and I'd texted her stuff about you."

"You told her?"

"No! Not about us, not about that night! I wouldn't do that! I'm not stupid!"

"No, I guess not. But I don't get it."

"For God's sake, Luke! She's my sister. We're really close! She knows… Well, she guessed something about us. She just sent me a few texts. Teasing me about you. You know. And I replied. And Danny saw them, and jumped to conclusions, I guess."

"Oh. So that's why."

"Look, Luke, I'm really sorry about what happened. I mean, it was - partly, I guess - my fault. You'll be all right, won't you?"

"I reckon so. I'm a tough kid! No worries! No, seriously, Naomi, don't worry. It'll be fine. I'll be out of here within a week."

She picked her bag up from the floor and hunted through it, pulling out a white envelope.

"Here. I got you a card. Don't open it until I've gone, though. It's a bit naff. I got it from that Christian Bookshop. I thought you'd like one with a bible verse or summat on it."

She handed it to him. As Luke took it, their fingers touched. Her skin was warm and smooth; her steady dark eyes on his face. It seemed a long moment, as she looked at him and he looked back. Then she dropped her eyes and reached back into her bag.

"I got you summat else, too. I asked the bookshop lady for something like Game of Thrones but Christian, and she nearly wet herself laughing! But she said try this. She said it had lots of angels, lots of action. It's by some American guy."

Luke looked at the muscular white-clad angel on the cover, brandishing a sword over its head. "Frank Peretti," he said. "Wow. Thanks. Looks good. It'll be a relief to have something exciting to read while I'm stuck in here."

"Sure. I'm reading another C.S. Lewis. 'Problem of Pain'. It's interesting. I'm really getting into it."

"Isn't it a bit, well, a bit heavy?"

"I'm not thick, Luke! I can read stuff! I've got 4 A-levels. I'd have gone to uni, like you, if it hadn't been for Jessica."

"Really? You stayed at home for her?"

"Yeah, well, Mum isn't that brilliant, sometimes, at looking after her. I thought she needed me. Maybe I'll still go, one day, when Jessie's a bit older."

"Good for you. I'm glad you like the book. Naomi…" He reached out and touched the pale line on her cheekbone. "That scar. Danny did that, didn't he? It looks like it was really deep."

"Yeah, my face hit the door latch, when he beat

me up. We're both of us a bit battered, aren't we? Is that where Danny stabbed you?" Naomi said, pointing at the large dressing on his stomach.

"Oh, yeah. Perhaps I should cover up. I forgot I'm only half-dressed," he said, tying the dressing-gown cord around his waist.

"Sexy pyjama trousers, though."

"You're not serious! They're awful! Old man's PJs!"

"Yeah!" She leaned forward to tug at the faded striped flannel. "All baggy. One pull and they'd fall down."

Luke laughed. "Don't try it, please! Hey, Naomi, there's something I've got to say to you. To tell you. About what I said in Leamington. I was wrong."

"Wrong about what?" she said, looking seriously at him.

There was a sudden cough from the other side of the bed. Luke looked up. A nurse stood in the doorway. Next to her was Luke's manager, Ms Johnson, from the supermarket.

"You have another visitor, Luke," the nurse said.

"Tell me another time. I'd better go," Naomi said, grabbing her coat and bag. "I've got to go to the gym. They said they might be able to give me some work, maybe even my old job, now that I'm back. Er, see you, Luke, OK?"

"Um, OK. Bye," Luke said. He wanted to add, 'come back tomorrow, please', but Ms Johnson had already sat down on the vacated chair and was pulling papers out of her briefcase. Naomi walked out. She didn't look back. But at least she was back in Merton, and she'd come to see him. He'd see her again, he'd make sure of that, he thought, as he tried to pay attention to what his boss was saying.

"You made the front page of the local rag, did you know that? 'Knife attack in town centre'. Just what they like. Meat and drink to them. And some of the staff got together to give you this."

She pulled out a big card. It had 'Get well soon' written on it in lurid orange above a cartoon of a grumpy man in a hospital bed, with a bandaged leg in a hoist, a bed pan on the floor and a fat matron taking his pulse and frowning.

"Bit old-fashioned, I know. But I'm sure you'll like these better," Ms Johnson continued, putting a box of Dairy Milk on the bed. "Now, I've spoken briefly to the consultant, and we'll get your sick leave sorted. Six weeks, initially, I think. Here's the form. And when you get back, we want you to go onto the tills. For a while, especially if you've still got the cast on. Now, let me go through the process with you."

After she'd gone, Luke climbed back into bed. He felt exhausted, and the aches in his side and ankle had magnified. Images of Naomi's concerned and gentle face flitted through his mind. He wanted to lie quietly, and remember everything she'd said and how she'd looked. The envelope from her was on the side table. He opened it. She was right, it was a pretty naff card. A depressed-looking kitten trying to climb out of an empty goldfish-bowl, for some reason. The photo had nothing to do with being ill. Unless the kitten had eaten the goldfish and was about to throw up. Inside it said 'I am the

Lord who heals you', and Naomi had written, 'Sorry about all this. Hope you get better quickly. Love, Naomi.' No kisses, just love, Naomi. Love Naomi. He had to admit it. He did.

CHAPTER FORTY

"Well, welcome back. Back to the house of God," Francis said, opening wide the etched glass doors into the new atrium. "You have had quite a journey, but in returning and rest you shall be saved. I believe so, anyway."

"Pardon?" Barbara said.

"It's a bible verse, Isaiah thirty something. I really ought to know but I expect Sophie would give you chapter and verse. Anyway, welcome back, my dear, into God's house. Such a relief to have you back! You have suffered, I know, but I hope that that is all over now."

"Yes. I hope so too."

"So, this is our new building." Francis gestured at the cream-painted walls, the sandstone-coloured tiled floor, the large windows. "The atrium, I should say. The cafe. Of course, the new path and paved area are yet to be done."

Barbara looked up at the clear skylights set into

the warm timbers and cross-beams of the roof. Scraps of late frost were clinging to the glass, partly obscuring the blue and pale grey of the early spring sky. There was a faint scent of not-yet-dry plaster and new paint. But the cool sunlight still shone onto the bookcases and reflected gleams from the polished brass door handles and fingerplates.

"It's beautiful," she said, running her fingers over the grain of the pale oak doors that stood open in the doorway of the church.

"Limed oak. Expensive, but beautiful."

"The space - it's huge. So big - but it seems so calm. Spacious."

"Yes, it is, isn't it?" said Francis enthusiastically. "We are all delighted. Even though it was not a popular decision to spend Ivy's money on this, I think she would have been pleased. It was such an innovative idea, to roof in the dead space - as the architect called it - between the church and the hall. And it's given us space for a small bookstall, as well as a cafe. Big enough for meetings, big enough for parties, you could almost have a ceilidh in here, it's so spacious. With that, and the new kitchen… You haven't seen it in all its glory, have you? Let's gloat over it together..."

He opened the hatches between the atrium and the church hall's kitchen.

"Goodness," said Barbara. "Wow! Oh, that is - that is wonderful!"

"Yes. Even I, inexperienced as I am about kitchens, think it is splendid. Just splendid. Daphne insisted. I gulp when I think of the cost - tens of thousands - but we believe it will be worth it."

Barbara nodded and sighed. She looked longingly at the three-minute dishwasher, the hot water dispenser and the massive double cooker. The kitchen shone with stainless steel and gleaming white tiles. She couldn't imagine it ever smelling of mice, unlike the old one. There was a polished steel fridge the size of a wardrobe, a commercial microwave, and even a semi-automatic espresso maker. She'd used one of those at Thomson's. It had made fragrant, strong, perfect coffee in minutes. She'd love to work in that kitchen.

Francis shut the hatches and turned back to gesture at the bleached wood tables and chairs, the squishy red sofas, the cream fleece scatter cushions, and the low coffee tables.

"And all this new furniture too. I must say, I'm very excited at the possibilities. We are right on a busy street, and if we can open the cafe every day, we will have such opportunities for connecting with the local community."

"Yes. And make a little money, too."

Francis laughed. "Yes, well, that too! Churches are always chronically short of money."

He opened the main door to the church. She looked round. Someone had clearly tidied up. Several massive new cupboards stood against one wall.

"As you can see, we have had a blitz," Francis said. "Although no one dared remove the ancient hymn books, or offend the flower rota posse by throwing out the used oasis, we've managed to hide most of the clutter in those new cupboards. I daren't open them. I suspect that would release a minor landslide of candle holders and used Christmas decorations. Anyway, Barbara, let me show you where I put your things."

"Thanks. I'm so sorry about all that. About leaving my stuff here, and…you know…"

"No, don't be, please. It was just as much my fault as yours, to have reacted so crassly and unsympathetically. I'm truly sorry. You thought that I, er, that I believed you to have helped the thieves, I realised afterwards."

Barbara looked down at the terracotta tiles of the floor, remembering the humiliation and misery of that moment, and nodded.

"What can I say? I did think, forgive me, just for a moment, that you'd forgotten to lock the door properly, and that was how they'd got in. But I never, not for one moment, thought worse of you than that."

"Oh. Oh, I see. Thank you," she murmured. "But I shouldn't have…"

"It was still a terrible thing for me to have thought. And, I keep thinking, what sort of church are we, if one of us can be in such trouble as you and not feel they can ask for help? Barbara, dear, I am so, so sorry." He took her hand. "I don't think words can express it."

"That's all right. It's, well, it's fine now. I think I'll get sorted, with you and Sophie helping."

"Good, very good," Francis replied, releasing her hand and going ahead of her up the stairs to the balcony. "But it is still regrettable. A reproach. You worked so hard at the cleaning and we barely thanked you, and paid you a pittance, and did nothing when you needed help. I'm sorry."

"Francis, it's fine now," Barbara said. "I think, maybe, we should stop apologising to each other, don't you? Otherwise, we'll never get anywhere."

"Yes, of course, I am sorry that I keep saying sorry. Oh - I said it again, so sorry!" he said, with the ghost of a wink at her. "You're right. One should say sorry, accept forgiveness, and move on."

Barbara smiled briefly, turned away to look round the balcony. "It's been tidied up here too, hasn't it? Did you ever find out who'd broken in? Who the burglars were?"

"No. Not a hint or fingerprint or scrap of evidence, sadly. Not even anything on the CCTV cameras in the street. The police suspect the builders - they appear to have been very lax about the keys, and one set has gone missing - but they haven't got very far in any investigations. I expect, given the fact that there are far worse crimes being committed and that they are under-manned and over-stretched, that they are not - how shall I put it? Putting their best men on the case."

"Oh. That's a pity."

"Well, never mind. We were insured, thanks to Marjorie, and very little was actually stolen. Anyway, there are your boxes. Behind that screen. Still safe."

"Thanks."

Barbara opened one of the boxes. Carefully, she took out the model Dakota and unwound its bubble wrap and foam. It looked forlorn. The broken wing was trailing, one wheel was missing and the tail fin was bent. She wrapped the newspaper back round it, paused, and looked at the other boxes. Only six. So few. She had so little left of any value. It was a clean start, perhaps. She scrunched up the Dakota and felt the plastic snap underneath the paper. Yes. Time to move on.

"Er, can you put that in the bin, please?" she said, passing it to Francis.

"Yes, but are you sure?"

"Oh, yes. Very sure. I need to… I think I need less unnecessary clutter in my life. If I'm going to be living out of boxes for a while, anyway."

"I hope you won't have to, not for long, at least. Yes, I'll take this and put it in the bin. What's that, underneath?"

"Oh. Er, nothing. Well, another model."

"Can I have a look?"

Barbara passed it to him. He gently removed the wrapping from the VW Camper van with its bright, fractal red, yellow, black and orange paint.

"Oh, goodness. How bright. How fascinating! What on earth is it? I've never seen anything like this."

"It's based on World War One dazzle camouflage patterns. From the ferry in Liverpool, called the Razzle Dazzle ferry. I, er, I thought it would look nice."

"You painted it? Well, Barbara, you are a surprisingly complex person. You do have hidden talents. What about everything else? What other secrets do you have tucked away in that box?"

"Nothing, honestly." She blushed slightly, and laughed. "Just more models, but nothing quite so interesting. I'll keep the rest, for a while. I'll take them to Sophie's house."

"I'll help you carry them. And what are your plans now, my dear?"

"Sophie's happy for me to stay with her for a few months, bless her. I'm looking for more work. I managed to sort out some benefits, and I'm going to save up for a deposit for another flat," she said, lifting one of the boxes. "And I was going to talk to Christians Against Poverty next week, see if they can help, give me advice, and so on."

"That sounds an excellent plan," Francis said, taking another box. "I'm so pleased you've returned to your job here. The church was, even to my uncritical eyes, in sad need of a little regular dusting and polishing. Especially after the builders had turned it into a dust bath. And painting too, as well as cleaning. Perhaps you could paint dazzle camouflage all over that dreadfully ugly font. And, of course, when we open the cafe, we will need a manager. I wonder if you would be interested in that?"

CHAPTER FORTY-ONE

The end credits for Portal Two rolled, the music played and Luke tossed the games controller onto the floor, yawned, stretched and heaved his ankle, with the cumbersome cast, onto the sofa arm. His phone rang.

"Luke, darling, thought I'd ring to see how you are?" his mother said.

"Oh, fine."

"Really?"

"Well, it's a bit boring to be honest. I'm getting fed up of watching 'Friends' and brain-dead quizzes."

"I bet you are, darling. Just be patient. Your cast will be coming off tomorrow, won't it?"

"Yeah. Can't wait."

"Are you eating properly?"

"Of course!" Luke thought, guiltily, of the small pile of takeaway containers in the kitchen. He'd tried to cook, balanced on one leg and a crutch, but it hadn't been easy.

"Don't lie to me, darling. I think I'll come over for a day or two next week."

"Just you?"

"Simon sends his love and prayers, but he's busy. So you'll escape the fatherly lectures. It'll just be me, coddling you and force-feeding you home-made casserole and fruit crumbles."

"That'd be nice, to be honest."

"So, tell me what you've been doing, who's visited, did that lovely girl Sophie come round? And, nagging mother that I am, I have to ask, have you been doing your physio exercises?"

After she'd hung up, Luke checked his phone again for messages. None. His Sheffield friends, Sophie, Francis, his work colleagues, the youth club kids, his parkour mates - all busy, he guessed. He tossed it onto the cushion, leaned forward and rubbed at the aches in his leg. Perhaps he should go out, try to hobble round to Sophie's cafe, just to see what was going on. She'd told him about Barbara turning up. At least that had worked out all right, despite his failure, even though everything else he'd been involved in had gone so pear-shaped. What a waste of space he was. He could barely walk, he couldn't work, he couldn't run, it would be weeks before his ankle was better.

He remembered what had Barbara had said at the Winter Shelter. That people thought he was worse than a failure, that he was a paedophile. He clenched his fists. No wonder he'd been asked to leave St. Bart's by that stiff-faced vicar, and turned down as a Winter Shelter volunteer. If people thought that about him... How could he do anything worthwhile here? All those kids at the youth club - in such trouble and need, yet there was no way he could get involved now, even if the youth club hadn't closed. Was there any point in staying? He couldn't even go to church. A pariah - a real pariah.

Start again, somewhere else? He stared up at the ceiling.

"OK, God," he muttered. "I give up. I don't know what to do, but I can't stay here, just stacking shelves, not doing anything useful. I give up. I give up!"

His phone buzzed. Listlessly, he picked it up. It was a message from Sophie.

Hi Luke. Hope you're OK, will call round soon. Praying for you lots, of course. I forgot to give you that bible verse I had for you. So here it is. Song of Songs 5:5. Be encouraged.

What was she talking about? He thought for a while then remembered. She'd said something about a random verse that she'd picked out when she'd was deciding whether to tell him where Naomi was. That must be the one she meant. Song of Songs? That was odd, he thought. It was not usually the book of choice for Christians giving each other bible verses. He looked it up.

'I arose to open for my beloved, and my hands dripped with myrrh, my fingers with sweet-smelling myrrh.'

He read through the verses before and after, dropped the book, breathed in deeply and leaned back against the sofa with his eyes wide. What? Sophie had picked that verse? That verse! Porn in the bible and he'd never noticed.

He remembered someone at Spring Harvest saying that 'Song of Songs' was essentially an erotic poem about romantic love. Fingers dripping myrrh…That night with Naomi: the warmth, the skin, the sweetness.

She was one, huge overwhelming reason to stay in Merton. He remembered what else Barbara had said. That he should talk to Francis and tell him all the truth. That Marjorie Fowler was the one who had started the rumours. That she hated him, and had spread the gossip about him on to Daphne and Ted. He sat up and phoned Francis's number.

"So, you see," Luke said, in Francis's study a few days later. "It was… It was rumours, gossip, slander. And a misunderstanding. I should have told you everything."

"Hmm. My goodness, what a complete muddle and mix-up we have all made of it," said Francis, standing up and going to the window to look out over the garden. The snow had long since gone, the ground frost had thawed, and early April rain soaked the trees and long grass. He stood, watching the raindrops trickling down the window pane, then turned back to Luke.

"I am constantly amazed by how easily small mistakes explode into giant disasters. I mean, look at Henry VIII. One menopausal wife and suddenly all the monasteries are destroyed."

"Huh?"

"A comparison with Henry VIII doesn't really help, does it? Not in this case. Hmm. You, Barbara… As I said, what a muddle. George had told me some of this, but there seemed to be nothing I could do. I owe you an apology, as does all the PCC, I think. And reparation, of course. What do you want me to do?"

Luke shrugged.

"Reinstate the youth club, although that would be difficult, give you your job back?"

"Um, I dunno..."

"Perhaps it was rather more dangerous than you expected...I mean, no one normally expects church youth work to involve running for your life from thugs and then getting beaten up, knocked unconscious, stabbed and kicked. Which reminds me, I'm sorry to see that you're still having to use the crutch."

"Yeah, cast's been off a couple of days, but it's still not quite right, not yet, anyway."

"We are praying for you. Well, me and Sophie and Barbara. I don't expect Marjorie is though... Anyway, what do you think about the youth club?"

"Um, to be honest, I don't really feel ready for it at the moment. I feel a bit too - too battered, I reckon. Like I've got my fingers really burnt. Maybe later."

"After the scars have healed? Maybe after a few more years experience in the real world? Is that what you want?"

Luke hesitated. What did he want? Apart from Naomi?

"Yeah. I think so. I reckon I need a bit more experience - maturity, to be honest, to do youth work again. Yeah, I still want to, one day. But not just yet."

"I understand. Wise, I think."

"But, even without going back, I hate this feeling that people think I'm a - well, you know. It was way out of line for them to say that!"

"Yes, you're right," Francis said, sitting on the sofa opposite Luke. He sighed. "I will have to talk to the PCC, and let them all know you have been falsely slandered, and there is no basis to all the gossip. To tell them - order them - to stop it and apologise. Oh dear, that will be difficult."

Luke nodded. "And Mrs Fowler?" he said, adding 'the cow' under his breath.

"Well, Marjorie must apologise to you too."

"Yeah, right - though I don't really want to see her or talk to her. I just feel like - well, to be honest, I'd rather not see her just yet. I'd rather punch her than talk to her."

"Goodness, I imagine you do. However, perhaps this is not the right moment to preach forgiveness to you. Er, what about the others? Daphne, Ted - they seem to have been involved as well."

"Yeah. Them too."

"Very well. Look, Luke, the complication is that you did admit to sleeping with one of the youth club. Although, technically speaking, Naomi Robeson isn't, of course. She was well over eighteen and was only coming to keep her sister company, as I understand it. Anyway, the point is, what shall I tell them in your defence? I imagine you and Miss Robeson don't want further gossip going the rounds."

"No, I guess not," Luke said, running his hand through his hair. "I don't know. Keep her out of it, if you can."

"Hmm. Yes, I think I can do that. You have told me all the truth, all the story, in confidentiality. And it was based on a misunderstanding, anyway."

Francis leaned back in his chair and gazed at the calm fish drifting in his aquarium.

"Oh dear," he murmured. "Community is so hard. Fish are definitely simpler."

He turned back to Luke.

"I am so sorry about the youth club. That is, of course, another casualty of this whole debacle. But, apparently, Barbara and Sophie are hatching some plans for the future. For some sort of young people's cafe in the new building. I'm sure they'll welcome your help."

"Really? Wow. Good for them," Luke exclaimed. "I'll talk to Sophie. But, listen, Francis, I don't want to have this shadow over my head. I want to come back to church without pointing fingers and whispering."

Francis nodded. "I understand. It must be completely cleared up."

"So I want you to talk to everyone, not just the PCC. Everyone in Holy Trinity. And the other church leaders in Merton as well."

"Yes, of course. I will have to eat a certain amount of humble pie myself, I think."

Luke shrugged. "Yeah, I reckon so."

"Mistakes… mistakes. To err is human…" Francis muttered, steepling his fingers together. "Anyway, you need a complete public exoneration. I shall arrange that…And perhaps a sermon against gossip. Now, it's James, isn't it, who talks about the tongue as a fire…"

He picked up a notebook from his desk and started to make notes.

"Er, see PCC, see Marjorie, see Ted, see Daphne, sermon; oh, and talk to all the other local church leaders about you. Explain everything to them."

"And the Winter Shelter leaders too. They refused to let me volunteer for them!"

"Did they? Oh, yes, certainly, I'll have to speak to them as well. Goodness, I will be busy. Which reminds me, how would it be if you came on the PCC? That would be a very public declaration of confidence in you. And your advice and comments would be welcome. You are still, technically, a church member. So I believe I can co-opt you."

Luke thought for a moment. "Um, yeah, that'd be brilliant. Yeah - really brilliant. I'd get to vote, wouldn't I?"

Francis laughed. "Of course. But I don't think many people would call joining a PCC brilliant!"

"Can you do that? Co-opt me? Marjorie and co would vote against me."

"Well, Barbara has returned. She's still on the PCC. And I can - let me see." He thought for a while, then chuckled. "Yes. Positively Machiavellian. I can see a way to arrange it. Once I've seen Daphne, Ted, Marjorie. Yes, pure Machiavelli."

CHAPTER FORTY-TWO

Marjorie knocked a rapid staccato on the door of the vicarage. There was no response and no noise from inside. She knocked again and tapped her feet impatiently. She had almost decided to leave when the door opened.

"Honestly, Francis, about time," she exclaimed. "You knew I was coming at four. It's five past!"

"Is it? I was just feeding the fish. My watch must be a bit slow. Anyway, come in. Let me take your coat. Er, coffee? Tea?"

"No, thanks. I hope that this won't take too long, whatever it is."

She strode into the study and looked around contemptuously. "As tidy as ever, I see," she sneered.

"You would be hugely disappointed if I changed my organic chaos for a namby-pamby alphabetical filing system, wouldn't you? What would you scold me about? Heaven forfend I should take that from you."

Marjorie shrugged, pushed a copy of the Church Times off an armchair and sat down. Francis followed and sat at his desk, rather than on the sofa opposite. For a moment Marjorie thought about changing chairs. He was slightly higher than her and she didn't like having to look upwards at him. But it was a trivial thing.

"Right, Francis, what's this all about? I wanted to see you anyway about Luke. It isn't at all appropriate that he is still living - rent-free - in the church house. I warn you, I'm going to raise this at the next PCC meeting, I'm afraid!"

"Ah, yes. Luke. Well, one small thing is that he isn't living rent-free. He's paying a moderate amount, slightly under market rates, I must admit, but a reasonable amount. I can't understand how you didn't know that. I'm sure it's in the treasurer's reports."

Marjorie snorted. "Well, you might have told me. You know I don't have time to read all the fine detail in Ted's reports. But that's beside the point. Luke shouldn't be in that house! Especially now he's got himself into so much trouble that he's getting revenge attacks in the street. God only knows what sort of crowd he's getting in with! I want him out, Francis! Out of that house and out of Merton!"

"It is about Luke that I asked you to come here," Francis replied mildly. "To discuss him. It appears that you have taken a quite unreasonable dislike to him."

"He was a mistake right from day one. He even

skipped the first youth group session, remember? Failed his driving test twice. Unreliable, inexperienced, liberal, underhand…"

"You see. You're attitude to him is quite vindictive, if I may say so."

"Vindictive?" Marjorie sat upright and glared at him.

"Yes, I think so. Marjorie, my dear, I am worried about you and about this unforgiving, harsh spirit." He leaned forward, his elbows on the desk and his fingers steepled together. "As your vicar, I need to speak to you about it. This is a serious matter. Please, will you be patient and hear me out?"

"Oh, very well!" Marjorie sat back down and folded her arms. "Carry on."

"It appears that Luke has been seriously slandered. There have been allegations and rumours of all sorts; hints of paedophilia, abuse of the boys at the youth club and the parkour group. These, I do not need to tell you, are very serious allegations."

"What of it? I told you, I warned you, about him."

"Well, there are the legal issues. There is no evidence, none at all. Luke's been completely exonerated. Whoever is responsible for this could face a charge of slander. But that is beside the point. I don't expect it to come to that."

"Slander?" Marjorie looked up, startled. But she was safe. It had been Daphne and Ted who'd started the rumours. Not her.

"Even if it is slander, I don't see what I've got to do with it!"

"The thing is, Marjorie, is that although I am sure Daphne and Ted did most of the gossiping, it appears that it all started with you and your dislike and prejudice against Luke."

"I deny it."

Francis sighed. "I'm sure you do. However, I have spoken, in private, to Ted and to Daphne. They have both agreed to leave Holy Trinity."

"What!"

"Yes. They are going to leave. To leave both Holy Trinity and the PCC. In fact, technically, they have already left."

Marjorie stared at him. He looked back, his hands folded under his chin, his face calm and unusually determined. She let her anger rise. How could he take Luke's side - again!

"How dare you! Making them leave? You can't do that, Francis! They were doing what was right! Trying to protect the youth!"

"I'm afraid I have."

"Throwing someone out of church?" she snapped. "You? Since when have you been so assertive? You've usually got as much backbone as a damp dishcloth, and suddenly you're practically bullying people out!"

"Yes, well, I am aware that I am, generally, too much of an appeaser. I am too concerned with peace, rather than justice and leadership. But this situation…Yes, I have had to be assertive. I spoke to the dean and bishop as well, and they have backed me up about this."

"But Daphne? Ted? He's the treasurer! You need them!"

"Nevertheless, they have agreed to go. I don't think they liked it here any more, anyway. They weren't too enthusiastic about traditional hymns and Book of Common Prayer, and they blame me for the falling congregation. The proverb about rats leaving a sinking ship comes to mind. And I am a bit too 'wishy-washy', as Daphne put it. We'll have to manage without them. Fortunately, I've spoken to George and he's agreed to have a go at being treasurer."

Marjorie clutched the arms of her chair.

"George? He hasn't said anything to me!"

"No, I asked him not to. We had a long discussion about you, Stephen, Luke; about all that has happened recently."

"How dare you! It's none of your business!" she said, leaping up. "How dare you discuss me and my son?" Her lost, dissolute, corrupted, beloved son.

"Marjorie, your well-being, your soul's well-being, is my business, I'm afraid."

"And what about the PCC? Its well-being? Honestly, you've just got rid of two key members. The church is disintegrating and it's your fault - your weakness, bias and liberal faffing around!"

Francis stood up and went over to the aquarium.

"We'll come on to that. But for now, I want you to think about something. Come here, look at these fish - they're all different, they have different needs, roles, food, colours; some like to mosey along on the stones at the bottom, some like to hide in the weeds; some swim alone, some in a group."

Marjorie glanced at the aquarium then turned contemptuously away.

"Just what has this got to do with anything?"

"Bear with me. You could say that it's a community, like the church. They don't eat or attack each other. Of course, the metaphor can be overstretched."

"And your point is?"

"That there's some fish you just can't mix. Daphne and Ted, I'm sorry to say, are like piranhas. One scent of blood and they attack. It wasn't what they said, as how much they delighted in it all. It was essentially a feeding-frenzy of character assassination. The bishop and I agreed that it was best for everyone if they left."

"Oh. And me? Am I a piranha too?"

"Maybe you are an angel fish and a little too territorial to share space, perhaps? I'm not sure. Though at the moment I think you are more like a puffer fish, all spikes, but they are protective spikes. You are seriously hurt by the revelation about Stephen, underneath it all, so you are lashing out to protect yourself."

"Thank you for the psycho-analysis!" Marjorie snapped back.

"No, please, Marjorie, please listen. I know you feel you've lost Stephen, but you haven't. He's just not quite what you wanted and you have to accept him as he is, that's all."

"That's all! Much you know about it! That's it. I've had enough. I'm going." She stalked to the door.

"In a minute, please, Marjorie! I have something important to tell you and to ask you."

"Are you throwing me out of the church too?"

She paused.

"No! No, of course not," Francis said, sitting back at his desk. "Marjorie, I - strange as it seems at present - I value your help immensely. Please - sit down."

She shook her head.

"Oh. Anyway, I wanted to say, it if hadn't been for your efficiency we would be in an even worse plight. You insisted we got the church contents insured, and you arranged all that, and now that we've experienced a burglary I am so grateful that you did."

"I should think so. You, I seem to remember, were not particularly keen on the idea of insurance."

"I wasn't, but I bowed to your better judgement on that occasion. Thank you. Anyway, do you remember that PCC meeting when we appointed Luke?"

"What of it?"

"There was a question in the Church Times that week, asking why churches were so full of difficult and disagreeable people. I've realised what the answer is. It is because they are faulty. Part of the league of the guilty. They are learning how to be truly human, and in the meantime, in churches, they are accepted, tolerated, even loved despite their unpleasantness. But sometimes you do have to look past the toleration and love and confront the difficulties and disagreeableness."

"So I'm an immature and disagreeable puffer fish, am I? Well, thanks. Your pastoral manner leaves a lot to be desired."

"I have to admit that you are difficult. So am I, for that matter. But what I'm trying to say is, think of all that you have done and given to the church, to God's house. Please, please, sit down and hear me out. I don't want you to lose your church. Or your relationship with God. I want you to stay."

Reluctantly, Marjorie sat down. Suddenly she felt very unsure of herself, and near to tears. If she lost George and Stephen and the church and God too, what would be left? She bent her head and bit her lip to stop the tears. There was quiet for a few moments.

"Marjorie, there's an emergency PCC meeting on Friday night, at half-past seven."

"Is there?" Marjorie took a deep breath and lifted her chin defiantly. "What are you playing at, Francis? Calling a PCC meeting without telling me? And, I assume, no Daphne or Ted?"

"I'm telling you now, Marjorie. I don't know if you know - but I expect that you do - that Barbara is back in Merton."

"Oh, yes. I heard all that. What a stupid mess to have got herself into!"

"Well, perhaps. But we won't go into that now. After all, we all get into messes, I think. Look at you and Stephen. Anyway, she will be there on Friday, since she is still a PCC member, and also Sophie and Luke will be there. I'm co-opting them onto the PCC."

"What! Honestly? Over my dead body, Francis!"

"I do hope it won't come to that! I know you will object, but Barbara and George and the others have already agreed to vote them on. So even if you and Henry vote against them, they will be co-opted."

"You conniving…No, I won't say it…"

"I'm afraid so, Marjorie. I have had to connive a little, in order to rescue the situation."

"I'm not coming on Friday. I'll leave. I'll resign. I'm not staying on the PCC with those two."

"Yes, I expected that you probably would, and that Henry would too. But I hope that you will stay in the church. That is what I want to ask you. George will stay, of course. Especially with the organ being restored."

"You think you've won, don't you?"

"It's not a competition, Marjorie! And even it if was, remember that you have gained something. You could say that you've won. You've rescued the organ, you've kept the church as you wanted it: traditional, robed choir, sung matins, BCP, no youth work, no drums, no guitars, no doughnuts, no modern worship songs."

"Well, it suits you better, Francis," Marjorie said acidly, drumming her fingers on the arm of the chair. "You're never going to be a trendy, motorbike-riding, tattooed modern vicar, are you?"

"Perhaps you're right. I thought you were wrong, last year, to prompt us to initiate a Compline evening service mid-week, but the number of people who come to it is rising every week. I myself find it surprisingly refreshing."

"You're a traditionalist yourself, face it."

"After all, there are plenty of other churches in Merton who do the trendy stuff: Alpha courses, electric guitars, Hillsong anthems and so on. Where will those who value liturgy, tradition, the older hymns, go to, if we don't provide for them? You were right, I have to admit. I think that the church will recover and might even prosper."

"I usually am right, Francis."

"But you were wrong about Luke and Stephen. He didn't seduce Stephen, and nothing that he did or said to the boy made any difference there."

"I'm still not prepared to discuss my son with you!"

"You will have to face up to Stephen's sexuality at some point. You will have to accept him and forgive him. You know that, so why not do it now?"

"No! Let him suffer for a bit!" she snarled. "I have! Right. I've had enough. Have you got any more to tell me? Any more advice, any bombshells, any more conniving?"

"Er, no, Marjorie."

She stood up.

"That's it, then, Francis. I'll send you my letter of resignation from the PCC tomorrow."

"Very well. Good. Are you going to leave the church too?"

She hesitated. No, that was a step too far.

"I, er, I might stop coming for a few weeks. Especially if Luke and Sophie are there. Or…"

"Well, consider coming to Compline, or to the early communion instead of the half-ten."

"Don't you dare give me any more advice, Francis!"

She strode out, slamming the door behind her. As she walked towards her car, her fists clenched in

impotent fury, Marjorie thought of Stephen.
Francis, the sheep-faced underhanded toe-rag, was
right, although she'd like to tear his dog-collar off.
She'd love to make trouble for him, if she could.
The plotting, conniving, little weasel. Oh, how the
worm had turned! But he'd got the bishop's
support, so what could she do? And what did
Francis and Luke and Daphne and Ted and
everything else matter, compared to losing
Stephen? Francis knew, and she knew, in some
deep place inside herself, that she would have to
forgive her son. She couldn't live permanently
estranged from him, and from George too, as
might be the case if she didn't unbend. But she
wasn't going to make it easy. Let him stew for a
while. For an instant, the memory of Stephen in the
choir at ten; his innocent childish face, his soaring,
unbroken voice; filled her mind. She blinked hard
and leant against the side of her car, trying to shake
the tears away.

CHAPTER FORTY-THREE

"Good recovery," said the physiotherapist, fingering and probing the muscles and bones in Luke's ankle. "Cast's been off five weeks, hasn't it? Not bad. Keep up with the exercises for a few more weeks. Right. You're officially discharged. Don't tangle with any other muggers for a while, right?"

"What about, um, running?"

"Oh, if you're sensible. Walk, jog, run, whatever. You're unlikely to do any damage. Someone told me you're a parkour fan?"

"Yeah, what about that? Can I do that?"

"Within reason. Just don't do base-jumping."

Luke grinned as he walked out of the hospital and into town, ran along the low wall by the Golden Lion pub, bounded down the underpass stairs several steps at a time, ran through and up half the steps at the other side, reached up to grab the rail and did a cat pass over the railings, stumbling slightly as he landed. His ankle twinged, but that was all. It was a great to be free-running again, even if he was a bit out of practice. And out of breath. It would be a few weeks before he was up to a half-marathon. Maybe he could do one, get sponsored, raise some money for the Winter Shelters, he thought.

He thought back to the morning, to his first shift at work since the attack. The store manager, Ms Johnson, had said to him, as he sat at the till, "You're doing well, there, right? Better than piling soup tins up, eh?"

Luke nodded. "Yeah. It's fine. Bit, um, brain-dead work on the tills, to be honest. Although I like helping out, at the customer service desk, you know."

"Good. If you feel up to it, we can give you some more shifts, move you to full time. Maybe think about your future in the store? I always felt you had potential. Anyway, come and see me tomorrow morning, about ten. OK?"

"Oh. Wow. Yeah, thanks!" Luke had said. "Ten tomorrow. Right!"

That hint of a possible future made him feel almost as good as he felt about being able to run again. He hadn't felt this optimistic for months, not since starting the youth worker job nearly two years ago. It had been a good couple of weeks. Especially being back in cahoots with Sophie: sharing ideas with her, plotting ways to help the kids in Merton and discussing all that had happened. Strangely enough, he'd actually enjoyed the PCC meetings as well. He appreciated being asked for his opinion and being allowed to vote. Barbara was there, taking the minutes like she'd never been away. She'd looked much more cheerful and, well, normal, than when he'd seen her in Coventry. Better still, Marjorie Fowler wasn't there. At some point, though, he knew he'd have to talk to her. He wanted a face-to-face apology from her, and he reckoned that perhaps he owed her and Stephen one too. He could see, now, that it would have been better if Stephen had told her before he went to uni. He should have asked Stephen if his parents knew, and if not, tried to persuade Stephen to tell them. That would have been more helpful. Not that the other advice Luke had given him was wrong, but he'd just not considered everything properly. If he ever got another chance, he would do things differently.

Luke was relieved to be back in a church too, after all those months as an outcast. Even though Holy Trinity had slipped back to traditional old hymns, King James' readings and the Book of Common Prayer, he didn't mind too much. At least Sophie, he and Barbara had plans to restart some youth work and even start an alcohol-free evening cafe for teenagers. Juice, smoothies, some board games. They could be ambitious and start a games cafe, playing monopoly - or better still, games like Munchkin, Eldritch Horror or Exploding Kittens. Jake might help: loaning some of his offbeat games collection, getting involved in something other than drugs. A games cafe could be very popular and pretty good fun, Luke thought, vaulting over the barriers at the pelican crossing. And Francis had asked him to start a more contemporary youth-led evening service, once a month, as well as helping with the Sunday School. Luke felt he was back in the flow.

Just one thing left, he thought, one final piece to sort out. But it was the most important. He phoned Naomi.

"I think I'll have the chicken with pesto. It sounds yummy," Naomi said, in the Pizzeria restaurant the next week. "You sure this is OK, Luke? You're going to treat me?"

"Yeah, sure! I want to. To tell you the truth, I've never done this before."

"What? No kidding! You've never taken anyone out for dinner? I thought you'd do that sort of thing lots."

"Nope. It's not really the sort of thing we used to do in Sheffield. More likely to go to a pub or nightclub than a restaurant."

"Well, it's nice. Sophisticated… Good thing you've put a posh shirt on, isn't it? No tie, though?"

Luke flushed, Was he supposed to wear a tie? He looked around at the various couples and family groups on the other tables. "No one else is…" he stuttered.

"Oh, come on, Luke. Joke!"

"Oh." He looked at her as she smiled at him. At her long eyelashes, soft lips, glittering silver earrings and necklace, at her floaty cream dress printed with turquoise flowers. "Um... You look nice, anyway. I like your dress. It's pretty…"

A faint red tinge appeared on her cheeks as she looked down. The waiter came up and lit the candles, then took their orders. Luke had decided to splash out with the last of his savings, since he was doing so well at work. Ms Johnson had put him on the management training program. That, and Naomi being here, was worth a celebration. The waiter came back with an ice-bucket and a bottle, pulled out the cork with a flamboyant twist, and filled tall flutes with Prosecco. Naomi took a sip.

"I've never had this. Mmm, it's bubbly, nice - isn't it?"

"Um, yeah. I thought you might like it. My Mum loves it. Naomi, I've got something I want to tell you."

"Sure, what is it?" She put the glass down and looked earnestly at him. The reflected candle flames flickered in her cool brown eyes. Luke paused, lost for a moment.

"Come on, Luke, what is it?"

"Sorry, um... About when we met in Leamington."

"Yeah…" she said cautiously.

"Well, you were right. I shouldn't have called it a mistake and gone on and on about how I wished we'd never done it."

Her eyes narrowed. "So?"

"So… I reckon if there was a competition, like X-Factor or something, for being the world's biggest twit, I'd win it."

"Well, if there was, I'd vote for you," she said coolly.

"Yeah, I deserve that. But, um, it wasn't a mistake, really, was it?"

"Depends what you think."

"I don't think so, not really, not now. I just wished… Well, this probably sounds stupid, Naomi. I wish we'd never got found out."

"What do you mean, got found out?" she said intently, leaning forward.

Luke fiddled with his napkin, folding it into a concertina. "I mean, losing my job because of it. You're right, it wasn't fair. It all got such a mess. But…"

"But what?"

"I'm really glad it happened!" he blurted. "Naomi, honestly, it was the best night of my life!"

She grinned.

"Oh, Luke, you idiot," she said.

"I know. Anyway, I just wanted you to know that. And to say sorry for what I said. I got stuff all a bit mixed up, I really did."

Naomi nodded. A noisy group of chattering people went past outside and Luke glanced at the window. It was getting dark and he could see Naomi's face reflected in the plate glass. He gazed at the flickering candle flames and how the light from them glowed on her cheeks and eyes and wine glass as she sipped her drink. Then the waiter came up to the table and put Naomi's bruschetta and Luke's chicken pate in front of them, along with a basket of artisanal bread.

"Yours looks nice," Naomi said.

"Want to share?"

"Yeah, sure. You can try some of mine too."

"Anyway, are you all right? Back home OK? I bet Jessica was glad to see you."

"Yeah, she was. Really pleased. I was too. I'd got so bored in that refuge place and I really missed her and my friends and my job."

"Oh, yeah, did you get that back?"

"Yeah, I did! It's just like before, in a way. Job, Mum... Except Danny's gone. Oh, and his dad too. Good riddance."

"What happened to him?" Luke asked, spreading pate on a piece of bread and passing it to her.

"Ta. Mmm, that tastes really nice, doesn't it? Yeah, Walter - he just went off to Birmingham, like before. Only that was weeks ago and he's not come back. My Mum's texted him and phoned him, but he only answered once. He told her to stop bothering him. I reckon he's got another woman there. Anyway, Mum's thrown out all his stuff. I think she's happy to get rid of him."

"That sounds pretty good."

"Yeah. He was a right mean sod. Danny, well, Danny was OK at first. He's nowhere near as mean as his dad."

"Oh - but, Naomi, he still beat you up!"

"Only once. Although once was enough. I'm not defending him! And I'm not going to go back to him, I'm not stupid! I'm really glad he's gone." She hesitated. "But he was really nice when he was young, before he went to secondary school. You know, he wrote to me from prison, and he said he was sorry. They've put him on a drugs rehab program, and he's going to try to stay clean."

"Oh. I suppose that's good," Luke said through

gritted teeth. 'Forgive us our sins as we forgive others' seemed impossible when he thought about Danny. He reached across and tentatively touched the scar on Naomi's cheekbone.

The waiter sidled up. "Everything OK?" he murmured.

Luke jumped and took his hand away as if he'd been slapped.

"Oh, yeah, yeah, everything's fine, isn't it?" he said.

"Yeah," Naomi said. "It's all fine."

The waiter sloped off.

"Um, anyway, Naomi, Danny - you said he was sorry?"

"That's what he said. You know what I think? All those drugs he took wrecked him. I think they fried his brain. Like cannabis-induced psychosis, you know? A bit like that. And those no-good drug-dealer mates of his."

"So do you reckon he'll be all right?"

"He might be. I don't care that much, really. I wrote back and said I didn't want to see him again, anyway, once he got released."

"How long has he got?"

"Five years, at least. Might be longer."

She twirled the remains of the Prosecco in her glass. "Do you know, Luke, that this time last year I was actually praying - really praying - that if God existed he'd stop Danny getting at me and make sure he never touched Jessie. I suppose God sorted that out for me. Do you think he did?"

By the time they'd chased the last crumbs of

chocolate fudge cake and vanilla cheesecake around their plates, Luke was sure. They'd talked, they'd laughed, she'd smiled at him, they'd discussed, argued, disagreed, and yet even while she was saying, "Luke, don't be so daft! How can you say that? The Hobbit was rubbish. It was just boring stupid rubbish!" he felt sublimely happy. He leaned across and took her hands.

"Naomi, let's do this more. Lots of times. And go to the cinema, and walking, and to pubs and stuff like that. Let's, oh, you know, bit old-fashioned, I guess, but let's go out together."

"Luke - really? Do you mean it?"

"Definitely! I just want to, I guess, be with you. Lots. Um, do you, I mean, is that OK?"

"Yeah, that's OK. That would be really nice."

"Brill!" He squeezed her hands gently. "Really?"

"Yes. Really really."

"Wow! I mean, um, I dunno what to say…"

"Me too."

Luke knew what to do though. He moved the candles out of the way, leaned further across and kissed her. It had been a long wait. But worth it.

CHAPTER FORTY-FOUR

As Luke walked into the church cafe a month later, Sophie rushed up to him.

"Luke! You've cut your hair!" she exclaimed. "You look so different!"

"Yeah. I got tired of the teenage grunge look. Especially now I'm going to become management. I reckon I need to look a bit more, well, smart. Dull, you know."

"Oh, it's definitely smarter. I think it's better. It isn't dull! You look pretty cool, actually. It makes you look older. Barbara, hey, Luke's here!"

Barbara was visible behind the hatch in the kitchen, taking a cake out of the oven. She turned, saw Luke and smiled.

"Hi, Barbara. I hear you're the cafe manager now?"

"Yes. I've been promoted, isn't it amazing? I really didn't expect that, but Sophie's been so encouraging."

"Oh, Barbara deserves it," Sophie said. "Babs is the boss of the bara brith. The queen of the cup cakes. You should taste her flapjacks!"

Barbara looked embarrassed, and turned away to fill up a milk jug.

"Well, congrats anyway," Luke said. "How's it all going?"

"Oh, really well, thanks," she said, putting the jug on the counter. "I love doing this and we get quite a few customers now. Oh, and I've got a flat at last. It's fairly small, but it's nice. Near the park."

"Great! I'm really pleased for you. So, how about a coffee?"

"Sure, I'll get one for you. And tea for Sophie."

The cake, cooling on a wire tray on the side, gave off a warm aroma of coconut and lemon.

"Can I have some of that cake too?"

"It's too hot. How about a slice of this - ginger and spice loaf?"

"Sure." He took a bite. "Good, really good. Nom nom, as Jake says. Can I have another slice - or two?"

"Honestly, Luke, I reckon you've got hollow legs!" Sophie exclaimed.

"Burn it off doing parkour," he said, leaning back on the counter to looked around. "It's pretty brill, isn't it, this kitchen, the cafe, the hall? I reckon it's fantastic. The hall looks miles better than when I came here."

"Yes, it does, doesn't it? It was worth waiting for. I'd been praying for, well, I don't know how many years. And now we've got it. But it's still a shame about the church splitting and all the youth work and stuff stopping. It really was a bit of a disaster as well as a blessing."

"But we're doing something now, thanks to you," Barbara said to Sophie.

"Well, yes. You know, I wasn't sure what the point was of that vision I had, back then, ages ago. You remember? About the church splitting. But I think God meant to warn me, to prepare me to stick with the church throughout thick and thin, you know? Anyway, Luke, what are you up to now?"

"Oh, you know I've got put onto the management training scheme at the supermarket." He shrugged. "To be honest, it's a bit daunting. There's loads to learn. I'm not sure – I'll see how it works out."

"You'll do fine, Luke, I'm sure," said Barbara. "Look at us both - management material now. We're going up in the world."

"And Naomi?" Sophie asked.

Luke grinned. "You'll have to ask her yourself how she is. Come round to see us. We're just about to move in together, into this tiny house on Warren Street. It's only a living room, bedroom, kitchen and titchy garden, but it'll be OK."

"Oh, Luke…"

"Yeah, Sophie, I'm going to be living in sin. Terrible, isn't it? Don't give me the lecture. I've already had it from Dad. Thing is - I don't reckon God minds. Anyway, we're going to get married soon."

"Luke! Really? When?"

"As soon as we've saved enough for the basic

church wedding. I'm going to ask Francis to do it. I reckon he owes me."

"Oh Luke, a wedding! A wedding! Fantastic! Oh, I'm so excited! That's wonderful! Faith, hope and love – but the greatest of these…"

"Is cake!" said Luke, with his mouth full. "Especially this cake."

"Honestly, Luke. OK. Cake it is. Cake and love. But love lasts longer, doesn't it?"

"Yeah, I guess so."

"Anyway, can I be a bridesmaid? Please?"

"Your cravat isn't quite straight, darling," said Luke's mother, tweaking the purple satin as they waited in the vestry. "There, that's better. Yes, very smart. Makes a change from t-shirts. Very sophisticated, actually."

"Ta. I don't feel sophisticated. Feel the opposite, to be honest."

She kissed his cheek. "You'll be fine. The sun is shining, it's going to be marvellous. And Naomi is lovely. I'm looking forward to seeing her in her dress."

"Me too."

"Of course you are. Oh, this is going to be such a fun day! Right, time for the final checks." She walked around him. "You did brush your hair, didn't you?"

"Yeah, Mum, of course I did! Leave it, it's fine," Luke said, shaking her hand off.

"Leave the boy alone, Petra," said Luke's dad. "Go and check that the flowers are all OK or something. Stop fussing."

Petra glanced at Luke and his dad, and raised her eyebrows. "It's probably a little late, Simon, to have the father-and-son talk," she said, "but I'll leave you to it. I'll go and say hello to Naomi's mother."

Father-and-son talk? thought Luke. He said nothing, but stared down at the new black shininess of his shoes.

"I don't know what she means," his dad said. "You know what you're doing, I suppose."

"Yeah…"

"Naomi seems a very pleasant young lady."

"Yeah, um, she is."

"I didn't expect you, the youngest, to be the first, I must say."

"Well, um…"

"Nervous?"

"I reckon so. A bit, yeah." An understatement. Luke slid his sweating hands into his pockets. The trousers felt too tight and the dinner jacket too hot. He could feel his face reddening.

"That's understandable. But stand up straight, take a few deep breaths, speak clearly."

Luke squared his shoulders and lifted his chin up.

"That's better. Your ankle's completely healed now, isn't it?"

"Yeah, fine, not even a limp."

"Thank God for that."

His father looked him up and down.

"Your mother's right. Very smart," he said. "Hmm, bit of lint there…"

He stepped close to Luke and picked a thread of cotton off his shoulder.

"I'm surprised Petra didn't spot that. Right, you'll do. Ready?"

"Yeah. As I'll ever be, I reckon."

"Good. I think you've got taller. It must be those shoes. You're taller than me now. You've been growing again, haven't you, my young apprentice?"

"Dad," Luke said, and paused.

"What?"

"Don't call me that."

"What? Oh, right. Right! Yes." He glanced at his watch. "It's time to go."

The church looked brilliant, Barbara thought. Nosegays of white carnations, roses and trailing ivy cascaded down the ends of each pew, and were echoed by flower arrangements by the altar and the font. The wood glowed, the brass shone, the gilding above the altar gleamed. The pews were full. Lots of teenagers from the youth group giggling and chatting and waving their phones above them to take photos; Naomi's mother in bright orange sitting by a sprinkling of grandparents, aunts and uncles; Luke's family, his father in a navy blue suit and his mother resplendent in a fitted red dress with a feather and net fascinator perched on her silvery hair; various church members and friends filling up the back rows.

Francis said "I now pronounce you husband and wife" and Sophie started clapping almost before he'd finished speaking. After the final hymn, Naomi and Luke turned to face the congregation, George triumphantly crashed his hands down on the keyboard and huge chords rang out. The tune started low in the deep bass notes, then grew, stately and celebratory, until suddenly the high notes took over so that it it brightened and resounded, filling the church with rejoicing. Barbara could see George's rapt expression in the mirror just under the organ pipes. He looked as though he'd been waiting years for the opportunity to play this glorious, climactic, thunderous tune.

Naomi and Luke came down the aisle. Naomi smiling beautifully, Luke's cheeks were red, and he grinned sheepishly. Behind them, Francis stood and looked on. Barbara smiled at the triumphant expression on his face. He looked as pleased as if he had arranged the marriage himself, but she privately thought that Sophie deserved most of the credit.

"You didn't mind not being a bridesmaid?" she whispered to her.

"Nah, I wasn't that serious. Naomi just wanted Jessica and Hannah, and that was fine. Doesn't she look gorgeous though?"

"Yes," said Barbara, turning to look with faint envy at the lace and cream train of Naomi's dress. "Lovely. Really lovely. And happy."

"You do too, you know. I'm not hitting on you or anything, you know! But you look nice. You've had your hair cut."

"And coloured." Barbara fingered her ash blonde highlights self-consciously. "Do you think it is OK? Not too - too bright?"

"No. It really suits you. It's just nice - subtle. You look like Helen Mirren."

"Really?" Barbara thought about asking Sophie if her makeup was subtle too. But she was sure it was. Just a hint of colour in her lips and cheeks, and a trace of silver eyeshadow. She smoothed the creases out from her pale green dress and straightened up.

Outside, after the photos and congratulations, Sophie grabbed Barbara's hand and dragged her over to where a young man, wearing a grey tweed three piece suit, stood by himself.

"Gerald! I thought I saw you at the back row," she said.

He nodded and flushed.

"Do you know Barbara?"

He shook his head.

"OK, well, let's do the intros. Gerald, this is Barbara Walters. Barbara, this is Gerald Sutton."

"Pleased to meet you," Barbara said, shaking hands with him. He had a thin, diffident face, straggly black hair and a reserved manner, and apart from the fact that he stared rather a lot at Sophie, Barbara couldn't really see him as a stalker. "Did you enjoy it?"

"Er, yes, I suppose so," he stuttered. "I d-don't go m-many weddings."

"Wasn't that last organ piece amazing!" exclaimed Sophie. "I was expecting the Wedding March, you know, the usual piece. Not that! It was wonderful!"

"I recognised the tune, but I don't know what it's from," Barbara said.

"It's from the film, Babe, you know, the one

about the sheep-pig. The one that the farmer sings, about 'if I had words I'd paint a day for you'. It's an odd choice for George, really. But it was wonderful!"

"From Babe? Is it?"

"Er, yes," said Gerald tentatively. "B-but it's actually Saint-Saens Organ Symphony."

"Really?" Sophie said. "Oh, that explains why George knows it! Well, I think it was great, wasn't it?"

She looked around, and suddenly pulled Barbara forward.

"Come on!" she said. "Naomi's going to throw the bouquet! Bit old-fashioned, I know. I suggested it."

"What? No…" Barbara said, but Sophie pushed her onwards. Naomi turned, threw and the bouquet sailed high, twisted, and tumbled down into Barbara's astonished hands, as Sophie laughed. Barbara gazed at it in surprise and looked across at Francis. He winked and lifted his hand to her. She buried her face in the gardenias and carnations, breathed in their bracing clove scent, and looked at the frilled, curled petals; white and delicate, like pearls.

Francis would take a great deal of looking after, she thought. She had seen his study. There would, no doubt, be a lot of organising, reminding and tidying involved. In the last few months, from things he'd said and done; hints, a hand taken and held for a moment longer than normal, a smile at the cafe counter; she'd realised that it was possible that she had a future with him. She might, or she might not, encourage him. It felt strange, but amazing, to be free to choose. But a tossed bouquet, no matter how scented and beautiful, wouldn't make the decision for her.

She turned back to look at the cheerful family groups. Jessica chattered to her friends, Luke's father stood with his arm draped proudly around his son's shoulders, George and Stephen were nearby with white carnations in their button holes, although Stephen looked slightly uneasy in an obviously new suit. Naomi looked calm but, well, glowing was the only word for her, and Luke had an expression of anticipation and excitement brightening his face. Sophie dashed, laughing, from group to group, her pink hair feathery and her mirror-embroidered Kutch skirt swirling in the breeze. Barbara laughed too, and threw the bouquet high into the cornflower-blue air.

The End

Printed in Great Britain
by Amazon